TH
SECRET
WITHIN

BOOKS BY LUCY DAWSON

The One That Got Away
Little Sister
What My Best Friend Did
You Sent Me A Letter
His Other Lover
Everything You Told Me
The Daughter
White Lies
The Memory
Don't Ever Tell

THE
SECRET
WITHIN

LUCY DAWSON

bookouture

Published by Bookouture in 2021

An imprint of Storyfire Ltd.
Carmelite House
50 Victoria Embankment
London EC4Y 0DZ

www.bookouture.com

ISBN: 978-1-80019-254-6
eBook ISBN: 978-1-80019-253-9

For GP, SD, CD and GD.
Four generations of inspirational women.

AUTHOR'S NOTE

The Exeter Memorial Hospital, the Royal Grace Hospital and the Goldtree Hospital group are fictional. The Westmare caravan park and the Fowles hotel in Lyme Regis do not exist in real life either.

PROLOGUE

'Shhh! I'm not going to hurt you! I'd never do that.' I loll back on the comfy hotel mattress and wait. Those big, anxious, baby blues stare back at me, shining in subdued lighting.

'We can stop this any time you like, OK?' I smile. 'This is about you being totally comfortable with everything we're doing. Is it all right for me to carry on now?'

A hesitation. 'Yes.' The reply is little more than a whisper.

I reach for the roll of thick tape. 'Shall I do your wrists first?'

As they are offered to me, I take a moment to marvel at how slender they are – the network of delicate veins running up the arm... such incredible complexity beneath that pale, almost translucent skin. Beautiful. True to my word, I bind them with care, but tight enough to do the job, cutting the roll free with my pocket knife before smoothing down the severed end. I like a neat finish.

'I'm not sure I want to do my ankles too?'

I swallow down a sigh. 'Well – it's up to you, but...' I shrug.

A nervous bite of the lip. 'OK – I'll do it.'

That's more like it. I move quickly while we're still in this decisive mode, before sitting back to admire my handiwork. 'Try and work yourself free...' I watch carefully for any loosening but I've done an excellent job. 'There we are! We're ready...'

'Wait!'

Oh, fuck me.

'I don't think I want to do this after all.'

Yup – here we go… My smile tightens. 'I've *just* finished binding you.'

'I shouldn't be doing this. Can you take me home? I want to go home to my family.'

'Hey, hey!' I soothe. 'This is what *you* said you wanted, remember?'

'I thought I did, but I don't anymore. Can you cut me free, please?'

I hesitate – and watch those eyes widen again: this time, with fear.

'You're cross with me.'

'No, no!' I say truthfully. 'I'm not at all. I promise.' Because this was entirely predictable; having doubts when it comes to the crunch is only natural.

'I did think I wanted to do this but turns out I'm not brave after all.'

I get up, walk to the door and double-check that it's locked.

JULY 2017

CHAPTER ONE

I needed the two men sitting on the other side of the table to trust me.

Our meeting had been billed as an 'informal' coffee, but I knew full well they had the final say in my getting the job. While there was a post in the department that had to be filled, if these two didn't want me joining their team, it wouldn't matter how well I'd done in the earlier rounds of interviews. They'd put a stop to my coming to the hospital – and that was unthinkable: far too much was riding on this.

As they put their phones on the tabletop and settled themselves, ready to begin, I tried to remain relaxed; smiling as I picked an imaginary piece of lint from my trousers, shifting slightly in my chair out of the direct sunlight shining in my eyes. I focused instead on the cloudy lines on the table, left by the last quick wipe down it had been given. It takes as little as a tenth of a second to form a first impression of someone's personality, based on their face. One of the most useful things I was ever taught as a rookie plastic surgeon, was to always smile at my patients – because then they will trust me and that will make them feel safe.

It's actually a false misconception, because there is no link between having a friendly face and being trustworthy, but we're all built that way regardless, so when I meet people before I operate on them, I look confident. I tell them I'll take good care of them, even though the very first thing I will do when they are laid out unconscious in front of me is hurt them – albeit for the greater good. Once anaesthetised you're defenceless; you can't blink, you can't breathe for yourself. You are at the mercy of other people, keeping you alive. So, patients are incredibly brave and the very least they deserve when they are frightened is someone to trust – me.

I lifted my gaze and let it rest on both men. The older of the two felt it, looked up and automatically grinned back. 'Right! Let's get started! So, I'm Hamish, I… oh, I've forgotten my sugar.' He frowned down at his drink. 'Hang on.' He jumped up, but as a man with a waist of reasonable girth, he accidentally jogged the table, making the liquid dance out of our mugs. 'Damn, sorry both! I'll get some napkins too.'

He hurried to the stand of sachets and spoons by the till, and I turned my attention to his colleague. 'This is a very swish new coffee shop!' I commented, lifting my cappuccino to my lips. It was tepid and tasted like the milk had been strained through the seat of one of the burnt leather sofas that were dotted artfully around the room. I wished I'd asked for the water I'd wanted, instead.

'Isn't it?' he agreed. 'We haven't got enough beds, but at least we have double roast.'

I shrugged helplessly, and he sighed. 'I know, right?'

Hamish returned, dumped a pile of paper napkins over the largest spill, wiped his hands on his trousers and sat down again. 'Where were we?'

You were just about to wonder – now I'm sitting right in front of you – if everything you've read about me in the papers is true.

Each of the headlines I'd memorised word for word flicked through my mind before I could stop myself.

'Arrogant' Surgeon Suspended

Spurned Surgeon 'Threatened Medical Director and Patient Safety'

Vindictive Surgeon Demonstrated 'Dangerous Lack of Respect' for Protocol.

Still squinting, I moved my chair further to the right so I was out of the sun's glare completely. I was starting to feel hot – despite sitting under an aggressive air-conditioning vent – but Hamish was too busy with his sugar to notice my discomfort, tugging at the corner of his sachet vigorously. We all watched the crystals fly everywhere, bouncing over the table to land in the sad coffee puddles. I stayed diplomatically silent.

Hamish bit his lip. 'Tan, can you take over, please?'

His right-hand man cleared his throat. 'Sure. So, I'm Tanveer Husain.' He repeated his earlier introduction, nodding at me. His voice was quiet and shy. 'I work closely with Hamish. I guess your first question is: do we think this is a *good* place to work?'

'It is really – yes,' I agreed.

'Well, regional posts in hospitals like this genuinely are…' Tanveer hesitated, before continuing delicately, 'dead man's shoes. They don't often come up simply because no one wants to leave. Hamish can vouch for that. He's one of the longest-serving team members in the department. How many years is it now, Hamish?'

Hamish had happily sorted himself out and sipped his coffee. The flesh of his neck bulged over his tight collar as he swallowed. He needed the next size up. 'Lord, more than I care to remember.' He brushed some rather unruly sandy hair out of his eyes. 'Tan's right – I'm part of the furniture now, but the good thing about the way everyone stays put, is we all have the chance to really get to know each other and function as a cohesive whole.' He smiled and placed his cup down, folding his hands in his lap. 'Although that's not to say the department is complacent, outdated or static as a result! We're definitely holding our own!' He looked dismayed and immediately moved his hands back into sight, on the table. 'If you get my drift.'

'Obviously, it's not perfect,' Tan caught my eye. I thought I saw a flash of dry humour. 'Personally, I was really unsure about moving to the area when we relocated from the Midlands – it's not exactly "ethnically diverse" down here.' He sat up a little straighter. 'But it's been great for my kids.' He reached out for his coffee. 'They haven't looked back.'

'That's really good to know.' I decided to acknowledge the elephant in the room. 'I just want to get it right this time.'

'That's understandable, given your recent experiences.' Tan's voice was sympathetic, but I noticed Hamish had crossed his arms. 'In lots of other hospitals, as you know, the dinosaur age is almost over,' Tan continued. 'The old-boy network will have retired within the next ten years; it's nowhere near so white, or so middle-class male anymore. Here, we're behind that curve in the hospital overall. While I can tell you that there is definitely room for improvement balance-wise, bullying or intimidation will not be tolerated.' He held my gaze unfalteringly.

'Thank you, that's good to hear too,' I said.

'It's actually very encouraging that we're attracting the attention of candidates of *your* calibre.' Hamish jabbed a finger in my direction, his jacket lifting, revealing deep-set wrinkles in the linen that suggested it hadn't been cleaned recently. 'We want to build on our reputation that this is a progressive department. You'd be sharing an office with both of us and one of the other consultants, a chap called Nathan. He's sorry he can't be here but it's one of his private practice days.'

'It's fine,' I assured them. 'I've met almost everyone else now. I've got enough of a picture to know I'd enjoy working here.' I could have punched myself in the face the moment the words were out of my mouth. I sounded desperate. No one is attracted to desperation.

Tanveer smiled. 'You'd be with the better of the two plastics teams, if that helps make your decision any easier?'

My decision? I froze for a moment. Was this as good as in the bag? I laughed. 'I've no doubt that's true.'

'You really would be warmly welcomed. I hope you'll come here,' Tan assured me.

I sensed a sincerity in both his words and demeanour, which was so comforting I almost began to relax, but not quite. That the Devon and Cornwall Trust were even considering employing me full stop was a miracle, given I'd legally and very publicly forced my last employers to reinstate me after I'd been escorted off the premises, handily tipped-off journalists shouting questions as cameras were shoved in my face. If I was now *this* close to securing a post here, I could not afford to trip up in sight of the finishing line.

So it was only once we'd warmly parted company, that I allowed a little spring in my step and my smile to spread as I followed the signs back to the main hospital entrance. They said it was my decision. They wanted me…

The automatic doors opened and I stepped out into glorious Devon summer sunshine. I took a moment to slip off my jacket and roll up my sleeves, feeling the warmth beating down on my face and forearms. We were going to *live* here. I would finally be able to close the door on one of the most horrendous experiences of my life, leave it all behind, move us away and start again! Feeling excited for the first time in months, I started towards the car, then paused and dashed back to the hospital shop, buying four celebratory ice lollies. Holding them upside down by the corner of the wrappers, I let an ambulance pass, then crossed the road and hurried to the shady corner of the car park where I'd left my poor family.

The doors were all open and I could see Alex's pale, shorts-clad teenage legs hanging out of the back. They looked even lankier than usual, given he'd kept his enormous trainers on. With socks. It was certainly a look.

'Hey!' I smiled, appearing alongside the door. 'It was too hot to go for a walk then? I'm sorry I was so long, but I've got treats?'

'Ooh. Thanks, Mum!' Alex removed his headphones and sat up, readjusting his slipping glasses and taking one of the lollies from my outstretched hands. Cassia vacated the front passenger seat, fanning herself grumpily, and took another without a word, before walking round to climb into the back again. I let the lack of gratitude go, given how long they'd been waiting and took my place in the front alongside Ewan. He looked at me expectantly.

'Really good!' I confirmed.

My husband's face split into a grin. 'So you think?…'

'Yes, I do.'

'I *knew* they'd want you! I TOLD you!' he exclaimed and leant forward to kiss me.

'Dad! PDA – never okay.' Cassia wrinkled her nose. 'Public display of affection,' she explained as Alex frowned and opened his mouth. 'Can we go now, please, and get the air-con on before I actually *expire*?'

Ewan ignored her, taking my hand in his. 'That's really great, Julia, but remember you don't have to say yes when they offer it to you, unless you *want* to. It's your call.'

I looked at his earnest face. I knew he meant every word, but if I accepted, it would mean he could take the local teaching job *he'd* been offered: a head of department role at a school he was excited about, which also had spaces reserved for Cass and Alex. We'd be able to exchange on the house we'd all viewed together and loved. We'd be in for the start of the September term. Our new lives could begin. And what was to say I *would* be offered anything else? The staff at the Exeter Memorial Hospital seemed nice. The department was busy and covered a large geographical area, so there would probably be some interesting enough work. I wasn't exactly looking for a high-octane environment in any case.

Most importantly of all, they wanted me, despite everything. 'I'm not going to look a gift horse in the mouth.'

Ewan frowned. 'They're lucky to have you, not the other way around.'

I was so grateful for his unwavering loyalty, but privately, I knew I had to be realistic about my options. 'Let's go and drive past the new house.'

*

The narrow, one-way street forming the main artery through the village we would soon be calling home, was busy with wandering holidaymakers licking ice creams and peering in small shop windows. We had to make an impromptu stop, pulling into the car park next to the boatyard so that Alex could nip into the nearby pub and have a wee, but miraculously, we found a space. As he shot out and Ewan and Cass started a lazy debate about what radio station we ought to be listening to, I opened my door and wandered to the edge of the harbour wall.

The smell of chips was wafting from the vent of the pub kitchen, and I breathed in hungrily, my tummy rumbling. A small sailboat was heading peacefully towards the mouth of the Exe and as it drifted past, I wondered if sailing might be something Alex would like to try. I pictured his reedy body swamped by a lifejacket, helming carefully while staring at the horizon through his thick, bottle-end glasses, and as ever when I thought of Alex bravely stepping out of his comfort zone, I got a lump in my throat. He'd had such a shit time of it recently. Maybe it could be something we would learn to do together, as a family.

Glancing across the river to the crumbling, rust-red sandstone banks on the other side, a fresh, welcome breeze lifted my hair. I was so glad that last interview was over and it seemed I was no longer damaged goods. Closing my eyes, I replayed the performance of my barrister, Charles, for the hundredth time; summing up to the jury, validating me:

'Those who run the Royal Grace hospital would have you believe my client was an unstable, spurned woman, hell-bent on destroying a fellow male surgeon who'd the audacity to rebuff her affections. The truth of the matter was Ms Julia Blythe was illegally forced from her job amid a campaign of smears and intimidation. Why? Because she highlighted the unsafe practise of said male colleague… and he didn't like that one little bit. He sank into the ranks of his 'fraternity' when Ms Blythe blew the whistle, whereupon they all opened fire.

'She should have been praised, thanked and congratulated for her bravery. Instead, she was treated in the most heinous of ways: dead animals sent to her home, bloodied sanitary materials left in her office, suspended on the most spurious of grounds, excluded from theatre, which is known to be disastrous for a surgeon who relies on the constant practise of their skill-set to stay at the top of their game, as Ms Julia Blythe undoubtedly was.'

He'd furiously removed his glasses at that point, as if it was all too ludicrous for words. I don't know if it was a staged gesture or genuine.

'All while her accusers continued to spread their lies in an attempt to discredit her, *because they knew she was right*. Julia Blythe did everything expected of her, yet this was her reward?'

My skin started to hurt, and I opened my eyes again. Looking down, I saw blood under my fingernails. I'd been absently scratching the delicately scabbed eczema on my arm and wrist, which had flared up. Mentally revisiting what had happened ahead of today's meeting; planning how I'd explain about the devastating time I'd had if asked by my prospective new colleagues – had proven unsettling.

But it was done now. Hamish and Tan understood. They'd been kind. It was time to leave my painful experiences behind, if this relocation was going to be a success. I didn't want what had happened to play any further part in my life. I didn't want it to have any more power over me.

'Mum?'

I turned and Alex was standing uncertainly behind me. 'I'm done.'

'Me too.' I held out my arm to shepherd him back to the car.

*

We paused outside the new house once we'd driven round, cut the engine and listened to the sleepy sound of buzzing lawnmowers and seagulls calling overhead. Ewan sighed happily and took my hand as we looked up at the last of the afternoon sun catching the upstairs windows, firing them golden and lighting the foiled estate agent's logo on the 'Sale Agreed' sign.

'That's my bedroom there, the one on the right, isn't it?' Alex leant through the gap between us and pointed up at it.

'Yes.' I winked at him.

'And mine is the middle one?' Cass asked.

'Certainly is,' Ewan agreed, and she smiled suddenly.

'I like it.'

That was it. Decision made. I was taking the job.

We were ready to be happy again.

CHAPTER TWO

Nathan

I took the stairs rather than the lift – two at a time, my footsteps echoing pleasingly – and passed a husband and wife on their way down, looking lost and clutching a bulging plastic bag full of food: visitors. Sure enough, they asked me where Hampton ward was. They were at completely the wrong end of the hospital and two floors higher than they needed to be, so I set them right. The wife blushed and shot me a furtive last look over her shoulder as, whistling, I carried on up to the office and they descended into the bowels of the building.

I could pretend I'm not aware of the effect my looks have on women, but that would be ludicrous when I've spent most of my adult life taking full advantage of it. I'm not of Spanish or Italian descent, contrary to popular assumption. My mother is American, my father English and there's a touch of Scots in the background. I only appear swarthy when I've got a tan… at which point I will gleefully ham it up. Not so much now as when I was a bored junior doctor, when for my own amusement, I used to put on a heavy accent in the manner of Antonio Banderas. I got caught out eventually, of course, when I simply forgot to do it one day and was rightly told to pack it in.

It would also be disingenuous to moan that looking this pretty means I'm never taken seriously; I couldn't give a fuck. I've heard patients call me Dr Fit – or suggest I'm giving them all sorts of fever – on the phone to family when they think I can't hear. I don't care; it means I get away with a *lot* more than most colleagues because people are too busy staring at me. I stopped bothering with full explanations of patients' surgery years ago; they weren't listening. I realised all I had to do was sweep into the room, smile, flirt a bit, tell them they looked amazing and that I *really* enjoyed doing their op – because who doesn't like to feel special? No hassle, no tedious questions... just in, out, on to the next.

'Afternoon!' I smiled at the new breast care nurse – whose name I couldn't quite remember: Maeve? Maura? better not risk it – as she approached down the other side of the corridor, clutching an oversized envelope. 'Hot enough for you?'

She stared at me like a rabbit caught in the headlights.

'Outside.' I nodded at the window as I passed her. 'It's warm out there today.'

'Oh! Yes – very!'

'Have a nice weekend.' I laughed, knowing she was checking out my arse.

'You too, Mr Sloan!'

I was still smirking as I breezed into the office to find Hamish sitting inches from his whirring desk fan, eyes closed, forehead shiny and cheeks like blanched tomatoes. Tan was busily sorting through some papers, the sleeves on his otherwise spotless white shirt rolled up.

'Hello children!' I flopped down into my chair and put my feet up on the desk. 'Hamish, you look as hot as a dog. Busy day?'

'Very.' He eyed me. 'You, on the other hand, look fresh as a daisy.'

'I've been on the RIB this afternoon,' I confessed. 'I only had a couple of ops at the Goldtree this morning, so I thought I'd pop down to the marina and bounce around the bay for a bit. Beautiful day for it. You should come next time.'

'You're not getting me in that hairdresser's motorboat, thanks.'

'Too fast for you?' I teased. 'You stick to your sails then, yacht-boy. Anyway, how did you get on earlier? That's really why I'm here. That and to see if you want to grab a quick beer on the way home?'

'Can't, unfortunately. Cecily's mother is coming to stay for the weekend. It's her ninetieth on Sunday.' Hamish sighed. 'So, I'll be rushing home to listen to the television at ear-splitting levels and making endless cups of weak tea. By earlier, I assume you mean how was our chat with Julia Blythe, while you were busy tending to your privates?'

I laughed as I settled back into my chair. 'That's exactly what I mean. So what's she like?' I waited, my eyes gleaming. When Hamish frowned and scratched his head, but said nothing, I turned to Tan instead. 'Well?'

'She's one of those women you couldn't describe as pretty…' Hamish appeared to have collected his thoughts after all. 'She's got dark, straight hair. Very direct blue eyes, thin face. No tits or hips. Wouldn't be surprised if she's a gym bunny; she looks the type. Not had any work done on herself at all, I don't think. Shorter than I expected. Power suit. She's attractive, I suppose, if you like that sort of thing.'

I stared at him. 'I know what she *looks* like, you fool. Although that was an alarmingly comprehensive precis. I mean, how did she play it?'

'Oh. I see. Sorry.' He hesitated again. 'She was… polite, direct – but she told us she'd enjoy working here. It was obvious she really wants the job, which Tan practically offered her on the spot.' He raised an eyebrow at Tan, who looked embarrassed and shrugged. 'She's very comfortable in her own skin. I spilt my coffee and she looked a little pained – just watched me clean it up while I slopped about under her nose. I imagine she makes a lot of people feel flustered. If I had to choose one word it'd be – crisp… or smug.'

'I didn't get that feeling at all,' Tan cut in. 'I thought—'

'Aloof, brisk: there are two more,' Hamish continued. '*If* she's got a sense of humour, I've no doubt it will be very dry and terribly sophisticated.' He rolled his eyes.

I sat back, delighted. During her trial, I'd imagined Julia's barrister telling her to look unapologetic, focused and driven at all times. When I'd watched her walk from court to a waiting car on TV, I'd wondered if the way she'd so confidently held herself might just be part of the performance, so to hear that she was the real deal and everything I'd hoped she be was intoxicating news. Well, well, well…

'So you didn't like her then?' I asked Hamish, who began to fumble around in his pocket.

'I didn't warm to her, put it that way.'

I considered that with interest. I'd read in more than one newspaper that Julia Blythe was 'difficult' – although that's often a criticism levelled at women who don't automatically smile. 'Arrogant' was another popular description of her; but might that not just be a professional woman simply too busy to indulge the worn-out anecdotes of her extremely dull and – evidentially in the case of the Royal Grace hospital – inept colleagues? Most men know when a woman isn't ever going to be taken in by their 'charm', at which point they dismiss her as having a certain froideur – a la poor Hamish, forever the fat kid who never gets the girl – but *I* find that kind of woman's refusal to accommodate mediocrity both refreshing and intriguing. So what if she wasn't big on small talk? Personally, I loathe it; unless it's entertaining – rare – or about me.

Real life Julia Blythe sounded like a delicious amalgamation of Kristin Scott Thomas, Cate Blanchett, Tilda Swinton and Gillian Andersen. A grown-up, experienced woman with a cool and collected sexual allure. A proper challenge.

'What's her voice like?' I asked. It would be unbearable to have perfection ruined by a pedestrian accent.

'Her voice?' Hamish looked up from his mobile phone. 'Borderline posh. Why?'

Lovely. I sat up, decided. 'OK, so do we think we can make this work? The powers that be are going to plonk *someone* new in the team with us – we have no choice over that – but we can at least influence who we get lumbered with and Julia Blythe ticks the boxes for me; she can't afford to rock any more boats. Tan,' I pointed at him, 'she gets your vote too?'

'Of course she does. He thought she was *very* nice,' Hamish cut in. 'As I said, he got positively animated at one point.'

Tan glanced at Hamish, then down at his desk. 'Yes, I liked her.'

'For the record, she wasn't a horror.' Hamish chucked his phone down and crossed his arms. 'But I'm not sure you're right, Nate. I don't think she's anyone's fool, and I don't think she'll obediently keep her head down for one second.' He looked at me pointedly. 'You're assuming her now-screwed CV means she'll be meek, mild and choose to look away if she sees something she ought not to once she comes here. *I* worry she'll do the exact opposite. There's a real danger we might be biting off more than we can chew. It'll be a bloody nightmare if we saddle ourselves with some trigger-happy rabid #metoo-er. What if she's only too happy to snap on the surgical gloves and give the department a painful examination? Who knows what she might find?'

'As usual you're completely missing the point.' I swung my legs round and got up, walking to the window to look out at the car park below, watching several cars searching fruitlessly for a space. 'It's precisely *because* she's got that trigger-happy reputation that I want her here. The whole Royal Grace debacle was ridiculous. They all came out of it looking batshit, if you want my honest opinion, but the fact remains, *she* blew the whistle. You cannot blow it again in a completely different location without it looking like it might be *you* that's the problem. She's got form now – and that's what makes her so useful to us.' I turned to face them again. 'I'm not suggesting we sit her down on the first day and tell her everything we like to do here; I'm simply saying should she open a cupboard, something a bit grubby tumbles out and she trots faithfully off to the management… we've got a compelling defence. We gently suggest making up bullshit about male colleagues is exactly what Julia Blythe likes to do; precisely why she had to leave her last job.' I shrugged.

'So to recap, given we have no choice that someone is going to be foisted on us, having *her* coming into the department – ready gift-wrapped in scandal – is far less of a threat than some unknown quantity. If she's a bit up herself, so much the better. No one likes a know-it-all. However, I'm sure we can think of something to do to her once she's here that will *guarantee* she holds her silence, if you're really worried?'

'Hmmm.' Hamish was still sceptical. 'You're sure she hasn't piqued your interest for some other reason?'

'Well naturally, I'm also going to fuck her.' I deadpanned and Hamish laughed. Tan winced miserably.

'Oh Tanny!' I sighed, heading back to my seat. 'Come on, don't look like that.' I waited until he met my eye. 'You're right – I'm an insufferable arsehole, I'm sorry. Don't be cross with me.' I stuck my bottom lip out then winked at him before grinning.

'She's had a very difficult time.' He spoke so quietly I struggled to hear him.

'Well, I'm sure she has, but I still think it would be wise for me to at least *check* how big her balls really are?'

Tan closed his eyes, and Hamish snorted.

'Nathan, please,' Tan began. 'She—'

'No one gives a toss what you think, Tan,' Hamish interrupted. 'Although, you're not actually going to get involved with her, are you?' He turned to me. 'I don't think it would be wise to muddy the waters. Better that you give this one a wide berth.'

I gave him a bland smile. 'If you say so.'

He looked relieved. I saw no reason to break it to him that I had every intention of pursuing Julia Blythe, finding the crack in her armour and prising it open. 'Honestly, you just need to think of her as an insurance policy. If it's there, you don't have to use it. That's all this is about, I swear,' I lied easily. 'We need someone we can manoeuvre, nothing more.'

'I'm not saying I don't like the concept.' Hamish looked at me and shook his head slowly. 'You're a clever old sausage, aren't you?'

'Stop it. You know I like a lot of praise. Am I better than you?'

'You're the best.'

'And you're not just saying that?'

'Oh, shut up... go on then,' he conceded. 'Let's give her our thumbs up.'

'Excellent!' I said cheerfully. 'Because I think she's perfect.'

*

Back in the sultry, airlessness of my car, I undid the front windows but it barely made any difference at all, it was so hot. I searched on line for Julia Blythe, surgeon, pulling up some stills of her walking from court. In one, she had her hand outstretched in irritation, as if pushing the reporter away.

I was going to relish conquering a woman who had brought a whole Trust to its knees. There was no sport to be had in picking off little brown sparrows, fluttering around my head. Real seduction lay in something altogether more exotic than that. I sighed, leaning my head back, taking pleasure in the pleasingly lush green of the beech copse at the back of the car park against the very bright, deep blue of the almost-Mediterranean sky. Nothing was moving; there was no wind at all. It would be a long couple of months until the leaves started to fall, signalling Ms Blythe's arrival at the hospital, but I was more than prepared to lie in wait at the foot of the tree for someone as special as her.

SEPTEMBER

CHAPTER THREE

Julia

It was sod's law that on my first on-call weekend at the new hospital, I was summoned halfway through dishing up Sunday lunch. I wiped my hands free of lamb fat, passed the carving knife to Ewan and hurried in to work, crossing the car park with a shiver. I'd misjudged the bright sunshine and blue skies from the warmth of my steamy kitchen. It was much colder outside than it looked. Driving in with bare arms meant my skin was unattractively mottled with goosebumps and my fingers almost stiff by the time I joined the rest of the trauma team; but it was nothing a little heat wouldn't fix, unlike our poor casualty.

The twenty-five-year-old girl we were assessing had accidentally severed her hand while trying to hack the stone from an avocado she was holding. She'd brought the large blade down towards it with force, missed and cut right through her palm. It was at least a clean cut, but also a surprisingly deep wound with tendons, nerves and the blood supply all affected.

I quite enjoy the rare emergency surgery I get to do. The adrenaline is addictive – things can change very, very quickly – but there is also a pleasing simplicity and clarity to danger. You don't have time to think about anything else. If you panic that's it – someone loses their hand function forever.

We got going with the deeper tendon repair before turning our attention to the microvascular surgery, but it took time and once we'd finally finished re-knitting everything, I was hungry and tired. I wanted to be at home already and was making my way down the main corridor leading to the car park, when I noticed a man striding briskly some distance ahead of me. He stood out simply by virtue of the fact that most hospital visitors are slow, nervous walkers with no clue where they are going. They'll often stop dead to inspect signs with no warning – or you come out of a lift to find them frowning at it in confusion, like they're not sure what it does – only for them to shout 'excuse me?', right at the last minute when you've just disappeared round the corner, to ask for directions. This man walked with a confidence like he knew the place inside out. A couple of passing nurses greeted him and he stopped to speak to them.

He still had his back to me but I watched their body language change in response to what he was saying. One of them made a face of mock outrage then pouted. The other put her head on one side and began to twist her hair flirtily round her finger, before he said something that made both women laugh louder than was necessary. I couldn't help rolling my eyes. The exchange lasted seconds before the three of them parted company, but as he turned the corner and stepped into bright sunshine, I got a glimpse of cheekbones sharp enough to cut something on, amused, heavy-lidded eyes and a definite smirk. I couldn't see if he cast a shadow or not, but the reputation behind him was clear as day.

I quickly accosted the nurses as they walked past me.

'Sorry to disturb.' I smiled. 'I don't want to hold you up, but that man you were just talking to. He is?'

They glanced between each other.

'Nathan Sloan. Just back from his holidays. He's—'

'…one of our top plastic surgeons!'

They were younger than I'd appreciated now I was up close to them; finishing each other's sentences, fancying the doctors, misguided and inappropriate familiarity… I was reminded of my own junior days and felt bad for judging them. 'Thank you, both.'

I didn't miss the 'top' reference though. Mr Nathan Sloan: the one consultant in the department I had yet to meet, with whom I'd be sharing an office…

I sighed and carried on my way.

OK, so one of my new co-workers was possibly a bit of a prick. This was not a problem. Pricks are everywhere; you can't avoid them, especially in surgery. And being a prick does not make you a dangerous and reckless maniac who deserves to be in prison. This was NOT going to be a repeat of my experience at the Royal Grace.

Nonetheless, I googled Nathan Sloan once I was back in the safety of the car and pulled up all of three lines of his NHS bio:

Mr Nathan Sloan, Consultant Plastic and Reconstructive Surgeon

A consultant for over fifteen years, his specialist interests include breast and microvascular reconstruction.

Another quick search revealed he had a private practice in Exeter, providing a full range of cosmetic surgery. From the testimonials, he focused on breast augmentations and uplifts, although he also offered reconstructive work after trauma and cancer. It was all very uncontroversial stuff, apart from the most ludicrously glamourous picture of him giving blatant come-to-bed eyes to the camera. It was more like a headshot for a movie casting than a normal surgeon's picture. But as private plastic clinics were entirely based on promoting enhanced appearances, I could hardly blame him from trading on his own good looks. It was all part of the package, so to speak. Even the nicest and most dedicated consultants undertook some private work. I saw nothing there that was cause for alarm. Plus, if he were to google *me*...

I shivered briefly in my stupid short sleeves – and decided perhaps it was fairer to assume nothing about him at all, until I'd had time to form an opinion based on fact, rather than impression.

With any luck, he'd afford me the same courtesy.

*

My unexpectedly full-on Sunday of surgery made me doubly glad I'd requested Monday off to take Alex and Cass in on their first day of term. Cass was particularly nervous. Unlike Alex, she had enjoyed a consistent popularity at their old school. She was putting a brave face on it, but I knew she missed her Surrey friends. We also now had the added complication of Ewan being on site, both in a professional AND parental capacity, which was a big adjustment for all three of them to make. We'd decided in advance that it was important for him to keep a bit of distance, at least to give Cass and Al a chance before the other pupils realised they were related to the new, year three teacher, Mr Wilder; although it was such a comparatively small school, I was sure everyone must know already.

Arriving horrendously early, as Ewan was due at a quick welcome coffee with the headmistress and another new member of staff before kick-off, the kids and I took ourselves upstairs to hang up their coats and orientate before everyone else arrived. Cass looked around the classroom in disbelief once we'd trailed up several flights of wooden stairs, polished from years of use, to the top of the school and found the door marked '8F'.

'It's even more tiny than I remember.' She wrinkled her nose.

'Cass!' I said quietly. 'Give it a chance.' I knew she was only being prickly because she was nervous. 'I think it's really sweet.'

'I think it's *mental*.' Cass glanced at the old-fashioned desks and the large sash windows overlooking the empty playground below. 'It also smells funny.'

That was true; the sweaty aroma of meat and vegetables already cooking, and on a large scale, had crept up the steep stairs behind us.

Alex shrugged. 'I like it,' he said simply, and my heart swelled with hope.

Please let this be the place where he would settle and make some kind, gentle friends.

Cass rolled her eyes. 'You would.' She held up her coat. 'So where am I supposed to put this?'

I looked around me as a stocky teenage boy dressed in a blazer suddenly appeared in the doorway and stopped dead at the sight of Cass. His mouth literally fell open, and she gave him a withering look before glancing away. It was Alex who smiled and held his hand out.

'Hi, I'm Alex!' he said cheerfully. 'I'm new here.'

Cassia's Nordic beauty seemed to have frozen their prospective classmate, however, and it was a few heartbeats more until he managed to tear his eyes from her and stare first at Alex's extended hand then up at its owner. I attempted to keep casual and busied myself with finding my phone, which was starting to ring in my bag, while I prayed with my whole being for this boy to take my son's gesture and not leave him hanging.

The wait seemed to last a lifetime. I declined the call just as Cass sighed and stepped forward.

'I'm his sister, Cassia.' She offered the boy her hand too.

He looked at her, flushed slightly and took hers first, then to my huge relief, shook Alex's. 'I'm Ben.'

Cass nodded coolly and returned her attention back to me. 'Like I said, where do I put this?' She held up her coat again, and I mouthed a silent 'thank you' before saying aloud, 'out here, I expect.'

'They have actual pegs? No lockers?' She was incredulous as we found a row outside the classroom. 'And when do I get *my* phone back?' She nodded at my bag as it began to ring again, before hanging her coat up with another sigh.

'At the end of the day.'

'What if there's an emergency with Al?' She folded her arms and looked at me, eyebrows raised.

'There won't be. It's not going to be like St James. You're not going to have to look out for him all the time anymore, Cass. I promise.'

'Are you actually going to get that?' she scowled at my bag.

'No. It can go to voicemail. Even if there was a problem, Dad's here now, isn't he? You could just find him. But it's going to be OK.'

I reached out and tucked a piece of her hair back behind her ear. She flinched and quickly ducked away from me. As always, it was like trying to stroke a wild pony.

'I'm all right,' she said. 'You can go now. But can you please take Alex down to his form room with you? At least I don't have to be in the same class as him here, I suppose.' She still looked worried though, thirteen going on thirty.

'He'll be fine, Cass. Remember how friendly everyone seemed when we came to look round?'

Just as I said that, an exceptionally slim and pretty woman in a trouser suit appeared at the far end of the corridor, called 'Ben?' impatiently, and when there was no immediate answer, stalked towards us at speed in her high heels, clutching a water bottle. She flashed the most perfunctory of smiles as she passed, enveloping us in a cloud of strong, floral perfume.

Cass coughed and flapped the air melodramatically as the woman re-emerged without the bottle. She glanced at Cass and raised an eyebrow as I said 'Morning!' and smiled.

She merely nodded at me, gave Cass another stare and walked off.

'Yeah, Ben's Mum seems super nice,' Cass remarked, once she'd disappeared.

'Point taken, but maybe just try and enjoy today? Give it a chance, you might like it?'

Her eyes filled with sudden tears and she shook her head. '*Enjoy* today? Only someone who has forgotten what school is actually like and can't imagine how it would feel to have to leave the one you were happy at, to start all over again, would say something like that.'

'Oh Cass!' I stepped forward guiltily, arms open.

'Don't!' she hissed, moving back and wiping her eyes with her sleeves as we heard more voices approaching. 'I'll be fine. Just go! Please!'

I did as I was told, taking Alex with me. My phone started up *again* as we made our way downstairs. I looked at the screen and sure enough saw 'Dominic'.

'Is that Dad ringing to speak to me?' Alex said, with his usual pinpoint accuracy, trailing behind on the stairs.

I took a deep breath. 'Yes, it is. But you know what, Al? I think let's call him back later. Don't you? You're a bit busy right now.'

'He'll have probably called me on my phone, but I gave it in at the front desk when the lady said "no phones allowed in school hours". That's why he's trying you, I expect. Sorry, Mum.' He pushed his glasses up his nose then gave me a spontaneous hug as we reached the corridor, his lanky arms wrapping tightly round me, before he pulled back and patted me affectionately on the head.

'It's fine, love, don't worry about it.' I declined the call as it began to ring again and smiled as another set of parents passed us. 'The most important thing is that you have a great day – and I know you're going to, OK? Now, let's hang your coat up too, shall we? Well done! And where's your bag?'

I kept smiling even as I left the school, crossing over the busy car park, past small knots of parents who were catching up and chatting, feeling very conscious of my new role as Mr Wilder's wife, not just Alex's mum and Cass's stepmother. My little family were *all* going to be OK, weren't they? I thought about Alex being cheerful and Cass trying not to cry and felt suddenly near to tears myself.

My phone began to ring for the hundredth time and I made a snap decision to bolt back to the car, rather than go in search of a quick coffee, as I'd planned. It simply wouldn't do to have a row with my ex in front of everyone on the first day.

I slammed the door shut and answered breathlessly. 'Hello! Yes – I'm here!'

'Finally!' Dominic exclaimed. 'I've been calling and calling! I want to say good luck to Al for his first morning.'

I closed my eyes and mentally adopted the brace position. 'He's already gone in, Dom.'

'What? But it's not even eight a.m.! I've called *loads* on your AND his phone! You must have heard it! So you just ignored me?'

'Of course not.'

'I don't believe this! You've been down there a *week* and already everything I said would happen, is happening. I'm being cut out!'

'No one is cutting you out of anything. Ewan had to be in early today to have a coffee with the headmistress. That's all.'

Dominic laughed. 'Whoa – hold up. So actually, I didn't get to speak to my son on his first day – a really big deal – because your husband had a prior social engagement?'

'A professional appointment. That's different.'

'Wouldn't the easier thing all round have been for Ewan to get a job in one of the multitudes of schools in Surrey, so I could keep seeing my son and not have to live two hundred miles away from him?'

'No, because MY new job is in Devon,' I said patiently. 'They've all come with me, not the other way around. You know this.'

'Don't do the patronising doctor voice,' Dominic snapped. 'And don't make out like I'm overreacting either. I have every right to be concerned about my son's education.'

I sighed as I prepared myself for one of his rants, looking across the car park at the door of the school opening. Ben's mother marched out, long black hair flowing behind her as she checked her watch, scowled and blipped a shiny Range Rover, before roaring off. The number plate was STORM 1. Did that refer to her name or nature?

'You're running away from your problems rather than facing them, which is forcing me to have to give up my relationship with my son,' Dominic continued. 'You'd done the hard part – they'd taken you back!'

'But that's the point, Dom! I forced them to acknowledge publicly that I wasn't any of the terrible things they said I was, and *that's* what made it possible for me to finally leave. No one would have employed me ever again if I hadn't cleared my name first.'

'No – you've taken Al away – you've deliberately manoeuvred me out of his life and I'm not going to stand for it.'

'Oh, come on! You *know* that's not true!' I waited but there was no response. 'Dominic?'

He'd gone, hung up on me.

I drove slowly home. As usual after an unexpected run-in with Dom, I felt jittery and slightly nauseous. I ate a couple of plain crackers from the box, standing up next to the larder because I couldn't be bothered with making toast, only to regret my laziness when I decided to sit down to read the Sunday supplements I hadn't managed to get around to the day before, with a cup of tea. Unfortunately, by the time I'd found my hydrocortisone cream and returned downstairs – I'd absently scratched and picked the eczema on the back of my hand until the red patches of skin were throbbing – the tea had gone cold. I gave up and looked around, distracted, unable to settle.

I shouldn't have taken his call – except he would only have kept on and on until I did. The newly naked branches of trees dancing madly around on the other side of the kitchen window caught my eye. The wind had picked up from nowhere, swirling golden leaves about our new walled garden. The sky had darkened against the old red bricks and it was obviously about to rain. So instead of going for a walk to clear my mind, as I'd planned, I started to attack the unpacking. I managed quite a bit and was making some good headway, as well as feeling calmer… until, while washing up my plate after lunch, I stopped dead at the sink, when Lise's song suddenly came on the radio.

I didn't move – my rubber-gloved hands submerged in bubbles – just listened to the words telling me she loved me and hoped I would love her forever too. My sight blurred and I shook free of the gloves, wiping my hands first on my jeans, then the tears from my cheeks.

I'm too old and jaded to believe in signs anymore – but I still closed my eyes, wrapped my arms around myself and imagined her hugging me. Before the music ended, I hurried out into the hall and picked up her picture, newly unpacked and on the sideboard; Lise cuddling a cherubic Cass, contentedly snuggled on her mother's lap, sucking her thumb while my beautiful best friend flashed her killer smile for the camera, her naughty eyes dancing.

Lise would tell me that the move was the right thing to do. I was certain of it. She'd say Dominic would calm down. She would also point out that life is too short to worry about things you cannot control.

I wiped my eyes again, returned the photo and pulling on wellies and my mac to brave the stair-rod rain now determinedly falling, picked up my bag. I wanted to get something special for tea before heading over to collect the kids. I'd promised to take them out for a coffee shop cake, partly as a treat to mark the achievement of the first day, and also to allow Ewan enough time to finish up before coming to find us. It would be a back-to-front meal, pudding first and out, rather than at home, but it was good to shake routines up occasionally. I forced myself to breathe out steadily as the echo of Dom's accusations rang in my ears.

Nothing stays the same forever, thank God.

*

I did the food shopping faster than I'd allowed for, but didn't have quite enough time left to mooch around any of the nice clothes shops I'd noticed, so pulled up in the school car park early instead. Irritatingly, the sun had come out from nowhere, the sky had completely cleared and I was now uncomfortably warm in my boots and mac. On starting to slip my arms free, however, I noticed I had a small spill of something down my front. I stopped, sighed and reluctantly pulled it back on – and why on earth had I worn *wellies*? I inspected myself in the rear-view mirror. At least my eyes weren't the slightest bit puffy from crying earlier. That was something. I took a deep breath and glanced up – to see Nathan Sloan lounging against the wall by the gates, frowning down at his phone.

My heart sank. Although it was, of course, perfectly reasonable that he might also have children at the same school as mine… I would have *so* rather met him properly for the first time in a professional capacity; colleagues on a level footing in our to-be-shared office, rather than with me in school mum mode and dressed like I was going deep-sea fishing. I had no choice but to get on with it though, so I prepared to introduce myself and got out of the car. At least he was on his own; I didn't have to do a meet and greet with anyone else listening in.

Clumping towards him, I tried not to crossly notice that today he looked like he'd stepped from the pages of *Horse and Hound* magazine's polo pull-out special: 'Argentina's hottest export' perhaps? He'd called the weather correctly and was dressed in a blue, open-necked, sleeves-rolled-up shirt, tucked into sand-coloured trousers, while aviator sunglasses held back his dark hair in the now-*hot* September sunshine. He was only missing a massive stallion. Wanker.

ARGH! Was this giving the man a chance? No, it was not! I had a very firm word with myself to BE NICE. He couldn't help the way he looked.

'Hello, Nathan,' I said smoothly, arriving in front of him, trying not to mind that *I* looked ridiculous. He glanced up from his phone and gave me a social smile of zero recognition, probably assuming I was a patient.

'I'm Julia Blythe. I've just joined the plastics department at the hospital. Nice to finally meet you.' I offered him my hand, secretly pleased to have initiated the power handshake.

His expression lifted. 'Ah! Julia! Hello! Nice to meet you too.'

'I saw you from afar at work yesterday and didn't have a chance to say hi properly. It was my first on-call.'

'Oh, sorry I missed you. I popped in once we were back from holiday to pick up a couple of things. That was bad luck that you got pulled in.' He was well-spoken and the owner of a firm grip, shaking from the elbow rather than the wrist. I'd expected as much and kept my palm flat and fingers outstretched. Once my index finger was almost touching the pulse of his wrist, I held on just a second longer, then released *him*, rather than the other way around. 'You have kids here, I take it?' I nodded at the building behind him.

He laughed. 'Yes! I don't just hang around random school gates at home time. I have a sulky man-child in year eight, who goes by the name of Ben.'

I recalled the boy staring at Cass in the doorway with his mouth open. Oh, give me strength… but I nodded enthusiastically. 'I think I met him this morning. My stepdaughter and son are in year eight too.'

'Terrific! Well, it's a fabulous year. Lots of good kids – they'll settle in well, I'm sure.'

'What a small world!'

'Well, not really,' he shrugged, 'that's just Exeter for you. Half of the hospital consultants have kids at this school. Anyway, how are *you* settling in? Liking it thus far?'

'The hospital you mean?' I shielded my eyes from the sun. 'Or the Devon weather, which seems to be all over the place!' I laughed and motioned at my mac and wellies. 'Spot the out-of-towner!'

He smiled. 'It's the proximity to the sea. The weather here can change very quickly without warning. You'll get used to it. They are very shiny, new wellies, though. You need to go for a proper walk and rough them up a bit.'

'Yes... yes I do. Anyway, the hospital seems great.' I paused and peered at him more closely. He had heterochromia – his left eye was blue and the right dark brown.

He grinned and pointed at his face. 'It's not a heterochromia, in case you were wondering – it's an anisocoria. I was bullied when I was a kid; one of the little sods punched me in the eye and my pupil stayed dilated. See?' He suddenly leant in close enough for me to catch his aftershave. He smelt expensive. I was immediately reminded of his equally olfactorily blessed wife, roaring off in her Range Rover with her personalised number plate.

Oooh – did that mean she might be *Storm Sloan*? What a preposterous name! I couldn't help my resulting flicker of a smile, but he noticed it immediately. I saw him scan my face again with more interest as he drew slowly back, but I very firmly told myself not to read into that. He was simply trying to get the measure of me.

'It doesn't affect my sight, obviously...' he continued, leaning back on the wall. 'Oh, sorry – of course you'd know that – it's just my one cool thing in common with David Bowie. Anyway, I'm glad you're enjoying the hospital. Better than the last place, I hope?' He spoke lightly, but watched me tense, waiting to see how I was going to answer.

'Well,' I began carefully. I was prepared for this and knew exactly what I wanted to say to defend myself *without* slagging off the Royal Grace. 'Depending what you might have read in the papers, I—'

'JULIA!'

The loud shout caught me completely by surprise, and I turned, to see my extremely drunk ex-husband inexplicably staggering towards me.

CHAPTER FOUR

Julia

My whole body contracted with shock as my brain tried to process what I was seeing. This wasn't some hideous hallucination – Dominic really was weaving towards us, not just tipsy but properly inebriated, outside our son's new school, my husband's new place of work and in front of my new colleague. All other thoughts fell away from me as I turned very, very hot indeed, leaping forward in my mind to where I knew this was going to go, and the humiliation it would involve. How, *how* could he do this to Alex? It had been at least five months since we'd had an episode like this, and he'd decided to pull it *today*?

'What are you doing here?' was the best I could gasp as he arrived alongside me. 'You're supposed to be in London!'

'Came up on the train, straight after we finished talking this morning.' He reached out and put an arm briefly round my shoulders, squeezing tightly. The very particular sweet and sour yet stale smell of the hardened drinker, and the softness of his unwashed clothes, elicited such an enormous wave of anxiety within me, I felt sick myself. His face was pallid and his forehead shiny with sweat as his body tried to rid itself of the booze in his blood.

He pushed back a lock of lank, greasy, dark hair, glanced to his side, noticed Nathan and drew himself up like a sentry in response – legs together – before oddly leaning slightly to one side, extending his arm and hand right out in an exaggerated gesture of greeting, almost like the jerky movements of a clockwork doll.

'Hello, mate! I'm Dom, Alex's dad. I see you've already met my lovely ex-wife, Julia?'

'Dominic, please...' I breathed. I couldn't draw the air into my body properly. Horrified, I watched Nathan assess Dom then glance at me... before shaking Dom's hand. 'I'm Ben's dad, Nathan. Good to meet you.'

'Ah, well, I couldn't miss my boy's first day at his new school, you know what I mean? You need be there, don't you?' Dom was speaking slowly, enunciating carefully, trying hard not to slur. 'You have to make the effort.'

'Dominic, can I talk to you privately, please?' I put out a quick hand, smiling, to lead him away – but he pulled back roughly at my touch.

'No, you can't! Ha – this is a blast from the past!' He wagged a finger at me and laughed. '*This is inappropriate.*' Adopting a whingey, teary, high voice, presumably intended to be me, he added: '*Can I talk to you in the other room where he can't hear?*'

My face burned. 'Please,' I whispered, desperate to stop him from going any further. 'Alex can't see you like this. Other people, parents,' – I couldn't help shooting a look at Nathan – 'can't see you like this. Or if you don't want to talk, just go.'

'Go?' He pulled his face back like I was crazy, then laughed. 'I just got here!' He threw his arms wide and the expansive gesture made him wobble on his feet.

'I'm begging you.'

'No.' He shook his head defiantly. 'I want to see my son.'

I couldn't believe this was happening... and yet it was only going to get worse. More people would start to arrive at any moment... he was going to destroy it for us before we'd even had a chance. I stared at him, a lump of fear like a huge wodge of bubble gum in my mouth starting to expand, making it hard to breathe. I didn't know what to do – how to stop it.

'Right, well I think *I* might go for a quick smoke before they come out.' Nathan straightened up, looked at his watch. 'We've got ages before the kids make an appearance. Coming, Dom?'

A *smoke*? What was he doing?

Dom squinted at him too, trying to think clearly… despite his skinful, instinctively wary.

'My car is just over there.' Nathan pointed down the road, yawned and stretched.

Dom yawned too, wobbled on the spot again, then gave a random shake, before blinking. 'Yeah – go on then.'

Nathan nodded. 'Good man. Let's go.'

He started walking away from the gates and Dom followed after him, only to pause about fifteen feet away from me when Nathan stopped suddenly and patted his pockets.

'Shit! I left my keys on the wall!' He laughed and doubled back, reached past me to collect them and muttered urgently under his breath: 'Tell Ben's teacher to put him into homework club and I'll be back to get him in a bit… Got them!' He waved the keys in the air and ambled back over to Dom.

'So what part of London are you from?' I heard him ask conversationally as they walked off, Dominic zigzagging the pavement. I watched, powerless and horrified. I knew from experience that if I went after Dominic when he was this bad, it could easily escalate. I imagined him losing his temper, kicking in the front of cars, smashing windscreens, the kids all coming out – other parents watching, appalled. The police being called. Ewan appearing and trying to hold him back; Dominic ineffectually attempting to punch him – Alex watching other dads and staff restraining his father – the obscenities Dominic would scream at me, at everyone. Adrenalin was now roaring around my body, my pulse fluttering so fast at my wrists I felt faint as I stared after the two men. They turned a corner and disappeared out of sight.

A stillness descended, despite the blood crashing in my ears. A bird started singing in one of the trees above while I stood there with *no idea what to do.*

The lone song was broken by voices behind me as a group of three mums, holding the hands of much smaller children in uniform, appeared, chatting. A minibus came around the corner and pulled up outside the school. The teacher who had been driving threw open a sliding door and children in games kit began to leap down, disappearing through a side entrance in the brick wall as more parents materialised. It was quickly becoming very busy. A second minibus came up the road, and this time Ewan jumped out, jogging round. He scanned the area carefully for cars before releasing his pupils, and as they streamed past him, noticed me standing across the way. He beamed and gave me a quick, happy thumbs up. He couldn't have seen Dominic then? So where had he and Nathan gone?

Despite my skin prickling with anxiety, I gave Ewan a wink, and he waved before locking the bus and disappearing through the door in the wall after the children. No sooner had *they* vanished, than a teacher came out through the same door holding a register, leading her class towards the railings. Ben was at the front, talking to a couple of other boys and looking around him excitedly. At the back of the group was Al, slightly detached from the others. He looked quite happy though. Still no sign of Dominic or Nathan.

I made my way over to the teacher as quickly as I could and introduced myself as Alex's mother.

'He's had a super day, I think.' She beamed at me. 'Such a lovely boy. He's going to be an asset to the year, I can tell.'

'Thank you.' There was so much I wanted to ask her. Had he eaten lunch? Talked to anyone? Joined in with the lessons? Did she think he was going to need any extra tuition to catch up? But instead, all I blurted was: 'I've got a message for you from Nathan Sloan. He's asked if Ben could go back into homework club? He'll come and get him in a bit.'

Ben was within earshot and his smile faded. 'But it's the first day! We haven't even got any homework! He said he'd be here.' His shoulders sagged as he looked down at his feet. The poor boy was obviously very disappointed.

I felt terrible but also couldn't help glancing behind me again. Still clear. All I wanted to do was get Al and Cass into the car as quickly as possible. Once I'd done that, I could make a plan. I needed to text Ewan to let him know what was going on... what the hell would Dominic be saying to Nathan? What intimate secrets would be tumbling from his uninhibited booze-soaked lips? I swallowed, nauseously.

'Could I just ask,' I turned to the teacher again, 'do the other year eights come out of this door too, or do I need to go somewhere else to find Cassia Wilder? Oh, here she is!'

Cass appeared, talking to another girl. Ben immediately straightened up as she arrived alongside us.

'Hey Cass!' he blurted, and she frowned at him, before turning to me and looking at my feet.

'Why are you wearing wellies?'

'It was raining.'

She glanced at the bright blue sky. 'OK,' she said slowly. 'Can we go now, please?'

'Yes. Slight change of plan, though, we're back to the car first. It's just over there. Let's go! Quick! Quick!' I pointed and smiled apologetically at Ben as we made to leave, but he didn't notice at all, too busy staring after Cass as she walked away. Alex loped after her and called out cheerfully, 'Bye Ben!' He laughed loudly, and a few people turned around to stare. 'See you tomorrow!'

'Al! Stop laughing! Nothing's funny,' Cass hissed.

'I'm just pleased, that's all.'

'Can you be pleased more quietly? Everyone's looking.'

'Come on, Al!' I tried to jolly him along without revealing I was every bit as eager to leave as Cass. She thought this was embarrassing – it would reach levels of humiliation she hadn't dreamt possible unless we got away before Dom came back.

CHAPTER FIVE

Nathan

We finished our cigs in silence, skulking by the car in the side street like teenagers dodging their teachers, and as Dominic ground his fag butt into the ground, wobbling with the effort but looking altogether calmer, I cleared my throat and said casually, 'I've got a proposition for you. Let me drive you back to the train station, put you on the one minute past four back to Paddington and I'll give you a hundred quid in cash.'

He looked at me, confused.

'A hundred pounds to quietly go home, which is what you'll have to do eventually anyway, so you might as well get something out of it. You can't see your kid when you're like this, my friend.' I gestured at him. 'No one wants to be that dad.' It was a risk, but it seemed to resonate.

He looked down at his faded and slightly stained black jeans then rubbed his face as if thinking carefully.

'You'll get it out when we get to the station?'

Ah – so it was just the money talking. Well – whatever it took. I nodded.

He shrugged, wavered on the spot and admitted defeat. 'Go on then.'

I opened the car door before he changed his mind, and he climbed in. I drove fast to the train station. Dominic looked like an experienced drinker to me – his eyes were slits in puffy grey skin and he was sweating like a husky in summer. Nonetheless, I didn't intend to overestimate his capacity. I wasn't up for a pool of vomit swimming in the footwell. He sat back, his head heavy on the seat rest and closed his eyes. I tried not to grimace. His hair was unwashed enough to be practically slick. I wanted him out of my car.

'I've got a joke for you, mate,' he murmured, as if reading my mind. 'A Porsche driver crashes. The police find him crying in the front seat, going "oh my beautiful car!" They're all "You tit! Crying over a Porsche – you haven't even noticed your arm has been ripped off." The driver looks at the bloody stump and goes "Shit! Where's my Rolex?"' He sniggered to himself.

I forced a laugh. 'It's my wife's car, to be honest,' I lied. I don't know why I felt the need to explain anything to someone like him.

He opened one eye, looked at me and closed it again, grinning widely. 'If you say so.'

Being rumbled like that pissed me off – but I gritted my teeth, particularly when he burped suddenly and I was assaulted by the smell of flaccid hamburgers. The sound of his own bodily emission seemed to wake him up a bit. He began to fidget restlessly, sat up suddenly and looked around him, confused.

'Where are we?'

He'd forgotten already? I began to wonder if he was just very good at appearing more sober than was actually the case. 'We're driving to the train station, remember? You're going back to London.'

He rubbed his stubbly face with both hands. 'For a hundred quid.'

'That's right,' My voice was soothing. 'For a hundred quid. Like I said, as soon as we get there, you can have it.'

We lapsed into silence. He watched the students milling around outside Exeter College as we stopped at the lights, then turned his head to me and said, far more precisely than I was ready for: 'Yeah, but why? Why are you paying me off? Who is Jules to you? Are you seeing her?'

I glanced sideways at him. Tempting though it was to wind him up, he might turn ugly. In my experience, it's the wiry little blokes you really need to watch out for – they're the proper thugs. Nonetheless, I couldn't help being deliberately vague to pay him back for the Porsche comment. 'It's not up to me to explain our relationship. I'd better leave that to her.'

He stared at me and blinked a couple of times. 'Fuuuck. So *this* is what the big move's been about. That poor bastard, Ewan. First Lise cheats on him, now Jules? This'll gut him.'

I noted that with interest.

He wrinkled his nose. 'That doesn't sound like Jules, though… wait – so *you're* the reason I'm losing touch with my son?' He pointed at me accusatively.

'No – I just work with her!' I corrected quickly.

'So why are you paying me to go home?' He yawned involuntarily and gave an odd, sudden judder, like you do after taking a piss. I glanced at the floor of the car, horrified, but all seemed OK. 'I don't understand,' he concluded.

It couldn't be simpler: doing a good deed for Julia of this magnitude – smoothly getting rid of her troublesome ex – was going to make me appear *very* likeable and fast forward me through several weeks' worth of earning her trust via smaller-scale gestures. It was a bargain for a measly £100.

'A hundred quid. No questions asked,' I said. 'Deal?'

He sighed heavily. 'We both know I need it…' He shrugged and looked so bleak for a moment I almost felt sorry for him. He scrunched his eyes closed the way children do when they think that means you won't be able to see them anymore.

'Deal.'

That's right, I thought, as we lapsed into silence again. You just focus on how much vodka you can get for that, there's a good chap. I briefly wondered what he'd been before the booze took over, but then realised I didn't care.

We pulled into the station. 'Stay here,' I ordered, stopping in front of the entrance, jumping out and pulling my wallet from my pocket. I withdrew one hundred pounds from the cashpoint, returned to the car, opened his door and held out the small fold of twenties.

He took it slowly, counted it, the cheeky git, and undid his seat belt, tucking the money in the pocket of his denim jacket as he climbed out.

'Nice to meet you, Nathan.' He offered me his hand, swaying slightly.

We shook and I held him steady when he nearly wobbled over, but when I let go, he just stood there uselessly.

'Yeah, I'm going to need to see you board the train,' I said. 'Come on, it'll be here in a minute and you need to get through the barrier. Where's your ticket? You *have* got one, I take it?'

Luckily, he found it after a stressful – for me – hunt through numerous pockets; but it was so creased from being sat on that it didn't work when he tried to feed it into the slot with the exaggerated slow motion of extreme concentration. He missed twice before getting it right, straightening up with all the smugness of having successfully threaded a needle. He lurched through onto the platform and blankly stared up at the monitor, straining to read it, scratching his head, then visibly losing what little focus he had, pulling out the money, starting to count it again and looking around him – no doubt for a platform café selling tinnies.

I swore under my breath and approached the guard on the gate.

'Sorry, could I just come through to put my friend safely on the train?' I nodded over at Dominic who had dropped one of the notes and was bent over, struggling to pick it up off the floor, missing repeatedly.

The guard frowned. 'He's intoxicated, isn't he? I'm afraid I can't let him on the train in that condition.' He drew himself up self-importantly. 'I shall have to alert the Transport Police. I also can't let you onto the platform without a valid ticket for security reasons.'

I eyed him coldly. 'See it, say it, sorted' seemed rather to have gone to his head. Everyone is such an officious *wanker* these days. Dominic wasn't a walking bomb: he was a bit tipsy. We'd all been there. Well, maybe not at four in the afternoon on a school day, but still, whatever happened to kindness? Plus, someone like him didn't get to tell me what to do.

'You think my friend is *pissed*?' I said softly. 'Are you aware that cerebral palsy sufferers spend most of their lives having to deal with people like you, mistaking their disability for drunkenness?' I paused to give that statement time to sink in. 'I'm astonished that someone in a customer-facing role, in this day and age, hasn't had sufficient staff training to recognise the difference between the two. Actually – I'm *appalled* by what you've just said. I might have to tweet about this. What's your name?'

The guard paled, glanced at Dominic and swallowed nervously. 'I'm sorry, sir—'

'Doctor,' I interrupted, demoting myself from my 'Mr' status – as befits a consultant – to make the point. He was nearly sick on the spot.

'So sorry, doctor.' He swung the gate open. 'Please let me know if I can be of any further help, to either of you.'

I gave him a final glare – now actually outraged – until I remembered it wasn't real. Still, the point was a valid one, and perhaps next time he decided to be an unpleasant little jobsworth, he might stop and consider if the 'evidence' in front of him was really the whole picture.

I swept through the gate then hurried over to Dominic, who had finally managed to pick up the cash. The train was pulling in.

I led him over to the quiet-zone carriage, assuring him that the buffet trolley would come around once the train had left the station. He settled down very nicely and appeared to be already snoring, his face mashed onto the window, as they departed. The first stop wasn't until Taunton – and I was confident he'd sleep past that too… all the way through to Basingstoke. We were home and dry.

I sauntered out to the foyer, nodding curtly at the guard who immediately swung the gate open for me again, and climbed back into the car, which *didn't* have a ticket, despite my having dumped it on a double yellow. The gods were smiling.

I thought for a minute, drumming my fingers on the steering wheel, and called the school as I pulled away. The secretary answered and in my best Bond voice I asked her to pass an important message to Julia Blythe, mother of the new boy, Alex, in year eight, that the packet had been returned to its original destination.

It was fun – I nearly called her Moneypenny but managed not to. As I hung up, a euphoria swept through me at having set Julia's world right that was so thrillingly visceral, I sped up and accidentally ran a red. Hesitation is the cause of most accidents. Once you're committed, you've no choice but to go for it. I heard the squeal of brakes, a blast on a car horn and earned myself an angry man shouting silent obscenities through his car windscreen as I sailed past him, unperturbed.

*

When Julia had – out of nowhere – driven into the car park in a white Mini, I'd found myself temporarily thrown. My brain had gone into overdrive as it attempted to assimilate this unexpected, brand-new information. She was here, at pick-up time? She had kids at the school too? I silently cursed my wife's insistence that I collect Ben on his first day back. I'd already planned my first meeting with Julia – and it was me busily sweeping into the office before a full day's list – not hanging around the school gates like some self-employed, made-up-job dad with too much time on his hands. I'd crossly looked down at my phone in an attempt to appear busy and important, thinking that if I didn't catch her eye, maybe she wouldn't come over and start chatting. I wouldn't then have to do the excruciating bit of admitting I knew who she was, when she had no idea who *I* was. It was too annoying for words. Not the start I wanted at all.

But then something quite extraordinary happened. She walked right up to me, introduced herself, told me entirely unselfconsciously that she'd noticed me the day before at the hospital and reached out to take my hand… simply holding it in hers, quietly and gently. It was astonishing. My heartbeat slowed right down and I could *feel* her goodness transfusing through my skin as she touched me. I am not a spiritual man but it was a moment of complete, calm connection. I stared into her kind, make-up free eyes in amazement. They were utterly without guile. She withdrew her hand, and I blinked. She was frowning slightly.

Immediately worried that the strength of my reaction had unnerved her as much as it had me, I was about to pretend she had something on her face to excuse my looking into her soul, when it dawned on me that she had simply noticed the mismatch of my eyes.

I quickly – and far more breezily than I felt – gave her the usual explanation, leaning right in so she could get a closer look, and I could smell her… Pears soap – I didn't even know they made that anymore. I was suddenly in my grandmother's house as a child on summer holidays, and when I pulled back, Julia gave me the sweetest smile of recognition – as if she'd seen straight through to the small, floury boy chattering away happily, shaping offcuts as my kind grandmother methodically kneaded bread at the table, her skilled hands turning the dough this way and that. I felt completely exposed but oddly unafraid of the honest intimacy – although I garbled some conversational cardboard about hoping she was liking the hospital, while I tried to recover myself. She started to talk but I didn't hear what she was saying. A million thoughts were exploding in my head. I wanted her to touch me again… I wanted to make her smile like that again too.

Where was the woman as cool and intellectually slippery as running water that I'd been expecting? I was ready for the usual dance to begin, prepared to lure her into submission against her better judgement… but watching her mouth move softly as if she was in silent prayer, I realised this was going to be like corrupting an angel; a prospect which at once both terrified and enthralled me.

I was still shell-shocked when Dominic arrived seconds later – I didn't hear a word he said either – I was only able to focus on her face. She was obviously deeply distressed at the prospect of her son seeing his father half-cut on his first day, and quite simply, I wanted to help. The strength of my urge to protect her was overwhelming, in fact. I swung into action, determined to get him as far away from her as possible, as quickly as I could.

*

Putting my foot down and roaring back up the hill to collect poor abandoned Ben from after-school club, however, I began to gather my thoughts a little. I don't subscribe to the concept of 'the one'; it's a notion I have always scoffed at. Both of my wives were right at different times of my life. The first, Serena, wanted a Catholic wedding, which meant several meetings with the parish priest while he puffed fruity smoke from a pipe and asked me what I thought made this relationship so different to all of the others. The truth was, I had no idea; everyone around us was getting married – it just seemed the thing to do. Storm, I took to Vegas – her mother has never forgiven me – where I suggested she have a tattoo of my initials either side of a heart, in lieu of a permanent wedding band (we used my signet ring for the impromptu service). To my enormous surprise, she agreed – although it hurt… fingers do, the skin is so thin… and the wide platinum band I had to buy her to cover it up on our return because she wasn't feeling quite so rebellious by then, cost a bloody fortune. On neither of my wedding days did I experience any rush of emotion, certainty or a binding of souls.

As I thought of Julia now safely able to drive her son home, having been rescued from Dominic, however, the sense of purpose I felt was – I had to admit – very gratifying. That said, now I wasn't stood directly in the glare of her dazzling purity, I began to wonder if I was simply going to have to recalibrate my pursuit. Less a duel to the death, more a chase through a verdant forest that would see her caught and vulnerable, panting in my arms, eyes wide. Both are enjoyable in different ways, of course.

Except, I shivered involuntarily at the thought of holding her. It was something akin to being ambushed with an injection – writhing in protest – finding myself unable to prevent a sting then shock at *feeling* medication coolly infusing the blood, soothing the stomach, finally arriving as a taste in my mouth. Sensations over which I had no control but could acknowledge as a desire to be a better man, for her, while simultaneously feeling like a king.

My God. For the first time in my life… was I falling helplessly in love?

I laughed, but the sound was tinny and uncertain. Almost afraid.

CHAPTER SIX

Julia

'So tell me about your day!' I said brightly as we stopped at some traffic lights, trying not to panic as it occurred to me that just because we were no longer at the school, it wouldn't stop Dom returning and making a scene anyway. What if he was at this precise moment walking around the car park, yelling drunkenly for Alex by name? I swallowed anxiously.

'No one really talked to me,' Alex said, cheerfully. 'I think they will, though. It just takes time.'

I glanced at him quickly in the rear-view mirror. 'Is that what someone said to you or what you think?'

'Both,' he said, but didn't elaborate further.

'The headmistress made us stand up in the whole school assembly so everyone could get a better look at us.' Cass stared out of the passenger window. 'Which was really great of her and not at all epically embarrassing.'

'What?' I glanced at her in dismay. 'Why would she *do* that? What about all the new year threes having their first day too? Did she make them stand up as well?'

'Nope. Just us. Then she said Mr Wilder was our father, and *Dad* stood up, so Al said "He's actually my stepdad; my real dad is called Dominic and he's an artist but not a famous one." Everyone laughed – not *all* at him, I don't think, just most of them – and the whole time, I'm just standing there with everyone looking at me, so it was *awesome*.'

'I'm really sorry, Cass. I don't know what to say.'

'Well, now they all know who we are, and that we moved up from Surrey and two *more* things… technically, three… because the headmistress also said we had to tell everyone a fact about ourselves. Al said he wants to be an artist or photographer and he believes guinea pigs are the ideal pet' – she shook her head in disbelief – 'then I said "my mother died from cancer when I was eight and I don't want to talk about it".' A brief, triumphant smile flashed across her face and she looked out of the window again. 'That shut her up.'

My mouth fell open in amazement. 'You didn't really?'

'She did,' Alex confirmed. 'Word for word.'

There was a moment of silence. 'I think you're brilliant, Cass,' I said, truthfully.

'Thanks.' Cass leant her head back and closed her eyes. 'Can we just go home, then you come back later to get Dad? I don't want any cake.'

'We're not going to go home just yet, actually.' Dominic had the new address. What if he was already on his way there?

'But I'm really tired!' she complained, lifting her head up and scowling at me.

'Me too,' agreed Al. 'It was exhausting today. Actually, someone *did* speak to me. I think Ben likes me. Although he mostly asked about you, Cass. I said you don't tell me stuff like if you have a boyfriend and he should ask you himself.'

'Quite right, Al. Well done,' I said. 'Cass can absolutely talk for herself.'

Cass swung round in her seat. 'Don't tell him anything,' she ordered, before turning back. 'Urgh. I hate boys.'

'Except me,' Al said.

'Yes, but *please* stop talking to people about guinea pigs, OK?' She sighed again. 'I heard you at break. They weren't asking you because they were interested; they were teasing you. Tell them about your photos, or your art – whatever – just nothing about animals, all right?'

'Good to know, thank you.' He nodded.

'You're welcome.'

My heart broke a little for both of them, and I had to bite my lip to stop my eyes from welling up. Damn Dominic. We drove in silence for five minutes while I tried to think of a plan. I couldn't go back to the house. I simply wasn't prepared to let Alex see his father that way, when he was still learning to feel secure in his new surroundings.

Cass pulled a face. 'Where are we even going? It looks like we're just driving around in circles. Why can't we just... Oh – your phone is ringing.' She reached into my bag in the footwell by her feet and pulled it out. 'It says "Newschool".'

'Can you answer it? It'll be Dad.'

'Hey Dad – oh – sorry – hello. Nathan who did you say?'

'Can you give me that, please?' I reached out immediately. 'Now!'

'No! You're not hands-free!' She leant away, then glared at me. 'Six points and a fine. It's never worth it. Sorry, can you repeat the message again? The original what? OK. Yes, I will. Thank you.'

She hung up. 'A message from Nathan Sloan. He wants you to know the package has been returned to its original destination.' She spoke carefully and precisely. 'What does that mean?'

I caught my breath. 'You're sure that's what he said?'

'It wasn't a man. She said she was the school secretary. What package? What's she talking about?'

He'd put Dominic on the train home? Because that's what that message meant, didn't it?

I was astonished. How on earth had he managed that?

*

'Has the time come to block Dominic from seeing Al for a bit?' Ewan took his trousers off and dropped them in the dirty clothes basket.

'A restraining order, you mean?' I'd had a bath in an attempt to relax before bed, but accidentally made it so hot I'd had to climb out after a few minutes, feeling sick. My skin was still livid pink; crossing our room in my pjs to pull the curtains, I briefly leant my forehead against the cool window as raindrops cascaded down the glass, distorting my reflection.

'I don't want to do it.' Ewan sat down on the bed to take his socks off, balled them up and threw them in the basket too. 'But he can't turn up drunk out of his mind at school like that. It's unacceptable.'

'I know. If it hadn't been for Nathan Sloan…' I turned and stepped round a couple of boxes we hadn't yet unpacked. 'Although the fact that *he* had to help is obviously horrendous. I spoke to Dom's mum earlier. He's back at hers now, sleeping it off, apparently. She couldn't have been sorrier.' In fact, poor Sorcha had cried down the phone. All that money, yet none of it able to fix her son. I peered at a scribble in black marker on one of the boxes.

'Do you know what's in these? It says "loft" on here. I don't think they've been opened since the *last* move.' I tried to push one of them. 'They weigh a tonne.' It was almost certainly CDs or DVDs of *Friends* from a time when boxsets were cutting edge and streaming was something kids still did with welly boots and a jam jar. 'Do you mind moving them a bit more out of the way for now?'

'Sure.' Ewan put his weight to the first and then the second, shoving them tightly into the corner. 'But just to finish what we were saying – today can't happen again. I want us to have a chance to settle properly.'

'Agreed. Can I have a think about the best way forward as far as Dom goes?'

'Of course.' Ewan stretched his arms up then behind his back. 'Those are really heavy.'

'Did you see the kids much at break time? Were they mixing with the others in their year?' My face must have looked more anxious than I realised, because Ewan drew me into a hug.

'I watched them from the staff room window for a bit. Cass was OK – in a big group of the year eight girls. Al was very much on the outskirts of things, chatting to himself. He took a football to the head—'

My eyes closed briefly.

'…but I genuinely think that was an accident. I saw a few younger kids go up to him, say something and run off a few times – eventually Cass went over. I'm not sure what was going on. I didn't want to go down and get involved, but some other boy came across too. Quite a big lad, not tall like Al, but beefy… Al's year, I think; I'm not down with the names yet. He gave the younger kids an ear-bashing by the look of it, because they all scattered.' Ewan let go of me and took his T-shirt off. 'Then the same kid took Al over to another group of year eight boys. Al sat on the edge, but he was sort of interacting.'

Ben – it had to be – stepping in to look after Al because he could see it was important to Cass. He'd worked out a strategy quickly. 'Well, it could have been worse, I guess. Although I have no idea what I'm going to say to Nathan Sloan tomorrow. When I think about what Dominic might have told him… *that* along with whatever Nathan will have read about me and the Royal Grace…' I exhaled slowly. 'Do you think I should buy him something? A thank you for his help today?'

'No, because you're not responsible for Dominic. You were just married to him once. Just say thank you when you next see

Nathan and try to leave it at that.' He shrugged and got into bed. 'Nathan's a parent too. He'll appreciate the situation, I'm sure.'

*

Nonetheless, I arrived at ten to eight the following morning, hoping to catch Nathan alone before he headed off to start consenting his patients, but annoyingly Tan and Hamish were already there too, laughing at something. The noise died down when I walked into the room, and I immediately wondered if Nathan had told them what had happened the day before.

'Morning, Julia.' Hamish smiled. 'How are you? Disappointing news, I'm afraid. Firstly, this is the Scarlet Pimpernel – Nathan Sloan – regrettably, back from his holidays. Secondly, it's his birthday today and the tight sod hasn't brought any cakes in.'

'We met yesterday, actually.' I smiled. 'Happy birthday.'

'Thank you.' He nodded at me and immediately turned back to Hamish. 'I just forgot – that's all. I swear.'

Tan raised an eyebrow, and Hamish laughed again. 'He was so busy remembering that this is one of the two days a week he graces us with his presence,' Nathan flicked him a V-sign, 'that everything else flew from his mind. How often *do* you drive to the Goldtree Hospital car park by mistake only to realise it's one of your NHS and not private days? Just out of interest?' Hamish crossed his arms and waited.

'Yeah, yeah, yeah.' Nathan glanced up at the clock and sighed. 'I ought to go down, really.'

'A full list awaits the hand of God,' teased Hamish. 'Do you think you'll make it unassisted? Should we call for a porter and a chair now that you're at such an advanced age?'

Tan smiled and moved to his desk to leaf through some papers, pausing to sign them.

'How old *are* you, anyway?' Hamish asked, obviously knowing full well.

Nathan yawned. 'Old enough to know better—'

'...pissed enough not to care,' Hamish finished the quote, and Nathan shot a quick glance at me. I looked away first.

'I might go and get a proper coffee from downstairs.' I reached into my bag and pulled out my purse, wondering if he'd take the hint and come with me so I could apologise for Dominic and find out what exactly had happened, but he didn't say anything. 'Nathan? Treat you to a birthday latte?' I tried again. 'Have you got time for me to get you one before you go down? Can I get anyone else anything?'

Nathan hesitated. 'Go on then, thank you very much. I'd love one, if you don't mind.'

I smiled, slightly frustrated at his simply giving me his order. Men could be so dense. 'No problem. I'll bring it right up.'

'One sugar, please,' he added.

'He's definitely not sweet enough already.' Hamish stared at his mobile and frowned. 'I'm fine thanks, Julia.'

'I'm OK too,' Tan confirmed. 'But thank you for asking.'

I was only halfway down the corridor when I heard Nathan call my name.

'Hey.' He caught right up to me and I breathed in an intense, heady aftershave. 'I told the others I'd changed my mind and fancied a cappuccino instead, so we could grab a quick word. About yesterday—'

'I'm so sorry,' I began and scratched the back of my hand. 'I can't tell you how embarrassed I am.'

'No, please, don't be.' He stepped forward and lowered his voice. 'There's nothing to be embarrassed about. *I'm* sorry that the best way I could think of getting the message to you that I'd put him back on the train was via the school secretary. I didn't want anyone from this place involved.' He gestured behind him at our office. 'It seemed the least intrusive way to get in contact. I hope it all made sense. I thought you'd want to know what was going on? Did I do the right thing?' He looked troubled.

'Yes! I don't know how on earth you persuaded him, but whatever you did, it worked. Although when you made that comment about going for a cigarette and just disappeared off, I don't mind admitting I was pretty unsettled.'

'Well, I'm pleased to have unsettled you.' He stared at me and his mouth flickered into a smile.

I raised an amused eyebrow. He obviously couldn't help himself, and clearly men were not impervious to his charm either, but he'd been kind and I was very grateful. 'Whatever Dominic might have said, I just want you to know that—'

Nathan held up his hands. 'When we got in the car, he seemed to very suddenly hit a wall. He barely said a thing, just asked me to take him to the station because he wanted to go back to London. He didn't tell me anything of substance.'

I found that hard to believe. 'Really? It's not like him to give in without a fight. He honestly didn't say anything indiscreet to you, some allegation I might need to correct? Whatever must you think of me, thanks to my ex-husband and the newspaper reports.' I laughed lightly, scratching harder until I realised what I was doing and stopped, clasping my hands behind my back instead. 'I promise I'm not everything that people say about me.'

'You have nothing to worry about. We might have chatted a bit, but nothing controversial. I did find myself wondering how a man like him was ever married to a woman like you.'

My mouth fell open. That was a bit...

'I'm fascinated by how we're all a couple of wrong decisions away from life catastrophe,' he continued, 'but you don't have to tell me anything about Dominic's backstory at all – obviously. Anyway – we'll just leave it there.' Luckily, he hadn't noticed my misunderstanding him. 'I've not breathed a word about this to anyone – I hope that goes without saying?' He looked at me sincerely. 'This stays between you and me. As for what I may or may not have read in the papers, you work here now, you're one of us. That's all that matters.'

Before I had chance to respond to that, the clinical nurse specialist joined us. 'Morning both! Happy birthday, Mr Sloan. Another year gone! I remember when *you'd* just joined here. My goodness, that makes me feel old!'

'Nonsense, Joan, you're the lifeblood of this place. We'd be lost without you.' Nathan placed an affectionate hand on her shoulder. 'I also know what you're after and yes, I have signed it – give me *two* seconds and I'll dig it out. Julia,' he turned back to me, 'thank you, it's really kind. Decaf, one sugar.' He let go of Joan, spun on his heels and returned to our office.

'Ah, that's nice!' Joan said, approvingly. 'Mr Sloan is one of those people who always looks after everyone else, so you're a good deed, doing something for him for a change. It's the little things, isn't it? Just letting people know they're appreciated. Such a gorgeous man,' she sighed. 'I must say, it's very nice to see you're not above doing a coffee run either – you're going to fit in beautifully.' She beamed at me. 'Ooh! You've a bird on the line!' She nodded at my trouser pocket, which had started to ring. 'I'll let you get on.'

I waited as she walked briskly towards our office, brandishing some forms, and pulled the phone out: Dominic.

'Jules? Are you there?'

'Yes.' I walked down the corridor towards the coffee shop.

'I'm so sorry. I don't know what to say.' As usual, the morning after the night before, he was contrite. It was like talking to a completely different person. 'I was angry that I'd not had chance to speak to Al. I miss him so much.'

'So you thought the way to show that was turning up drunk to abuse everyone instead?' I kept the emotion from my voice. Stick to the facts.

'I know, I know.' He sounded wretched. 'There's no excuse. I'm just – really struggling at the moment with him being so far away.'

'When we were living twenty-five minutes away from you, sometimes Al didn't see you for several months at a time. You'd often say you were coming, then simply not turn up, leaving him very disappointed.'

'That's fair,' he admitted. 'But I really want to be a good dad to him now. He's all I've got.'

'That's not true,' I said, 'and even if it was, it wouldn't be OK to put the weight of that neediness on Al's shoulders. He's thirteen. He's not responsible for your happiness.'

'Look – you're angry with me.' He sniffed. 'I can hear it in your voice. I get it and I'm sorry. I shouldn't have rocked up a bit merry.'

'You were barely able to stand; you were rude to me in front of another parent—'

'Nathan,' he said immediately, and I stopped walking.

'You remember him?' I held the phone to my ear and listened carefully, stepping to one side so a trolley could be wheeled past me.

'Yeah, of course. He drove me back to the station.'

'What did you say to him?' I'd betrayed myself as too interested though, and practically heard Dominic sit up. He forgot he'd rung to apologise and changed tack completely.

'Why do you care?' he said curiously. 'Who exactly is this bloke to you? Are you up to your old tricks, Jules?'

I shook my head incredulously. His jealousy and paranoia were astounding. It had always been there, under the surface, but now it floated openly on the ever-present pool of alcohol he spent so much of his time slipping into. 'Stop playing games. There are no "old tricks" and you know it. I'm married to Ewan.'

'You were married to me,' he shot back.

'Hi there! Morning!' I smiled as I passed another consultant on their way up to the department. 'I'm not getting into this again. You know what happened, why I left you. It had nothing to do with Ewan. You can choose to rewrite history or face reality, it's up to you, but while we're on the subject of Ewan, he asked me last night if I think the time has come for a restraining order against you, to stop you from seeing Alex.'

'Bastard! It's nothing to do with him!' he exclaimed. 'Nothing at all!'

'He was asking me what *I* think,' I continued, ignoring that unpleasant outburst. 'What would you say if you were me? You were abusive, drunk and unpredictable yesterday – outside a *school*. Should I let you go on seeing our son when you're like that?'

'Don't, Jules, please!' he begged. 'I'm sorry!' As ever he came full circle all over again. It was so sad and such a waste of both of our lives. 'Please don't go back to the courts. We don't need to involve them. We always were a good team, weren't we, eh? Remember? Please, Jules. I'll sort myself out, I promise.'

I hung up. I could spend the next thirty, forty, fifty minutes on the phone to him. It wouldn't change anything. He'd genuinely just asked me if I was having an affair with Nathan Sloan and that's why we were here? He was *so* manipulative.

I shoved my phone back in my pocket as I arrived at the coffee shop, disquieted, uncomfortable and angry, and began to queue for Nathan's cappuccino, one sugar.

CHAPTER SEVEN

Nathan

I drummed my fingers on the cool surface of my desk, glancing up at the clock. I should be going downstairs to start the meet and greets – Tan had already left to do his – rather than waiting for Julia to bring the cappuccino back up, yet my legs would not move. I wanted to make sure she was OK, that I hadn't upset her. I'd overdone it with the remark about not seeing how Dominic had ever been married to a woman like her. Julia had been unnerved.

'Must you make that noise? It's bloody irritating.'

I looked left to discover Hamish was frowning at me. I didn't answer; just flicked up the middle finger that had been drumming, instead.

'Charmed, I'm sure. Go on then, I'll bite.' He crossed his arms. 'What's wrong?'

I sighed. 'Nothing.'

He turned in his chair to face me properly. 'This is reminding me of the day when you almost didn't go in for your final exam. You were "convinced" you'd fail it. Remember I told you I was sick of paying for you and you couldn't live in my parents' flat forever – so you were going whether you liked it or not? And I actually stood over you while you got dressed?'

I sighed again. 'Yes. You've always been both bossy *and* a pervert.'

Hamish raised an eyebrow. 'You placed in the top five per cent *nationally*. Do I *really* need to have a similar pep talk with you now? Is it the big op this afternoon… or,' he looked at me slyly, 'something to do with our new girl?'

'Julia?' I scoffed quickly. 'You do talk crap sometimes, Hamish. On the subject of Julia though, it turns out her kids are at school with Ben. I forgot to tell you.' I began to rifle through my things absently as if my mind was very much elsewhere, although I had no idea what I was pretending to look for. 'She's got a boy in the same class. Might prove useful.'

Hamish put his head on one side. 'You know you said about checking her balls?'

'Yes. What about it?' I regretted making my cheap anatomical remark about Julia. My veneer of niceness sometimes wore a little too thin. It was better when I wasn't allowed to be myself.

'Well, that was a joke, wasn't it? You also said you were giving this one the swerve, remember?' Hamish has a ridiculous memory for detail. He would almost certainly have lined up rows and rows of colour-coded toy cars as a child – only in our day, parents didn't consider that spectrum behaviour. They were too busy completely ignoring us.

'Why was she pointedly making a thing of offering you coffee, only for you to then leg it out of the room after her?' Hamish wasn't letting it go. 'One might think you were wanting a private word with each other?'

'Well, one would be completely wrong and seeing things that aren't there.' I was annoyed that it had been *that* obvious. I'd forced myself to stay at my desk when she asked if I wanted to join her, only to buckle at the last minute and run after her anyway, like an excited puppy, cartoon love hearts exploding in the air all around me. Fuck's sake.

'Anyway – yesterday,' I mentally scrunched up the humiliating picture, 'we had a situation at the school gates. Julia had just introduced herself when her ex-husband showed up from London. Drunk as a skunk, demanding to see their son. Julia panicked. I ended up taking him to the station and paid him a hundred quid to get back on the train to London.' I got up and began to gather myself.

'Well… did you now.' Hamish looked at me thoughtfully and crossed his arms. 'That was kind of you.'

'Well, *she* thought so,' I added crossly, 'which was the point. It was a tactical manoeuvre, obviously.'

'Of course it was.'

I looked at the ground before looking up at him. 'What is it you're very irritatingly *not* saying?'

'It was my asking you not to touch her, wasn't it? That's what's made her fatally irresistible.'

'Stop it.'

'Can you *please* not, just this once? You really don't have to mount everything in sight, Nate. I just don't think we should rattle her cage. Apart from anything else, it'd be like fucking a coat hanger.'

'I said stop it – wind your fat neck in!' I exploded. Hamish looked astonished.

'Sorry!' I said. 'I didn't mean to snap, Ham. You're right, I'm on edge about the op this afternoon. I feel out of my depth and it's getting to me a bit. I'll be all right once it's done, but this is really nothing to do with you – or Julia, who for the record, *doesn't* interest me in the slightest. Right.' I patted my pockets. 'I need to go.'

'Don't forget your coffee.'

I spun around at the sound of her voice and there she was, standing in the doorway, holding out a takeaway cup. For a horrible moment I thought she might have heard me, but rather she lifted the drink a little higher. 'You especially asked for a cappuccino, remember?' She gave me a flicker of her eyebrows, reminding me of our secret exchange in the corridor.

I hadn't offended her. I immediately wished I hadn't told Hamish about her husband and kept her confidence as I'd promised. I'd already let her down. 'That's very kind of you, thanks, Julia!' I deliberately avoided Hamish's eye as I walked forward and took the coffee. 'Have a good day.'

'You too.' She stood to one side like we were at the front door of our house and she'd just handed me my briefcase. As I passed, I caught an intoxicating waft of clean clothes, more Pears, and coconut shampoo. I managed to wait until I'd turned the corner at the end of the corridor before I moaned aloud.

*

It was my last op of the day that was the big one, and I was grateful to feel my confusion, discomfort, *everything* else melting from my mind as I scrubbed in. My patient had a bad case of lymphoedema that had caused a build-up of fluid around her waist. Gravity was doing its thing and dragging the skin down so badly she was struggling with basic tasks like urinating, walking and cleaning herself effectively, to say nothing of the recurrent infections she kept getting. Abdominoplasty – or tummy tucks – aren't normally funded on the NHS and she didn't meet the usual criteria, being grossly overweight, but I'd fought and fought for her to have her abnormality removed when the Commissioning Groups rejected my request the first time. It went way beyond being a cosmetic issue – it was adversely affecting the quality of her life and I wanted to improve it for her. Plus I was deeply pissed off that they'd said no. Having got my way eventually, I then realised I was actually going to have to get in there and do it. It wasn't just a case of slicing off a lot of tissue; there were some tasty blood vessels I needed to take care of. Nothing about the op was straightforward, apart from the fact that I might fuck it up and be left with an enormous dead woman on the slab.

When I finally had her unconscious, I couldn't help but take a moment to marvel at the sheer expanse of flesh before me. The skin had become crumpled and leathery in appearance, and her navel was so stretched it looked like a vertical letterbox. There were a lot of us in the room and, as ever when we're under a little bit of pressure, I went into full smooth mode, belying the pre-op panic beneath my own skin. I was smiley, made lots of little jokes, plenty of pleases and thankyous. I started to hum while the anaesthetist, Paul, made some last-minute checks. He wasn't looking as relaxed as usual either, poor sod. He was going to be glad when we were done and she opened her eyes again.

'Happy to start?' I asked him, and he nodded.

'Happy, Jim?' I checked with the surgeon assisting me.

'Ready.' He gave me the thumbs up. There was nothing for it but to cut. I made my first delicious long slice from hip to hip – wary of straying into her abdominal wall and the internal organs being protected below – to reveal a layer of snow white then yellow fat. It was like watching a painting well up from beneath the surface of a blank canvas as the red threads weaving through the severed tissue began to bead and shine under the theatre lights.

As ever, the moment I was in, I felt calm. When I was a younger man, the first cut would occasionally trigger a sense of euphoria that would necessitate my needing to lean against the operating table to hide the evidence of my excitement. These days, I experience a much more convenient equilibrium on entry. I made a second incision to free the belly button, and after that it was a question of working through my mental checklist; I separated the tissue quickly but slowed down as I turned my attention to the blood vessels. The last thing I wanted was heavy blood loss. Once they were safely cut and tied, I felt calmer still as I removed the remaining tissue, created a new hole for the navel, painstakingly realigned the abdominals and stitched it all back into place before pulling the skin together. Having closed, I allowed myself a tingle of exhilaration at having got away with it.

'Thank you everyone!'

We woke her up immediately because of her size, and although she was confused, she asked for her husband. I'd done my bit – now it was over to her. It had been almost four hours, but I'd barely noticed. I really am so much better at functioning in theatre than navigating the far more complex demands of everyday life. But I wasn't going to think about any of that. I wanted to suggest going for a drink to the team. Usually you can always rely on the anaesthetist to be up for a bit of trouble, but Paul was one of the rare breed who liked to push off back to his family, and while Jim was always polite – as the younger surgeon – I sometimes got the feeling he didn't much like me or was professionally jealous. Whatever, I was left with no choice but to head home once I'd checked the office and discovered Hamish had cleared off for the day too.

*

By the time I arrived back at the empty, dark and cold house, my equanimity had already dissipated. I checked my phone and remembered it was Ben's swimming night. Wandering into the kitchen, I ate a bit of ham, got myself a beer then mooched back into the sitting room. I couldn't be arsed to light the fire and only managed ten minutes of Gerard Butler saving the White House before discovering I wasn't in the mood for that either. I dicked around on my phone for a few minutes, but tiring of that too, threw it down on the sofa. I was restless and considered hitting the gym, only it was now peak after-work time. I'd have to wait for the machines, which would annoy the hell out of me and ruin the workout. I looked around the room, tapping my foot restlessly on the floor, then impulsively jumped up to go and find my laptop.

Sat at my desk in my study, I started it up, located a file within a file within a file called 'accounts and expenditure 16–17', paused and listened carefully to the empty house. Nothing. I was alone. I glanced at my watch. I still had a good hour until they came back.

I selected a thirty-second film of a half-naked woman, but it was tedious. The next patient had her legs spread. Labiaplasty. Unmoved I clicked on to the next... one of my favourites, who has no idea I look at her whenever I want to. I watched myself examining her, lifting the flesh, remembering how it had felt to touch it at the time... but it wasn't doing it for me tonight. I sighed tersely and moved on to my most recent addition to the collection: Stefanie.

It's always a bonus when the star of the show is someone you know socially. I settled back, watched her come into my consulting room – only to fast forward through the dull talky bit where we had discussed her possible augmentation. I let it start to play as Stef stood up to take off the top half of her clothes, unhooking her bra and sitting on the edge of the couch, ready for me to examine her, while I faffed around washing my hands. Hilariously, because she thought my back was turned, she quickly pinched her nipples to make them erect. I smirked. Yeah, stiff, that made all the difference.

I watched myself start to inspect her, tracing my finger round the edge of the breast where I was suggesting the implant would fill out the new shape, then laughed – the sound resonating around my empty study – as she immediately picked up my hand and moved it between her legs, the randy bit of old mutton. I bet she doesn't do that sort of thing for poor old Steve. Handy that she'd worn a skirt too. Almost like she'd planned it. I rolled my eyes and toyed with unzipping my trousers, but found I wasn't sufficiently interested.

Instead, I crossed my arms and watched as we began to fuck. She was lying back, legs splayed and eyes closed...

Nothing. It was no good. I hit pause – just as I winked over my shoulder at the camera lens – sighed and leant forward to pull open my drawer, starting to look around for my blade in among the papers...

'Hello? Dad? Where are you?'

My heart almost stopped. I slammed the drawer closed and the lid of the laptop down. Luckily, I didn't even have a semi, so was able to hurry straight out into the hall. Ben was standing there, a multitude of school bags hanging off him, framed by the car headlights beaming in through the open front door. He turned and gave a thumbs up, at which the wheels crunched the gravel before pulling away.

'Mum's gone to get some milk. She said could you put the lasagne in the oven?' He began to unload, kicking his shoes off and unzipping his coat.

'What happened to swimming?' I said, thanking my lucky stars I'd kept it in my pants after all.

'We got a message when we were arriving that the swimming teacher was ill, so...' He shrugged. 'Can I play *Fortnite*?'

'Yeah, sure,' I said, halfway to the kitchen before catching myself. 'After you've done your homework though.'

I heard him groan and smiled briefly. And it was ever thus. I located the lasagne, read the instructions and put it on at the right temperature – who says I never cook? – before remembering the laptop. I chucked the food packaging in the bin, before pausing to fish it out and put it in the *recycling*, as I'd been instructed to do on numerous occasions, and hastened back to my study.

'Ben? Are you upstairs?' I shouted, once I was in there. His distant and muffled response was affirmative. I had a clear window. I opened the laptop and winced at the sight of my own naked arse. That would have taken some explaining. I felt my pulse quicken slightly at the thought of being publicly exposed, grabbed my phone, took a quick pic of the laptop screen and sent it through to Hamish via our Snapchat, with the message:

some new content for you.

It was by way of an apology for calling him fat earlier. A message pinged back immediately:

hahahahahaha!

I smiled. I was forgiven. I could practically hear him running to log in to the practice cameras.

I deleted the downloaded file on my laptop without a second thought. There would be others. I got up and went to find Ben, who was diligently doing his homework, tapping away on *his* keyboard. The whole house was nothing but bloody devices.

'Hey buddy, I'm going to jump in the shower. Will you tell Mum the lasagne went in at quarter past when she gets back... Ben?'

He nodded silently but didn't look up. I raised my hands in surrender and drifted off. Far be it for me to disturb a genius at work, and God forbid we should have something actually approaching a conversation.

I stripped off in our en-suite and climbed under the shower, starting to soap myself while contemplating the next few tricky days ahead. I'd packed a bit too much onto the private list, and a former NHS breast cancer patient of mine had popped her tightly permed head back up again. The implants I'd given her had fucked up, and she was scheduled to have them removed on Friday – my private surgery day – so I wasn't going to be around to correct my own work. While her implants going wrong wasn't my fault, I *was* uneasy that I hadn't taken enough of the surrounding tissue when I'd removed the bulk of the cancer during her original op. At the time, I knew I'd rushed it, but had put it from my mind, given that there was just enough of a border and the chemo would probably catch anything that was still there. It was a worry that my carelessness might be about to bite back, depending on who was down to do her op. If it was Hamish, I'd be fine. Julia, on the other hand…

And there she was. Back in my head, holding out my coffee.

I carried on cleaning myself. Her smile… I exhaled, closed my eyes and saw myself removing *her* clothes, rather than via Stefanie's brazen manoeuvres. I tried to focus on Stef instead, only for Julia to return. I was kissing her – it was all practically virginal – but then… I pictured us in bed; me on top of her, moving slowly, an expression of wonder and rapture on that angelic face of hers. An intensity crept up on me out of nowhere. I exhaled with a gasp of surprise and after a second or two, rested my forehead on the wet tiles; the longing of a mere moment ago already having morphed into something pathetic and desperate, post release.

Still her face swam in my head. Oh, this was not good, not good at all. Hamish was right, she was *nothing* to look at… but the way she looked at me… shit.

I must have muttered that aloud because I heard a voice behind me say: 'Yes, that about covers it.'

I half jerked round, my back still to the door, to see my wife standing there, watching me, arms folded in disgust. 'I've just come back to a kitchen full of smoke that your thirteen-year-old son is trying to sort out because you put the lasagne on to grill, not cook. The alarms didn't go off, so I assume that means you still haven't replaced the batteries after I asked you to the other day, when you removed them because the "bleeping" was annoying you. But I can see you're "busy".' She shot me another revolted look. 'So *I'll* sort it out, shall I? Ben said he called you, but you didn't answer him. He's in tears down there, just so you know.'

'Well, I'm sorry, but perhaps if we had a little more time together, I wouldn't be up here doing—' I began defensively.

'Ah, of course,' she cut in before I could finish. 'It's my fault you can't even put the oven on properly, then snuck up here for a wank.'

'I'm just tired. I didn't do it on purpose!'

'You *accidentally* found yourself having a wank?'

'No! The lasagne! I didn't grill it on purpose. I've done a major operation this afternoon – the obese woman. It went well though, thanks for asking. She didn't die and I think I've vastly improved her quality of life, so…'

She hesitated, regarded me for a moment and sighed tightly. 'Just get dressed and come down, all right?'

I heard her calling Ben, jollying him along, asking if he'd like fish fingers and chips instead, as I climbed out and started to dry myself. Winding the towel tightly round my waist, I walked through the bedroom to our dressing room. Looking at myself half-naked in one of the full-length mirrors, I flexed my arms then drew my already flat stomach in further, turning sideways to examine myself in profile. Good for any age, not just my own, but… I leant forward, closer to the glass, inspecting my hairline before looking myself deep in the eyes. I suddenly had one of those hideous moments when you blink and twenty years have passed. The hopeful boy you were only yesterday is – just for a moment – somehow there again, inhabiting your sagging old skin with a sense of disbelief. I reached out and touched the cold glass, then drew my fingertips back and placed them on the lines under my eyes, before running them incredulously down to the sharp stubble on my chin, now flecked with grey… then the boy was gone again and I stared at everything I had become.

I'd just admonished my wife for not putting out, when I'd shagged someone else the day before we went on our family holiday, in the private practice room *she* designed for me… and I'd filmed it. I didn't give a thought to her – or Stefanie. I felt no guilt. I rarely feel anything these days. The older I become, the more I worry I'm not a very nice man at all.

So how had *Julia* apparently cut straight to a taut, infected part of me, so deeply buried I hadn't even known it was there, and simply lanced it? I'd just imagined us, for want of a better phrase, 'making love'… Christ. I shivered and sat down on the edge of Storm's cerise velvet chaise lounge, despite hearing her voice in my head telling me to get up because my towel was damp.

I was already craving that release again. It was akin to the sensations I'd experienced outside the school when Julia held my hand, and in the corridor at work as she passed me the coffee – only on steroids. Just feeling *something* was exhilarating.

But *why* was she doing this to me? It couldn't be anything as disappointingly predictable and teenage as simply wanting what Hamish had told me not to have?

On the other hand, that was preferable to fancying myself falling in love on the strength of two meetings lasting mere minutes, as I had done in the car after 'rescuing' her.

I lifted my head and looked in the mirror again. A frightened man stared back at me. Privately struggling with unfamiliar feelings that seemed to have just temporarily overwhelmed me was one thing. The prospect of totally giving in to them, and where that might lead, was quite another.

It was imperative that I immediately disengage any fanciful notion of 'feelings' for Julia Blythe. I wanted to have sex with her – that was all. But now I might not even bother with that. Hamish was wrong – I actually could take it or leave it. I was perfectly capable of walking away and *not* pursuing Julia Blythe. Then again, I might just do it for the hell of it. Either way, *I* was in control. No one else. Me.

CHAPTER EIGHT

Julia

I frowned, looking critically at the bloodied cavity in the chest of the unconscious sixty-year-old woman on the table. 'Just move the retractor back a bit, please?'

As one of the team assisting me obliged, I got a better look at what had been cut away during my patient's last operation. Her cancerous breast tissue had been removed and implants inserted into the space left behind to create volume again. Her body had responded naturally to this foreign object by forming an internal web of scar tissue around the implants. Unfortunately, this pocket had then started to tighten, causing a severe capsular contraction that had deformed her new breasts and left her in a lot of pain. It was unusual for encapsulation to occur only four months after the original surgery and a particularly cruel blow given everything she'd already been through... Her grown-up daughter had been very upset and wanted answers as to why it had happened.

'I read online that too much touching of an implant before it's put in can raise the risk of infection. Is that true?' she'd demanded before the surgery. Her mother reminded me of a dinner lady I'd had as a child. Tight, springy grey curls, glasses and fierce demeanour. You held out your plate to her, got what you were given and were thankful for it. Her daughter was cut from the same cloth. 'So it could be the surgeon's fault this happened?'

Litigious alarm bells rang, and aware from her mother's notes that Nathan had performed her double mastectomy and reconstruction, I chose my words carefully. 'There are lots of potential causes of encapsulation, but when I remove the implants today, the pain that your mother is currently in, will stop.' I turned to Mrs Dowden herself. 'You've decided that you don't want more implants, though?'

'No, I don't!' she'd said. 'I'd rather be flat and get on with it. I've got things that need doing.'

'I'll take good care of you,' I said and smiled.

'Yes, you do that,' her daughter remarked, pointedly. Quite the charmer.

Once I'd got under way, however, I forgot about her attitude and now, with the first of the troublesome implants out, I was almost ready to do the other side. Except I was concerned to see quite so much of the original breast tissue. Still frowning, I began to trim it back carefully, right up to the muscle. While I was sure that Nathan was confident he'd left a safe border, I wouldn't have been happy with that much remaining in situ had she been my patient – and now she *was* mine, I thought privately, I was going to be a bit more thorough.

It took longer than expected, but by the time I was closing the incision on the right breast, I was feeling much happier. 'Good.' I looked down at the edges of the skin I'd carefully joined back together. She'd have neater scars now too.

'We're done. Thanks, everyone. Have a good weekend.'

I walked away from the table, past the tray containing the redundant bloodied breast implants and went to scrub out. Glancing at the clock, I prayed the traffic wasn't too bad. I wanted to get home in plenty of time to catch up with the kids over their tea before the babysitter arrived and I had to start getting ready.

I was tired and didn't feel like going out to dinner, but a school mum from home had kindly put me in touch with someone she knew, who lived in Exeter… *she* had equally kindly invited me and Ewan to dinner to meet them and some other local couples. It was a good opportunity to start building a social life and important to make the effort. Mindful, however, of how aggressive – probably frightened – Mrs Dowden's daughter had been, I went down to recovery before leaving, to find what I hoped would be a much more relaxed and relieved family.

I could hear them talking as I rounded the corner, which was always a good sign, but as I slipped around the curtain, I discovered Nathan there, chatting away like an old friend.

'Hello!' I said in surprise. 'It's not your day here, is it?'

'I wanted to pop in and check on Mrs Dowden.' He had his arms crossed. 'I did her original reconstruction, of course, and was only sorry I *couldn't* be here today, but thank you for stepping in, Julia. All's well that ends well. You'll be much more comfortable now, Mrs Dowden, and home again in no time. We'll let you get some rest. Shall we?' He gestured for us to leave, but I held up a hand. I hadn't had a chance to—

'Thank you so much, Mr Sloan, for all you've done,' the daughter interjected. 'And for taking the time to explain what could have caused Mum's reaction to the implant so thoroughly.' She glared at me.

'Not a problem at all. Pleasure,' Nathan said. 'You can always reach me if you have any more concerns, but I'm sure this is going to mark a real turning point. Now, if you've no further questions?'

They shook their heads.

'Well, you both take care. I don't want to see you back here again, OK?' He pointed warningly at Mrs Dowden and grinned, pulling the curtain back. She actually *giggled* and after that, there didn't seem anything for me to add.

I simply said, 'Glad you're feeling more comfortable now.' They briefly glanced in my direction as if I was an extra in *Casualty* who hadn't really warranted a line, and we left.

To my surprise, Nathan marched off ahead and had reached the double doors when I called after him, still trying to make sense of what had just happened.

'I didn't explain to the family about what could have caused the encapsulation because the daughter started asking if excessive handling of the implant might have been responsible,' I explained as I caught up with him and we pushed through the doors together. 'I wasn't being lazy. I just didn't want to get into that.'

He looked appalled as we made our way back to the office. 'Excessive handling? What's wrong with these people? Always looking for someone to blame. I did what I always did: out of sterile conditions, straight into her. No messing. Did they say anything else?'

'No. Nothing at all.'

'Good.' He exhaled. 'I certainly don't think you were being lazy, and I don't want you to think I was checking up on you, either.'

That hadn't occurred to me until he said it.

'I came in because – and this is going to sound daft – old Ma Dowden *really* reminds me of my mother. They're both of the generation that dismisses the opinion of other women completely, but if a *man* says exactly the same thing, it's gospel, so I hope she wasn't unpleasant to you? I was worried she might let rip...'

'Well, that was nice that you wanted to back me up.' So that was why he'd more or less taken over? We arrived back and he stood to one side to let me through the door first. 'It obviously meant a lot to them that you came in too.' I hesitated, but before I had the chance to say anything else, one of the nurses appeared, putting an envelope on Tan's desk.

'Nice new colour!' Nathan remarked as she passed him. 'That really suits you!'

'Thanks Mr S!' she called over her shoulder, patting her hair as she left, and I stared at him, rather thrown by that unexpected comment.

'There's something else I needed to mention.' He didn't notice my stare, just carried on. 'You're out to dinner tonight to meet some new friends, aren't you?' He held up a hand and pointed at himself. 'Me – I'm one of the "new friends".'

'Oh!' I exclaimed, before I could help myself.

'I know, sorry. It only clicked when my wife said Stefanie and Steve had invited us to dinner to introduce a new couple to the area. "She's a surgeon at the hospital; he's a teacher at St Ben's… " I told you – Exeter is a *very* small world. Anyway, I'm going to cancel. No one wants to hang out with their colleagues when they've been at work with them all week.'

His tone was brusque, and I paused. 'Well, you're honest, at least!' I tried to laugh.

He blushed. 'No, no – I meant *you* probably don't want to hang out with *me*!'

'Oh!' I laughed properly. 'I thought you were just being forthright that you find me boring. Please come. It'd be nice to have a familiar face there.'

He scratched his head. 'Well, I guess I might see you in a bit then.' He picked up a very nicely tailored camel coat, slung casually over the back of his chair. 'You going for a run on the way home?' He pointed at my trainers poking out of my gym bag under my desk.

'No, I went before work. I'm more of a morning person. Hang on – are Stefanie and Steve smart?' I called after him as he went to leave. 'I've never actually met them before.'

'He's a partner in a local law firm. She's a barrister at the chambers around the corner from him. Think three courses at the dining table, special china.' He slipped his coat on. 'Take the good wine and don't wear your wellies.'

'Oh ha ha.' But I smiled as he disappeared. I'd missed being able to joke around with colleagues. It felt good.

'Hi, Julia,' another surgeon, Eleni, walked in and looked around. 'The men have all gone home, eh? It's OK, we will finish up! Has a scan just been brought into here that was meant for me?'

'Something just went onto Tan's desk?'

'Ah!' She walked across and peered at the envelope over the top of her glasses. 'That's the one. Thank you.' She picked it up then paused to rub the back of her neck and groaned. 'I'm getting too old for all of this hunching over! Was that Nathan I just saw leaving?'

'Yes.' I smiled.

'On a Friday?'

'That's what I said!' I laughed. 'But he came in to check on a patient of his, so I guess we can't be too mean.'

'Yes, he likes taking care of people.' She hesitated, seeming to consider something and took her glasses off. 'You know, in all my years as a surgeon, I've put up with walking down corridors in scrubs and people saying "excuse me, nurse?".'

I smiled encouragingly, although this was sounding like the start of a longer-than-I-had-time-for anecdote.

'A man puts on scrubs and bam – he's a surgeon, the big man, yes?' she continued. 'And it's the little things too – surgical instruments are made to fit a man's hand. The damn gloves are too big. I don't need to tell you – you've got children… you've missed first steps, school plays… this job has tried to make a man of you. Years ago, I had a friend who was a nurse. She said to me, "why is it all female registrars are lovely, so approachable, but then they become surgeons and it stops? They won't talk to the nurses anymore".' Eleni shrugged. 'I protested – but she was right, we have to become like the men. For survival.'

I smiled, still clueless as to where she was going with this. She looked at me steadily as if she was trying to assess something, and then said, 'So just today, let's go *all* the way and talk like they do! Nathan is so pretty, isn't he? But you know what I think is *really* hot in a male surgeon?'

My eyes widened. I hadn't seen that coming. Eleni was a beautiful but steely sixty-something Greek grandmother. 'What's "hot"?' I repeated, making sure that was really what she'd said.

'Yes,' she said, impatiently. 'Attractive, sexy. I'll tell you,' she put her glasses back on, 'it has nothing to do with how they look. It's the way I hear them speak to their patients and the way they *listen*. Tan, for example. He is a gentle and sincere man – and oh! Be still, my heart!' She clapped her hand to her bosom. 'They are the authentic ones. They don't need to be "seen" caring.

'Now Nathan Sloan is *very* attentive. And recently I notice things, that someone about to retire doesn't want to see.'

She placed a hand briefly on my shoulder. 'You didn't get to this point without knowing how things should work. You spoke out. You were a public champion. I read about you in the papers and I cheered. So perhaps you will keep your eyes open in this quiet little place.' She looked at me meaningfully then her face broke into a broad smile. 'You look dismayed. I know, I know – but what do I care anymore? Just days, Julia and I'm *outta* here!'

I thought about the hair colour comment I'd *just* heard Nathan make, the nurses I'd seen him flirting with before we'd even been introduced, and cleared my throat. 'I'll be honest, Eleni. It took me about five minutes to work out Nathan is "popular" with the female staff, although I'm grateful for the warning. You're very kind to think I still feature on the radar of men in *that* way.'

She stared at me for a moment. 'We women! Who needs the men to do it when we put ourselves down so well, eh?'

I blushed. 'Fair point, but Nathan has been a good friend to me since I arrived here. I will say that.' I held up my hands as if in surrender, as I thought about him leading Dom away.

'Attentive, yes!' She was becoming impatient with me. 'This is what I'm saying. Listen Julia, you are female – he's interested, OK? He has an agenda.'

Wow. She was really pushing the point. 'Well, thank you, but even if he did have an "agenda" I'm not some med student whose knickers will fly off for Dr Handsome because *everyone* falls hopelessly in love with him. I would have some say in the matter, and I'm very happily married, thank you.' My tone was tarter than I'd intended, but Eleni's face broke into a wide smile.

'That's more like it!' She patted me on the arm. 'Have a good weekend.'

*

I was still thinking about Eleni's warning when Al found me putting on a bit of make-up. 'Mum – Cass is looking for you.'

'OK. Well, she'll find me, but thank you, darling.'

He watched me sweep mascara over my eyelashes curiously.

'How's the settling in going?' I asked conversationally, as it seemed he was staying put.

'Um. Someone pulled my chair out, so when I sat down it wasn't there and they laughed. Ben told them to leave me alone.' He scratched his head. 'They haven't actually touched me though, which is good.'

I paused, wand in mid-air, stomach lurching at the thought of him sprawled on the floor, confused and humiliated, as everyone pointed and jeered. Not being able to be there to protect him at all times was the hardest part of parenting. I put my hand down and looked at him in the mirror, sitting on the bed behind me. 'Alex, you will tell me if you aren't happy and things become too difficult again, won't you?'

He nodded. 'It'll get better,' he said, decisively. 'I'm just not the sort of person people notice. Or if they do, it's for the wrong reasons. I'll make some friends when people get to know the real me.'

I couldn't speak for a moment. Eventually, I cleared my throat and turned to face him. 'I think you're very brave.'

'And that's a good thing?'

I nodded, my eyes shining. 'A very good thing indeed.'

'Oh – so you're both in *here*.' Cass appeared in the doorway. 'Al says you've got us a babysitter.' She crossed her arms. 'Is that true?'

Al left the room hurriedly.

'We're *thirteen*!' she continued. 'It's so embarrassing! Who even is this person?'

'One of the gap students from school?' I confessed.

Her mouth fell open melodramatically. 'You are kidding me? So now everyone at school will know too? How could you do this to us? Do you know *nothing* about how it works?'

'We're in a new area; I'm going out for the evening past your bedtime. Alex sometimes needs a bit of support. This isn't about you.'

'I can look after myself *and* Al,' she insisted. 'I always do. This is unbelievable!' Her eyes filled with tears.

'Is this just about the babysitter or is there something…' I trailed off as she simply flounced out without letting me finish. Not for the first or last time, reminding me of her mother.

*

'She'll be fine,' Ewan assured me in the car on the way to Stefanie and Steve's. 'Just try and relax. I'm really looking forward to meeting some new people.'

'About that. Nathan Sloan's coming with his wife, Storm.'

Ewan's face fell.

'It's OK. He won't have told anyone about Dominic.'

Ewan shot a glance at me. 'I meant more that they're parents at the school, so I better mind my p's and q's.'

'Oh, I see. But I don't think you have to worry. Nate's not like that. You'll like him.'

Ewan raised an eyebrow, not missing the 'Nate', but he didn't comment further and, slightly embarrassed, I didn't either. My informality had surprised me as much as it had him.

*

Nathan was right. Stefanie and Steve were extremely smart. We were the first to arrive, and once we'd done the introductions and passed over the wine we'd bought, we were ushered into an immaculate sitting room – a properly grown-up, luxurious space that wouldn't have looked out of place in a boutique hotel. The fire was lit, with a huge mirror hanging over a mantelpiece carrying lots of handwritten cards and stiff formal invitations: evidence of busy, full lives.

I perched on the edge of a very plumped-up dove-grey sofa and prepared to begin the excruciating business of blind-dating the couple whose home we were in, but I needn't have worried. Stefanie was a borderline professional hostess. Her small talk was as polished as the silver picture frames sitting on the piano and sideboard, displaying black and white pictures of beautiful, long-limbed, almost adult children, captured with tousled beach hair in various exotic locations. There was one of Stefanie at the centre of the arrangement, taken some time ago, laughing into the camera on board a yacht, dressed in a swimsuit, displaying endless legs.

'Honestly, don't,' she remarked, finding me looking at it. 'It's high time that went into the attic – it's not doing any good down here; people keep thinking it's my eldest, Flora – it's too depressing for words! What a lovely jumpsuit you're wearing!'

I looked down at myself.

'Thank you. I had to take about five yards off the hem, but...'

'Well, you wouldn't know,' she said. 'It looks like the whole thing was made for you, and navy is *so* flattering. Now tell me, how are you finding life in the South West?'

'I love it,' I said, truthfully. 'This is such a beautiful part of the world. Open countryside five minutes out of the city centre, right next to the sea, close enough to Cornwall to pop in for day trips. What's not to like?'

She nodded in agreement. 'We're very lucky, aren't we? And how are you liking being "out" of Exeter, rather than "in"?'

She proceeded to smoothly grill me, asking interested questions, but making genuinely helpful suggestions. Had I joined a gym? She'd recommend hers. I was a runner? There were excellent running clubs and the indoor climbing centre was fabulous. Were the children settling into school? Had I considered some out-of-school clubs for Alex, in that case? That might take some of the pressure off everything being centred around the one environment; give him a little respite and help him feel more 'involved' locally, all at the same time. Was he sporty? Arty? She'd send me some links... I didn't get the chance to ask her a thing about herself in return, and felt gauche when the bell went again and she jumped up to let in a heavily pregnant woman whose name I didn't quite catch and her accountant husband, followed by Nathan and his wife. I knew she'd arrived because I smelt her perfume before she even came into the room.

When she did appear, clutching a glass Stefanie had already handed her, she smiled tightly at us. 'Sorry we're late! We've got builder issues at the moment. Nice to meet you all – I'm Storm.'

So I'd guessed what she was called correctly. I raised my glass of wine in greeting. She was dressed in a beautiful, black cocktail number. I hadn't appreciated Devon would be quite so chic.

'I missed your name?'

I realised she was talking to me and I was staring at her. 'Sorry – I'm Julia. I think we might have children in the same class? I'm Alex's mum.' I decided not to do the 'we met outside the kids' classroom on the first day of term, actually', as she'd obviously forgotten me. Fair enough as I hadn't seen her since then. Ewan had done most of the subsequent pick-up and drop-offs – the joy of having him on site.

'Ah – Alex and the much-discussed Cassia.' She smiled, but her tone was cool.

Surprised – I opened my mouth to say, 'All good I hope?' but Ewan had come back into the room from the loo and her face had already lit up. '*Hello*, Mr Wilder!'

Oh, she was one of them; the mum who prefers to talk to the dads.

'Mrs Sloan. Nice to see you.' He shook her hand, and she laughed prettily. 'Please – you must call me Storm. We're all off duty tonight. Isn't that right, darling?' she addressed Nathan as he appeared in the doorway.

'Isn't what right?' He looked wary.

'I was just saying we're all off duty tonight. Don't worry, you're not about to agree to something I might hold you to later!' She laughed again. 'Nathan and I have just been having a discussion in the car about the new bath we're going to put in the en-suite. He can't see the point, he's more of a shower person, but when we were in Venice recently our hotel room had the most *amazing* free-standing bath beneath the window. I'm trying to recreate the look in Exeter, to Nathan's dismay!'

'Mostly because for the same cost, I'd be able to pay for her to have a bath in a hotel every night for the rest of her life!' Nathan smiled and we all laughed politely, except Storm's went on just a little too long – which was when it dawned on me they were in the middle of a whopping row. I shot a quick glance at Ewan, who looked diplomatically at the floor.

'Yes, well, dinner is ready!' said Stefanie quickly. 'Come on through!'

We followed her into the dining room and sat down to a table laid, just as Nathan had predicted, with some very beautiful china and glass. I was sandwiched between Nathan on my left and Geoff, the pregnant lady's husband, on my right. Ewan, Storm and the pregnant lady were opposite us with Stefanie and Steve at each end. A starter appeared, glasses of white wine filled, and Storm looked straight at me and kicked off with 'How are you enjoying working with my husband? Everyone always tells me what a puppy dog he is at work!'

So she did know who I was? I put my glass down carefully and said: 'The whole team have been lovely, actually. Really welcoming and friendly.'

'Oh, I am pleased! It must just be at home he's a miserable git then!' She winked at me and took a large mouthful of wine. Nathan chuckled and picked up his own glass but didn't pass comment.

'Were you pleased to move here?' Storm continued. 'Nathan was saying you had quite a difficult time at your last hospital?' Her eyes were wide with sympathy. She had an extraordinary face now that I was able to examine her up close: pale, perfect skin, deep blue eyes, a rosebud mouth and when she blinked innocently, she made me think of a china doll. Her long dark hair certainly gleamed as if it had been brushed very carefully by the little girl who owned her. There was nothing costume jewellery about the enormous diamond ring sitting on her third finger though, glinting in the light of the candles Stefanie had set everywhere around the room. They were reflected in yet another vast mirror above a mantelpiece and against the backdrop of more dazzling white walls… making it appear as if there were hundreds of flickering flames everywhere. 'An internal row became very public, I think?' Storm continued, her voice becoming syrupy, inviting a cosy confidence. 'Lots of jealousy and infighting. Sounds dreadful, you poor thing.'

I hesitated. She was younger than me, but it was hard to tell by how much. I didn't want to get into this with her.

'Julia took her former employer to court,' Ewan said suddenly. 'She whistle-blew on a male colleague's poor practise. My wife is a surgeon,' he explained to Geoff, who was looking confused. 'They tried to bully her out of her job – all the boys together. They didn't really like being held to account.'

'You didn't tell me that bit!' Storm looked at Nathan and, surprised, I wondered what he *had* said. 'Good for you, Julia! Us girls have got to stick together!'

'It was a very stressful time,' Ewan said. 'I was really proud of her for not giving in but standing her ground.' He smiled at me.

Storm's mouth fell open. 'Oh, stop it!' She fanned invisible tears as if she was welling up, while I watched her quietly. 'It's so rare to hear a man talk unselfconsciously about his love for his wife! How did you two meet?' She took another innocent sip of wine, and Nathan carried on studiously eating. 'You were married before, I believe, Julia?'

This time, Nathan paused and looked up at her.

'Sorry – that's what you said, isn't it, darling?' She then turned back to me, whispering, 'Don't worry, we're members of the second-time-around club too. Anyway, I interrupted – you were about to say?' She smiled encouragingly.

I took a deep breath. 'Ewan was married to my best friend—'

Storm's perfectly shaped eyebrow raised in delight. That was even better than she'd hoped for, obviously.

'…who died when our children – I have a son and Ewan has a daughter – were both eight. I was divorced by then from my husband, and while it was nothing that we planned to happen and indeed we had to get past quite a lot of feelings of guilt – we fell in love.' I reached for my glass and raised it to Ewan, my eyes suddenly full of tears. He smiled sadly back. Nathan put his knife and fork together, and looked up at Storm who, chastened, refused to meet his eye.

'How about you two?' I turned in desperation to Geoff and his pregnant wife. 'Is this your first baby?'

'Yes,' she said, nodding.

'Oh – how lovely! Congratulations!'

'Thank you. It took us a long time to conceive,' she continued, earnestly. 'The man's ball sack has to stay at a constant temperature.' She made a cupping gesture with her hand. 'Geoff might have been getting a bit too warm, we think? Anyway – we got there eventually!'

There was a bark of laughter next to me from Nathan, who turned it into a cough, grabbing for his napkin, as Stefanie blinked and I bit my lip so hard I tasted blood. Did she just say ball sack?

A pause followed in which I'm sure I wasn't the only one being treated to a mental image of the inside of Geoff's hot pants, before Stefanie leapt in with a bright, 'Now, are we all ready for some beef Wellington? Steve? Would you like to get the red?'

Steve nodded, leapt to his feet and rushed from the room as Ewan gamefully cleared his throat and turned to Geoff. 'So, do you know what you're having then?'

I loved him for that.

Over the main course, the tension eased slightly thanks to Clemmie's – as her name turned out to be – scrotal diagnosis and Geoff deciding to take full advantage of his wife's encumbered state to get cracking on the red wine. He obviously wasn't a man used to drinking, however. Before long, his cheeks were flushed and his eyes shining – he was enjoying himself.

'You know how you two are surgeons?' he slurred slightly, pointing at Nathan and me. 'What made you decide you wanted to do it?'

Nathan barely hesitated. 'I'm fascinated by the human body and I don't feel fear, so it seemed a no-brainer to channel that combination into something positive.'

'He means he doesn't *allow* himself to feel fear,' Storm interrupted. 'He's not got some genetic mutation or something.'

Nathan laughed. 'The kind of school I went to, if you showed fear, they ate you for breakfast. How about you, Julia?' He turned to me.

'I still feel it, but I agree that it can be helpful to contain it at the right moments. Although if you switch off your emotions too often, sometimes you can't turn them back on. It's about a balance of fear, I think.'

'I meant what made you want to be a surgeon?'

'Oh.' I felt foolish. 'Well, I'm quite little and most of my life people have said things like "Look at your tiny hands!"' I waved them and everyone smiled. 'My mother used to say it made me so cross I became a surgeon to prove I could still do something with them.' I shrugged self-consciously and took a sip of my water.

'Wow,' said Geoff admiringly. 'I mean what you two do is a *proper* job. I think it's amazing. If I don't go into work, the world doesn't stop turning, but what you do? I mean. Just, wow. What does it feel like when you cut into someone?'

Nathan wiped his mouth with a napkin. 'It sounds an awful thing to say, but I don't think about it at all.' He shrugged. 'It's just part of my job. That's partly why you dissect cadavers in medical school, to help condition you for surgery. You'd be useless in theatre otherwise. It has to feel normal; you have to not panic – it's actually dangerous to allow yourself to empathise with someone you're about to operate on. This is a small town; the law of probability says that sooner or later I'm going to have to operate on someone I know, might really care about, or is related to someone I know or care about. I'm no use to them if I let that connection or emotion cloud my judgement. You have to have a coping mechanism or you'd never survive.'

Geoff gaped, hanging on his every word. 'That's *fascinating*!'

'Oh, I don't know.' Nathan smiled. 'It's just what we do, really.'

'I actually meant what does it feel like to cut into someone, pressure wise?' Geoff persisted. 'Like if someone is really fit, is it a firm cheese, or if they're really fat, does it feel like trifle?'

'Oh, I see,' Nathan said. 'Cutting through fat people… hmmm. Yes, a little like trifle, but it holds its shape. It easily parts with gentle strokes of a knife—'

'…Or diathermy – which is like a hot, cauterising pencil they mostly use,' Storm interrupted, her cheeks sweetly flushed from the wine she was steadily drinking. 'It cuts and coagulates at the same time.' She met my surprised gaze with a hint of challenge. 'I got as far as registrar but stopped when Ben was born. I wanted to be a mum more than a consultant. Some women manage both,' she raised her glass to me, 'but I couldn't. That's how we met.' She nodded at Nathan. 'Across an unconscious patient. I expect you thought I worked in PR or something; it's my name – confuses everyone.'

'I didn't think anything about you, actually.' It sounded more dismissive and rude than I'd intended. I meant I hadn't made any assumptions about her, but Nathan shifted in his chair. 'What I mean is, I don't like to define people by their jobs.' I tried to dig myself out of the hole. 'You've never wanted to come back to medicine?'

She shook her head. 'No. I don't miss it at all. I have my own interior design company now. I do projects with local hotels, private individuals, that sort of thing.' She tossed her hair back, defiantly. 'I can fit it around Ben – plus too much water has gone under the bridge. I've forgotten more than I learnt.'

'But all that training!'

'You sound like my mother!' She laughed, and I raised an eyebrow. Touché. 'She still tells everyone I'm a doctor, but I've learnt to live with her disappointment. It could be worse; I could be Nate.' She nodded at him. 'Imagine what it's like to be a surgeon and *still* be the underachiever in your family!'

Steve coughed awkwardly, and Stefanie's eyes widened. Bloody hell. The gloves were really coming off. Only Nathan himself didn't seem the slightest bit perturbed by what she'd said, simply carrying on eating his food.

'Nathan's mother is like an American Mary Archer,' Storm confided in us, touching Ewan's arm briefly. 'Very glamorous, very capable, very academic. She was a child movie star and now teaches drama and English.' I thought about Mrs Dowden and how Nathan had told me she reminded him of his mother. She was formidable, for sure, but I wouldn't have said she was the image of Mary Archer? Or glamorous. Maybe it was her mannerisms that had rung a bell with Nathan? I forced myself to concentrate on his wife, who was still talking. 'His father is a professor of physics at Harvard.' she continued, 'and his younger brother is the CEO of GENEUS. They provide those home DNA tests that everyone's been doing, only to find out they have different fathers than they thought – devastating families all over the place, but it's made him *super* rich.' She took a slug of her wine.

'I say all of this like I know them well, but we've never met because they're VERY religious – "God has seen fit to bless me with a million-dollar company" – and they don't recognise me as Nathan's wife. We are, as they say, estranged. Hey – maybe your brother would buy me my bath for Christmas!' She widened her eyes like she'd just had the best idea ever, and Nathan shrugged.

'I think you'll find that like lots of super-rich people, he's tight as arseholes.' He swallowed his mouthful. 'Excuse my language. Plus the last time I tried to phone him, I didn't even get past his army of support staff, but you go for it! Not just a pretty face, are you, my darling!' He grinned at our hostess. 'This beef is sensational, Stef – Ted's farm?'

Stefanie tore her astonished gaze away from Storm and cleared her throat. 'Yes, yes it is.'

'Thought so.' Nathan carried on eating. 'We really are spoilt for good quality local meat round here. Now, you two.' He turned back to Ewan and me. 'How are Alex and Cass getting on at school? Ben is certainly very taken with them… that's our son,' he explained to Geoff and Clemmie. 'He's got a bit of a crush on Cassia, I think, if truth be told.'

Storm stood up suddenly, bashing the table with her knees and making the cutlery jump. 'Sorry,' she said, her voice trembling, 'I suddenly feel a bit sick. I think I need some air.' She turned tail and fled from the table. We all stared at Nathan, who carried on eating, only to look up when he felt our eyes upon him.

'Oh, right – of course. Will you excuse me? I'll go and check if she's OK. It's just this ridiculous fasting and time-restricted eating thing she does – it means the second she eats normally, she feels queasy.' He wiped his mouth on a napkin and stood up.

They didn't return and while we tried our best to keep the conversation going, once we'd finished our food – their half-finished plates remaining pointedly on the table – it petered out completely.

'Would you excuse me if I pop to the loo?' I asked.

'Second on the right by the stairs,' Stefanie said automatically. 'Steve – would you help me clear? I hope you've all got room for some roulade!' she added as I escaped, leaving poor Ewan to fend for himself.

I found it immediately – Stefanie having thoughtfully left the door ajar and the light on – and closed the door behind me, starting to wriggle out of my jumpsuit only to hear voices drifting in through the open fanlight window above my head. Someone was outside in the back garden; I could hear the click of heels on paving stones as their owner walked around – while arguing. I froze, not because I was intending to listen in, but rather as an automatic reaction to standing in my bra and pants; although that was absurd, as nobody couldn't see me, and had no idea I was there, given what I heard them say.

'I am *not* making a scene!'

'You are.' Nathan's voice was quiet. 'Everyone gets that you're pissed off about the bath – you've made it very clear.'

'It's not just about the bath and you know it. You're making me out to be one of those Cheshire housewives and I'm not. I'm NOT!' Was she crying? It sounded like it. 'You think I'm as stupid as you paint me, don't you?'

'I would never underestimate you or your appetite for drama.'

'You think I *like* this? Look what you've made me into, what I've become!'

Yes, she was definitely crying.

'A mother to a lovely boy?' Nathan said pointedly. 'Who lives in a very nice house, wants for nothing and is sulking because I've raised objections about a bath that costs enough to feed a family of four for a year, which in my opinion is immoral... but yes, I'm a monster, I see your point.'

'It's not about the bath!' she hissed furiously. 'Don't you get that? Do I really have to explain it to you?'

'I'd rather you didn't. Can we go back in now? It's going to look rude, even by your standards. Maybe don't have more to drink, either.'

'I'll do what I want! You think I don't see it?' Her voice was trembling with energy. 'Well, I do. I know what you're up to and you better watch out with this one. She's not going to—'

I jumped as my phone began to ring in my pocket and swearing under my breath with embarrassment – knowing that they could hear it and would think someone was spying on them – I yanked up the gathers of loose material to try and find it and make it stop.

Only when I looked at the screen, I saw it was Molly, the babysitter, and forgot about everything else instantly.

'Hello, Molly – is everything OK?' I answered immediately, no longer caring if Nathan and Storm heard me or not.

'Hi Julia, um. Sort of. There's a man here? He says he's Alex's dad? He's in the house with us. Is that OK?'

CHAPTER NINE

Julia

'You've done absolutely the right thing in calling me,' I began to wriggle my arms back into the jumpsuit while holding the phone, 'but I'm coming home anyway. Where is he now?'

'Just watching TV and chatting to Alex and Cass.' Molly sounded anxious. 'I did say I needed to phone you first, but Alex told me you wouldn't mind and let him in.'

It wasn't worth alarming or panicking her by asking if Dominic was drunk, given he was apparently sitting quietly. 'And they're just chatting?'

'Yes. He's got some big bags with him, so I thought perhaps he must be staying with you, or something?'

Sorcha chucked him out? Surely not? 'Don't worry. I'll sort everything when I get back. Where are you now?' I tried to keep my voice nice and casual. 'I take it they can't hear you talking to me?'

'No. I'm in the kitchen.'

'Great! Well done. I'll be ten minutes. You don't need to bother telling them I'm on my way.'

'OK.' She sounded uncertain, but relieved. 'See you in a bit.'

I ended the call and yanked the zip up so hard and fast I almost dislocated my shoulder, before bursting out of the loo, and crashing straight into Nathan on his way in from the garden.

'I've got to go,' I announced.

'I heard.' He looked tired. 'You don't have to pull the 911; I'll take Storm home when she stops crying. Sorry you had no choice but to overhear.'

'I didn't 911. I really do have to go. Dominic has just turned up at our house.'

'Oh Christ. They're all at it. Is there a full moon tonight?' He sighed before leaning on the wall for a second. 'Ex-husbands and wives, eh?' He moved his foot to straighten up again and there was an unpleasant scratching sound. We both looked down and noticed a large arc on the pale oak floor.

'Shit!' He looked alarmed. 'Did I do that?' He lifted the bottom of his shoe. Embedded in the sole was a small and sharp piece of grit. He tried to pull it out with his fingers, but it was too tiny for him to get a purchase, so reaching into his pocket, he pulled out an antique folding knife with an elaborately jewelled handle. Opening out the blade, he picked at the piece of grit, wobbling on the spot. I held out a hand to steady him but he shook his head.

'You go, I've got this. Thank you though. Hope it goes OK when you get home.'

'You too. That's a very flashy penknife. Are those real rubies?'

He nodded. 'A gift from my parents for my eighteenth birthday. You're meant to tape a penny to the blade if you give a knife as a present or it severs your relationship. The receiver then has to return the penny to the giver straight away as "payment". We didn't do any of that – as Storm so kindly pointed out tonight. I apologise that she decided to wash my dirty linen in public. I hope—'

'I've already forgotten everything she said,' I assured him. 'But I really ought to go now. I won't say anything about the floor either.'

He snorted. 'Thanks. See you on Monday.'

I turned and fled back to the dining room, where Stefanie was carefully dividing a giant swiss roll. 'I'm so sorry,' I announced, 'but we've got a situation at home we really need to get back for. The babysitter just called.'

Ewan looked alarmed, but Stefanie nodded, faintly, the knife paused mid-air. 'I quite understand. I expect one of the children is ill? There's a lot about at the moment. It always happens at this time of year with the temperature change. Don't worry at all. I'll get your coats.'

'Please don't get up.' I held out a hand to everyone else as they began to scrape the chairs under the table, poor Clemmie puffing as she attempted to rock herself to standing, Geoff wobbling uncertainly on his feet. 'It was very nice to meet you all. Have a lovely rest of the evening.'

Storm, who had appeared in the doorway, openly gave a snort of derision at that, but I didn't care as I slipped past her. I just wanted to get home.

Ewan ushered me down the path to the car in silence. Only once the car door was shut and I was pulling away sharply did he collapse his head back onto the head-rest and groan aloud. 'OH MY GOD. That was horrendous. Ball sacks, bathtubs and bastard brothers! What have we done? They're all mental! Thank God for you. If you hadn't pulled the SOS call, I was going to! Did I look suitably concerned?'

'I didn't make it up. It really was Molly calling. Dom is at the house—'

Ewan sat up straight immediately. 'What?'

'He just turned up. They're all watching TV, apparently.'

'She let him in?' He put his hands on his head. 'Is he pissed? Do we need to call the police?'

I pictured the new neighbours twitching their curtains; flashing blue lights outside the house on a Friday night… and Molly recounting the whole story to the other gap-year students at the school on Monday, if not before. 'She said he's calm. I don't want to antagonise anything.'

'We're going to *have* to get an injunction. He rocks up unannounced at half nine on a Friday night, when he lives two hundred miles away? That's not normal.'

'I know!' I shouted suddenly, and Ewan turned to me in surprise. 'I'm sorry,' I said immediately. 'I'm just frightened, that's all. I want to be there *now*.'

We continued in silence, only punctuated by Ewan placing a gentle hand over mine. 'Slow down, we can't do anything if we don't get there in one piece.'

I gritted my teeth and said nothing more until we pulled up outside the house with a jerk. 'Let me handle it, OK?' I jumped out and slammed the door.

Leaving him to pay Molly in the hallway, I went to find the others.

All three of them were sitting on the sofa, Dominic in the middle, watching *Top Gun*, of all things, like it was totally normal.

'Hey guys!' I said quietly, closing the door behind me, but they didn't hear me.

'Dad, I don't understand why that man has sunglasses on in the dark?' Al put his hand on Dom's arm and left it there. I winced at the sign of affection.

'Because it's cool.'

'No, it's because he's a silly show off,' I said, louder this time, and they all turned around.

'Oh hi, you're back!' Dom got to his feet.

'Sure am!' I looked at him pointedly, taking in a neat haircut, clean trousers and a shirt.

'Sit back down, Dad, you're missing it.' Al patted the sofa next to him.

'No, Dad's just going to come and have a quick chat with me in the kitchen.' I beckoned to Dom, smiling, but Al's face fell and he sighed heavily.

'Cass? You all right?' I looked at her and she nodded silently, totally absorbed in the film.

'I wonder if they'll make a *Top Gun 2*?' Dom sounded nervous as he followed me out into the hallway and through into the kitchen. 'I'm not sure how I'd feel about that. You shouldn't mess with perfection.'

'I can't watch it anymore, all that "best of the best" competitive crap. Swap planes for scalpels and there's my working life for the last fifteen years.' I closed the door behind us. 'Dominic, what are you doing? It's—'

'I'm sober! I'm totally sober. Look!' He took a step closer to me, but I stood my ground. 'I've been concentrating on going to meetings – that's why I haven't been in touch. I crossed the line, I know that, but—'

'Haven't been in touch? What are you talking about? It's Friday. You were here on Monday. That's just five days ago. You know that, right?'

'Of course I do! The point is, I don't have any alcohol in my system. I'm in recovery! Why would you say I'm not, when I am? I don't understand?' He gave a brief shake of his head, like he was tipping toxic fairy dust from his hair that he'd not noticed me sprinkle on him – and stepped away.

'While I'm obviously delighted that you're as much as four days sober, it's still Friday night, nearly ten p.m. and you're in my house with Al and Cassia without my permission, so you—'

'I need your *permission* to see Al?' He pulled such an exaggerated expression it was almost a caricature of confusion. He was becoming angry. 'Since when?'

'You need permission to be in my and my husband's house, yes.'

'But I phoned Al earlier! I didn't just turn up! Didn't he tell you any of this?'

'It's not Al's responsibility to tell me anything. *You* should have called me, not him. And you're not supposed to ring when you're on your way or have actually arrived. We've been through this!'

There was a pause, and just like that, he crumpled in on himself, leaning on the side and covering his face with his hands. 'You're right, of course, you're right – I'm sorry. I was just so excited to see him.'

'It unsettles Alex hugely when you just appear out of nowhere, then inevitably go again without warning.'

'I can see that. I'll leave. I'll leave now.' He stared up at the ceiling, bewildered. 'I need to start getting this right, I know I do.'

'Come on, I'll drive you back into town. Where are you staying?'

'I haven't sorted anything yet.'

I swore internally. 'There's a Premier Inn right opposite the station. I'll make sure it's got availability while you say goodbye to Alex. I'll pay.'

'I know what you're thinking,' he said suddenly, 'and you're right, but I AM sorting myself out. I'm going to get a job, be in his life properly and responsibly. He's such a good kid – the best.' His voice broke and his eyes filled with tears. 'He deserves my best too.'

I waited patiently for him to gather himself. It wasn't that I didn't believe he meant what he said. I'd spent years wanting him to change, willing him to, helping him to. Maybe this would be the time that was different... I really hoped so, but I'd heard it before and I wasn't going to hold my breath.

'I mean it, Jules,' he said, 'I'm going to show you I can change.' He looked at me pleadingly.

I hesitated. 'Perhaps as you're going to be around tomorrow morning, I could bring Alex into town and you could have breakfast with him? How about that?'

'That would be great! Except... I haven't really got the money for that either.'

I didn't let my expression betray my thoughts. 'There's a cashpoint at the station. I'll get you some when I drop you off.'

'Thanks so much. I'll pay you back, of course.'

I ignored that, as I didn't see how he could, so it seemed churlish to comment.

'I'll grab my stuff from your music room.' He patted his pockets. 'I put it out of the way so no one tripped over it. It's a nice space. Do you still play the piano, by the way? It looks good in there.'

I shook my head. 'Not as much as I'd like. No time, really. Why? Do you want it back?'

'No!' He coloured. 'It was a present to you.'

I straightened up, suddenly having had enough of the ghosts gathering in the room around us and walked to the door. I found Ewan on the other side, sitting on the love seat in the hall, head in hands, waiting. He had a black rucksack and two large, empty canvas holdalls on the floor next to him.

'Ah – you've got my things,' said Dom. 'Thanks, mate. Sorry to drop in like this.' He walked past me and bent to pick them up from my husband's feet.

'No worries,' Ewan said with difficulty, but to his eternal credit, didn't say anything else.

I frowned as Dom shook out the enormous canvas bags, carefully folded them and shoved them in the rucksack. 'What are they for?'

He flushed. 'I bought Al and Cass a present each.'

'What did you get them, a couple of giraffes?'

He scratched his head awkwardly. 'That's not far off, actually. They've taken them upstairs. I'm sure they'll show you. Sorry – they're a bit over the top, but I know how much Al likes animals and I didn't want Cass to feel left out. Can I go and say goodbye to him?'

I nodded, and Dom disappeared into the sitting room.

'What the hell?' Ewan mouthed immediately, and I put my finger to my lips. He closed his eyes and shook his head in disbelief. I couldn't blame him. How would I feel in his position? He waited in silence, saying nothing while I checked online to make sure there was room at the Inn.

Dom reappeared with Al trailing behind him, chattering away. 'But you can just stay here! Mum and Ewan won't mind!'

'That's really kind of you, pal, but I'm going to get a hotel. I snore *really, really* badly and I'll keep you all awake if I stay here.' Dom shrugged. 'Whatcha gonna do?'

Al grinned. 'To be fair, Cass wouldn't like that. She needs her sleep. I'll see you tomorrow then?'

'Yes!' Dom widened his eyes and pointed right at him. 'For breakfast. Waffles, pancakes, anything you like. In fact, all of them!'

I made a mental note to get at least fifty quid out.

Alex smiled and clapped his hands excitedly, a baby bird in a stork's awkward body. 'Yay! You're the best, Dad!'

I saw Ewan look away as my boy threw his arms around his father and hugged him tightly, resting his head on Dom's shoulder and closing his eyes, his glasses slipping slightly. His smile was totally blissed out. His capacity for such simple and complete trust frightened me for him.

'Love you, mate.' Dom's voice was choking up as he patted Al's back then let him go. 'Cheers, Ewan.' He offered him his hand. 'Cass is on good form. Nice to see everything working out for her. She's looking so much like Lise all of a sudden, hey?'

Ewan took a deep breath. 'Yes – she is. Take care, Dom. Travel safely.'

'Will do.' Dom swung his bag on his shoulder.

'I'll wave from the window.' Alex ran excitedly into the sitting room, and Dom opened the front door. I walked out into the dark, pulling my coat more tightly around me and gasping as a gust of wind so cold it must have come straight from the sea blew through my very bones, taking my breath away. Seconds later it began to rain. I shivered and unlocked the car, pausing only to wave at our son, framed in the window, watching us leave.

CHAPTER TEN

Nathan

'You lost control in front of them all.' I drove the knife in mercilessly as I concentrated on the dark road ahead, the windscreen wipers whipping back and forth while Storm cried next to me on the passenger seat. 'Why do you think we've all ended up leaving early?'

'We can't go on like this anymore,' she whispered.

I rolled my eyes. 'You're drunk. You'll feel better in the morning. This is the booze talking, not you.'

She twisted her head and looked at me, aghast. '*That's* what you think this is?'

'I think you made an embarrassment of yourself this evening, yes. It was very obvious to everyone that you were angry about the en-suite.'

'*It's not about the fucking en-suite!*' She shrieked so loudly that I almost swerved.

Stef had managed to behave impeccably. No one would have spotted any intimacy between us at all, yet Storm was incandescent about a bath. The contrast was damning.

'Oh God.' She covered her face with her hands and started to sob. 'What have I done? How have I let us get to *here*?'

I sighed tightly. I found Storm's navel-gazing and complete-emotional-collapse episodes particularly tedious. Her usual flinty disapproval was vastly preferable. She was a heartbeat away from declaring that I didn't love her anymore and probably never had, pushing for me to tell her in return that she was being ridiculous. It was absolutely the booze talking, whether she liked to admit it or not.

'Is there something going on with you and Julia?'

I glanced at her, shivering and staring out of the window at the raindrops blowing down the glass, arms wrapped around her body in *abject* misery. 'What the hell are you on about now?'

'There was an atmosphere tonight,' she continued. 'It didn't feel right from the moment we arrived, and I saw the effect it had on you, being sat next to Julia at dinner.' Her voice became calmer and more resigned as she spoke. 'You went all fidgety, like it was uncomfortable for you to be that close but not touch her. Are you in love with her?'

There was a moment of silence before I laughed. 'Even for you that's quite something! I met the woman four days ago!'

'Deny it then! Swear on our son's life that you don't have feelings for her.'

'That's a hideous thing to say,' I replied. 'You've seen for yourself how fragile life is – before you decided to start plumping cushions to occupy your mind. I won't do anything of the sort and don't ever ask me to again.'

'So you're not denying it.' She was triumphant.

I swerved into a lay-by and twisted to face her. 'If you think my working with Julia is going to be a problem for you, if she's going to become the next woman you start to obsess over and develop some strange girl-crush on, it would be helpful for me to know.'

'I don't develop "girl-crushes". I just know what you're like, that you're capable of having your head turned,' her voice was trembling, 'because I turned it once. But I think it's more than that this time. I think you've actually fallen for her.'

I stared at my wife. 'She's a senior colleague that I've barely known a week. How *could* I be in love with someone I've known for that little time?'

'I saw the look on your face at dinner when you were talking about Ben having a crush on their daughter. You were staring right at Julia. You were subconsciously telling her you have feelings for *her*. You think I don't know you! That I don't see!' She started to weep.

'You know *nothing*.' I was suddenly so angry I could barely get the words out. 'You're just pissed. Has something else happened that you're not telling me? Is that why you're behaving like this? Have you had another row with your mother?'

'No! Of course not! Because it's never you, is it, Nathan? Nothing could ever be your fault? You—'

'I think we should just get home, go to bed and in the morning *I'll* go and pick up Ben and take him to hockey.' I cut across her. 'You can sleep in and have the whole day to yourself if you like. I'll even see if I can book you a massage. How about that?' I pulled back onto the road and put my foot down.

'A massage… lucky me. You still haven't said you don't love her.'

'I don't fucking love her!' I roared.

Storm winced and closed her eyes.

'The kind of fairy tale shit you're talking about – love at first sight, eyes across a crowded room – it doesn't exist! That's attraction, not love and it doesn't last!'

'Well, maybe that's for the best,' her voice trembled. 'Because I can tell you she doesn't feel the same way about *you*! She loves her husband. Any fool could tell you that.'

I concentrated very hard on the white lines and cat's eyes running up the centre of the road. I would not dignify that with a response.

'Do you love *me*, Nate?'

I shook my head. 'Not right now, if I'm honest.' Friday nights used to mean the pub, laughter, catching someone's eye, uncomplicated sex in some pretty girl's flat. I hadn't known I was born.

Storm sniffed and turned away from me.

'There are tissues in the glove compartment.'

'I'm just a bit under the weather at the moment, as well as being upset,' she whispered. 'That's all. I'm sorry my sniffing annoys you.'

'I was trying to be nice! Can I not even offer you a tissue without doing something wrong?'

Storm pointedly closed her eyes again, like she was having to block out the pain of listening to her unreasonable, ranting husband. Well, she'd finally got the reaction she'd been pushing for. I drove too fast for another minute or two until we lurched to a stop at a red light. I glanced at Storm, who was now apparently so emotionally exhausted she'd passed out. That'd be right; she'd flop into bed the second we got in and I'd be left pacing the house all wound up with nowhere to go.

I flashed my lights furiously at the red and it flipped. I pulled away, glancing across at the other side of the road, to see *Julia* about to drive past me in her little white Mini, apparently on her way back into town, some man sat alongside her in the passenger seat. I couldn't see who in the dark – he was looking out to the left and had a hood up. Dominic? I imagined so.

Julia didn't notice me as she sailed by – it was a split-second thing. I twisted quickly to try and get a longer look at her, swerving enough to make Storm open her eyes briefly.

'Nathan! What's the matter with you?'

Where was she taking him? Back to the station again? On her own? Was that even safe? Had I been alone, I would have swung the car round and followed, to make sure she was all right, but – I glanced angrily at Storm, blinking, as if she wasn't sure where she was and yawning – I was not.

*

She staggered into the house when we got home, kicking off her heels and making straight for the stairs as I closed the front door and put the chain across. In times gone by, we would have relished a child-free evening; it would have meant being able to make noise during sex. Sex with the light on. Possibly sex more than once if we were feeling *really* racy. Now that Ben was more regularly staying over at friends' houses, it wasn't nearly so much of an event to have the place to ourselves. I went for a piss then padded upstairs. She'd be out cold by now. I crept into our bedroom to get my book for the spare room later, but to my surprise she was awake, obviously naked – albeit covered by the duvet – and waiting for me.

'I'm sorry,' she whispered. 'Come to bed.'

I looked at her, lying there, her once intriguing violet eyes fixed desperately on my face. What man would refuse? I knew I was expected to say yes – to prove I still had feelings for her, but why the hell should I? Women, quite rightly, aren't expected to perform when they don't want to. Putting sexual pressure on your spouse simply isn't the done thing anymore.

'A kind offer, but you don't have to do that. Go to sleep.'

'I *want* to, Nathan.'

Yes, I know you do. A husband refusing his wife sexually – when girls are taught from an early age that boys are only after one thing – must feel like the ultimate rejection… but frankly she deserved it for humiliating me so deliberately at dinner.

'No, really,' I said softly, 'I couldn't possibly expect you to suffer an underachiever like me.'

Her eyes filled with tears. 'I really am sorry. I shouldn't have s—'

'Get some rest.' I made for the door. 'I'm going to watch TV for a bit. I'll go in the spare room when I come up, so I don't disturb you.'

'Oh, please don't!' She sat up and winced at the movement. 'Promise you'll come in here? Would you mind bringing me some water when you do?'

'Don't I always?'

She smiled gratefully. 'Yes. Don't make a special trip but just, if you could not forget. My mouth is dry. You were right: I *did* drink too much.' She lay down again slowly. 'Why do I do this?' She put her hand to her head.

Because you're unhappy, I could have said. We could have sat and talked like adults, but I'd already been through one arse-shattering divorce. I didn't fancy round two. Things suited me as they were. Or at least they had up until now.

*

I went to the bathroom first and cleaned my knife before heading to my study to sit in the dark and watch a couple of new films; two patients from the day before. A therapist would no doubt tell me because I wasn't hugged enough as a child, I now punish all women – who represent dear old Ma – by deliberately making my female patients vulnerable without *actually* confronting them, or her. Essentially, making up for what my mother failed to give me and to spite my father.

I would say I like looking at tits. I reached into my pocket and flicked the blade open, laying it down in preparation on my desk. I removed my trousers, folded them up and, taking my seat again, slipped my hand down the front of my boxers. I picked up the knife and restarted the film, watched myself marking the breasts of the patient on the screen with black pen, to identify where the incision points would be. My hand and breath started to quicken, and as I watched myself sweep the curve under the left breast, I gasped and darted the point of the knife into the skin of my right thigh. It wasn't deep – barely more than a paper cut really. Superficial – and that was the problem. It wasn't doing anything for me anymore. The films felt like experiences I'd already used up. Frustrated, I tossed the knife onto the desk and pushed the laptop away. I craved something stronger, fresher – more authentic.

My mind instantly returned to Julia; her kindness and understanding when I'd apologised for Storm's behaviour. She'd backed me up to the Dowdens too, refusing to indulge the daughter's speculation that I'd caused her mother's implant failure.

I'd felt her body tremble next to me with suppressed laughter at dinner, when the pregnant woman had made her extraordinary comment, and I'd failed to contain my own amusement. I hadn't gone looking for the shared moment – but neither did I make anything of it. I didn't take her hand when she reached out to me in the hall afterwards either. Storm was talking out of her arse.

I balled my hands into fists, and leaning my elbows on the desk, dug my knuckles into my temples. As if my wife's unwanted presence in every other area of my life wasn't bad enough, she now demanded ownership of my thoughts too? Her comments were grossly intrusive. She hadn't *seen* me. She hadn't read my mind and discovered that I'd fallen for Julia at all. It was Julia's troubled professional background I was interested in. Nothing more, nothing less.

In fact, perhaps I would make things even stickier for Julia – properly wind her in my web until I was ready to make use of her, because I did NOT have feelings for her, therefore could do as I pleased. If that also involved my needing to get physical with Julia – well, there we were. Fuck Hamish telling me I couldn't do it and fuck Storm telling me I already had. I released my hands, heat prickling in my spread fingertips as I thought about touching Julia properly. Reaching out, I snatched up the phone.

'Hello. I thought it was dinner at Stef's tonight?' Hamish yawned, and I imagined him stuffed into his beloved saggy old chair in front of the fire; hard to see where the chair left off and Hamish began.

'Already done and dusted.' I put the phone on speaker so I could pull my trousers on. 'Things got a little tasty so we came back early.' I picked the handset up and headed off to the kitchen to get some water. 'Listen, I've been thinking. Now that Julia is here, perhaps you're right – her difficult past isn't quite enough. I'd like to have something really meaty – so to speak – in our back pocket that we can use as leverage at a later date, should she unwisely step out of line.'

'Ah ha!' I imagined him shifting position in his chair, becoming more alert and interested. 'We have some departmental admin to do! Excellent! Do you have a particular scenario in mind?'

'Yes. I do. I won't go into it now, but we'll start laying the foundations first thing on Monday.' I paused as I regarded the glass I'd automatically filled for Storm, then tipped it back down the sink after all, leaving it on the side and picking up my own before walking to the door.

'I assume you will be playing the active role in proceedings and I'll be watching?'

'Indeed.' I saw myself running a finger softly down the skin of Julia's stomach, her muscles contracting involuntarily at my touch. I flipped off the light.

'Lovely!' I could tell Hamish was smiling. 'I shall look forward to that.'

CHAPTER ELEVEN

Julia

I was enjoying a coffee at the kitchen table over the Saturday papers when my mobile buzzed at precisely nine a.m. It was a local number I didn't recognise, but I picked up in case it was something to do with Dominic.

'Julia? It's Stefanie. I'm sorry to be calling early. I just wanted to ring and apologise for last night. I don't blame you for one second, pulling the babysitter routine. It was an awful evening – I'm so sorry! What you must think of us?'

'Oh no, it really was an emergency,' I said. 'I wasn't staging anything.'

'You're kind to pretend, but both Steve and I were saying we'd have done exactly the same in your position. Storm can be such a sweet girl, then inexplicably she's... like last night.'

'She honestly wasn't the reason we left.'

'She was very rude. I won't pretend otherwise. Nate's an old friend of ours, you see – and since he married Storm, we've rather inherited her by default. His first wife, darling old Serena, is a brick. You'd like her a lot. Unfortunately, it was the classic story: married young; Serena supported Nate while he worked his way up; she ran the house, did everything with the kids; he was spending all of his time at work... and suddenly his very pretty registrar was pregnant... In fairness to Nate, they weren't right for each other in the first place. I did try to tell Serena... Anyway, I hope you'll come and see us another time, and I'll send you the links to some of those clubs I was talking about for your son. Have a *super* weekend, won't you?'

I felt bad as I hung up, but also pleased that none of them had an inkling why we'd really left, only for my phone to bleep with a text from Dominic himself. Up by nine and making breakfast arrangements? Maybe this really was a new start.

I began to read the message as Ewan wandered back into the room, clutching the kids' damp, clean school uniforms, ready to hang over the rack. He jumped when I suddenly dropped my phone on the table, grabbed a section of the paper, flung it across the room and shrieked with anger.

'What's happened?' Ewan looked at me in astonishment.

'What always happens.' I got up and went to find Al.

*

'Can I come in, love?' I pushed his bedroom door open only to be confronted by two very large, plush toy guinea pigs on the floor, next to one another, each about the size of a small sheep. 'Goodness!' I said. 'Did Dad get you those?'

'Yeah!' Alex was already dressed and wandering around his room excitedly, packing a backpack. 'He knows pigs are animals that need company – they don't like to be alone – so he bought me two.'

'Where did they come from?' I sat down on the edge of his bed. 'I've never seen anything like them.'

'Japan, I think.'

'Dad was in Japan?'

Alex shrugged. 'I suppose so. He could have ordered them on the Internet, though? I'll ask him at breakfast.' He beamed and my fury with Dom glinted within me, like the sharp edges of crystals, undiscovered until the rock is split open.

I watched Al pack a pencil case and a sketch pad then took a deep breath. 'I've just had a message from Dad actually. He's really sorry, but he's had to go back to London.'

Alex stopped dead. 'But what about breakfast?'

I felt the muscles in my jaw grip as I tried to smile. 'He's going to have to miss breakfast this time.'

I watched our son's shoulders sag. His eyes started to shine and he quickly turned away.

I diplomatically looked in the other direction, at the bloody guinea pigs, sitting there lifeless on the floor as I listened to Alex try to swallow his tears. They were Dom all over – stuffed, useless wastes of space that you couldn't actually *do* anything with. Alex gave a desperate gulp, then began the heartbroken sobs that I couldn't ignore.

'Oh sweetheart!' I jumped up and tried to pull him into my arms, but as he was now taller than me, I couldn't comfort him properly.

'It's OK. It's OK!' Alex tried to say. 'I'm OK.' For the first time ever, he drew back, freeing himself and huddling miserably in the corner of his room.

'Dad said someone he knows is ill and he needed to go and see them.'

Alex nodded and fell silent for a moment before blurting tearfully, 'but he promised *me*!'

'Yes, he did and I'm sure that he absolutely meant it when he said it.' I tentatively walked over to Al and tried to put a hand on his arm, but he leapt away from me.

'I'm really OK, Mum.'

'You don't have to pretend this doesn't hurt, Al. You're allowed to feel disappointed and let down, even if Dad didn't mean you to feel that way.'

'I want to be on my own.' The tears started again.

'Can't I just?…'

'No!' he almost shouted, desperately. 'Please just leave me alone!'

I did as I was told, feeling sick as I gently pulled the door to, powerless to stop my son's pain as Dom's thoughtlessness threw him across the gap between childhood and growing up… the same agony I had felt when Dom used to recklessly chuck Al too high in the air as a squealing baby – his delight laced with fear – only breathing again when Dom caught him at the last moment and I could steal him back into the safety of my arms. Dom would give an incredulous and slightly slurred 'now what? He loved it! You heard him! Give him back to me! I'm *fine.*'

'Julia?' I turned to see Cass on the landing in her dressing gown, looking worried. 'What's up with Al? Is he *crying?*'

I nodded. 'Dominic had to go back to London, so he's missed the breakfast they were going to have.'

'Oh.' Cass looked down at the floor. 'That's not good.'

'No.' I glanced in through the open door of her bedroom. A giant snow leopard – sitting on her floor with its front paws crossed – stared back at me. 'Whoa.'

Cass looked back over her shoulder. 'Yeah. I called it Whisper. Dominic bought it for me. She's very pretty but I think I'd like it to sleep in the spare room tonight? It creeps me out a bit.'

'I can understand that.' Whisper looked as if she might spring to life and eat us at any moment. I'd die of pure fright if I woke up in the night and saw that thing staring back at me. 'I'll put her in there now. Cass, would it be OK if we all went to Dartmoor after breakfast? I know it was going to be your and Dad's trip, and I don't want to get in the way, but I wondered if,' I lowered my voice, 'it might help cheer Al up?'

'Yeah, of course,' she said. 'I'll go and tell him.' She moved past me.

'I think he wants to be on his own,' I tried to explain gently.

She pushed the door of Al's room open and stuck her head in. 'Hey Al? It's just me. Can I come in?'

I heard a muffled response and she reappeared. 'We'll be down in a bit… Maybe make some pancakes?' she mouthed the last bit, and I nodded, blown away by the expert mothering from the girl who had lost her own, as she gently shut the door on me.

*

The rain re-covered the windscreen in a fine mist the second the wipers cleared it.

'This is stupid,' Al muttered in the back.

'The forecast said it's supposed to clear by late morning?' Ewan offered.

'Well, the forecast is stupid too.' Al folded his arms. 'This whole thing is dumb. I don't understand why I couldn't just stay at home and play *Fortnite*. I told you, there are new skins.'

'Remind me, what exactly *are* new skins?' Ewan asked conversationally.

'You *know* that means new characters; you're just trying to get me to start talking and I don't want to.' Al glowered out of the window.

'Al…' I began, but Ewan put a hand on my leg, before moving it back onto the gear stick.

'When are we even there?' Al began complaining again. 'This is taking forever.'

'It *is* taking a long time, to be fair,' Cass agreed. 'I'm starving. Can I have something to eat, please?'

'It's quarter past eleven,' I pointed out. 'Bit early for lunch yet. And it just feels longer because we've taken the scenic route through the villages rather than go the main road way. Isn't that stream pretty the way it cuts through the edge of that cottage garden? And look at that little stone bridge! It's just like Billy Goats Gruff, isn't it?'

'Didn't Mum used to tell me that story?' Cass said.

'Yes, it's a Norwegian fairy tale,' Ewan confirmed. 'The troll is pushed off the bridge by the biggest goat and washes away – or ends up in a cave. I can't remember.'

'What a really stupid story,' said Al crossly. 'Who cares about goats? I don't.'

'Hey!' said Cass, affronted. 'And er, hello? Who has two giant stuffed guinea pigs in his bedroom right now?'

'I don't even want them!' Al shouted, and Cass drew back in surprise. 'I'm going to throw them out of the window when I get home! They're just – dicks!'

'Alex!' I spun round. 'You don't need to shout at us or use language like that.'

'I just want to get out of this car!' he yelled. 'You're all dicks. All of you!'

'We're nearly there. You can get out then.' I turned back and shook my head. On the one hand it was genuinely sweet that the worst word he was prepared to use was 'dick'. On the other hand – I could practically *feel* his pain, squashed into the back seat along with his lanky legs.

Cass sniggered suddenly. 'You called your guinea pigs dicks!' She grinned and nudged him. Ordinarily, Al would have laughed too and pushed his glasses back on his nose, but he exploded at her touch.

'Shut up!' he yelled. 'Just *shut up* – all of you! SHUT UP!' Then he leant across and thumped her hard on the arm.

'OW!' shrieked Cass in alarm and fright – shrinking back against the door, away from him. 'He just hit me!'

'Pull over!' I shouted at Ewan. 'Now!'

Ewan swerved left into the verge and rammed on the brakes as we all jerked forward against our seat belts. Mercifully, the roads were so quiet nothing was coming in either direction. I swung round and grabbed Alex's skinny little wrist. He yelped in fright.

'That's unacceptable,' I said. 'You never, *ever* hit a girl.'

Cass was crying, holding her arm.

'Especially your sister, who you love,' I continued. 'No matter how angry you get. Please tell her you're sorry. Right now.'

Alex stared at me, his eyes wide. 'I'm sorry!' he shouted.

I shook my head. 'Like you mean it. And not to me – to her.'

Alex looked away then twisted to face her. 'I'm sorry, Cass.'

'It's OK,' she said in a small voice as I let him go.

We drove in silence for the next ten minutes. The rain intensified as we passed the visitor centre and a few dejected people standing by their cars: hoods up, zipping coats, damp dogs on leads. Even the sheep were mournfully huddled against the gorse bushes. We pulled into a gravel clearing further on and Ewan finally stopped the car. Alex unclipped his seat belt immediately and shot out in his hoodie and jeans, running as fast as he could, up the side of the hill, away from us. I watched him slip slightly on the wet grass and stumble, but he kept going.

I went to open my door and Ewan shook his head. 'Leave him. Let him run it off.'

Cass leant through the gap between us and watched Al scrambling up the slope. 'He's going to get soaked.'

'I'm so sorry he hit you.' I turned to her.

She shrugged.

'It wasn't that hard, and he's normally the kindest person I know, so…'

'That still doesn't make it OK, and I won't let him behave like that, Cass. No one is allowed to do that to you.'

She nodded. 'Oh! He just fell over properly. Shouldn't we go after him?'

'No,' Ewan said. 'He'll come back when he's ready.'

He was right – Al returned to find us eating our lunch. He shivered out of his sodden hoodie and huddled under the blanket I handed him without a word. I glanced at him starting to eat his pasty, only pausing to wipe his misted glasses. His usual happy smile was still missing.

*

True to the forecast, albeit a little late, the clouds cleared as we drove further on after lunch, desperate for a glimmer of good weather. 'Just enough blue to make a sailor a pair of trousers, as my granny would have said!' I tried cheerfully, but no one answered. We drove to the stretch of road on top of yet another hill, alongside Hound Tor, and pulled up on the verge.

Ewan pointed to the huge outcrop as we climbed out and pulled our coats on. 'It's called *Hound* Tor because according to local legend the rocks were created when a pack of dogs was turned to stone.'

'That's cool,' said Cass generously and the two of them headed off to check it out. I walked for a couple of minutes behind them, gratefully breathing deep lungfuls of rich, damp air, then turned back to see where Al had got to.

He was crouched down, staring at the grass. Sighing, I wandered back and smiled as I neared him.

'What have you found, love?'

'This,' he said absently, pointing to a small, perfectly intact bird's skull almost hidden within some gorse.

'Oh wow!' I watched as he picked it up carefully and balanced it on his palm. 'The beak is quite long. I wonder if it's a baby seagull?'

He pulled a clean tissue out of his pocket and wrapped it up. I thought he was going to pass it to me to keep it safe for him until we got back to the car, but instead he dug a divot with his heel, chipping away at the soft earth until he had a deep enough hole. I passed no comment on the state of his shoes as he placed the skull tenderly in the ground, then pulled the tufts of grass back over it like a blanket, patting and squashing it down. He wiped his muddy hands on his trousers, said 'Amen' and walked off to join the others.

I stared down at the disturbed ground, then up and around at the acres and acres of lonely land spreading out beneath the thickening cloud. Somewhere around here – Ewan knew where – were the remains of a medieval village: several longhouses and a few smaller dwellings. I watched Cass stomping off ahead, hands in her pockets, long legs striding, white blonde hair catching on the breeze. I could see her, with all of that wild, ethereal beauty, ruling moorland like this, hundreds of years ago. Dominic was right: she was turning into the image of Lise.

I glanced at Ewan and remembered Lise holding my hand as she lay in bed, looking at me with those beautiful, but uncharacteristically tired eyes. Lise was always the last to leave the party, except for the one that really mattered.

'I want you to be happy. I'll be really cross if you don't meet someone.'

Someone, though. Not her actual husband… but she must know, wherever she is, that I never had feelings for him while she was alive. It never crossed my mind beyond thinking he was a nice man and I could see what she saw in him – but that was it. *He belonged to her.* The best thing had come from the worst. I sighed and looked around me again at the exposed landscape. What it must have been to sustain life up here as a young family?

Perfect place to bury a body, though. I looked down at the shallow grave Al had made – and thought about Dominic again, blithely buggering off to London, my fifty quid burning a hole in his pocket. He wouldn't be giving a second thought to Al right now. I watched our son, walking miserably across the exposed ground, and began to follow him, just as he stopped to rummage around in his coat pocket. I glanced up, noticing a circling flock of seagulls, wheeling high above his head, apparently innocuous but watching carefully from afar. Al pulled out his pasty bag, ate one of the larger bits and tipped the remains on the ground. The birds began to fly faster and cry to each other, the circle darkened as they moved more closely together.

'Al!' I called warningly, but it was too late. He unwittingly walked away.

The effect was electric. They barely let him get two feet from the scraps before one broke and dived, and the rest followed. They weren't interested in Al, but neither were they scared of him. It was so unexpected that he screamed and dropped to the ground, covering his head with his arms as the extraordinary flurry of flapping wings, bright eyes, and sharp beaks swirled on the ground next to him, tossing up the scraps. I started to run to him, and Ewan began to sprint from the opposite direction. Cass stood still with her hands covering her mouth. It was horrible. I couldn't get there fast enough as Alex panicked.

He didn't stop screaming, even when they all took to the air, his cries echoing across the moor.

CHAPTER TWELVE

Nathan

'So, good weekend?' Hamish asked her on Monday morning, not looking up from his computer as he scratched some livid stubble rash. God knows what he'd shaved with – his chin looked like salami.

'Great, thanks!' she replied, beaming. That was an outright lie, I could tell. Her eyes were puffy. She'd been crying on the way into work.

She cleared her throat. 'How about you, Hamish? Get up to anything nice?'

'Had the mother-in-law for lunch yesterday – but I struggled to finish her.'

She blinked then laughed. 'Oh right, I get it. Good one.'

I rolled my eyes and got up. How Hamish had *ever* had sex in his life was beyond me. 'Julia, can I grab a quick word about Mrs Dowden before you disappear into theatre? That encapsulation on Friday?'

'Sure. You can ask me now, if you like?' She followed me over to the kettle. 'Is there a problem?'

I glanced across at Hamish who had picked up a ringing phone and started talking. 'No. I actually just wanted to ask if everything went all right on Friday with Dominic when you got home?' I lowered my voice discreetly.

'Oh right. Yes, thanks. All sorted.'

'It's just you look like you've been crying?' I pushed it. It worked. Her eyes filled. 'Excuse me.' She exhaled. 'I hope this doesn't make you feel uncomfortable. You don't need to say anything because I'll be fine in a minute. Alex didn't want to go to school this morning. We had quite a difficult drop-off and I'm still a bit upset.'

I was actually very impressed. It was the most professional handling of crying at work I'd ever seen. I blinked, refusing to become distracted and recovered myself. 'It's completely my fault. I shouldn't have asked. I'm sorry he's having a rough time. Listen, after you left on Friday, Stef was asking if Ben does any good clubs out of school because you're looking for some extracurricular stuff for Alex? By coincidence we're doing a mini rugby tour this weekend and—'

She blanched, probably imagining her son being mashed into the pitch by a load of heavily set teenagers. 'Al's not really a rugby sort of boy but thank you.'

'It's not geared towards contact and scrums when you're kids. It's more about running and letting off steam.' I leant on the side and folded my arms. 'I was like Alex at school – light and tall – so I was useful in the second row. The camaraderie made me feel good – and I used to get rid of a lot of pent-up anger running around in the mud.'

She hesitated. I could see her considering that. So Alex was angry as well as upset? That smacked of issues with Dominic. Had to be.

'Let me make you a cup of tea.' I straightened up and touched her arm briefly. A shiver of anticipation rippled across my skin. 'I've seen Alex a couple of times at the school gates now, and he so reminds me of myself at that age. It's tough being thirteen and vulnerable. Like I told you the first day we met,' I pointed at my dark eye, 'I was *not* the cool kid at school! In fact, Storm's right – I ended up an underachiever – and because I was bullied so much, I'm sure.

'I remember being sent to a fifth form class once with a message for the teacher. I was terrified – the whole room stank of sweat, threat and testosterone – and someone threw a shoe at me. It hit me on the side of the head; actually knocked me over. They all pissed themselves and the teacher did nothing. Absolutely nothing, the bastard, just carried on reading the letter.' I sighed and flicked the kettle on. 'I got up, trying not to cry and after that, when any of them saw me, they thought it was huge fun to knock me off my feet. My nickname was shittle – a highly original version of skittle.'

'That's horrible,' she said. 'Was it a boarding school?'

I laughed. 'How did you guess? My mother was offered an opportunity in the States. I was at school over here. My father wanted me to have an English education, so they switched me to the kind of boarding school that creates a loneliness in your soul you never lose. They moved to Massachusetts with my brother. He was too young to board, lucky sod. Was Alex bullied at his last school?' I reached for two cups.

She nodded. 'That's partly why we moved.' She took a deep breath. 'A group of boys stamped on his head.'

'Jesus! And this was while you were being bullied at work too?'

She nodded. 'I was very involved with the court case. I took my eye of the ball with Alex and I feel very guilty about that. We don't think there has been any lasting physical damage, but it's quite hard to be sure because he had some social challenges and additional needs anyway. They're mild, but enough to make life difficult for him sometimes.'

Tan was right; she *had* been through the mill.

'Anyway,' she tried to laugh, 'can you stop being nice to me, please? I refuse to cry again.'

'Sorry. For what it's worth, it's when we *stop* feeling stuff we need to worry. Especially in this game. I don't think it's a sign of weakness at all, just so you know.' I smiled at her and she held my gaze… but then Hamish hung up and came lurching into our moment like a bison on ice skates as he swung round on his chair, stretching up to reveal faintly yellowed arm pits on his shirt. He yawned unnecessarily loudly.

'Oh excellent! You're making tea. I'll have one, please!'

Julia instinctively turned away so he couldn't see her face, wiping her eyes as I shot him a look, but the stupid arse didn't take the hint. 'Everything all right?' He looked between us.

'Yes fine,' I said smoothly. 'We were just discussing Julia's experiences at the Royal Grace, that's all.'

'Ah.' Hamish hesitated. 'Is it true that you were sent a dead animal in the post?'

'Hamish!' I admonished. He was going to undo all of my good work. And upset her again. 'Come on, mate!'

'No – it's OK.' She turned back to face him. 'Yes, it is true. Not a whole one; bits of a rat – a not very subtle message. I also had a sex doll delivered to my home address with the face all cut up, mugs of urine left on my desk at the hospital, a used tampon placed on my chair, and bags of dog's mess on the windscreen of my car while it was parked at the Royal Grace.'

I was appalled. What a bunch of unimaginative arseholes. I'd have at least gone with something like a box of live locusts that would have jumped out at her when she'd opened it. A bag of dog shit never made anyone scream.

She went back over to her desk and sat down. 'A junior told me she'd witnessed a male colleague of mine remove a healthy breast before going on to remove the one with the malignant tumour in it. The junior was certain it was supposed to be a single mastectomy and even queried it during the op. The surgeon got shitty with her, told her it was evident that the cancer had spread and he'd had no choice but to perform a double mastectomy. She didn't believe him and came to me.

'He had a reputation for getting juniors to do his ops for him, not supervising them properly, and rushing surgery because he was always prioritising his private clients.' She crossed her arms. Getting defensive. I leant on the side and watched her quietly.

'Anyway, I reported what she'd told me. He went ballistic and said I was making trouble because he'd rebuffed my advances towards him,' She laughed and I glanced briefly at Hamish. 'He told the Medical Director that I was seizing my chance to make what was no more than a "bad day at the office" into a huge, unfounded negligence case because I was an angry, spurned woman. Clever, really – it turned it into a he said/she said when it ought to have been all about the facts; he removed a healthy breast in error. He *should* have been suspended immediately while they began an investigation to make sure he hadn't done it to anyone else.'

'They obviously didn't?' I guessed.

'I was gobsmacked to see him at work two days later, actually operating. I kicked off about *that* too. I said the system was broken if we were going to let surgeons damage patients and not only *not* hold them to account but let them carry on doing it. I asked them what they were so afraid of; why they weren't investigating him properly?'

Hamish nodded emphatically. 'Good for you!'

'Which is when rumours started flying around about my aggression and my propensity to "throw my weight around" when I didn't get my own way, all of which was crap, obviously. I was told everything was being looked into – my "conduct" as well. They hoped I'd be scared enough about my own future to leave it alone, so they could shove everything under the carpet... I threatened to go public – that's when the hospital suspended me and I took them to court to force them to give me my job back.

'I had my whole professional life looked at under a microscope, while *he* quietly retired – full pension – no further investigation, no action taken.' She threw her hands up. 'And now here I am. Was it all worth it, you ask yourselves?' She laughed uncertainly. 'Someone said to me afterwards the case shone a much-needed light on sexism in our workplace, but I disagree. I think it probably put a lot of young women off joining the profession and that makes me really sad.'

'Well, on behalf of the *patients* he didn't get to butcher because you stepped in to prevent it, I'll say an emphatic thank you.' I made sure my smile was the correct blend of sympathy and reassurance.

'Thank you.' She flashed me a grateful glance. 'I'm not a troublemaker, honestly I'm not – and I promise I won't try it on with any of you.'

Hamish laughed heartily. 'Well then I feel safe to check that you're coming to the rugby with us at the weekend? I take it Nathan's asked you? Ah, Tan – just the man!' he exclaimed as Tan walked in, looking slightly harassed. 'Friday – there's still another space, isn't there? And a spare caravan now that the Mottrams aren't coming?'

'I think so, yes.' Tan dumped some papers on his desk. 'I'll double-check later. Why?'

'Julia's coming!' Hamish turned back to her. 'When I say caravan, don't panic. It's more a static home in a holiday park next to the beach. There's an indoor swimming pool and "nightly entertainment", but don't let that put you off. It's fun. The kids love it.'

'Tan's coming with his wife, son and two daughters. Ben and I will be there, and Hamish is bringing his stepson,' I said. 'An informal departmental social! Just do one night if you prefer? Head on over after school and work on Friday, back on Saturday. Bring Ewan and Cass with you too. We'd be delighted to have your company. Ben really likes Alex – he'd be made up to have you all come along.'

'I'll ask Ewan but thank you for the invite – that's really kind of you. Whoa!' She looked at the clock and jumped up. 'I must get on! Thank you for letting me vent.'

'No problem! Have a good morning!'

We waited until we were sure she wasn't coming back, and the smile fell from Hamish's face. 'She's a lunatic. Although you're right, Nate, the Royal Grace lot also sound certifiable. Bags of shit and mugs of piss… bloody amateurs. *That's* not how you get things done. Anyway – all set. Nicely played.'

'What's all set?' Tan said quickly.

'Nothing!' Hamish grinned at me, leant back in his chair and happily patted his tummy. 'I must get rid of this. It's not attractive.'

He waited for me to disagree and tell him it wasn't that bad, but I didn't because it's an inescapable truth. He's much too fat. If you were marooned on a boat in the middle of an ocean with Hamish and were forced to kill and eat him to survive, you'd do very nicely indeed. I crossed the room and sat down at my desk. Julia would come, she'd do it for Alex, I was almost certain of it.

'What's all set?' Tan asked again. He was worried. 'Something involving Julia? What are you going to do to her?'

'Nothing,' I lied. 'Nothing at all.'

CHAPTER THIRTEEN

Julia

I crossed the room to get my pjs from the drawer. 'We've been invited to a camping and rugby weekend on Friday night.'

Ewan put his book down on the duvet and waited to hear more.

'The blokes in my department are going with their families. They've all got sons similar ages to Al – but there are some girls that Cass might like to meet. I was telling them about Al struggling and needing to make some friends.' I sat down on the bed. 'We'd be staying in a caravan.'

'I know Dom messing around has set Al back,' Ewan reached for his water and took a sip, 'but he'll make some friends eventually. You can't do it for him. Plus…' Ewan gestured around at the large boxes still stacked in the room, 'we could blitz a lot this weekend if we stay here.'

'I've done the kids' rooms and the essentials,' I reminded him, taking my top off. 'We could just throw everything else away.' I was only half joking about that. I didn't want to have to go through all of the crap from the old house. 'I like having less clutter.'

'Clutter is one thing – it looks clinical at the moment. I want to put some pictures up, make it look like we're actually staying.'

I sighed. 'I don't want to go on a rugby weekend for me. I just thought—'

'…if you want Al to do more exercise to let off some steam, *I* can sort that out.' Ewan picked up his book. 'Unless it's important we spend some time with your new work lot, I vote we have the weekend at home.'

*

We swung open the caravan door and stepped in. At the far end was a Formica table with four stools, a built-in L-shape bench sofa topped with brown, rigid cushions and thin tartan curtains at the window. A large, flat-screen TV dominated the small space. 'Well, it's nice and warm!' I said cheerfully, putting the bag down in the middle of the floor.

Cass wrinkled her nose. 'Where am I sleeping?'

'There's a twin room for you and Alex to share.'

She stalked off to have a look. 'Is this a joke?' I heard her call, and breathing out deeply, I went to find her. She was staring at two short, very close together beds. One was covered in a blue nylon bedspread that looked like it was poised to give some cracking electric shocks the second it was touched, the other was smothered in a Disney duvet, complete with Belle, Snow White and Cinderella. She looked at me challengingly, eyebrows raised.

'It's for one night. That's all.'

She snorted in disgust and pushed past me.

'The bathroom is a *cupboard*,' she announced as I followed. 'I'll be able to wee and wash my hands in the sink at the same time.' She turned on the tap and an apologetic dribble coursed down the plug. She sniffed and shut it off quickly. 'Urgh! Eggy. That's disgusting.'

'This is small.' Alex appeared behind us.

'Yeah, I know, so can we not all cram into the tiniest part of it?' Cass snapped. 'It stinks and I'm starting to feel claustrophobic.'

'Ewan's talking to Ben's dad,' Alex announced. 'They're outside. Do we want to go and have food at some pub called The Pilchard or something? Ewan says we've got hot dogs and to check with you first?'

'I don't want to go to a pub. I'd rather stay here,' Cass said contrarily. 'Please, Julia, tell them we'll see them later. Ben just stares at me.' She shuddered. 'It's gross. *He's* gross.'

'Can *I* go with them?' Alex said suddenly.

I was taken aback. Alex had never asked to do something like this before – but wasn't it exactly the reason we'd come, so he'd mix with people, start making friends? 'You really don't want to go, Cass?'

She shook her head and pulled her jumper sleeves down over her hands, before crossing her arms defensively.

'OK, Al, if Ben's dad doesn't mind taking you.' I smiled. Nathan would look after him. 'Ask Ewan to give you some money for your meal.'

Alex brightened immediately and disappeared.

'And take a coat?' I called, but there was no response.

I went back into the main area of the caravan and sighed as I watched Alex through the window, walking off down the lit-up path between Ben and Nathan in just his hoodie. Nathan had his hand resting on my son's back as they walked, and Alex was already chatting away animatedly while Ben trailed slightly behind them.

Ewan appeared and followed my gaze.

'He'll freeze,' I said.

'He'll be all right – the pub's not far away, well within walking distance. Nathan said to go and meet them at someone's house when they get back at nine p.m. Hamish. He's the other one you share your office with, isn't he? Apparently, it's right on the beach.'

I was confused. 'They're not in the caravan park too?'

'I don't think so?' Ewan held up his phone. 'I've been given the address. It's very easy to find, apparently. A little white stone cottage, a hundred yards from the beach. Sounds lovely.' He looked around dubiously. 'As I'm sure this will be.' He sniffed. 'What's that smell?'

'The drains, I think. It'll be fine. Let's go and make the hot dogs, shall we?'

*

We could hear laughing and chatter as we approached the front door. Feeling shy, I knocked, but it pushed open – not properly on the latch – straight into the open-plan downstairs space, where everyone was congregated. Tan had his arm around a very pretty woman, and two more couples I didn't recognise were sitting at a kitchen table chatting, while a dozen children were spilt over squashy sofas watching *Guardians of the Galaxy 2*. Ben looked up and flushed violently as Cass crossed the room and perched on the edge. Al didn't notice us at all.

Tan kindly stood up in welcome, but Nathan bounded down the stairs holding a beer and reached us first.

'You've made it! How were the hot dogs?' He came across, offering Ewan his hand, before leaning in and briefly kissing me on either cheek. He smelt different today – a sharp, breezy lime mixed with a peppery warmth I couldn't put my finger on – he must have a bewildering array of aftershaves. 'I'll introduce you to everyone. Julia, you need to meet Tan's wife, Trishna – she's lovely. What can I get you both to drink? We've got practically everything open, so tell me what you'd *like*.'

I scratched my arm. It was always a bit awkward seeing colleagues socially like this, kissing them hello when you'd never do that on Monday morning at work. 'Just a white wine, please.' I looked at the bottles on the side – there was a lot of booze for a kids' rugby weekend. Unless it was just the front for what was actually a jolly for the parents. 'Thanks so much for taking Al to the pub; that was kind of you. Was everything OK?'

'He was no problem at all. We had a great old chat over burger and chips about drawing – and sloths. He knows a lot about them, doesn't he?'

'He knows a lot about most animals,' said Ewan. 'Art, animals, *Star Wars*, photography and *Fortnite*. Those are Alex's big loves.'

Nathan nodded gravely. 'Yes, we covered *Fortnite* in some considerable depth too, but it was a genuinely interesting chat. Normally, I'm lucky if I get a single word out of Ben. Now – beer, Ewan? Wine, Whisky?'

Ewan hesitated. 'I'll grab a whisky if it's open? Thank you. I feel bad we've turned up empty-handed.'

'Don't,' said Nathan, dismissively. 'There's far too much here as it is. Hamish always goes rogue on weekends like this – he's never quite stopped being the naughty kid who swipes the contents of his parent's booze cupboard, shoves it in the back of the car and roars off to the party. This cottage is his big sister's. Personally, I think she's mad to let him anywhere near it.'

I looked around me. 'It's very nice.' With its white walls, bleached beams, driftwood cupboard doors, butler's sink and blue stripy curtains it had definitely received the cottage-by-the-sea brief and stuck to it faithfully. 'She rents it out, I take it?'

Nathan nodded. 'She's one of those irritating people who started flipping properties and building a proper portfolio back in the early nineties. When we were all getting pissed at the Roundhouse, she was snapping up fisherman cottages in Salcombe for a song. We all laughed at her. Ha ha us.' He took a swig of his beer. 'She's got something like about thirty places now, from little ones like this to actual hotels. Hamish's parents own a pretty chunky amount of property too. Student houses, offices – in fact, my private practice is in a building owned by the Wilsons. Hamish just ponces around whichever holiday home or hotel room is vacant at the time.'

'You and Hamish go back a long way then?' Ewan said. 'He's in both of your department, right?'

'Yes, we were at medical school together,' Nathan confirmed as we moved slowly towards the table. 'When he comes out of the loo, I'll introduce you. His family are all around here, so he was always coming back to the South West. I followed him, hoping to be adopted into the fold and it worked. They had any number of spare rooms going begging and, as you know, my folks were – and are – in the States. The location of this one is stunning though, you'll see in the morning when it's light; sparkling sea for miles. There are some amazing runs along the shoreline, Ewan, if you've brought your trainers. I'm going first thing tomorrow morning – want to come along?'

'Thanks, but it's never done much for me, I'm afraid,' Ewan said. 'I'm more of a swimmer and a footballer. Julia is the runner in our relationship.'

Nathan turned to me and grinned. 'Well, you'd be very welcome tomorrow too… if you think you can keep up?'

*

Nathan was right. It was glorious along the coast. The tide was right out and the damp sand – striated with silver slivers of water running down to the sea as they caught the light – was far more forgiving on my joints than pounding pavements. Reaching the path again, I stopped, exhausted, breathing heavily in the cold morning air, and dropped my hands to my knees as I stared out at the horizon line. Clouds were starting to blow in.

'Morning!' said a voice behind me and I turned to see the man himself; unlike me, fresh as a daisy in pristine gym gear.

'What time do you call this?' I teased. 'I'm done already!'

Nathan looked impressed. 'Wow – what time did you start?'

'Only three quarters of an hour ago. I was out here for sunrise.' I straightened up and wiped my brow. 'Sorry, that sounds insufferably smug. But yes, I'm finished – so at least you won't need to worry about me "keeping up".'

He laughed. 'I knew that would bug you and that you'd *have* to come down this morning – if just to prove me wrong.'

I flashed him a grin. 'I don't know what you're talking about – if I had wanted to make a point of showing you up, I'd have arranged a specific time to run with you, but I'm not that unkind.'

'Thanks. Big of you to let me off the hook.'

'You're welcome. On a serious note, Alex had fun last night. Thank you for inviting us here.' I picked up my left heel to stretch my quads, wobbled and instinctively put out a hand, which he caught.

'Steady!'

'Sorry.' I let go of him. 'I probably just need something to eat, that's all.' I put my foot down, pulled my sweaty hair from its band, shook it out and then picked up the other leg.

He glanced sideways at me. 'Do you ever wear make-up?'

I laughed out loud and wobbled again. 'Excuse me?'

'I don't mean that as a bad thing!' he said quickly. 'You just don't seem to be into "artifice" for want of a better word. You're very straightforward – happy in your own skin. That's what I mean.'

'Well, I'm not going to put on full slap and have it drip off my face into a patient during surgery, am I?' I pointed out. 'And I don't tend to wear make-up when I go for a run either.' I put my leg down and turned towards him. 'Are you saying I *need* to wear make-up?' I teased. 'Thanks very much!'

He hesitated, looking at me – then to my surprise, he turned and started to walk away. Bewildered, I wondered what I'd said to offend him, but just as I was about to call after him to stop so I could apologise, he suddenly came back.

'I'm saying I spend a lot of time with women trying to change the way they look and I think you're beautiful. You're perfect,' he said simply, leant forward and kissed me. Instinctively, I closed my eyes, for less than a second I even kissed back – it was a physical response – but then my mind caught up. I placed my hands on his arms, pushing him back.

'What are you doing?' I gasped, covering my mouth with the back of my hand. 'I'm married! We're both married!'

He looked as stunned as I felt. He just stared at me in silence before blurting, 'I've fallen in love with you!'

I instantly heard Eleni's voice in my head. *He has an agenda.*

'What are you talking about?' I exclaimed. 'I've been at the hospital for three weeks! That's nothing!'

'I know.' He put his hands on his head. 'I know! I've been telling myself the same thing! But now I've kissed you, I'm sure of how I feel. I think I've loved you pretty much from the moment you shook my hand outside the school in those ridiculous wellingtons on that baking hot afternoon.' He laughed and stepped forward eagerly, taking my hand in his. I was so shocked by the words I was hearing, I just stood there like a fool.

'The more I learn more about you, the more I realise you're the most incredible woman I've ever met. You're kind, you're passionate, you simply say how you feel – there are no games. You're everything.' He reached out with his other hand and ran the back of his fingers down the side of my face in apparent wonder.

It made me shiver and I stumbled back away from him.

'I'm married,' I repeated.

'I can't help how I feel.' He put his hands together in a praying position and rested them on his lips, as if he couldn't believe the words falling from them. 'Someone like you could save someone like me.'

'No, don't do this.' I shook my head, finding my feet on the sand again. 'Don't feed me crap lines. We work together, Nathan. I've just started here after a really, really difficult time in my professional life – and you know my personal life is complicated at the moment too. I don't want drama and I don't want awkwardness.

I've enjoyed being part of a team again, feeling like we were *friends* as well as colleagues. I thought you understood that?'

'I do. Of course I do! But I want to make things better for you. I want to… *protect* you and Alex.'

'Protect us?' I was confused. 'You mean when you dealt with Dom? That was kind of you, but I don't need a—'

'Come away with me,' he said suddenly, before I could finish. 'Just for a night somewhere. Somewhere where we can talk!'

'What?' I wrapped my arms around myself instinctively and stared at him for a moment. I simply couldn't make any sense of what he was saying. 'You want me to spend the *night* with you somewhere?'

'Yes!' he said eagerly. 'Not like *that* – just some time together.'

I laughed in disbelief. 'You're joking, right? This is just you messing around?'

'No.' He shook his head emphatically. 'I'm serious. I didn't think I was, but I am and – you're incredible.'

I'm not saying he can't be very attentive to those round him. Again, Eleni's warning resounded in my head. So she was right. This was what he did, how he worked. What was it he really wanted from me?

The wind gusted suddenly. I turned my head away from the sharp sand lifting into the air, waited for it to pass and when I looked back at him, my voice was cold. 'I really *am* too old for this routine, Nathan. Did you think I'd fall swooning into your arms, we'd go "somewhere for the night", you'd have your wicked way with me, then by morning I'd have fallen desperately in love with you too?'

He frowned. 'I didn't think anything. I've only just realised this myself. All I know is I want to be with you.'

'Do women you can't have do it for you? Is that it? Or is this a needing to dominate women you work with thing?' I asked. 'I'm genuinely interested. Like Storm said: is it because you feel you're the underachiever – so you've always got to be top dog?'

'What? Of course not! I told you, I wasn't looking for this! I've never felt this way about anyone.'

'Not your first or your current wife?' I shielded my face as another gust of wind attempted to blow more sand in my eyes. 'I'm sure they'd be delighted to hear that. I'll say it again. You don't love me. True love develops quietly over time; it's not showy gestures and overused words. I'm really insulted that you think I'm naïve enough to believe otherwise. I thought we were friends.'

'Why are you so *angry* with me?' He took another step closer. 'I don't understand.'

'Because you've broken it!' I shouted. 'I just told you – I felt like we were all getting on really well and now that's gone! Now it's going to be weird and uncomfortable at work – all thanks to you. Just… don't talk to me about this ever again, OK? I want you to pretend you never said this to me. If you really "love" me' – I met his gaze furiously – 'that's what you can do.'

I turned and started to run back along the path, away from him. Once I was sure I was out of his sight, I stopped and yelled aloud, wiping my lips with the ball of my thumb and fingers where he had touched me. I looked over my shoulder, double-checking that I was alone. All I could see was the empty beach, a couple of gulls wheeling overhead. Thick cloud had turned the sky a flat, dull white. I started to walk. I was going to have to tell Ewan, but in the caravan, where the walls were paper-thin and the kids would hear everything? Perhaps it would be better to wait until we'd left, in any case, otherwise he might try to have it out with Nathan. I continued to put one foot in front of the other, forcing my mind to methodically sort through the facts and potential outcomes. Nathan was a parent at the school. Ewan might lose his job there if things became heated.

My eyes filled with tears. Since marrying Ewan, I had only kissed him; had only *wanted* to kiss him. Nathan couldn't possibly have been given the impression that I was unhappy in any way, or that I had encouraged him somehow. He had no right to alter the dynamics of my marriage like this! Ewan was going to be devastated. This was going to push all sorts of buttons for him. Love? Nathan didn't know the meaning of the word.

I wanted to leave immediately – without having to see any of them. I could fake illness? Yes – that was the thing to do. I rounded the corner, decision made – to find Cass standing on the step of the caravan in the doorway, arms protectively wrapped around herself, her hair lifting on the breeze, as Ben spoke earnestly to her. I watched him place his hand on her arm only for her to shake him off.

'Hey!' I shouted and he turned, frightened, immediately stepping away from Cass as I marched up to them. 'What's going on?'

'Nothing. He's just leaving,' Cass said. Ben looked between us then pulled his hood up and nodded politely at me. 'Mrs Wilder.'

I watched him lope away, disappearing between the vans, and turned back to Cass. 'What was all that about?'

'He just asked me out.'

'You said no, though?' I couldn't help myself, horrified at the prospect of them dating and being further linked to Nathan. 'Because you don't like him, do you?'

She shrugged. 'He's not as mental as I thought he was.'

'But that's not a good enough reason to go out with him. You only do that if you *want* to. You don't *have* to do anything.'

'Yeah, I know.' She shivered. 'It's cold. Did you bring any hot chocolate?'

'Julia!' A voice called out behind me and I turned to see Storm walking towards us, immaculate in a wax jacket and jeans tucked into nut-brown riding boots.

'I've just arrived. I wanted to surprise my boys, but neither of them seems to be around.' She looked the caravan up and down then fixed her gaze on me. 'Ben's not at the cottage, and Nathan has apparently gone for a run. Hamish's stepson said he thought

Ben had come to see Cassia? I didn't know you were here too, until Tan enlightened me.' She smiled tightly. 'What fun!'

Cass snorted rudely – just for a second it was as if Lise was right next to me – and disappeared back into the van.

I briefly considered telling Storm what 'her boy' had just done at the beach, but unlike Nathan I respected the mechanics of other people's marriages. For all I knew, she chose to turn a blind eye to his behaviour. I couldn't possibly be the first woman he'd spun that story to while married to her.

'We're going home, actually.' I cleared my throat. 'I don't feel very well, all of a sudden.'

'Oh, I'm sorry,' she said, not sounding sorry at all. 'Such a shame. Would you like to leave Alex here with us and we'll bring him back tomorrow so he doesn't have to miss out?'

'That's very kind of you, but he's seeing his dad tonight,' I lied; the irony of my using Dom when it suited, not lost on me. 'So I'd be having to ask you to come back a day early, which of course I can't do. But thank you so much for the offer. Ben *was* here by the way. You just missed him.'

'Yes, he seems to like Cassia,' Storm said. 'He's mentioned her a lot at home. It's the classic giveaway, isn't it?' She held my gaze. 'He does this all the time: falls head over heels only to lose interest just as quickly when they start going out with each other. Cassia probably ought to know that. I'd hate her to get hurt.'

Yeah, she knew what Nathan was like for sure. I hesitated and looked down at the ground as I considered my response carefully. 'She just wants to be friends with him, that's all. I think he realises that now. Perhaps you can tell the others we've left early and send our apologies. I'm sure they'll understand.' I looked up and held her gaze coolly.

To my surprise her eyes filled with tears, making her appear even younger than she was and it occurred to me she might have seen what just happened at the beach. I took a deep breath. 'Is there anything you want to say, Storm? Do you have any questions for me?'

She gave me a strange, slightly anguished look and shook her head. 'But thank you for asking.' She turned on her heels and left.

CHAPTER FOURTEEN

Nathan

'It's so perfect!' Hamish crowed, standing over me. 'Look at it – just bloody look at it!' He tapped my shoulder with his phone as I sat on the cold sand, my elbows on my knees, hands on my head. I ignored him for a moment, staring at the waves rolling in while I tried not to think about Julia running away from me.

'I admit I had my doubts and I didn't think you should use your wily charms, but I'm delighted to be proven wrong. It looks like she's grabbed you for a quickie in the dunes. She's not going to want her husband to see this!' Hamish shoved the screen under my nose.

I glanced at it and there she was – captured – my mouth touching hers. I snatched the phone from him, both horrified and aroused by the image. What had I done? I pulled at the pixels with my fingertips, enlarging her face.

As Hamish had suggested before we'd made our separate ways down to the beach, in deliberately keeping my arms down by my side, it looked like Julia had instigated the kiss; she appeared to be holding on to me when, in reality, she was pushing me away. She *had* kissed me back, however, if just for the briefest moment – I'd felt it. Her eyes were closed, her lashes sweeping her cheeks, her face tilted up to me, her mouth on mine. The crashing sea and darkening clouds were swirling behind us, her hair was lifting on the wind, but we seemed to be oblivious to everything, caught up only in what mattered – each other. Anyone looking at the image would have believed we were in love, that this was undoubtedly a grand passion. My lips parted slightly in amazement as I studied the picture and, incredibly, I felt near to tears. I hadn't cried since the headmaster informed me of my grandmother's death.

And yet… I blinked and swallowed, passing the phone back to Hamish – she had pushed me away. She had been angry, *really* angry. She thought I was mocking her, but I'd never been more sincere in my whole life – I just hadn't known it until the second we kissed and it became impossible to ignore; like pretending the sun doesn't rise in the East and set in the West. I love her.

I squinted out to sea again and remembered a story I was taught at school but hadn't thought about for years: a beautiful bird – the Caladrius – owned by the king to take away the sickness of any ill personage within the royal household. As white as snow, the Caladrius would look at the sufferer and, in doing so, draw the affliction from the person into itself, before flying away with it. The higher the exquisite bird flew towards the sun, the more the sickness would burn away, healing both the Caladrius and the sufferer on earth. It being school, they gave it a quasi-religious spin, likening the ill person to an unrepentant sinner and the Caladrius to an angry God, turning His head away, but I preferred the medieval version.

Julia. I balled up my hands and placed the fists on my forehead; she was my Caladrius: her very presence gave me hope, made me want to be a better version of myself. Yet I had held open the door to the cage and knowingly closed it behind her, watching her wings beat in fright when she found herself caught.

'It's a total result. Bang up-to-date *evidence* that Julia Blythe causes trouble for her male colleagues wherever she goes! A serial seducer!' Hamish sat down next to me with a little gasp of effort. 'She'll turn a blind eye to whatever the hell we tell her to now!'

I hadn't fed her cheap lines – she could be the making of me. She already had been. I hung my head. I should have carried on walking away. I was *so* close to doing the right thing for once – possibly the one selfless act of my life – but I failed. I turned back to get a deliberately damaging photo of her… and yet the second my mouth touched hers, I realised the enormity of my mistake. I put my hand on the back of my neck and rubbed the tight muscles. My stomach felt full of wet elastic bands, slipping and sliding all over each other.

'Nate? Aren't you pleased?' Hamish was beginning to deflate. 'I don't think I could have got a better shot, could I?'

'You didn't do anything wrong.' It was my fault. I was to blame.

'Right, well, you're welcome.' Hamish scratched his head. 'Come on then! Buck up! Smile, at least?' He threw his hands wide in exasperation, still holding the phone. 'Has someone died?'

Me. I've died. I was aware of the wind on my face, I could taste the salt in the air, but I felt nothing. It was already not enough to have kissed her. I wanted more. My comedown was gathering speed, and the bleak reality of what my callous, selfish plan had cost me – and her – was becoming clearer by the second. I shivered and glanced at my oldest friend, desperately sad that I'd cheapened such a profound moment in my life and sold it to him, crouched in the distance, snapping away.

We were never going to get that back. I was never going to get a second chance at that first kiss. And what the hell would happen if she were to ever find out it had been deliberately staged and photographed? She would never forgive or trust me again. I was terrified at the thought.

'Nathan!' Hamish changed his tone, becoming firm. 'I'm getting worried now. You're practically catatonic! Talk to me! Tell me what you're thinking!'

'We've made a mistake. We shouldn't have done that.'

Hamish stared at me. 'Okkkayyyy. Are you worried about Storm's reaction if she were to see the picture, because it really does look like Julia is leading everything? I honestly don't think you've got any worries there. No one but us is going to see it anyway. Julia should want to keep it under wraps, that's the whole point. *She'll* never know it exists, unless something goes wrong.'

I thought about that and sat up a little straighter. 'That's true. Suppose we just stop everything now? No more films. No more collecting. No girls. No events, no networking. Maybe it's time? We've had a bloody good run of it. Perhaps we *should* quit while we're ahead?' I felt my mood lift instantly. I could salvage this yet. With nothing for us to protect, the picture was worth nothing. Delete it and it never happened. I would be free to start repairing my relationship with Julia in good conscience. 'I want to stop.'

Hamish looked at me in astonishment – then laughed. 'God, for a minute I thought you were serious.'

The elastic bands tightened. 'What if I am?'

'Stop completely? And do what? Be ordinary?'

I nodded, my smile fading.

'But... Nathan... you're not doing anything wrong! *We're doctors!* We simply look at films of patients we've already been given permission to view in real life!'

Patients *I've* been given permission to view. But I didn't say it out loud.

'What's responsible for this misguided pang of conscience, eh?' Hamish attempted cosy confidence, but it sounded more like a demand as he crossed his arms. 'It's her, isn't it? *Julia.*'

He spoke her name like it smelt rotten. I frowned and opened my mouth.

'No,' he held up a hand, before I could speak. 'You're wrong. *I* have no strong feelings about Julia either way.' He raised his eyebrows pointedly. 'But what about you?'

I looked out to sea. 'I've fallen in love with her.'

'Oh God.' Hamish let his head hang. 'No, you haven't!'

I twisted to look at him. 'Yes, I have. Why is this so hard for everyone to believe?'

'She's the first woman to reject you. That's not the same thing as love.' He rubbed his brow, apparently exasperated.

'I want to be with her.'

'Like you wanted to be with Storm? And Serena? They're just the two you married!'

'I don't ever remember telling you I was in love with Storm, or Serena,' I snapped. 'Because I wasn't. This is the first time this has happened. I know. I'm me.'

'You were "fascinated", "bewitched", "intoxicated" – by Storm especially,' Hamish countered. 'It broke poor Serena's heart and you know it.'

I blinked in astonishment. 'You're not still holding a candle for Serena? You *are* kidding me!'

'Of course I'm not!' he almost shouted, and I drew back in surprise. 'Sorry,' he added tightly. 'I'm simply pointing out that we've been here before.'

'No.' I shook my head. 'This is different.'

'"Love" is no more than the poor man's description for complex biological drivers designed to further the human race. You are innately drawn to people you are a good genetic fit with. The higher the likelihood that a female will give your offspring the greatest chance of survival, the stronger the pull towards her. That's all this is and you know it: a set of predetermined behaviours. Nothing more, nothing less.'

'Why did you marry Cecily then?' I retorted. 'Kids were hardly on the cards; in fact you got lumbered with someone else's and it wasn't as if you needed her money. You married her because you love her!'

Hamish ran a finger lightly around the edge of his phone. 'It's what normal people do. It's what society expects you to do. People are suspicious of a man who has never married or doesn't have a long-term partner.'

I stood up. 'I want to take the cameras in my office down. Things are going to change.'

He paled but after a heartbeat's pause, shrugged, 'OK. Sleep on that for a couple of nights and then if that's still what you want, we will.'

'It is. Delete the photo, please.' I nodded at his screen.

'The one we *just* took? No!'

'Do it, Ham. I'm not kidding.'

He swore under his breath and got his phone out. 'There. Done. Ridiculous!'

'I want to cancel the Christmas meet-up too.'

His mouth fell open. 'We're hosting! That won't go down well.'

'I mean it. Don't book any girls.'

'This is crazy! All you need to do as far as Julia goes is exercise a little bit of self-control and—'

'Really, Hamish?' I put my head on one side. 'You're going to lecture me about self-control?' I looked pointedly at his gut.

He flushed. 'You're a nasty bastard sometimes, Nate. Body shaming is—'

'Oh, you can fuck off with your body shaming.' I was starting to get angry. 'Firstly, the majority of our income is derived from exactly that and secondly, telling someone they're obese is the ethical responsibility of all health care professionals. I *care* enough to tell you, even though it would be easier not to, and you make out like that's a bad thing?'

'Fine. Message received. I'm fat. Thanks. You do not love Julia; you need to trust *me* on this.'

I ignored him. 'I'm so angry with myself for what I've just done to her, I can't—'

'Nate?'

I clambered to my feet at the sound of a woman's voice – but disappointingly, it was my wife.

'There you are!' Storm was posed behind me, smiling widely, hands on her hips and dressed in the most ridiculous outfit for the beach. The leather of her no doubt eye-wateringly expensive boots was already sand stained. 'I've been looking for you everywhere!'

'Well, obviously not *everywhere*, because here I am!' I smiled. I could practically see the blackness of decay creeping into the edges of the perfect picture she thought she was making, destroying it. 'Have you lost your horse? And what are you doing here anyway? Checking up on me?'

'I just missed you, that's all. Have you seen Ben? Julia told me he'd just left their caravan. I wondered if he'd come down here. Julia's going home, by the way. She doesn't feel well. Nathan?' She waited for me to say something,

She was *leaving*? My jaw clenched. 'I need to go for my run.'

Storm's face fell.

'Can't we just go and have breakfast together for once? I've driven—'

I turned and ran off, leaving her mid-sentence. It was hard to see how my plan could have backfired more spectacularly, even if it had led to my finally gaining an understanding of how I truly felt. I was disgusted with myself. I'd behaved like a child.

CHAPTER FIFTEEN

Julia

'But I want to stay!' Alex repeated angrily. 'I don't care that Dad is coming to visit. I don't want to see him! And don't lie and say he's not, because I *know* that's why we're going back – I heard you tell Ben's mum. You're not ill at all! You've just been running!'

I sat with my elbow on the passenger window ledge of the car, head on my hand and eyes closed. 'I wouldn't worry about having to speak to Dad, Al. It's really not going to be an issue.' *Because I made it up.* As Al fell silent, I tried not to think about Nathan's mouth on mine – all the ridiculous things he'd said. I was so angry at the thought of having to tell Ewan; the unnecessary tension and stress it was going to cause.

'So when did you find out Dom was coming?' Ewan said casually, staring straight ahead, his gaze on the road. I could tell he was making a huge effort to stay calm in front of the kids, but that he was furious too. Not even half past ten in the morning and already everything had veered wildly off course.

'I'm not going to speak to Dad. You can't make me,' Alex interjected from the back. 'He can take his stupid giant guinea pigs away too. And that dumb tiger.'

'No!' Cass said. 'I like it.'

'You can't even sleep with it in your room.' Alex glared at her. 'Just admit it.'

'Julia, I don't have to give Whisper back, do I?' Cass leant forward and pulled my sleeve. 'That'd just be rude to Dom, wouldn't it?'

'All of you – please!' I shouted suddenly, and they looked at me in surprise. Cass drew back into her seat.

'I'm sorry,' I said immediately. 'I really do have a headache. Could I just have a moment of peace and quiet, do you think?'

'Well, as we're almost home, I think that's unlikely.' Ewan looked sideways at me. 'Can I just ask how you want to play this? You want me involved or do I just say nothing and leave it to you?'

'Look, I'm sure we won't need to—' I began but the sound died on my lips as we turned into our drive only to see Dom *actually sitting on our doorstep*. I sat forward in my seat, peering incredulously as if I was hallucinating.

My rage reached boiling point, instantly. No build up – just there, like him. How many times must I tell him? Was no one hearing me anymore?

'I think let's just try and get him inside.' Ewan took off his seat belt. 'I don't want a scene outside for everyone to hear.'

But it was too late; I had already thrown open the door and was marching towards Dom. He was holding an iPad in his hands and waved it with a delighted smile. 'Hey, you're home after all! I thought you might be…'

'What are you doing here?' I hissed at him, with a fury that took even me by surprise. 'Why? WHY are you here?'

'Hey!' He stumbled to his feet. 'I only wanted to drop this off for Al.' He held the tablet up. 'Someone gave it to me and I thought he might like it. It's a bigger screen than his phone. We could FaceTime on it. It would feel a bit less remote.'

'You live two hundred and fifty miles away!' I exclaimed. 'You don't just drop something off! You *arrange* to come up!'

Ewan and the kids had climbed out too. Al looked down at the floor as Dom held out the iPad. 'Hey kiddo! Look what I've got for you?'

'Let's do this inside, shall we?' Ewan glanced around us and smiled at the couple who had stopped in the drive entrance with their small dog and a bag of shopping.

'Good news, Dom!' the man called. 'You weren't locked out for too long then?'

'I know, right?' Dom reached down beside him, picking up an empty mug I'd not noticed, before jogging over to hand it back. 'Thank you so much for the tea and biscuit though, Ian!'

I was so stunned by this exchange, horrified at what Dom might have told the neighbours we didn't even know by name ourselves yet, as they waved and disappeared into the house opposite, that everything slowed right down. I simply stopped as if I had hit pause. I imagined what that would feel like: everything static – no moving cars; no sound of birds; leaves suspended in the air as they fell from the trees; Dom frozen halfway back to us, tablet tucked under his arm; Ewan with his hand lifted, key in the lock. Cass looking down and Al trying to hide the fact that he was crying. I stepped outside of myself and regarded the scene calmly for a moment. I could walk up to Dom and scream my frustration in his face – but what good would that do? I took a deep breath, regained control and everything started up again. Dom arrived next to me; the front door opened. 'Get inside,' I said to Dom, keeping my voice low. My expression didn't change. He frowned but did as he was told.

I turned to Cass and Al. 'Go upstairs, please, to your rooms. Put some music on, watch some TV in our room if you like. I'll come and get you in a bit.'

They filed past me without a word.

'Don't forget your new iPad!' Dom said, holding it out to him in the hallway as Al passed. He grabbed it without a word and ran upstairs as Ewan and I came in and closed the front door.

'OK, so you're angry with me for saying I was locked out when I don't actually live here,' Dom said, hands up defensively as I stared at him. 'I needed to say *something* to explain why I was just sitting there. They don't mind, anyway. Ian said it was lovely we all get on so well together that I've got my own key.' Dom looked at me hopefully, and I laughed in disbelief. What was it with these men? Dom repeatedly turning up out of the blue; Nathan's ridiculous declaration at the beach; Richard calmly sitting on the edge of my desk at the Royal Grace telling me no one would believe me and everyone would trust HIM.

I was sick of it – sick of them all.

'You're less trouble when you're pissed or sleeping it off,' I said out loud, and Dom's eyes widened in shock. 'I told you not to come here. Your son does not want to see you at the moment, but you still think you know best and come anyway. It's great that you've been sober for a couple of weeks but stop thinking about yourself and what YOU want. You are damaging Alex with this behaviour and I won't let it continue. Get out now, before I call the police and tell them you've been stalking our property, trying to convince the neighbours you live here, and harassing us for access to Alex that we haven't agreed with the courts. You'll be hearing from my solicitor about the next steps I'm going to take.'

Dom looked like he was going to throw up. 'You're going to stop me from seeing him?'

'Get out,' I repeated.

'I came to bring him a present,' he said desperately. 'I just wanted to—'

'Get out!' I said it again, like a stuck record, and Ewan stepped forward alongside me.

'You really do have to leave now, Dominic.'

Dom turned on him. 'This is nothing to do with you!'

'Becoming aggressive is not going to help your cause.' Ewan switched into teacher mode. 'Think about this: see it from Julia and Alex's point of view.'

'Oh, do me a favour.' Dom laughed. 'Like you understand her so well, when she's moved you all down here for some other bloke. She's doing to you exactly what she did to me, only you're too dumb to see it. After being married to Lise, I would have thought you'd learnt to spot the signs, *mate*.'

Ewan's jaw clenched. 'Do not talk about Lise like that.'

'Yeah, yeah, never speak ill of the dead, even when they liked to mess around on the side and we all knew it.' Dom deliberately taunted him, but somehow Ewan managed not to react. 'Jules will leave you for this flash git, Nathan, just like she left me for you.'

'Nathan?' Ewan looked pityingly at Dom. 'That's who you mean? He's her work colleague, that's all.'

The blood had stopped moving around my body.

'And she didn't leave you for me.' Ewan didn't raise his voice. 'Lise was still alive when you two separated. Julia left you because your marriage broke down. I didn't become involved with Julia until after Lise died. You know that's true, so why pretend otherwise? We've moved *here* for a new start, all of us together. You have to accept that. We want you to be a part of Alex's life, but not like this. We'll work everything out, OK? But right now, you need to leave and go home.'

Dom hesitated, then wiped his chin and mouth with his hand, before looking at me, his expression haunted. 'You really mean it?' he said softly. 'I'm less trouble pissed? Jesus!' He looked up at the ceiling and his eyes filled with tears. 'I've worked so hard, Jules. This is the toughest thing I've ever done. I can't believe you'd say that to me.'

He pushed past me, yanking the door open and banging it so hard behind him that the whole fragile fabric of the old building shook.

*

Upstairs in his bedroom, I put my arm round Alex's thin shoulders as he cried, hating Dom with a passion for making our son feel so confused and helpless, for not giving him the space to be angry – while simultaneously wondering how on earth I was supposed to tell Ewan what had happened at the beach now? Dom's ridiculous assertion wasn't going to seem quite so laughable in the context of Nathan having just kissed me.

'Are you going to stop him from seeing me, like Dad said, before he shouted at Ewan?' Alex clutched the tablet to his chest.

'I want Dad to remember that he has to ask before he comes here. He can't just show up whenever he likes – even if it's to bring you a present. Otherwise, I'm going to have to make some new rules that he'll have to stick to, yes.'

'I don't even want this now.' Al held out the iPad to me. 'It's caused too much trouble. Can you look after it?'

'Sure.' I took it from him.

'I should have told him that I was angry with him instead of just ignoring him, but I didn't feel brave enough.' Alex looked down at the floor, fresh tears falling from his face. 'I'm not very good at saying how I feel.'

'I think you're *really* good at it.' I took his hand, only for him to pull back away from me.

'No, I'm not. Can I just be on my own for a bit now, Mum?'

Having just spoken about respecting boundaries, I could hardly insist I stay, even though I wanted to, very much. I got up.

'I'm going to go and start fixing some lunch. What do you fancy? Burgers, maybe? I was thinking too, we might go and check out the sailing club later this afternoon. I've always wanted to learn to sail. I wondered if you might like to try it with me?'

'Maybe,' he said miserably and turned away from me. He was still crying when I closed the door quietly.

*

As I shoved the wretched iPad on top of my wardrobe and finally began to strip my still-clammy gym gear to go for a shower, I decided then and there not to tell Ewan what Nathan had done. Dom's absurd allegations would only make the kiss seem more significant than it was. What the hell had Nathan been *thinking*? It couldn't just be about sex. I threw my leggings in the dirty clothes basket and stared at my reflection in our full-length mirror. No make-up, lank hair. No kidding I wasn't into 'artifice'. Although I took Eleni's point about not putting myself down, I still looked like a normal, pretty tired woman in her forties; hardly hot enough to be driving someone wild with desire. That was just fact. Nathan's absurd declaration *had* to be motivated by something else. Power? Was it about him needing to be in charge of me? He wanted to be top dog? In which case, that made him no different to pretty much all other male surgeons I'd ever worked with, except Nathan had gone to slightly more trouble with his *X Factor* backstory of bullying and his intriguing eyes. Worst-case scenario, Eleni was right and there was something even more significant in play. What had she said? *Keep watch in this quiet little place?*

Well my eyes were wide open now.

CHAPTER SIXTEEN

Hamish

Watching the two of them prowl around each other like cats on Monday morning was exasperating as it was inevitable.

Julia arrived first and smiled in relief to see me – so obviously didn't want to be on her own with Nate.

He blew in like a whirlwind five minutes later. She didn't look up, just ignored him and frowned at her screen as if there was something particularly demanding she had to concentrate on. I saw him glance at her, hesitate and open his mouth, so I jumped in quickly.

'What time do you call this?' I joked. 'Want me to pop down and consent your patients and do the team brief for you?'

Nathan gave me a wintery smile. He still hadn't apologised for what he'd said to me on the beach. 'I don't want to bugger my day up completely, so no thanks. Morning, Julia.' He hung up his coat. 'How are you feeling?' He turned to look at her, his face a picture of sympathy. 'All better? We were sorry you had to leave us so suddenly on Saturday.'

'I'm fine, thank you.' She glanced up and held his gaze coolly, then smiled. It was a twist of pure steel. 'Everything's back to normal.' She might as well have said *Don't ever try to fuck with me again*, out loud.

'Good!' he said after a moment's pause. 'Delighted to hear it.'
He looked at the door. He wanted to talk to her alone. I didn't get
it. I simply didn't understand how he could be married to Storm
and want a snotty bitch like Julia instead. When he'd abandoned
Storm mid-sentence on the beach and run off, leaving me to pick
up the pieces, I'd been incredulous. I'd held her tightly as she cried,
stroked her hair and reassured her – when she pulled back – that
Nathan was definitely not sleeping with Julia Blythe. I love Nate
dearly, but I really could slap him sometimes. If Storm belonged
to me, I would cherish her. The girl is exquisite. Perfectly formed.

Nathan cleared his throat. 'Could I just grab a quick word with
you, Julia?' He pointed at the door.

She glanced up. 'I'm so sorry, I really need to finish this.' She
nodded at her screen. It was a battle of wills. 'I'm afraid it will
have to keep.'

Ouch.

'Of course.' He smiled at her and after that put-down, obviously
felt the need to remind her – or himself – of his genius. 'Right, I
must go rebuild a hand! See you both later!'

He might as well have pissed around her desk to mark his scent
before leaving.

I sighed inwardly. It was all so frustrating. I'd been careful
to *slowly* put my foot on the brake – outright telling Nathan
what he can and can't do is always catastrophic. Suggesting that
it would be better if he didn't shag her was perhaps unhelpful,
but Julia had made me uneasy from the moment I met her. I
just shouldn't have allowed Nate to persuade me that she was
the right person to back as the next member of our team. We'd
have been better off pushing for some innocent newbie, like Tan
had been when he'd arrived. In all honesty, I also didn't expect
Nathan to be quite *so* drawn to a woman as asexual as her – she's
not his usual type at all – and neither did I expect *her* to reject
him so emphatically when he tried it on. It's really as simple

as that. I've never known anyone not fall for him when he has them in his sights.

I should have trusted my gut instinct and shut the whole thing down before it began. He would have been none the wiser if I'd made some manoeuvres behind the scenes. She would have applied for the post anyway, but she wouldn't have got anywhere, and Nate wouldn't now be in such deep conflict with himself. One minute he was setting her up, the next passionately declaring 'love'. He certainly believed himself to be suffering, and it was also very clear he was now going to pursue Julia at any cost.

It was equally obvious to me – as someone well used to being rejected by women – that Julia was not going to change her mind… all of which presented me with a problem. I'd been alarmed by Nathan's heartfelt and insistent vow at the beach that we needed to radically change our 'wicked' ways. I didn't want to. I liked my life the way it was and I wasn't going to change a thing – certainly not on Julia Blythe's account. So, what to do?

Julia herself wasn't much of an issue. Her position only needed reinforcing. It was Nate who required more active management to make sure he wasn't about to chuck the baby out with the bathwater. He needed a distraction.

I checked my phone and glanced at the image I *hadn't* deleted; the two of them kissing. On the plus side, we'd achieved our aim – we had dirt on Julia – which was the main thing. Now, I just had to make sure he wasn't about to mess it all up.

As usual, it was going to be down to me to sort everything out.

CHAPTER SEVENTEEN

Julia

Once Nathan left the room, I quietly exhaled with relief. Awkward though our brief exchange had been, it was at least now done. I'd made it clear to him that I wasn't going to be difficult about things. I'd been polite but firm; he had misjudged the moment at the beach but there was nothing more to be said about it. Nathan had got the message, I was certain of that, while Hamish had remained none the wiser that anything was out of the ordinary. A good result all round.

It had actually been an easier encounter than I'd expected – almost as if the kiss hadn't happened at all – which was exactly how I'd asked Nathan to behave… but so much for 'love'. I shook my head lightly and returned to my notes. It had been the right call to keep it to myself – we still had to work together. Least said, soonest mended, while now keeping my guard well and truly up.

My phone began to ring in my pocket and when I saw it was my former mother-in-law, I forgot about Nathan – steeling myself for a far more difficult conversation. No doubt Dominic had told her about my legal threats. I hurried out into the corridor – but again, I was wrong-footed.

'Julia dear? It's Sorcha. I didn't expect you to pick up. I thought you'd be at work?'

'I am – but I'm glad you called. I was going to—'

'Darling, Dom relapsed again yesterday. Very badly. We've talked and he's going into a residential rehab in Scotland for twelve weeks as of Wednesday, if we can get the admissions forms completed and sorted in time. He agrees it's the best course of action. We can't carry on like this. I wanted to let you know, obviously, so that you can discuss whatever you think is appropriate with Alex.'

'Twelve weeks? Wow. Of course and thank you for letting me know. Are you taking him?'

'Yes. He got into a scuffle last night and his face is a little battered this morning, but it'll be fine.'

I closed my eyes. 'I'm so sorry. That's my fault. I shouted at him. Is he OK?'

'It was at Paddington Station, and you're not responsible for the decisions he makes. They patched him up in A&E and he'll be grand. He's sleeping it all off now.'

The poor, poor woman. 'Are *you* all right?'

'Bless you for asking.' She sounded shattered. 'You know, I have a good feeling about this place. He'll be out just before Christmas but like most clinics of its kind, they don't let them have mobile phones, so once I get a landline for the place – in case you need to reach him, or Alex wants to talk to him – I'll pass it on and I will, of course, keep you posted. I'd love it if you and Alex would come and stay for a weekend or two while Dominic's away. We could do the Natural History Museum – all of the sights. I could spoil both of you for a change. Anyway, we can sort that when you're not at work. All love to you.' Her voice began to wobble.

'You too, Sorcha.' I hung up and leant on the wall for a moment, disorientated. Nathan dealt with and twelve weeks Dom-free. This was turning out to be a far easier Monday than I'd been expecting. I slid my phone back in my pocket and, for a second or two, I simply didn't know what to do, until I reminded myself of the very full clinic ahead of me. I blinked and went back into my office, sitting down at my desk and staring blankly at my screen.

'You all right?'

I looked up to see Hamish watching me. 'Just won the EuroMillions?'

I gave him a bland smile. 'How did you guess?'

'Excellent! Well, I've always liked you, Julia, and while no thanks are necessary for the good word I put in after your interview, if you felt you wanted to buy me a hugely extravagant gift with your winnings, who would I be to say no to such a kind gesture? I'm partial to yachts, or there's a Jeff Koons Balloon Swan, Monkey and Rabbit coming up at auction soon. The estimate is about 30k for the trio but I reckon it'll come in just shy of 45k. That'd do nicely!' He beamed.

'Is that all? Bargain,' I replied. 'We can choose one each and flip a coin to see who gets the one left over?'

'You like Jeff Koons?' He returned to his screen.

I hesitated. 'I don't know much about him really, other than he likes to be deliberately provocative. Isn't that right?'

Hamish stopped typing and reached for his phone. 'Here – this is the set.' He got up and brought it over to me. 'They're made of porcelain with a chromatic coating and based on huge, original stainless-steel sculptures that are over three metres tall.' He leant over me, pushing the screen under my nose. 'He first made the swan in ceramic form when he was just nine years old. Amazing, isn't it?'

I hesitated; Hamish was closer to me than I was comfortable with, but I attempted to relax. He was just trying to be friendly. That was a good thing. 'I wouldn't describe them as subtle, or particularly complex – if I'm honest? But that's probably my ignorance.'

'No, no – not at all,' he insisted, drawing back, to my relief. 'It's all about interpretation. Nothing is wrong or right, but I think if you take the swan, for example, obviously the neck is phallic, but viewed from the side, it's very female. The surface has been said to symbolise desire, acceptance and sexual harmony. The viewer is reflected in the surface, making you part of the piece somehow. *I* love the fact that they have been twisted by unseen hands; some might say it's pretty much the perfect gift for a plastic surgeon.'

He returned to his seat. It was the longest conversation I'd ever had with him and a surprising one. I wouldn't have had Hamish down as prone to artistic reflection.

'Thank you for putting in a good word for me,' I said. 'I appreciate that.'

He gave me a mock salute. 'Well, you were very much our first choice – Nathan's *only* choice.'

Was it my imagination, or did he say that pointedly? I didn't comment but stopped what I was doing completely when he started whistling 'There may be trouble ahead…', and crossed my arms.

'Hamish, did Nathan talk to you about me over the weekend?' I felt comfortable enough to ask him outright, given the cosy conversation we'd just had. Was he trying to tell me he knew what had happened? What Nathan had said and done?

He looked up at me, confused, but an expression of pity quickly spread across his face. 'Ah. I'm sorry to say, Julia, that he hasn't and if you don't mind taking a word of advice from an old fool who has been there, seen and done it all before, in my experience these "work things" are better left alone. They always become complicated and the grass is rarely greener. Nate's a super chap, and very obviously not happily married, but I still wouldn't recommend you go there.'

My mouth fell open. 'Oh, no – I'm sorry. I didn't mean *that* – I—'

'It's OK.' He held up a hand. 'You don't need to explain. I saw it coming as soon as he told me he'd "rescued" you from some encounter with your alcoholic ex?'

I caught my breath. *Nathan told him about Dominic?* Oh God. Did everyone now know about my private life?

'He does love playing the hero. Always has – and with good reason. He *is* extraordinary. I've told him so for years. The man has a genuine gift – women *cannot* resist him. Now, it would be simplistic to say it's because he's a surgeon and the power makes him attractive. After all, I'm hardly batting them off with a stick!' He chuckled. 'Of course, it helps that he's very pretty and the different colour eye thing makes him seem edgy and a bit danger- ous – but it's not even that. It's the damage... *that's* what women sense in him. He's a charming, good-looking, but a deeply broken boy. You all want to fix him – I understand – but take my advice, steer clear – not even someone as skilled as you could put him back together again. The second you devote yourself to him, he'll be off. I'm afraid to say I've seen it happen many times before. I'd hate to see you walk the well-trodden road too.'

'I wasn't asking if you think I'm in with a chance. I meant did he?—'

'Honestly, it's *fine!*' He held up a hand. 'Never apologise, never explain.' He reached for his mobile. 'Sorry – I need to take this.' He got to his feet and made for the door. 'Hamish Wilson...'

I had no choice but to let him leave the room. I'd misjudged our confidence, overstepped the line *and* given him the wrong impression. Marvellous. I waited anxiously for him to come back in, but by the time he did, Tan had also arrived. I ended up leaving it completely, for fear that it would sound as if I was protesting too much and hoped Hamish would think and say no more about it.

CHAPTER EIGHTEEN

Nathan

I had a terrible afternoon in theatre, my worst for years, and it was all Julia's fault. Our morning confrontation had thrown me completely. I'd been excited to see her. I'd assumed her anger would have cooled and she'd be ready to listen to an apology – but instead, I'd been met by a detached, controlled and patronising version of her. She hadn't even let me speak – just addressed me like a mother talking to a child caught deliberately scribbling on the wall. I was to behave myself going forward... or else.

Her sudden distress at the beach was one thing. She hadn't known what to do with her feelings – I understood that with hindsight – but I'd thought carefully about how best to defuse the situation *all weekend*. I had been going to take her to one side, apologise that my emotions had got the better of me and explain I'd no intention of hurting her. But she'd given me no chance whatsoever to explain, simply turning away from me as if I didn't matter at all. I wasn't sure who she thought she was, to be perfectly honest.

The more I thought about it as I'd cut away at the cancerous breast tissue belonging to a woman in her forties, the more convinced I became that Julia had been deliberately and unnecessarily hard on me. It was as if another person had slipped into her body. If I could rewind the whole weekend and reset everything, I would, but—

'Er, Mr Sloan?' the specialist registrar assisting me interrupted, in one of those irritating 'being jolly when I'm actually serious' voices. 'You're trimming back quite a bit there?'

I stopped immediately and gazed at him over the top of my mask. 'I'm sorry?'

I saw his eyes dart nervously to the nurse on his right, who wisely looked down. He didn't get the hint though, little prick, and cleared his throat. 'It just looked like, for a second, you might be going to go the whole hog and remove the chest muscles too, when we don't do that anymore, do we?'

The temperature fell away as if someone had opened a fridge door. 'You realise you're in theatre now?' I said icily. 'This isn't like being at the hairdressers when you're watching them absent-mindedly go shorter than you asked for but thinking at least it will grow back? This is cancerous tissue.' I pointed at the mess of bloodied flesh on display in front of us. 'I've no desire to leave this poor woman concave, but I also want to minimise the chance of reoccurrence, so I'll shave it as close as I think is necessary. I'm going to take the lymph nodes too, if that's all right with you?'

'Of course.' He swallowed.

'Sure?'

'Yes.'

'"Yes, Mr Sloan, I am happy for you to continue,"' I said. 'Just so we're all clear.'

A blotchy redness had begun to spread across his neck. 'Yes, Mr Sloan, I am happy for you to continue.' He whispered it.

I held eye contact for just a little longer to make my point, before resuming, but as I stared down at the hole in the woman in front of me, I realised I had now completely forgotten the fucking plan for her. I remembered Julia telling us about her colleague removing the wrong breast in error at the Royal Grace, before covering it up by pretending he needed to remove both breasts, and I had to stop myself from flinging the instruments down in exasperation. I *was* supposed to be removing the lymph nodes too, wasn't I? My mouth hadn't just said that out of nowhere? And *had* I just been about to remove her chest wall by mistake in a lapsed moment of concentration? I experienced a stab of clear and sharp panic. I could feel everyone watching me, wondering what was going on. I swallowed and saw bloody Mrs Dowden lying in front of me again, and her daughter smiling gratefully on the other side of the table. I hadn't taken *enough* there and I knew it, but Julia had smoothly sorted that out too. *Julia Julia Julia.*

I blinked. I needed to ask the status of my real-life unconscious patient, to double-check I was about to proceed appropriately, but I didn't want to give everyone in theatre the excuse for believing the SpR had been right to stop me. I was, however, scared of pressing on and making a huge mistake. It left me no choice but to escape the hellish no-man's land via the only route available.

'I tell you what, why don't *you* finish?' I turned to the SpR. 'You seem to be very sure of what's required here, so over to you now. I'll just observe the master at work, if you don't mind.' I inclined my head slightly and stepped back, gesturing at the inert body in front of me.

I thought he was going to pass out with fear, but he did as he was told, shouldering the public bollocking of being forced to complete the op with my standing over him, arms crossed – thus saving my arse in the process.

No one dared to speak to me as I scrubbed out afterwards. I wasn't entirely sure if I was still furious or maintaining appearances for my now-cowed audience. As I swept off back to the office I realised I was frightened. Irritating though the SpR had been, *really* I'd doubted myself at the table because of the way Julia had made me feel. I was going to have to speak to her about everything now, whether she liked it or not.

I blasted into the room – to find it empty. She'd left for the day. So apparently had Tan. Both of their desks were clear. I leant against the wall in frustration. I'd really wanted to talk to her. I'd wanted to—

'Ah! Good! You're back,' said a voice behind me. I turned to see Hamish, stood alongside an exceptionally pretty girl – mid-twenties – holding her hand out to me. 'Can I introduce our new secretary, Michelle? Michelle, this is Nathan Sloan, the last of our team for you to meet. He's been down in surgery all day.' Hamish withdrew back to his desk and sat down as we shook.

Her strong, slightly sickly perfume was already filling the room – reminding me a little of Storm. She was wearing too much make-up, but her wide eyes were eager, mouth generous and her slightly plump figure pleasingly ripe, so I gave her the benefit of my full smile, holding her gaze as I watched her openly wilt, which made me feel slightly better, but not much. In fact it was remarkable how little it meant to me.

'Welcome to the team!' I sounded more enthusiastic than I felt.

'Thank you.' She had a high breathy voice that would become irritating very quickly. Better if she didn't speak at all, really.

I turned away again, catching Hamish's eye, who was regarding me slyly.

'No!' I said, irritated as he shrugged then chuckled. Poor Michelle laughed brightly too – clueless – then trailed off uncertainly.

It all made me feel very tired and old.

'I'm off home. See you all tomorrow.' I knew exactly what the reality of sex with Michelle would be: squeally and sugary, ultimately unfulfilling and leaving me with a nasty headache afterwards, as she undoubtedly had some grunt of a long-term boyfriend lurking in the background. But it was irrelevant anyway. I only wanted Julia.

I was halfway down the corridor when Hamish caught up with me, panting like an old bloodhound, spare flesh swinging.

'OK, I'm sorry,' he said. 'Michelle's a pretty girl. I thought she might cheer you up a bit. That's all. Want to talk about it?'

I glanced at him. 'I'm not sure you want to listen.'

'Ah, Julia,' he said. 'I see.'

'I don't know what to do to fix it,' I blurted. 'I told her I love her and she thought it was a line. She thinks I'm everything I *have* been until now. She doesn't trust me and I'm frightened that she's never going to give me a chance to prove myself.' I paused; my heart was starting to race. I felt suddenly quite sick at the memory of how close I'd come to chopping out all of that woman's chest muscle earlier – the kind of error Julia would never make. 'I did some thinking last night; maybe I should do something to make her realise I'm a good person. What do you think about MSF?' I loosened the top of my shirt. 'It's like a bloody oven in here today!'

Hamish frowned. 'It's no hotter than usual. And you mean Médecins Sans Frontières? As in, going off to be a medic in a conflict zone?'

I nodded. 'I looked on their website. I speak pretty decent Spanish, French and Latin thanks to the sadistic efforts of the public school system, all of which is to my advantage, apparently.'

Hamish stared at me. 'I know they have a very distinct hierarchy in place, to keep their staff and volunteers safe. If they say you can't leave the compound, even if you are desperate, you have to do as you're told. I think you'd hate that. There's also the small matter of going somewhere that would put your life in significant danger, when you have a young son and wife who need you here. And two daughters who hardly see you as it is.'

'MSF have lower risk missions too. I checked. It's not all up to the wire stuff.'

'Sure,' Hamish shrugged, 'but I think there are… less dramatic… ways of making Julia appreciate your intentions towards her are genuine.' He smiled. 'I think you're just going to have to give her some space.'

'I want to show her I can change for her; that I already have!'

'Of course you do, but softly, softly catchy monkey. She knows how you feel now. Sit back and let her come to you in her own time.'

'You really think she will?'

'I know so. You're YOU!' He offered me a fist bump, which was just… the saddest thing. I was bloody glad no one was in the corridor to witness my being forced to return it.

'You don't think I've already blown it then?'

'Of course not! I know it isn't a strength of yours, but you're going to have to be patient. Let everything calm down and then let's see where the land lies. It's just going to take time. Come back in and grab a quick glass of water. You look a bit—'

'A bit what?' I blinked and wiped my face. My skin was slightly clammy. The stress of having nearly ballsed up that op… I exhaled.

He smiled. 'Nothing. Forget it. You'll be fine. Just take your time driving home, yes?'

I nodded. 'Thanks for listening, Ham. And I'm sorry I was a shit to you over the weekend.'

'It's OK,' he said. 'You're right. I do need to sort myself out.'

'Will you also come to the office and take the cameras down this week, please?'

'Absolutely.' He patted my back. 'Remind me if I forget, but of course I will. No problem at all.'

*

I thought about what he'd said as I stepped out through the double doors of the hospital and made my way to the car. I wanted Julia to understand me, that was all. My phone rang as I was putting my seat belt on. Stefanie. I declined the call and closed my eyes briefly.

I really did need Julia, so very, very badly, in spite of how she'd treated me earlier. Reaching for my phone, I messaged Hamish, asking him to forward the beach picture to me. I was almost certain he would still have it – despite my asking him to delete it. I assured him I wasn't angry that he'd kept it. I just wanted proof that I hadn't imagined her response.

Sure enough, the image followed. I looked at us kissing. There *she* was… in that split second before everything changed. I started to feel calm. She had kissed me back. There was no doubt in my mind.

If I was patient, she would come to see that I wasn't teasing her and that I meant every word; I was in love with her.

I could do that, no matter how long it took. I could be good.

*

For the first few weeks doing a lot of exercise got me through. I was at the gym every day before or after work. I'd suddenly explode with energy and anger in the middle of a session on the treadmill; headphones jammed in, music loud enough to deafen me, as a track would drop and I'd start pounding, like the devil himself was on my tail and catching up fast. Or I'd suddenly sprint like a mad thing along the very long, very straight path by the river under a sulky sky while out for a run; somehow seeing myself from above, getting faster and faster – pushing and pushing… until I'd literally drop, panting, sweating – exhausted. It was the only way I got a moment or two of release and the only thing that stopped me from marching up to her on a daily basis at work and sweeping her into my arms.

It was torture being in such close proximity, glancing across from time to time to see her frowning in concentration at her screen when we were in the office together. Even worse, were the evenings when she'd appear on the doorstep of my house, having come to collect Cass from ours because the children had started hanging out together. It took every ounce of my self-control to simply smile at her, shout for her daughter and *not* blurt something like, 'I'm so sorry that I screwed everything up. Can you give me a second chance to prove that I'm not the man you think I am, but someone who loves you?' Instead, we would stand there in silence, waiting.

October became November. I dreamt about her regularly. I hadn't had sex with Storm since just before the rugby weekend – although that wasn't unusual for us. I told Stef that Storm was becoming suspicious, so we needed to take a break. As the weeks passed, increasingly frustrated, I drifted back to watching some of my old patient films late at night on my own, just as a physical release. My legs were crisscrossed with cuts, admittedly, but I didn't sleep with anyone. I was waiting for her.

November turned into December and I was almost at breaking point. Unusually for the milder South West, the temperature plummeted and there was the feel of snow in the air. Confused, everyone became festive slightly too early – yet I was only aware of the year madly slipping away with no apparent progress, no nearer to Julia realising that she loved me too. My desperation ramped up sharply, despite Hamish's continued assurances that all would be well.

'The point is, something's got to give,' I said to him, nursing a drink in the nook of a quiet little backwater pub we regularly slipped away to when we needed a moment of decompression after particularly draining operations. I stared at the rows of different whisky bottles lined up on the shelves above the landlord, their reflections gleaming on his shiny head and the polished mahogany bar. 'I'm starting to go crazy. I've put the time in; she can't argue we've only just met anymore, can she?'

'No, she can't. I'm hungry.' Hamish rubbed his stomach. 'I want another of those cakes that Michelle brought in. They were very good. Did you know she made them herself? Talented girl.'

'I didn't have one. They looked like a diabetic coma waiting to happen.' I bit the quick of my nail. 'I just need something to break the impasse with Julia.'

'You missed out. They were delicious.' Hamish downed his drink and stood up. 'Right, well this was fun, but I'd better get off.'

'Hang on! I've just had an idea!' I put a hand out.

He sat back down again with a sigh.

'That big two-consultant op you're doing with Julia on Tuesday…'

Hamish folded his arms warily. 'What about it?'

'Suppose I did it with her instead? Can you call in sick?'

Hamish closed his eyes. 'You did *not* just ask me to do that. And you didn't just come up with it on the spot either.'

'Ham, please!' I begged. 'I'm the only other person with the right skill-set to step in for you. It'll give me the opportunity to show her I'm not a total twat, and she'll be forced to be in my company for a good six hours. Please?'

Hamish opened his eyes again. 'You were supposed to get bored of this and move on. She's not going to change her mind, Nate. I think you have to let this one go. Give up the fight.'

'I can't.' I picked up my drink and drained it. 'If I could, I would. Please, Hamish. I really need you to do this for me.'

He looked at me, then shook his head and glanced away. 'Fine – but this is only going to happen once. Don't ask me again.'

'Thank you!' The relief was enormous. 'I only need this one chance. Can you take the Wednesday off too? If it's two days, it'll make it look more authentic?'

He let his head drop. 'Nate! I've got a full clinic on Wednesday! People who actually need help.'

'Julia could cover that for you; I already checked. No one is going to miss out or suffer. They'll do better actually, they'll get her not you!' I joked, but he didn't smile.

'You've got it all planned out, haven't you? I thought you'd decided to play things with a straight bat?' He stood up.

I was bewildered. 'I am? I'm not doing anything wrong?'

'No. You never are, Nate.' He picked his keys up from the table, turned away from me and, to my surprise, left without saying goodbye.

CHAPTER NINETEEN

Julia

I was pretty stressed but determined to keep it to myself and not panic the team. A surgical procedure lasting six hours and counting is a long time for anyone, and I'd hit a slight snag with the massive procedure we'd undertaken: removing both of the patient's breasts and constructing new ones from flaps of fat taken from her abdomen.

'It'll be OK, won't it?' Kerry had said to me beforehand. 'I'm just worried about how I'm going to look, which is just me feeling sorry for myself, I know, but I can't help it.'

'You're not feeling sorry for yourself at all. Having your breasts removed is a major decision, but they're going to look great,' I'd reassured her.

'And hey – I get a free tummy tuck!' She'd tried to smile. She knew that I wasn't able to offer her a guarantee that it would work. We'd been through the pros and cons at length and decided using her own fat was a better option for her than implants; it would feel more like her because it *was* her.

Nathan – Hamish had been taken ill at the last moment – had worked painstakingly to assist me with sweep after sweep of his blade, to take out every single bit of breast tissue he possibly could, to prevent the cancer from returning. I'd been far from thrilled to discover he would be stepping in, but for this type of complex procedure, a two-consultant team gave the best patient outcome, and Kerry was all that mattered. After Mrs Dowden, I'd watched him carefully, but I couldn't fault his work, even if I was uncomfortable on a personal level to be operating with him.

Once Nathan had finished, we'd weighed the removed breasts to see how much fat we were going to need from Kerry's stomach. As soon as we'd cut the two right-sized flaps from her abdomen to put into the cavities Nathan had created, it was a race to get the blood vessels connected to the ones in Kerry's armpits, to reinstate a blood supply. We couldn't insert them under the skin otherwise, and I was having a slight issue with my plumbing. Some blood vessels are better than others – although still only three millimetres wide – and these weren't quite as good as they could be, more fragile than I'd have liked.

'Nearly done.' I was still working on my tiny sutures. Nathan had already joined the left artery and vein: the flap was on, it was my right side that wasn't playing ball. I needed to work fast but with control; one simple mistake… 'Bit messy, but we're getting there.'

Finally, to my huge relief I got the right side connected and the blood was flowing well. All that was left was to insert the flaps under the skin and shape them to form the breasts. We trimmed the excess tissue carefully to get the contours and symmetry right for Kerry, so that she would feel really confident afterwards. Once we'd finished I was very happy with all we'd achieved.

As we scrubbed out, Nathan turned to me. 'That was an excellent result, Julia. She'll have no idea what she's been through and hopefully, with only the areola reconstruction remaining, it won't be much longer before she'll be able to get on with the rest of her life.'

'Thank you,' I said. 'And for stepping in, too.'

He'd surprised me. I'd expected him to use it as an opportunity to show me how shit hot he was, given it was our first big procedure together, especially when things had started to get a bit sticky for me. I couldn't have been more wrong. He'd been calm and patient, not attempted to take over or say anything patronising, just been a reassuring presence.

'You're very welcome. Want to come and grab a coffee?'

'I can't, I'm afraid. I was supposed to meet someone ten minutes ago.' I hesitated. 'But another time. Thanks again.'

I legged it off to meet Eleni's possible replacement – a female surgeon considering moving to the area with her young daughter from London. She'd emailed me to ask if I might have an informal meeting with her, and I'd readily agreed.

'Given twelve per cent of all consultant surgeons across *all* specialties are female, if you join the plastics team here, you'll singlehandedly put us ahead of that shocking statistic, because there'll be *two* of us!' I smiled at her on the other side of the same coffee shop table I'd sat at for my interview with Tan and Hamish, almost six months ago.

'That's great!' She'd given me a tired smile in return and set her tea down carefully.

'Julia, I read about what happened to you at the Royal Grace, what you went through. Can I lay my cards on the table? I know this is informal, but is it OK to be *really* informal? Off the record?'

I nodded. 'Yes, it is.'

'How alpha is the rest of department here? I just want to be able to do my job. If their priorities are *all* knife before wife, I can't do it. I'm not fighting that macho shouty crap again, day in day out – or taking another post where I get constantly bitch-slapped by a bunch of bonkers old men for wanting to occasionally pick my daughter up from school. If that makes *my* priorities "all wrong", they can find something more manly to shove up their vacancy.'

I smiled. 'I hear you. It's not full silverback. There are some genuinely nice younger surgeons here, but on the whole there's a way to go yet.'

'And from a letchy point of view?' she continued. 'In my current place on my second day, one of my colleagues told me he wanted to make it absolutely clear that if I felt him touch my arse, it was because he meant to. Where does this place fit on that scale? Is there any sex harassment stuff I need to know about? Anyone suspended, about to be or ought to be?'

I hesitated, thinking of Nathan trying to kiss me, but that had been two months ago. Earlier, he'd been completely professional and polite. We'd moved on, got past it. 'There *are* a few on their second wife who they "met at work", but then I'm on my second husband, so…' I shrugged and smiled ruefully.

Holly flushed. 'I'm sorry. I didn't mean to offend you.'

'It's OK, you haven't. My first marriage ending had nothing to do with my job. As far as attitudes in general here go, have I stood alongside a handsome junior doctor and had the patients direct their questions to him rather than me? Yes, I have. If we keep working to change that, will it? I think so. I hope you come here.' I meant that. I sensed a potential friend.

She looked relieved. 'Thanks. Roll on the day when we don't have to have these conversations, hey?'

*

I was still thinking about Holly the following morning as I made my way to cover Hamish's clinic because he was off sick for a second day. How *were* we supposed to attract more women to a career in surgery, when women as qualified and able as Holly were still having such an appalling time at the coal face? All she wanted to do was her job. It wasn't exactly much to ask.

My first patient was an anxious twenty-five-year-old woman sitting in a hospital gown on the edge of her chair, waiting for me, when I knocked and entered the consulting room. She told me she'd had a bit of a problem with some private surgery, performed locally. A breast augmentation five months previously for cosmetic reasons had 'gone wrong'.

'I was pleased at first, although they were bigger than I thought they were going to be.' She spoke fast and was obviously nervous. 'The surgeon said there would be swelling that could take a while to go down. I waited but it didn't. They started getting tighter and hard and really painful. Now they feel like two balls stuck to my chest, and they hurt all the time.

'I didn't want to go back to him, so I went to see my doctor and she referred me to see you. I wish I'd never had it done in the first place.' Her voice trembled as she clutched the front of her gown together. None of the patients were ever sure if they were supposed to do them up with the opening at the front or the back.

I looked at her notes. Nathan had performed her surgery. I frowned. 'OK, do you mind if I examine you now?' I gestured to the hospital examination couch.

She stood up and glanced at the un-curtained window, apprehensively.

'Don't worry,' I assured her, pointing to the sign attached to the window. 'This is glass that we can see out of, but people outside can't see in through, unless the lights are on, and they're not. Only Kay and I can see you.' I nodded at the nurse alongside me and turned away to wash my hands. 'I'm sorry,' I said conversationally, 'my hands are a little cold. I'll try and warm them up as much as I can. OK, can you just open the front of your gown? Thank you.'

I wasn't surprised the poor girl was in pain. Her breasts were grossly deformed. Her description of two balls stuck to her front was very accurate. What on earth had Nathan been thinking? Even without the obvious encapsulation, the implants were much too big for her tiny frame.

'These were definitely the size of implants you asked for?' I double-checked.

'I'm not sure?' she said. 'I think so? We looked at a few options but he told me it was best to let him pick the implant profile?'

'OK.' I decided not to comment on that any further. 'Is it all right to put my hands on you now?'

She nodded.

'I'm just going to check your neck too, as well as the right and left breast.' I began to palpate the tissue, and as was often the case when a patient was embarrassed, she started to talk.

'It's really funny, that glass,' she said desperately. 'I can see people getting in and out of cars and they can't see me! Ow!'

'I'm sorry,' I said quickly. 'They can't see you, I promise. Can you put your hand behind your head there for a moment? I'm just going to push my finger briefly in your armpit too.'

'How come you don't have to have cameras in here, though?' she said, nodding at the ceiling and the corner of the room.

'Cameras? Can we swap arms now? Thank you.'

'Yeah.' She looked at me innocently. 'At the private clinic, he had cameras in the corner of the room.'

My hands momentarily slowed. 'In the waiting room?'

'Yes, and in the room where he examined me.'

I glanced up at Kay who widened her eyes.

I finished my examination in silence and stood back. 'If you'd like to close the gown again, thank you. He had cameras in the room where you were undressing, and he examined you like I just did?'

'Yes.' She started to look worried. 'That's OK, isn't it?'

'I think it's unusual.' I picked my words very, very carefully. 'You can sit up now. Did you ask what they were for?'

'Yeah. He said for legal reasons, he had to have a record of what we'd said in the consultation but that no images would be shared – like before and after photos – without my consent.' She spoke more confidently now.

'OK.' I tried to keep my tone even. 'Had he mentioned these cameras before you spotted them?'

She considered that. 'No – he didn't, actually.'

Whoa… I smiled at her. 'So tell me why you didn't want to go back to him when these problems started occurring? I'm not saying we won't help you, by the way – we will. I'm just interested to know why you didn't want *him* to deal with this?'

She looked anxious again. 'When I phoned him to say there was a problem, he wasn't very friendly about me going back in. He made me feel like I was making a fuss over nothing, and he got a bit nasty to be honest. It really upset me, and the more upset I got, the more I felt like I didn't want him operating on me again. I told a friend and she said I could just go to any doctor. It didn't *have* to be him.'

I smiled. 'OK. Thank you. So here's what we're going to do to help you…'

*

Once she'd left, I sat and stared out of the window. Nathan had cameras in his consulting rooms.

I reached into my pocket, pulled out my phone and did a quick search on his company name. He'd changed his website since I last looked and the home page was a picture of him smiling dashingly into the camera, dressed in a traditional white coat alongside a button entitled *Ask Dr Sloan!* I had a quick scroll around. It explained Nathan specialised in cosmetic breast surgery, including 'uplifts, augmentations and reductions', but offered a full range of aesthetic services. There were a lot of images of smiling women captioned 'Dr Sloan's patient'. They were all what I would call big-breasted and that would have set my alarm bells ringing right there. It was clear what his personal preference was, and how he liked to make women look. I could see nothing at all, however, which referred to any part of any consultation being filmed.

Kay came back into the room uncertainly.

'Could I ask you not to discuss what she just said with anyone?'

'*Yes!*' Kay looked hugely relieved. 'I agree. I really don't want to upset Mr Sloan, and she's probably made a mistake anyway.'

She'd misunderstood me. I'd been about to say I'd take it from here. 'I expect you're right. Hey, listen, can you give me two seconds before the next patient? I've got a quick phone call to make?'

Kay nodded happily and left the room, closing the door behind her. I picked up my mobile again and selected the 'contact us' option. 'Oh hello!' I said brightly when the call was answered. 'Is that Mr Sloan's secretary? Great – could you buzz him for me and ask if he can do coffee after all? My name is Julia Blythe. I could come to him for about five thirty today? Thank you so much.'

I waited, my heart thumping.

'Hello – yes, I'm still here. He will? That's great. Thank you for your help.'

I hung up, rested my elbows on the table and placed my fingers thoughtfully on my lips, staring at the wall in front of me, beyond which I could hear the muffled voice of Tan, holding *his* clinic. Please God, the patient had made a mistake, because while I had to check out what she'd told me, I felt physically ill at the thought she might be right and where that might lead.

*

I looked up and down the street of town houses, now mostly all occupied by high-end dentists and upmarket estate agents, before finally locating the sign for Nathan's private practice. Climbing several steep stone steps, I rang the bell, looking at the thick, warped trunk of an established wisteria while I waited, following its weaving branches up the wall. It must look stunning in summer. The door opened, but to my surprise as much as hers, Stefanie emerged, wrapped in a belted wool coat, chocolate-coloured leather-gloved hands clutching her handbag. She quickly rearranged her features into a delighted smile.

'Julia! What a lovely surprise! Ooh!' she exclaimed quickly and lowered her voice, 'are you coming to talk to Nate about working here?'

'I'm here on business, yes.'

'How wonderful! I'm not surprised. He's so great but with more work than he can handle at the moment. He's only just managing to squeeze me in before Christmas and I've known him for years!' She laughed.

'What are you having done, if you don't mind me asking?' I kept my tone light.

'Well, I'm not shouting about it – but it's you – you do this sort of thing every day for a living. Boob job, on Friday. I'm driving poor Nate *mad* though – keep changing my mind about the implant sizes, although I've just *finally* come to a decision.' She winked at me. 'It's time. Plus it gets me out of hosting Christmas. The lengths we mums go to for a rest, eh?' She laughed again. 'That reminds me, we must fix that rematch dinner soon. I'll buzz you in the New Year when the bandages are off, and *good luck*!' She nodded her head in the direction of Nathan's clinic and crossed her fingers, before kissing me briefly on each cheek and hurrying down the steps.

As if I was coming to Nathan for a bloody job interview. I gritted my teeth and stalked into the predictably plush waiting room; thick grey carpets, vibrant purple velvet sofas and armchairs – the colour of foil chocolate wrappers – either side of a spikey arrangement of white lilies in an ornamental fireplace. A pretty receptionist sat behind the desk, dressed in a black healthcare tunic; Nathan's initials stitched onto her breast pocket in white to match the piping on her collar and sleeves.

I smiled. 'Hello, I'm Julia Blythe. I think we spoke earlier? I'm here to see Nathan.'

'I'll just let Dr Sloan know you're here.' Her small teeth were absurdly white and neat. I wondered if she knew that Nathan was a Mr, as befitted his professional status in this country, or if she had been asked to call him Dr, to reassure potential patients. I didn't correct her, just took a seat and reached for one of the thick glossy magazines on the table.

She put the phone down. 'He'll be with you in just a moment.'

I pretended to start flicking through the pages, very briefly lifted my gaze and scanned the ceiling. I caught my breath – two small black devices sat in either corner. Was he watching me right now? I got out my phone, held it up and started pretending to adjust my hair, but I wasn't using it as a mirror. I was snapping the cameras – images that I immediately emailed to myself.

I heard a buzzer go, and the receptionist beamed at me. 'He's ready for you now.'

Following her through the hall of what would have been a well-to-do family house in a former life, I waited as she knocked at a door.

'Come!' said a voice, and she opened it to reveal Nathan in his usual uniform of shirt and chinos, sitting at a desk by a window overlooking a back garden – the bare branches of the trees motionless against the white sky – as he tapped away busily at his computer. 'Are you OK to take a seat?' he said absently, motioning to the chair next to me as if I was a patient. 'I'll just be a moment, then we'll go.'

'Sure,' I replied easily, more than happy to play whatever shitty power game he was into today. It gave me the chance to look around properly… and take in the same, small black devices in the top corner of this room too. I felt giddy and swallowed as I got out my phone and pretended to text, while quickly photographing the cameras.

'Sorry, one second.' I held up a hand as Nathan finally turned to me. I WhatsApped the photo to Ewan. He wouldn't understand, but it didn't matter.

'No problem at all.' Nathan jumped up and patted his pockets. 'So where would you like to go? There's a good deli just around the corner. Or…' he looked at his watch, 'we could go for a proper drink if you like?'

I put the phone back in my bag and cleared my throat.

'One of your private patients was in clinic today.' My heart started to thump. 'She has a severe encapsulation. Her surgery was five months ago.'

He sat back down slowly.

'I would actually question if the implants you gave her were the appropriate cc and might have contributed to her issues now, but that's not why I'm here. She told me in passing that she noticed cameras in your consulting rooms, which you said were for "legal reasons". Now that I'm here, I can see them.' I pointed up. 'Why would you have surveillance cameras where women are undressing and you are examining them? It's not medically necessary. What are you using the recordings for? Where do you store them? Do these women know you're filming them?'

He went very, very still and twisted in his chair to face out of the window.

'Nathan, I'm giving you the opportunity to tell me it's not what it looks like and that I've made a mistake.'

He continued to stare straight ahead. 'So what *does* it look like?'

I exclaimed aloud. 'Oh come on! These women come to you because they trust you, and you're filming them without consent – presumably, in most cases half-naked. Why would you need films of your patients in a state of undress? How do you *think* it looks?'

He leant forward suddenly, widening his legs so he could rest his elbows on his knees. 'I've done exactly as you asked. Acted as if nothing ever happened, haven't I?'

'You mean after the beach incident?' I frowned. 'Yes, you have. And thank you for that, but—'

'It's the hardest thing I've ever had to do.' He spoke conversationally. 'Do you know that I look forward to coming into work on my NHS days with an irrational excitement, but I dread it at the same time because being near you is almost more than I can bear? The days when I get home and Cass is at our house, and I know you'll be coming to get her, or I'll bring her back to yours and get to see you – it's like getting some kind of hit.'

He turned to face me. 'The way I feel about you is flying around my head constantly, in my eyes, on my tongue. I can't get any sense of peace at all. It won't settle and rest. I carry it with me everywhere I go in this heart-shaped void. I don't want to look at other women!' He gave a desperate laugh. 'Why would I want films of strangers? I only want you! There's no one else but you, Julia!'

I stared at him in disbelief. For a moment, I could almost believe him; it was such a convincing picture he was painting: a man used to getting everything he wanted, who had finally fallen in love… but also a man filming women without their knowledge. I thought about how I would feel to discover that my doctor was watching films of me naked any time he felt like it; maybe showing me – at my most vulnerable – to God knows who else.

I thought about men watching films of Cass being touched and examined intimately, and the wave of revulsion that rippled through me began to push out through my skin and harden like armour. I would not allow him to fire his lies at me and let them hit home.

'So you're saying you have never recorded or watched your patients being examined, via those cameras?' I adopted the same emotionless and factual tone that I used with Dom. 'Tell me the truth, Nathan.'

CHAPTER TWENTY

Nathan

My panic was fluttering like a butterfly stuck inside the glass roof of a very tall building. I wished I could reach up to squash it. 'You really don't have a very high opinion of men, do you?'

Julia shook her head defiantly. 'That's not true. I think there are lots of very lovely men. But you don't love me, and you're not answering my question.'

'I do love you! I don't understand! I've done it – I've waited and waited and you still don't believe me. Hang on!' I began to feel around desperately for my phone. 'I want to show you something!'

'You know I'm going to have to take this further? I can't know about these cameras and not say anything. I have a duty of care to the patients themselves. I'm going to have to report you, Nathan.' She picked up her bag and got to her feet.

'Look!' I scrolled through the pictures and found the one of us on the beach. 'See?' I got to my feet, held it up for her. 'You can't tell me this couple have no feelings for each other? Look at us!' I could hear the triumph in my voice. Now she would have to believe me; she was witnessing it with her own eyes.

She gasped and covered her mouth. 'Who took this? Was it Storm? Did she see us?'

I couldn't possibly tell her the truth. I'd be as good as dead to her. 'I'm not sure. It was sent to me anonymously, so *someone* is unhappy with us, yes. Please don't report me, because apart from anything else, if this picture comes out it's going to look like you've pretty much pulled a rerun of what happened in your last job – trashed a colleague you were involved with.'

'I'm not involved with you!' She exclaimed. 'You kissed me!'

'But *you've* just told me, it's what it looks like that matters, not the truth.' I reminded her, pointing at the cameras in the corner of the room. 'I don't want another scandal for you,' I pleaded. 'No one will touch you with a bargepole professionally if that happens.'

'Are you threatening me?' Her eyes widened. 'If I report you, you'll make that picture public?'

'I'm not the only one that has it, am I?' That was, of course, true and in the heat of the moment I believed the story I was telling her, the danger she was in. 'And, of course, I'm not threatening you! I'm trying to say you can't have it both ways! You can't insist my having cameras in here MUST mean I'm doing something wrong, yet a picture of you kissing me apparently means nothing? Don't you see?'

Her eyes filled with tears. 'You ARE threatening me.'

'No. I would never do that.' I shook my head emphatically. 'The cameras were installed for protection. You know what kind of litigious nutjobs wind up in here! If I don't do exactly what they want, or God forbid I get it wrong – it's my head on the block and *my* insurance policy! If I'm going to put some stupidly sized implants in a woman at her insistence, I want proof that I only did what she asked for!' It was a truth of sorts. That is why I put them up to start with.

'But that's absurd! You just tell them no!' Julia exclaimed. 'You refuse to perform the surgery!'

'I have an ex-wife, and ex-house, a current wife, a current house and three children at private school. You do the maths. I don't refuse anyone's money.' I took a step towards her. 'This isn't how it looks. I swear to you. Don't say anything, please. I don't want you to be damaged, of all people. I love you so much!' I hesitated, twisted to my desk, grabbed one of my surgical pens and reaching out quickly, drew a small purple heart on the back of her hand. It was meant to lighten the tone, a cute gesture, but she looked down at herself, horrified.

'What the hell is *wrong* with you?' She pulled away from me. 'You have NO idea what love is. None at all!'

Turning and grabbing for the door handle, she rushed out into the hall.

'Julia!' I called, bolting after her, 'wait!' but she was already past reception, had flung the front door open.

I clattered down the stone steps, the cold air hitting me as I frantically looked left then right, to see her sprinting up the road towards her car.

'Julia!' I yelled, but she didn't look up, just fumbled with the door handle and jumped in. The brake lights flickered on and the car lurched before she roared off, leaving me staring after her, shivering in my thin shirt as a few desultory flakes of snow floated past me, landed on the pavement and vanished.

CHAPTER TWENTY-ONE

Hamish

'Everything I've worked for!' Nathan was pacing the room. 'Julia was thawing until *this* happened – I know she was! Operating together on that patient was amazing. She's such an incredible surgeon. It felt so intimate!'

'Apart from the other twenty-odd people in the room, you mean?' I reminded him, pulling a chair over to the corner of the room and climbing on it to an ominous creaking.

'I thought she was coming to see me because she wanted to.' He continued to march up and down. I couldn't remember the last time I'd seem him so agitated. 'It was perfect timing! Stefanie left as Julia arrived – shutting the door on my past to welcome my future. It felt like a pivotal moment, Ham.' He fell back wretchedly in his chair and looked out of the window. 'It was like finding a deer in the snow at the last, cold, blue light of day. Outwardly serene but with muscles poised, you know?'

What on earth was he talking about? I said nothing, just wobbled and felt in my back pocket for the screwdriver. He wasn't waiting for me to respond anyway, that much was clear.

'She could have bolted into the dark forest behind her at any moment. I could tell she was nervous when I watched her in the waiting room.' He sat up again – still staring into space as I looked at him more carefully. Was he having some sort of breakdown? 'So, when she came in here, I pretended to be calm and not bothered. I let her sit down and gather herself… but that was when she started *accusing* me! She started shouting and holding her head like it was a… a *watermelon* exploding over the walls and—'

'Nathan, shut up now!' I wasn't doing him any favours, letting him dramatically grandstand. 'The point is that she's said she's going to report you.' I reached up and began to unscrew the casements. 'That's what we need to focus on here – formulating our response – not guffing on about deer and melon.'

Nathan twisted round and stared up at me. 'Thanks for that. Whose fault is this, by the way, Hamish? Who didn't remove the cameras when I asked him to *at least several weeks ago!*' He shouted the last bit so suddenly, I actually did jump, but carried on loosening the fixtures without comment. He could be such a petulant child when he wanted to be.

Moments later, there was a timid knock at the door. '*Not now!*' Nathan roared. 'Just go home! I'll see you in the morning!' I watched him out of the corner of my eye as he jumped up and walked to the window. 'A good receptionist pretends not to hear,' he muttered. 'This one's going to have to go if she can't get something so basic right.'

One of the casements fell to the floor with a thud, and I sneezed as some dust dropped down with it. 'Of course, had you not asked me to call in sick for two days, so you could operate with her, *I* would have been the one the patient spoke to about the cameras. Not Julia. We wouldn't be having this conversation now.' I rubbed my nose and stared at the light, feeling like I was going to go again.

Nate turned around very slowly. 'You're saying this is all my own fault?'

I sneezed for a second time. Once a wish, twice a kiss… 'At least we've still got the photo of her. You wanted to destroy that, remember?' I pointed the screwdriver at him.

He shook his head in disbelief and opened his arms out to the side as if offering himself up for crucifixion. 'Shall I hold still so you can shove that blade right through my palms? Make me really suffer? Go on! Say it again – I've only myself to blame – *except I asked you to take the cameras down ages ago.* I was trying to be good!'

'You could have just taken them down yourself. You weren't trying that hard.'

'*You're* the fucking landlord!'

'OK, enough now,' I warned, my patience starting to wear thin. 'Stop with the self-pity. We should both give up the blame game. It's happened. We've just got to deal with it.'

'Argh!' He suddenly shouted aloud again and kicked out at his desk in anger. It thudded up against the wall behind it, everything on top juddering, the remains of a coffee lurching up the white insides of the mug,

I sighed and stopped what I was doing. 'Get on with it and trash the room then, if you're going to. Fling the papers around, throw your cup at the wall so hard it smashes, get up here and rip the cameras out with your bare hands if it'll make you feel better, but I'm warning you now, I'm not clearing up after you.'

'I'm not asking you to clear anything up.' He collapsed down onto his chair, glowering. 'I'm well aware that this is a moment which requires clarity, thanks very much.'

I clambered down, the rest of the camera in my hands and placed it on his desk. 'Look, you've shown her the picture, which was a good move. She's no fool. She knows how that will look if it gets out. Kissing the colleague she's accusing of dirty deeds? And how does she explain it to her *husband*? I bet you she's at home thinking through her options right now and deciding to keep her mouth shut.'

'I honestly don't want to use the picture publicly. It'll make real trouble for her.' He leant to one side, rubbing his forehead with a hand.

My eyes narrowed and the stirrings of real anger began to swirl in my gut. 'Well, as I just said, let's hope you don't need to, but if she does come after you, make no mistake, we *are* going to use that photo to protect ourselves.'

'If I were her, I'd say the picture was a set-up anyway.'

I shrugged and sat down opposite him. 'At which point everyone is going to think she's certifiable. Her whole story is going to reek of bullshit. They'll all start talking about her, wondering if this is the same stunt she pulled in her last job – the one they tried to fire her from, remember? Meanwhile, *I'll* be telling everyone it was clear from the start that she had a sexual interest in you and the picture proves it. I'll remind them about the allegations her former colleague made. Gossip will do the rest. We'll have her discredited, borderline destroyed within days of her reporting you – that's IF she goes ahead with shooting her mouth off. You can argue the cameras are dummies, for God's sake.' I rubbed my lower back and grimaced.

'I already told her they were installed to protect me.'

I gave a tight sigh. 'OK, well that's not the end of the world. We'll deal with your laptop.'

He chewed on his lip. '*My* laptop? You're not worried about yours?'

'Well, right now, it's you she's got on the hook, isn't it? They'll only know you sent the films on if YOU tell them. There's no trail at all. We've been very careful.'

There was a pause while he looked at the now-redundant cameras, then up at me. 'You're not going to let me weather this alone, are you?' He was frightened.

'Of course not! I'll be there every step of the way. Haven't I always been?' I reached out and briefly patted his arm. 'But you don't *want* them to know I'm involved? You'll protect me like I'd protect you – won't you?'

Eventually, Nate nodded. 'I think you should get rid of your bits and pieces though.'

'Don't worry about me.' I smiled. 'I'll sort everything out my end. Just make sure you go for a run tonight so you can slip your laptop into the estuary.'

'It'll look like I have something to hide if it disappears.'

'But you *do* have something to hide! Better than them finding a load of films of half-naked women and you shagging some of them. You can't just delete the files. I think they leave ghosts on the hard drive. Someone who knows what they're doing could get them back, is what I mean.'

I glanced up at the clock. It was time for me to get back. Cecily was going out and I'd promised not to be long. 'A mate of a mate in London knocked someone off a bike, deleted his dashcam and swore he was blameless, even though several witnesses said otherwise. The police took him to court; but *not* because he deleted the dashcam – they said if he'd admitted he panicked, they would have been fine with that – but because he still insisted he'd done nothing wrong *after* that point. So, what YOU do is this: slip the laptop in the Clyst, then when plod comes calling, admit you were filming the patient consultations to legally protect yourself – as you've already told Julia. You panicked when Julia challenged you, took the cameras down and shoved the laptop in the water, which you now realise was a really stupid thing to do. They're not going to immediately think there were naked women on it and we've been having a happy private view any time we feel like it, are they?'

'Except that's exactly what Julia is going to allege.'

'Well, she's got no proof of that, has she? Pictures of the cameras themselves, yes. Pictures of what was on them, no. Anyway, you pull out the photo of her forcing herself on you and you say to plod: "yes, I'm sure that's what she says and this is why. She's very jealous. She doesn't like her lover looking at other women, even when it's my job. I had to end it with her. She's unstable." Plus, everyone is going to break up for Christmas in two days. Is Julia really going to report you as soon as tomorrow? And if she does, will they in turn tell the police before packing up shop for the festive season? Both very unlikely, in my view.'

I stood up stiffly. 'You've got the best of two weeks before the powers that be get back to work and on the case. Dump the laptop in the water tonight and don't worry, Nate. We've got this.'

I smiled at him again, keeping it in place until I'd closed the door quietly behind me and left him sitting in his room, still staring out of the window like the lovesick teenager he seemed determined to be.

I was prepared to let him wallow in it a little bit longer, but after that, I was going to expect him to pull himself together, and take the gloves off.

CHAPTER TWENTY-TWO

Nathan

'You're going for a run now?' Storm looked at the dark window, droplets running down it. 'It's freezing cold and raining!'

'It's fine,' I replied absently, rifling through the washing pile on the spare room bed, looking for my skins.

'They're in your top drawer. I thought the girls were coming over tonight?'

'I cancelled them.' I yanked open the chest of drawers I kept exclusively for my sports gear, and sure enough she was right.

Storm frowned. 'I'm not Serena's number one fan and I know the feeling is mutual, but I'd be pretty pissed off with you if I was her. This is the second time in a row you've ditched your daughters at short notice.'

'I haven't ditched them at all.' I started to unbutton my shirt, and Storm looked away. 'It's perfectly normal for Child Arrangement Orders that were made when the children were toddlers to have less relevance when they become teenagers. Serena appreciates I've got a lot of work to cram in before Friday.'

'But you're not at work. You're going for a run,' Storm pointed out.

I looked up at the ceiling and mentally counted to ten. 'She doesn't mind! The girls don't mind! They're fifteen and up to their eyeballs in parties at the moment. We're going to see them next week anyway! The only person with a problem here is you.'

'Shhh!' She looked at the door. 'Can you please not shout? Ben will hear you.'

'I'm not shouting?' I said, puzzled.

'That's the problem. You don't even know you're doing it anymore. Would you raise your voice to a female work colleague like this?'

Er, yes, I would. But that obviously wasn't the right answer. I had a feeling nothing would be. I pulled the skin over my head. 'Are you due on?' I waited patiently for her to answer.

'Am I *what*?' Her face hardened. 'That's your way of apologising for shouting at me? You know you're teaching your son some really appalling patterns that are not OK?' She was gathering steam, her skin angrily splotching with high colour. Maybe she was perimenopausal? I opened my mouth to suggest that, but she talked over me. 'He hears you and this is how he learns to speak to women. As a father of two daughters, are you OK with that?'

It was all so tedious I couldn't be bothered to answer. Plus, I could defend myself all night, it wouldn't make any difference, so I saved us both the trouble and simply left the room. I had things to do, places to go. Laptops to slip into rivers.

*

Once I was finally on the path – my backpack shifting around uncomfortably – I started to pant, my eyes fixed on the beam created by my head torch bouncing up and down as I ran. Why was Julia so blinded by this apparent desire to search for the truth and expose it? Please God she was going to be sensible enough not to say anything. I didn't want to have to hurt her.

Are you threatening me?

I pushed her voice out of my head, stopped running and turned off my light, pausing as my eyes adjusted to the dark. I was completely alone. I pulled off my backpack and unzipped it, lifted out my laptop and examined the surface of the inky-black water hesitantly. Was it deep enough? I crouched down and peered in. Would the evidence sink without trace? Julia just needed to get back to what she was really good at: patient care. She was a stunning surgeon – such a light touch.

My headlight suddenly randomly flashed on again, making me jump. I reached up and fumbled with the switch, wobbling slightly on my haunches, but overbalanced forward onto my knees as I managed to switch it off, which was when I saw her quite clearly: Julia lying beneath the surface of the water. Her eyes were wide and staring, mouth open, her dark hair floating eerily on unseen currents, pulling in the direction of the sea. I blinked in horror, but once I'd scrabbled to my feet, she was gone. A premonition? I felt sick and tried to steady myself.

It began to rain again, breaking the quiet and shaking me out of my reverie as fat droplets smacked onto the surrounding reeds and plopped into the water. I swallowed uneasily and stepped away from the edge as I slid my laptop back into my bag. I needed more convincing depths… and for Julia to see sense.

CHAPTER TWENTY-THREE

Julia

'I don't want this fight for you.' Ewan stared at the whisky in his glass as he swirled it around slowly, sitting at the kitchen table to my right. 'I don't want this fight, for *us*. The kids are settling, I like the school, there are opportunities. We've got a beautiful house.' He gestured around him. 'Your work is going well. Do you really have to report him?'

'You know I do.'

Ewan sighed.

'We share patients. He's been filming women semi-naked without their consent. I know he said it was to protect himself from litigation, but if that's true, why didn't he just tell them what he was doing? Or audiotape them? He's abusing them! If a doctor had secretly filmed Cass half-naked, how would you?—'

'Don't!' Ewan spoke through gritted teeth and with his eyes closed. 'Please.'

I shut up. All I could hear was the low noise of the TV from the kids' den and persistent rain against the dark and still-bare kitchen window. Ewan put his head in his hands.

'I'm so sorry,' I said sincerely. 'I don't want this all over again for us either, but I can't turn away.'

'I know.' His face was still hidden. 'I just wish it didn't always have to be you.'

'It doesn't,' I said truthfully. 'This sort of stuff is everyone's fight.' I thought about Eleni's potential replacement asking me how letchy the department was just *yesterday*, what I'd blithely told her in my ignorance. 'I don't want to draw attention to myself all over again, but now I've seen it, I can't pretend it's someone else's responsibility and let Nathan hide in plain sight. That patient told *me*. What sort of doctor – or woman – would it make me if I ignored her? I'd be no better than everyone at the Royal Grace who tried to ignore what I told *them*.'

Ewan looked up and eyeballed me steadily. 'You're going to do it tomorrow then?'

'Yes. He'll have taken the cameras down, but it doesn't matter. I've got the images I emailed myself and sent to you. He can't deny it.'

'Who do you have to tell?'

'The Medical Director at the Goldtree Hospital group. Nathan's practice is affiliated to them and he does his private operations there, so it's on their watch. It's tricky though, because private hospitals aren't regulated in the same way as NHS ones are. You'd be amazed how many of them don't even offer patients the right to complain about their care. They *should* recognise that what Nathan is doing is a threat to patient safety, suspend and investigate him, but they don't *have* to. It's farcical, really.'

'Hang on. They didn't even act properly when you reported Richard Norris at the Royal Grace and he was endangering life in an NHS hospital.' Ewan sat back in his chair. 'You're saying because this is a private hospital you could go through all of this for nothing?'

'Potentially yes. People don't like questioning "experts" like Nathan. They want to trust them; they don't want to believe they're up to no good. There's also every chance that because he's important to the business and makes them so much money, they won't suspend him because he's too valuable to them. Listen, there are a couple of other complications I need to tell you about too.' I tried to ignore the faint heart Nathan had drawn on the back of my hand as I swallowed a large swig of my G&T. 'Remember on that rugby weekend I went for a run before we left on the Saturday morning? Nathan found me on the beach. He told me he'd fallen in love with me and he tried to kiss me.'

Ewan went very still. He put his glass down and waited for me to continue.

'I pushed him away, obviously. One of the other surgeons at work, a woman called Eleni, had given me the heads-up that he tries it on with everyone, so it wasn't a total shock when it happened. I made it clear that we are very happily married and after that, nothing more was said about it. I didn't tell you because I didn't want you to get angry with a parent at the school, when I felt I'd handled it. In retrospect, I wish I'd told you, because this afternoon in his office he pulled out his mobile, and showed me an image of him kissing me, taken at the beach that Saturday. Only the way it's been taken, it makes it look like I'm kissing *him*.'

Ewan began to rub the back of his neck as if it was sore. He appeared calm, but I knew it was simply years of practise at keeping his temper with hundreds of unruly pupils. It didn't mean he wasn't feeling anything.

'Obviously, I'm *not* kissing him, but Nathan basically went on to say that if I made any allegations about him, the picture would come out and it'd look like I was up to my old tricks.'

'Blackmail?' Ewan picked up his glass and drained it.

'Pretty much.'

'And who exactly took this picture?' Ewan got up and reached for the whisky bottle again. I forced myself not to say anything. He wasn't Dom. This was an altogether different situation.

'Storm, I think. She appeared at the caravan moments after me, looking for Nathan and Ben. They didn't know she was coming. Her visit was meant to be a surprise.' I watched Ewan pour another large measure.

'I can see this is making you anxious.' He lifted up the glass. 'I won't if it bothers you?'

'It's fine,' I said. 'Sorry.'

'Cass!' Ewan shouted so suddenly that I jumped.

Seconds later she appeared in the doorway. 'Yeah? What's up?'

'I need you to do something and not ask why. Is that OK?' He leant on the side and looked at her as he crossed his arms. 'Could you do that?'

'What's going on? You both look freaked out?'

'I need you to stay away from Ben,' Ewan said. 'No more going round to his house.'

'Why?' she said immediately.

'Sometimes, just the fact that I've asked you is a good enough reason to say yes.'

'He's my friend. That's not fair!'

Ewan took a deep breath. 'OK. I forbid you to see Ben outside of school from now onwards, and if I see you talking to him socially *at* school, I'll be coming over and splitting you up in front of everyone, so unless you want a very embarrassing scene, I suggest you do as you're told.' He grabbed his glass of whisky, slung the contents down the sink and walked out of the room.

'Is he serious?' Cass turned to me, her voice wobbling. 'I'm not allowed to see Ben anymore? Why does HE get to decide? He's not the boss of me!'

'I appreciate this seems really unfair, but just at the moment, it isn't a good idea for you to see Ben.'

'Can't he come here? I don't always have to go to his? Does that help?'

I shook my head gently. 'I'm really sorry. Let's see how things are after Christmas.'

'Is it your fault?' she asked outright, and I shook my head. 'No. And it's not Ben's either, but for now, please can you do this for us? Dad doesn't mean it when he says you can't talk to Ben at school, that would be crazy, but he doesn't want you near Ben's dad for the time being. Is that OK?'

'Oh. It's Ben's *dad*.' Cass paused. 'It would have been a lot easier if you'd just said that?'

'We want to keep you safe, that's all. It's probably better we don't talk about it anymore. If I don't tell you, you won't feel you ought to tell Ben what you know, do you understand?'

'Yes.' Her voice was small and she suddenly looked much younger and more vulnerable than her thirteen years. 'Can I go now?'

*

I found Ewan in our room, lying on the bed, staring up at the ceiling. 'I'll support whatever you decide to do and I mean that,' he said as I walked in. 'I need to ask you something, though… what Dom said, that I'm too stupid to see that you and Nathan are having a thing right under my nose…'

I climbed onto the bed and knelt next to him, picking up his hand, which sat lifelessly in mine. 'Dom didn't know up from down when he said that. He was just about to go into rehab. He accused you and me of starting up behind *his* back and you KNOW that's not true. There is absolutely nothing in what he said. I promise you.'

'You didn't – I don't know – meet Nathan at one of these conventions or lectures you all go on and start something up then?'

'Ewan!' I looked at him aghast.

'He's a good-looking guy.'

'He's a predatory deviant.'

Ewan closed his eyes again. He squeezed my hand and pulled me towards him. I lay in his arms and he kissed the top of my head. 'Sorry. You're right.'

'It's OK,' I said. 'I don't blame you. You've only voiced what everyone will be whispering behind my back, once this gets out.'

'I have never met two women as brave as you and Lise,' Ewan said suddenly. 'She would say you were doing the right thing. She'd be angry that this has happened to you all over again, and she'd agree that you don't have any choice but to report him. I apologise that wasn't my first reaction. I just don't want you to get hurt. I want life to be easier for all of us. Lord knows we deserve it. What's that?' He peered at the back of my hand, noticing the sore skin where I'd scrubbed and scrubbed at the heart. 'It looks painful.'

'It'll be fine.' I sat up to look for my hydrocortisone cream. 'I understand how you feel, but I can't let him get away with it. That would only reinforce Nathan's opinion that he's untouchable – and he isn't. Men like him go into medicine because they're deeply insecure and they need a career that makes them feel superior to everyone else. They get to spend their whole lives being told by society that they're amazing; grateful patients doffing their caps; everybody worshiping them because they "save lives", doing something that "really matters". Like that bloke at Stefanie and Steve's dinner, remember? No one ever challenges them at work; they have whole teams hanging on their every word in theatre. They're used to being indulged and given total control… and it's *so* bad for them! Maybe it shouldn't be a surprise that sooner or later all that's left is a monstrous, narcissistic *ego*.'

I found an almost finished tube at the back of my bedside table and unscrewed the cap. 'Nathan's not special. He doesn't have a "gift". He's just a man used to getting his own way, preying on innocent women and it has to stop.'

I smeared the cream on my hand like butter and obliterated the remains of the heart completely.

CHAPTER TWENTY-FOUR

Nathan

'It's really hot in here!' My patient wafted her hand and fanned her face. 'I'm actually sweating.'

'I know, I'm sorry!' I smiled. 'I'm warming you up! It helps with the healing process. So I'm just going to mark you here...' I drew on her skin with my marker, under her left breast. 'And here...' I glanced to the right and made the second incision mark.

'Wow. This is crazy...' She glanced down at herself, delighted. 'I'm really doing this.'

'You really are!' I replied, forcing another grin. Most of the patients love it when I start drawing on them before the op. It makes it real – proof that it's finally going to happen. Maybe that's why I drew on Julia yesterday. I didn't mean to flip her out the way it did. I thought she'd like it. Most women do.

'If it's not a stupid question, why do you have to get busy with the Sharpie? You're only going to be able to go in under my breasts to put the implants in and it's pretty obvious where they are?'

'You standing up – when I can account for gravity – is the best position to get the symmetry right between your breasts,' I explained. 'You look totally different lying down on the operating table. Skin moves and I'd hate to make incision marks where I hadn't intended them. These drawings are my procedural map so

I can get the best results for you. It also,' I picked up a different colour pen, 'gives me a chance to relax you a bit. A happy, relaxed patient has a better anaesthetic experience, so it's worth a bit of colouring in.'

I drew a small upside-down smiley face on her tummy, and she smiled back at it. See Julia? People like it – it wasn't a weird thing to do. 'Plus, if I recognise my own scribbling, there's a pretty high chance I've got *my* patient in front of me and not somebody else's by mistake.' I winked at her. 'OK, you're done. You can put your gown back on, thank you.

'Now, *after* the surgery, I'm going to ask you to stay sitting up and alert while we manage your pain relief. I'll want you to move your arms around a bit, but you're going to be surprised by how little pain you are in, because we've chosen the right sized implants for *your* body. It's all going to be great and there's nothing to worry about, but do you have any other questions?'

'Did you get enough sleep last night to do this?' she half joked. The private patients are always more confident. Paying for my services tips the power balance in their favour. 'You look tired.'

No, I did not get much sleep – thank you for asking. I'm very possibly going to be suspended later today. It was on my mind last night. It's on my mind right now. My accuser might even be in the building as we speak, for all I know. You may not even get your operation…

'I always look this delicately bruised, but don't let appearances fool you, I'm fine.' I smiled. 'Hardy as they come. And YOU are going to be fine too. I promise. So shall we do this?' I beamed at her. 'Shall we make you feel great about yourself?'

She nodded and smiled bravely.

'Excellent.' I got to my feet. 'You're going to be *thrilled* with the results! Let's go meet your anaesthetist.' I would like to put myself under, wake up and find this was all over. Damn Julia! She could be in the Medical Director's office right now, beginning her story and the unravelling of my reputation and twenty-year career… Giles Creasy was exactly the sort of wimpy management twat completely ill-equipped to deal with Julia-in-legal-mode. 'Let's go!' I smiled.

*

I forced myself to concentrate as I made my first incision and began to create the pocket over the muscle. She'd have clinics this morning. Might she come in and report me this afternoon then, if she was going to at all, today? That would give me enough time to ditch the laptop after I'd finished up here. I only had two more ops to go… and I was ready for the first implant. My nurse, Sandra, passed me a wound protector so that the implant wouldn't touch the skin, and I placed it with care over the incision site. She lifted the lid on the implant package, but as I stared at it briefly, swimming in its sterile solution, I experienced a moment of panic. Was it my imagination or did it look considerably flatter on one side than the other?

'Grab me a surgical pen, will you?' I frowned at it.

Sandra quickly reappeared. I picked the implant up and briefly marked the letter 'O' on what I fancied was the flatter 'back' of it. I was almost certainly seeing issues that weren't there, but on the off chance I was right, I was going to put that side to the chest wall.

'What's that for then?' Sandra nodded at my mark.

'"O" for orientation,' I remarked. 'I want this to be the back of the implant.'

I began to push it into the incision carefully, teasing it into place, making sure, as much as I could, that the O was staying facing down as it moved from my hands into the patient's body. Just for a moment I was totally focused, no distractions, as I ensured it was in place. It was blissful not to think about Julia, but then there she was, creeping back into my head again. This really was such bullshit.

In the grand scheme of things, the cameras were simply not important. I had a woman in front of me, unconscious – and frankly mutilated – until I was ready to sew her up again. I could remove the implant right now if I wanted to, leave her with a useless flap of skin, no volume in the breast at all and an open incision – I could walk away, but I'm not *that* man. I am a good surgeon. I give my patients the very best of results, and that's why women come to me, because ultimately all they care about is how they are going to look on the other side of the surgery *I* will perform on them. I make them fabulous. What they don't need to know, doesn't hurt them.

*

I was still frustrated and edgy as I tried to concentrate on the regular click and hiss of my cautery pen while cutting away at the flesh of my second patient of the day. I glanced at the clock – I was on schedule, but twitchy, unable to settle. It *was* hot in the theatre. I could sense the impending threat – I was still half expecting the door to open at any moment, to reveal Giles in one of his cheap suits, flanked by security and Julia, as I was ordered to down tools and step away from the table. That was ridiculous, of course, but I couldn't help but be on hyper-alert and, given my distraction, I knew I had to be careful I didn't make a mistake… although dammit if the *next* wretched implant didn't look oddly flatter on one side when we opened the pack. Was it me? Was I seeing things? Two women with two slightly unusual implants in one morning? An unlikely coincidence – I was experiencing a loss of confidence, which was understandable given the circumstances – but I also wasn't going to take any chances.

I beckoned to Sandra. 'Surgical pen again, please.'

I marked the 'flatter' side with a 'W'.

Sandra looked confused.

'"W" for "Wall",' I explained. 'I want this side up against the chest wall.'

'Oh OK,' she said. 'That makes more sense. It's more specific than "O" for orientation, isn't it?'

'Exactly,' I said and moved the implant to the incision, stopping at the last second as I noticed the wound protector funnel wasn't in place. That was close. I swallowed, silently put it in and continued, making sure the 'W' was on the correct side.

'Although, now I think of it, maybe we should mark all of the implants this way.' I started chattering, trying to cover the fact that I actually felt nervous. It was insane. 'I don't trust that national database. It's begging for a data breach, something of that size, and then what? All of that information winding up in the wrong hands? It would be much better if we kept our own records – like GPs do – so if anything were to go wrong with one of my girls, we've got everything we need to hand *here*. I might give that some more thought. OK, let's close this side.'

I glanced at the clock. Time was marching on. I wanted to get finished and be on my way to the marina before 2 p.m.

*

I looked for Julia's white Mini in the car park once I was striding out of the building into air so cold it almost made me catch my breath, but to my relief there was no sign of it. No one stopped me. I headed casually off to Exmouth as if I hadn't a care in the world.

A couple of other boaties were having a pleasant faff on their RIBs when I arrived, waving cheerfully in my direction as I began to get mine ready to go out.

'Nice bright day for it!' one of them, a retired fund manager, called to me, pointing up at the almost blinding, clear-blue sky. 'Going to clear the head a bit? Blow away the cobwebs?'

'You've got it!' I gave him the thumbs up. 'Some peaceful time. You know how it is!'

'I do indeed!' He nodded mournfully. 'We've got the grand-children coming tomorrow night.'

'Ah – my sympathies.'

He shrugged good-naturedly and saluted as I pulled back off the mats, manoeuvred away from the pontoon and set out onto the open water. It was freezing. The faster I went, the more the wind snarled at my face, but it was good to be able to feel *something* as I bounced over the waves, occasional spray blowing up. Once I was far enough out that no one was around me, I stilled the engine, reached down to my feet and quickly unzipped my backpack. Pulling the laptop out, I glanced from left to right and jettisoned it over the edge, watching it sink down to the depths, never to be seen again. The relief was enormous. I floated on the quiet waves for a moment, closed my eyes, reached out my arms and felt the freedom. The sun shone on my face and I started to smile slowly, seconds before I yelled aloud with triumph, because I could. There was nobody to stop me. It felt good, like a war cry. I had done an excellent job against the odds for those three women today, improved their lives beyond measure and taken considerable care with them. Julia wanted to ruin that for the sake of films that no longer even existed?

I opened my eyes again and stared at the horizon.

I hoped to God Hamish was right; that now she'd had time to think about it, she would see *no one* had been caused any harm. I needed her to keep her beautiful mouth shut.

CHAPTER TWENTY-FIVE

Julia

'So these are the cameras in the consulting rooms, and this shot of them was taken yesterday?' The Medical Director stared at the image in front of him.

'Yes. I went to Mr Sloan's practice to tell him what my patient had alleged. I made it clear I would be reporting this irregularity.' I scratched my arm under the sleeve of my dress. I could feel the small scabs coming away under my nails. It all felt so horribly familiar – like sliding straight back down the snake to where I was over a year ago: reporting Richard, in an anonymous office just like this.

Mr Creasy peered at the cameras, clearly visible in the top corners of the room. 'And Mr Sloan responded by showing you an image of *yourself*, taken without your consent?'

'Yes. I suspect he's going to tell you we had a relationship, he ended it and in a fit of scorned rage I've turned on him – something along those lines – and *that's* what all of this is about. It's not true. I'm very happily married. I have no sexual interest in Nathan Sloan whatsoever. We've not had a relationship. He tried to kiss me, but I pushed him off.'

Mr Creasy hesitated, and I wondered what he was thinking. Did he already know about my background? 'It would have been much, much easier for me not to get involved when the patient brought this situation to my attention,' I said, 'but how could I not tell you about this? What kind of doctor would that make me? "Either help or do not harm the patient".'

He made no comment to my repeating part of the oath I swore when I graduated, just scribbled something on his notepad. He seemed to be taking this with a worrying calm.

'I'm sure you're aware the range of services that Mr Sloan offers includes labiaplasty?' I reminded him. 'If I were a patient of his and I was being filmed with my legs wide open, I'd want to know about it.'

He flushed violently, and I sat back in relief, to see at last some sort of reaction.

'Thank you, Ms Blythe.' He put his pen down. 'We'll be in touch. Thank you for also emailing the images ahead of our meeting. I will respond in writing, as you've requested, in due course. In the meantime, could I ask you not to discuss this with anyone?' He looked at me almost pleadingly, and I didn't blame him. I could see the news headlines too, maybe even the international ones. He'd probably thought he was almost done for Christmas, now this.

I stood up. 'I've no interest in gossip. I only want to make sure patients are protected. I'm confident you'll deal with what I've told you appropriately and quickly, so I'll expect to hear from you, if not tomorrow, by Monday.' I made my position clear. I was polite but firm. I wasn't going to let this go.

But after I left – just as the last time – I felt anticlimactic and flat, walking across the wet, cold car park. There was no going back now. From experience, I knew I wasn't going to feel 'lighter' for having done the right thing. It wasn't a case of a problem shared being a problem halved, but I'd not anticipated finding it quite so distressing to climb back into the cold bath; the soap still suspended in the water, its slimy tendrils like jellyfish, ready to cling to my exposed skin. And somehow this was even more an upsetting scenario than last time, mostly because of the purposeful nature of Nathan's actions. Richard Norris was an arrogant surgeon whose mistakes were potentially costing lives, but Nathan had deliberately violated these women time and time again. What had he done with all of the films of himself examining them? I didn't want to let my mind go there. I searched in my bag for my phone to text Ewan, but discovered I'd left it at work and had no choice but to drive back to the hospital and get it.

*

Climbing the stairs to the office, I felt double my age and oddly like crying – just sick of it all. I thought back to my original coffee with Tan and Hamish where they'd told me what a great place it was to work. Well, I'd torpedoed that in under one hour. Thank God we only had one day left. With a bit of luck, they might not find out until we'd all finished and they'd have time over the Christmas break to objectively consider what I'd done to their beloved team.

I pushed the door open only to swear aloud in shock. Rather than the empty room I'd anticipated, Tan, Michelle and Hamish were all pulling on their coats while *Nathan* waited for them.

I blushed guiltily as he looked at me.

'I know. Today's not my day to be here. I popped in to invite everyone for a quick Christmas drink. Join us?' He jumped up and rubbed his hands together. He was crackling with nervous energy.

A Christmas drink? Was he out of his mind – or here to make trouble? Had he come to confront me publicly? He couldn't know where I'd just been, not already?

'I won't, thank you. I need to get home tonight.'

'Ah, what a shame! We'll have one for you instead. Shall we, troops?' He held open the door and they all filed out, wishing me a pleasant evening.

I exhaled and sank down into a chair, when I noticed Nathan's scarf still on the table and tensed. Sure enough, seconds later, the door opened and he reappeared.

'Forget it on purpose?' I said. 'How long have you been waiting for me to come back so you could see if I did it?'

'And did you?' he asked.

I nodded. He closed his eyes briefly, then let his head hang.

'I have an obligation to protect patients.'

'I begged you not to!' He lifted his head and looked straight at me. 'You've made such a mistake.'

My heart thumped. 'That sounds like you're threatening me again?'

'Of course he's not!' Hamish – because when I turned to the doorway it was him standing there – gave a little chuckle and shook his head. 'Threatening you! Honestly! She's done it then?' He looked at Nathan.

Nathan nodded, and Hamish turned back to me, pleasant smile still on his face. 'You sanctimonious little cunt.'

CHAPTER TWENTY-SIX

Hamish

She gasped audibly and jumped up, covering her mouth with pretend shock. I couldn't imagine for one second it was the first time she'd had something like that said to her.

'I have a question for you, Julia,' I mused. 'What business is it of yours how Nate operates his *private* client practice and the measures he puts in place to protect himself from the patients who are never satisfied?'

I watched her hand start to slide up her sleeve, before she consciously removed it.

'I don't think it's appropriate for me to comment, other than to say things are rarely as simple as they appear from the outside.'

'Looks pretty clear to me.' I shrugged. 'A couple of months ago you asked me outright if Nathan had "talked" about you on our weekend away. I *told* you – very gently – to leave it alone, remember?'

'You misunderstood my question. That's all I'm going to say on that.' She walked over to her desk and picked up her phone, only to hesitate at the door and look back at Nathan, who was doing well to keep his hands clasped behind his back and a blank expression on his face. 'I can imagine what he's told you.' She gestured at Nate. 'I'd urge you to consider that there are two sides to every story.'

'I'm sure you would. I would also remind *you* of your promise to Nathan and me that you weren't going to try it on with us.'

'You're taking that comment completely out of context, as well you know.' She made for the door.

'I think you twist the context when it suits you.' I raised my voice, and she stopped, turning back. 'No wonder your last place tried to get rid of you. Quite the cougar, aren't you?'

Her eyebrows shot up. 'Cougar?' *And she laughed in my face.*

I had to grip onto the edge of the desk to stop myself from marching over to her. How dare she find this funny? This was exactly why I should have trusted my instinct and blocked her application. I should have tossed her back in the pool with the other small fry where she belonged! She was going to wreck everything.

'You think this is amusing?' I was struggling to keep my voice level. 'Making disgusting allegations about a dedicated surgeon who will now face, at the very least, the stress of being formally investigated – because of you? You're really playing this game all over again? We do like the warmth of the spotlight, don't we?'

She looked down at the floor. 'I *knew* you didn't agree with what I did at the Royal Grace. I saw it on your face when I was telling you what happened. Richard Norris was a—'

'...*man* who made one surgical mistake,' I interjected.

'How can you possibly know that's true? You weren't there!' she exclaimed. 'He had a reputation for—'

'Oh!' I cut in. 'A reputation! Well then! Sack him immediately! Discount years of excellent surgical outcomes! He had a *reputation*.'

'Filming women naked, without their knowledge, is not a one-off mistake. Cutting off a woman's healthy breast, making careless surgical errors is not a one-time mistake. How sad to see that my biggest barrier remains threatened men who refuse to support me.' She looked me right in the eye, the bitch.

'Hamish,' Nathan said quietly. 'Let's just go.' He put a hand on my arm, but I shook it off. While I was aware I had to be careful, she *really* needed to hear the sort of home truths people are becoming too afraid to say face to face these days!

'Nathan is an extraordinary surgeon with years of experience and hundreds of happy patients. He just gets on with the job and genuinely cares. This is how you repay him for giving *you* a job when no other hospital wanted to go anywhere near you? I'd heard you were standoffish and self-important, but this?'

She cleared her throat. 'I'm aware that I'm not always seen as likeable or warm,' she began, 'but—'

'I told you she'd be more trouble than she was worth,' I turned to Nathan 'sporting that little whistle in her fanny pack. Well, you know how to blow it all right, don't you?' I turned back to her and stuck my tongue in my cheek while making a wanking gesture with my hand.

'Hamish!' Nathan said sharply. 'That's enough! Don't speak to her like that.'

'You're being much too kind, Nate,' I said. 'She deserves whatever she gets.'

I turned back to see Julia had tears in her eyes. Of course she did, turning it on for effect. Double standards again. 'Nobody really wanted you here either. They were going to politely tell you they felt you were too qualified for this position and there wouldn't be enough high-profile work to hold your interest. It was only because Tan, Nathan and I argued your case. You might think on that – although I can see we underestimated you – you're very, very good at twisting the "female surgeon versus the patriarchy" narrative to suit your own end, aren't you?'

I watched a well-timed tear roll down her cheek and she briefly closed her eyes, as if my words were actually wounding her. She was good – I had to give her that.

'You can go to hell if you think you're going to force *us* to take it lying down.' I made for the door. 'I'll defend Nate every step of the way. Don't say I didn't warn you.'

I left her standing there and started marching back down the corridor. Tan and Michelle were nowhere to be seen, presumably having carried on downstairs.

'Hamish.'

I turned to see Nathan walking slowly towards me. 'While I'm grateful for the support, calling her—'

'...who do we send the beach picture to first?' I cut across him furiously, reaching into my pocket and pulling out my phone. 'I vote Joan. We can say someone forwarded it to me anonymously and I'm not sure what to do about it. That ought to be the fastest way to get it everywhere.'

He put a hand out. 'I told you. I don't want to use that picture.'

'You don't have a choice! You've got to start building your case, prove that Julia has a thing for you *before* the allegations come out; otherwise it won't be as effective. Open your eyes and start protecting yourself! Julia sold you out!'

'Yes – I'm coming to terms with that. Thank you.' He looked at my phone, hesitated, then nodded. 'OK. But tell Joan to keep it under her hat for now.'

At last! He was starting to see sense. 'There, it's done.' I slipped my phone back into my pocket.

Nathan exhaled and stared up at the ceiling. 'I can't believe she did it. I have tried so hard to change – and it's not enough, Ham. I have tried *so* hard.' His voice trembled.

'You shouldn't HAVE to change for her. She doesn't deserve you. Come on,' I put a hand on his arm, 'let's go and get that drink.'

CHAPTER TWENTY-SEVEN

Nathan

Tan shifted in his seat as I picked up my pint and tried to ignore the lyrics of 'Last Christmas', just audible over the hum and chatter of the hot and stuffy bar. When we'd arrived, we'd practically had the place to ourselves, before some kids had rocked up. They'd not even asked if we were waiting for more people to join us – just sat down at the far end of our large table like they owned the joint – then steadily the whole place had filled up with clones of them; shouting and shrieking, slopping their drinks everywhere as they hugged noisily and shoved us further into retreat, not even relenting when our food arrived.

I wished I'd ignored Hamish pushing us to stay for something to eat and gone home, especially when a couple of girls who looked younger than my daughters started singing loudly and tunelessly to each other, no consideration for anyone else around them. Their selfishness and overconfidence needled me badly. They hadn't even been born when 'Last Christmas' first came out – what would they know about giving their heart to someone, only to have it destroyed? It was hard to remember a moment when I'd felt older or lonelier.

'This is good.' Hamish licked his fingers as he swallowed the last of his burger, then picked an errant piece of food from his teeth. 'You're not eating, Nate?'

I stared down at my tasteless turkey bap and chutney, sitting on a sad square of brown paper, accompanied by a small metal bucket of greasy-looking fries, all served on a chopping board for the princely sum of £14.00. 'You have it.'

He shrugged and reached across the table, without offering any to Tan, and glanced at me as he bit into it, the juices dribbling down his chin. 'Look – Julia didn't say anything more than she'd reported you, did she?'

I shook my head.

'All she could have told them was you had cameras in your office.'

I glanced at Tan, but Hamish waved a dismissive hand. 'As if he's going to say anything. You've got no timeline yet, have you? No one has contacted you from either hospital?'

'Nope.'

'Well then put it from your mind for now.'

I turned and looked straight at Tan. 'I dumped my laptop out at sea. It was a stupid thing to do, but I just panicked.'

Tan looked confused and wary, but I'd already turned back to Hamish. 'That's the party line, right? I say that when asked? Yes?'

Hamish nodded.

'I imagine it'll all kick-off tomorrow,' I continued. 'I'm going for full suspension. Care to place your bets, gentlemen?' I drained the dregs of my pint. Suddenly I was pretty desperate for another.

'We don't have to think about it *now*.' Hamish was firm. 'Have a night off, for God's sake. You need another drink, pronto! Ah, look! And as if by magic, here comes the lovely Michelle with our next round!' He raised a suggestive eyebrow, and I turned to look at her crossing the room.

Her face was prettily flushed with the booze and heat of the packed pub as she concentrated on not spilling anything. I knew what Hamish was up to. Arriving back alongside us, she bent over to proudly place the glasses on the table, and I saw right down her top before she straightened up, still carefully clutching her bank card. With a sudden pang of guilt for letting her get a round in, I remembered when I'd been like her, trying to keep up with my bosses and feel equal when I wasn't. One particular consultant liked to dispatch juniors to the bar to get him cigars, with instructions to put it on his tab. The barman would stonily point out there was no tab and the hapless junior would just pay rather than face the embarrassment of asking the consultant for £7. A cunning ruse. The old bastard knew perfectly well what he was doing. I didn't want to be like him.

I reached into my wallet under the table, then bent down as if I was picking something up from the floor and handed Michelle a £20 note. 'This just fell out of your pocket.'

She frowned in confusion, then brightened. 'Oooh! I love it when that happens! You find one you'd forgotten about! Thanks, Nathan! Woohoo!' She gazed at me for slightly too long with open adoration and gratitude, her reactions delayed by the effects of the alcohol in her system.

I half smiled. She was sweet. She reminded me a little of Serena twenty-five years ago. Twenty-five years… and what had I achieved in that time, really? Two wives, three kids and a career about to end in disgrace. I thought of Julia looking at me with barely concealed disgust. How did she manage to make me feel so hollowed out by her disappointment? I picked up my drink and knocked it back in one.

'Wehay!' Michelle laughed, raising her glass and knocking hers back too.

Tan looked down at the table, briefly. 'Are you operating tomorrow, Nate?'

It was a reminder to go easy, but the genuine answer was, I had no idea.

I threw my hands up. 'Who knows, Tanny banany!' Was it because I'd not eaten – possibly – or because I found myself suddenly unable to cope and wanted to blank it all out – probably – but either way, that was the tipping point of the evening: *that* was the drink I finally felt spreading through my veins, loosening my anxiety, melting the tightness in my muscles and soul. I recognised Recklessness as he pulled up a chair at the table and sat down alongside me with a cheeky wink – and I knew how this was going to end.

I turned to Michelle and gave her the benefit of my full smile. She stared at me, Hamish smirked, Tan looked away and I could have stopped myself then and there... but I didn't, and that's always been my fucking problem.

*

In the back of the taxi I watched the road flashing past, the music from the tacky city centre club still ringing in my ears. Michelle had thought it hilarious that a '90's clubs classics' night had made me come so alive on the dancefloor, teasing me as I waved my arms in the air to 'Insomnia'.

'I saw Faithless do this live; they played at my then-girlfriend's student's union! They were amazing!' I'd shouted to her, only for her to gesture that she couldn't hear me, before leaning in closer. I said it again, right next to her ear, hands on her waist as she wobbled into me as someone dancing bumped into her. I smelt her perfume and the slippery heat of her body as the beat surrounded us. I was twenty again. Everything ahead of me! She lifted her mouth up to mine and I kissed her, just for a moment, before I came to my senses and realised we were in public. We needed to go somewhere more private.

I glanced back down at her, her head resting drunkenly on my shoulder. The taxi went over a speed bump and jogged her awake. She twisted her head up to look at me and our lips met again. She was warm; she wanted me. She wasn't complicated. Why did everything have to be so complicated? I kissed her back a little harder, put my hand on her thigh and in the dark, to the right of her, I caught the gleam in Hamish's eye as he smiled at me over the top of her head.

*

The house smelt of air freshener and dust burning off the radiators as Hamish put on the heating to take the edge off the almost-empty rooms. Michelle was drunkenly kissing me in the sparse sitting room, fumbling with my belt, unable to undo it. I pulled her upstairs and she trailed after me, holding my hand, giggling.

We found a bedroom. There was a bare bed in it. Just a mattress on a base. In seconds she was on her back – virtually passed out – but telling me she wanted me to fuck her hard, like she'd heard it in a film. I did as I was told because I was suddenly angry enough, but I couldn't get there. I stopped and reached into my back pocket – pulling my knife out, opening the blade in the dark, ready to nick it against my bare leg, only having had too much to drink, my hands were clumsy and it fell – towards Michelle's inner thigh. I gasped in horror – it could have punctured right through the skin into her adductor brevis – but *thank God*, it landed flat on her leg, the blade merely grazing the skin. There was the tiniest bit of blood – it was the sensation of cold metal that she hazily registered, lifting her head briefly before slumping back down and sighing, putting her arms above her head, her heavy breasts lifting. I shoved the knife away hurriedly. I'd got away with it – I'd got away with *something* – and then I thought of Julia, holding *her* in my arms, her beautiful face right next to mine. I returned to Michelle, only seeing Julia lose herself to me. I could hear Michelle gasping; I groaned and let my head hang briefly, before pulling out and turning to see Hamish stood in the corner of the room in the dark. Yanking my trousers up, I ignored him and went off to search for a bathroom.

*

Blinking under bright strip lighting, I cleaned myself up, washed my hands, put my dry mouth under the tap, then glanced in the cheap cabinet mirror over the sink. In seven hours I had to be up, ready to operate on Stefanie, unless they suspended me first. *Julia – how could you do this to me?* I turned the light off, desolate, and went to find Hamish and Michelle. She was still out of it on the bed while Hamish was on the phone ordering a couple of taxis. I didn't want to look at her.

'Take her back for me,' I pleaded, suddenly exhausted and placing a hand on his arm. 'I'm not feeling so good.'

'Sure thing,' he said easily, not remotely bothered. 'Sorry, yes.' He spoke into the phone. 'I'm still here. It's going to—' He gave an unfamiliar address.

'You know where she lives?' I frowned.

He nodded, and I decided I didn't want to go there. In every sense.

As my taxi pulled away, I watched him help Michelle into the back of their silver Ford, the small anonymous terrace house already locked up and in darkness.

*

Back at home, I drank a pint of water and showered before finally climbing in next to Storm, who stirred in her sleep, but didn't wake up. I thought briefly about Michelle, Serena and even Stefanie as I turned on my side, trying to push them from my mind… shags of Christmas past and present, but what future now? I turned on my back again as Storm reached a hand out and placed it on my chest, trying to hold on to me even when unconscious. My stomach was churning though and I pushed her off. I should get up and puke, except… couldn't be arsed… I was going to feel like shit tomorrow. Not that it was a big day or anything. And Stefanie… if she didn't get her op… I yawned, my eyes closing heavily. She'd be furious. Fucking Furious. Double F, too big really. Just Furious… like Julia. Everything came back to Julia.

Broken-hearted and confused, I was grateful to finally pass out.

CHAPTER TWENTY-EIGHT

Julia

I crept into the office early, hoping to find it empty, but unexpectedly, Michelle was there. She looked terrible – eyes puffy and make-up smudged beneath them. It was evidentially the hangover from hell. She opened her mouth to say something when I greeted her but covered it just as quickly with her hand. Her skin washed out, and she dashed from the room.

'Why don't you just go home?' I suggested, when she returned to her desk and sat down delicately. 'You obviously had quite the evening? Don't worry – we've all been there!'

She looked at me stricken and, to my surprise, her eyes filled with tears.

'Are you all right?' I grabbed a box of tissues.

'She's fine. Stop looking for drama and detail where there is none.' I turned to see Hamish had thumped his bag down on the table and was glaring at us. He pointed a podgy finger at me. 'What have you made her say to you? I know your game, and you can pack it in. She's a *secretary*!'

'What?' I exclaimed. 'I haven't done anything!'

'You just can't help yourself, can you? This is a place of work, may I remind you? In fact, you know what, Julia? We've got one day left in this office together before the Christmas break. I have nothing to say to you and would prefer that you don't attempt to engage me in any interaction, but please be warned that I will not tolerate you either attempting to manipulate or intimidate other staff members.' He nodded at Michelle. 'You clearly need to be reminded that we don't allow bullies here.' He was actually shaking with quiet anger. It was extraordinary.

'You're warning *me* not to bully people?' I was incredulous. 'Just what is it about women like me that so enrages reactionary men of a certain age, like you?'

He refused to answer. Just stared me down. I shook my head in disbelief, turned my back on him and walked from the room, only to hurry to the loos once I was out of sight, where I threw up at having confronted him: the adrenaline overwhelming me, just like old times. A couple of staff members came in and looked at me curiously, but didn't say anything, probably assuming I had a Christmas party hangover too. One of them whispered something to her colleague, who laughed. I'm sure she wasn't talking about me at all, but it felt like a taste of things to come.

*

I convinced myself everyone must have found out what I'd done and waited on tenterhooks for the rest of the day to be summoned by the Medical Director... but nothing. Five p.m. arrived and I was slipping on my coat to escape before Hamish returned from theatre, when Tan appeared.

He looked around him before whispering, 'You told them that Nathan has cameras in his consulting room?'

'Yes,' I admitted.

He gave a low whistle and looked at me in disbelief.

'It's true,' I began. 'He—'

He cut me off by simply holding up a hand. 'I really wanted you to come and work here,' he said quietly. 'I'd like you to remember that.'

*

Somehow Tan's gentle disappointment was worse than Hamish's abuse. He hadn't even wanted to hear my side of the story. As I parked on the other side of the cathedral to pick up Cass and Al, unable to get any closer because the city was full of Christmas shoppers, it was with a growing sense of disquiet that I walked across the green in the dark, towards the school. What if Ewan was right? Suppose they *didn't* investigate Nathan and everyone closed ranks? What would I do then?

I pulled my coat more tightly around me at the bitterly cold wind gusting across the path. Despite it only being the twenty-first of December, the Christmas market stalls were coming down, the clanking of poles from the glühwein tent hitting the grass as bolts were unscrewed, alongside the sharp snap of trestle tables folding up.

I passed the entrance to the cathedral, its warm light bathing the dark cobbles, and hurried on, towards the school car park, forcing myself to smile at the other parents spilling out of the gates with their children, ready to hurry home and get festivities underway. They all knew each other here. What would we do as a *family* if people turned their backs on us?

Half of the hospital consultants have kids at this school.

I heard Nathan's voice in my head as I glanced at the wall where he'd been leaning that first day.

I've loved you pretty much from the moment you shook my hand outside the school in those ridiculous wellingtons on a baking hot afternoon.

I swallowed queasily and ran the last bit up to the heavy wooden door. Inside, it looked a little like Hogwarts. I began to feel more normal as I stood next to the oversized Christmas tree and chatted briefly to the receptionist about where she'd be spending the big day.

'They're late tonight?' I remarked, checking my watch, before glancing up the wide mahogany staircase.

'Everyone's so overexcited it takes twice as long to get them to gather their stuff.' She smiled. 'I shouldn't think they'll be too much… ah, well, here's Alex at least!' She gestured up the stairs, although as I followed her gaze, my whole body tensed.

He was standing on one side of Nathan – who had his hand resting lightly on my son's back – with Ben on the other.

'Come down carefully!' I called out straight away, instinctively nervous. 'Hand on the bannister please, Alex. The stairs might be slippy; it's damp outside.'

I held my breath as all three of them descended slowly, ignoring me and chatting earnestly. The second they arrived at the bottom, I as good as grabbed Al and pulled him towards me.

He looked understandably surprised. 'Are you – oh no!' He patted his head in dismay. 'I've left my hat upstairs!'

Ben rolled his eyes. 'What a surprise.'

Alex grinned at him. 'Race you!' He turned and bolted, legging it up the stairs two at a time with his long legs.

'I said be careful!' I called again. I wanted to leave. I didn't want to be standing next to Nathan a second longer.

But Ben hesitated, then threw himself after Al – as they disappeared around the corner Nathan laughed easily. 'Boys!' he said, turning to me. 'You're never too old to get excited about Christmas. So you've got a few days off now I hope, Julia?' He smiled at me pleasantly and tightened the scarf around his neck, tucking it into his camel overcoat.

We were going to act like nothing had happened? 'I've finished until Monday the seventh, yes.'

'Lovely.' He beamed. 'Nice long break! Me too. Except I don't know when I go back yet. I was suspended just as I finished my third op today!'

Oh shit. My heart sank.

'As soon as they tell the GMC, I'll be obliged to inform the EM, who will no doubt follow suit, so thank you!' He continued to smile widely. 'Happy Christmas!'

I looked around me quickly, but no one was listening. 'I don't know what you expect me to say.'

'"Sorry"? That would be a start.' His smile faded.

I hesitated but glanced up to see Cass and Ewan standing at the top of the stairs. Ewan was watching us, and Cass was worriedly scanning her father's face.

'I'll wait for you outside!' I called up to them brightly. 'Al's just coming – would you hang on for him? I'm going to have a quick word with Ben's dad.'

I put my head down and walked out into the dark car park, tucking into a discreet corner. I knew Nathan would follow me, but I didn't expect to feel his hand on my arm and spun round in shock. 'I don't want to be touched by you.'

His grip tightened. 'What kind of man do you think I am?' he whispered. 'I'm a good person, Julia!'

I spoke much more clearly and calmly than I felt. 'Remove your hand.'

His eyes searched my face. 'Come away with me,' he begged suddenly. 'Please? I just want to walk away from it all – with you. I feel like I'm hanging on by a very thin thread now.'

'Oi!' Ewan called angrily behind Nathan, carrying Cass and Alex's sports bags towards us, while all three kids hung back awkwardly in the doorway, watching. 'I don't want a scene,' he said quietly, arriving next to us, 'but if you force it,' – he nodded at Nathan's hand, still resting on me – 'it's game on.'

'"Game on"?' Nathan repeated and turned to me. 'How can you even want to be with someone like this? I don't understand! He's such a pleb.'

Ewan dropped the bags instantly and took a step forward.

'No!' I said urgently, seeing what Nathan was up to. 'Don't! He's after a reaction he can report to the GMC and the press, when they come calling. It's all part of his "me and him" relationship strategy.'

'What?' Nathan pretended to look bewildered. 'No, I—'

'He's trying to make you look like the jealous husband,' I continued, glancing over my shoulder. 'Plus the kids can all see.' I placed my free hand on top of Nathan's, inclining my head forward so that it looked as if I was about to kiss his cheek. 'Don't ever touch me again,' I whispered next to his ear and dug my nails into the back of his hand – still clasping my arm – hard enough to make him gasp and let go.

'Happy Christmas!' I said loudly as I pulled back, stepping away from him. 'Come on, kids!' I beckoned them towards me. Confused, they hurried over as I waved to Ben, still immobile in the doorway. 'Bye, Ben! Happy Christmas!'

I put my arm around both of them, and Cass immediately shrugged me off, glancing over her shoulder at Ben. I did not look back.

'*Now!*' I said brightly, in my best 'changing the subject' tone, as we walked away from the Sloans. 'We're parked on the other side of the green; I couldn't get a space any closer than that, I'm afraid! How was your last day?'

I was walking so fast I could hear Al and Cass starting to pant as we marched past the dismantled market.

'Al, what was Ben's dad saying to you when you came down the stairs at school?' I said suddenly. 'You looked like you were having a serious talk about something.' In our urgency to keep Cass away from Ben, it hadn't occurred to me to do the same with Alex, but of course he'd leap straight into the gap left by Cass – or Ben had sought him out as a bridge to her. How stupid of me not to have considered that. 'What were the three of you discussing?'

'Nothing!' Alex was exasperated. 'We just…' He stopped and listened. 'Your phone's ringing.'

'It's OK, she'll call them back,' Ewan said. 'You were about to say?'

'None of your business!' Alex glared at him. 'I don't have to tell you anything. We're not at school now.'

'Don't speak to Dad like that,' Cass said hotly.

Alex shrugged. 'He's not *my* dad.'

'Why are you being so horrible? Oh my God!' Cass spun to look at me. 'Could you answer that or just – like – put it on silent? It's getting louder and louder.'

I rummaged around in my bag to find my phone. Unfortunately, we all saw the name illuminated on the screen in the dark. *Dominic…*

It was hard to see how the day could get much worse.

'Dad's back?' Al said immediately. We all heard the note of anxiety in his voice. 'I don't want to speak to him. Don't pick up, Mum. Please!'

'I won't say you're here.'

'No!' he shouted. 'Why don't you ever listen to me?' He shrugged his bag from his back, dropped it and ran off into the dark, pushing past people carrying Christmas shopping, shoving them off the path.

'Alex!' I called out desperately, but he didn't stop.

Ewan dumped the sports bags he was carrying and started to sprint after him. The phone was still ringing in my hand. To cap it all, some blokes tucked down in a dark corner of the cathedral began to sing 'We Wish You a Merry Christmas!' and cackle with laughter. Not at us, I realised, when I looked over to see they were surrounded by tins and empty bottles – it was just coincidence. I took a deep breath and started gathering up the discarded bags.

'Come on, Cass, let's get home and get you something to eat. Long day, huh?'

Her bottom lip trembled as she nodded and we started to head off down the path towards the car park, me puffing and staggering slightly under the weight of Al's belongings. I'm pretty sure it *wasn't* coincidence when the men started singing 'Little Donkey! Little Donkey, on a dusty road…' But I ignored them. I was learning to pick my battles.

CHAPTER TWENTY-NINE

Nathan

'Who did this to you?' Storm lifted my hand from the tablecloth, and examined the tiny, dark-red crescent moons left by Julia's nails.

I drew back, picked up my cracker and offered it to her. 'Pull me? It is Christmas, after all.'

'Nathan!' She looked embarrassed and checked to make sure no one around the table had heard, but unlike us they were all having a great time and busily chatting away. She took a sip of her champagne. 'Who made those marks on your hand?'

'When *was* the last time we had sex, in fact?' I sat back in my chair. I really couldn't remember. It was a rather unkind way to deflect attention, but – the truth? I shot a cold sideways look at her, gave her my best Jack Nicholson. As if she could handle the truth. I reached for my drink and took a large mouthful. 'It was Stefanie, this morning.'

She watched me put the glass back down. 'And *why* did Stefanie dig her nails into you?'

I sighed. The lady was not for turning. 'She wasn't so relaxed about having a GA after all.'

Storm raised an eyebrow. 'Which is why you shouldn't operate on anyone you know socially. They take advantage. You think she would have behaved like that with a stranger?' She sipped her drink again. 'You're sure that's what happened? Because you seemed a little off-colour this morning. Big night last night, was it?'

'Not especially. Just some drinks with the EM team.' I waited for her to ask…

'Did Julia go?'

Bingo. 'No.' I began to fiddle with a small bell on the cracker, undoing the knot and slowly deconstructing it so I could slide the contents out without detonating the snap.

'Why do you keep fidgeting? It's unnerving. Is there something you want to tell me?'

I stopped moving, seeing myself emerge from theatre after my third op, to find Giles Creasy and two more of the management team waiting. Giles had cleared his throat and almost stammered, 'Can we have a word, please Nathan?', like he was asking the teacher's permission to leave class and go for a wee. He'd gone through with it, though – told me the allegations, previewed what was going to happen, then formally suspended me.

'I had no idea the cameras were even there until Julia was in my office, photographing them.' I had put my hands on my head and closed my eyes. 'God, I wish I'd never met Julia Blythe!' My mouth had opened and the lies had automatically started to come out, but perhaps Hamish was right. I needed to protect myself.

Giles hesitated. 'Nonetheless, I think that—'

'It's OK, I know.' I patted his shoulder. 'You have to be seen to be acting, even when it's something as mad as this you've got to respond to. Can I just ask one small favour? Suspend me from practise – I'm off now for two weeks anyway – but could you possibly sit on doing anything more official in terms of announcements and kicking off investigations until after the Christmas break? I'd appreciate some time to explain to my wife and children why Julia has made up this vicious allegation about me – if you get my drift?'

I had looked at him wearily. 'You don't have to say it, Giles, never get romantically involved with a colleague, I know. No fool like an old fool, hey? You look at her and see this five-foot-two woman and you don't think someone like her could be a bully or a manipulator… I take it she's not shown you any footage from these so-called cameras?'

I watched him frown as he realised I was making a good point.

'The landlord has already removed them, by the way. I suspect they were dummy ones left in situ by the last tenants. I'm not asking you to ignore Julia's lies, just give me a moment to get my house in order personally. That's all.'

It had been enough to buy myself some time, but now what? What was I going to *do*?

'Nathan?' My wife's voice brought me back to the dining room. 'I said, you're sure there's nothing you want to tell me?'

'Nothing at all,' I lied.

'Are we about ready to order?' Hamish cut in from the opposite side of the table, looking up and down the gathered guests, his arm casually slung round the back of Cecily's chair as she sat alongside him comfortably. She was wearing the same black velvet dress and necklace as this time last year, and her hair was jammed back by a silver Alice band; although like a stopped clock, that was fashionable for once. She had at least bothered to change out of her jodhpurs and usual loose T-shirt. She has an ample bosom and rarely bothers with a bra – it must drive poor Ham nuts as she strides around their stud farm, swinging about the place. He often jokes he only gets attention if he wears a nose bag.

'Anyone need a little extra time? Nate? Still making your mind up?' He looked at me teasingly, and I shot him a brief deadpan look. 'I'm going steak and salad, of course,' he joked, moving on, wisely.

I could have made a crack about him liking it blue, but I didn't, mostly because I couldn't be bothered, but in any case, Sam got there first.

'Salad?' He snorted rudely, leant around his mother and poked his stepfather hard in the gut, adding in his deeply annoying mockney accent: 'That's ninety per cent pure lard, that. Not much point!'

Hamish tried to chuckle. Cecily rolled her eyes and said, 'Samsy!', but didn't follow it up, so, delighted, he simply slouched back, chair pushed away from the table, legs wide, hands on the back of his head, maintaining the confident pose as a pretty waitress arrived. I watched him swallow as she smiled down at him.

'Do your flies up, there's a good chap,' I remarked loudly. 'No one wants little Samsy to make an appearance.' I'd noticed he was flying low when we'd all sat down and hadn't wanted to embarrass him. I saw no need not to after the salad remark.

He jack-knifed immediately and we all laughed – the waitress included – as he flushed an unbecoming purple that clashed horribly with his strawberry-blond hair. Zipping himself up, he fled the table. I felt momentarily lifted and winked at Hamish, who grinned gratefully back.

I'd been looking forward to this evening, a regular fixture on our calendar: the last Friday night before Christmas was always spent at Hamish's sister's hotel in Lyme Regis for a black-tie meal. I had long been flattered to be included as an honorary Wilson – not least because it was always paid for and Fowles was one of my favourite places. But tonight, I just wasn't feeling it. My cheap triumph over Sam deflated, I was too out of sorts to enjoy myself. Not surprising really, given the day I'd had: Stef's op, followed by suspension, all topped off with the shitshow outside school. Julia's husband really was little more than a walking jockstrap. That said, her behaviour had been preposterous.

I glanced at the back of my hand again; no better than a little cat, hissing and spitting all over the place. *I* was the one who'd been suspended. I snatched the menu up and scanned it. Nothing leapt out at me except the elaborate *Fowles* at the top of it, in rather beautiful new calligraphy. Very ornate. I traced the sweeping F and O with my eyes, then onto the W – a bell rang in my mind, reminding me of the implants I'd marked yesterday, as well as Stefanie's this morning.

'You'll look after me, won't you, Nate?' She'd squeezed my hand tightly before the anaesthetist had arrived. 'You're still happy to do this? You look a bit – distracted.'

I'd glanced down at her, lying on the gurney. 'I'm absolutely fine. You trust me, don't you?'

'Always,' she had whispered.

I needed to end it for good this time and not just for Christmas – or Julia. I was fond of Stef and she was a fabulous fuck, almost unhinged if caught in the right mood, but she'd had her money's worth. I'd taken good care of her.

Very good, in fact. I'd been slightly obsessed with making sure the batch of implants we were using were up to scratch. Despite feeling rough as God's dog, I'd gone in bright and early to check the ones I was going to put into Stef; opening the packet carefully once alone in the supplies area – I didn't want the staff thinking I was losing my marbles – tipping the implants in the sterile liquid, watching them bulge like blancmange. Was it a trick of the light? Had I become so terrified of making mistakes I was now seeing things, because I was certain one of them was flatter, just like the ones of the previous day. I'd grabbed a surgical pen and marked Stef's with an 'F' to denote the flat side before covering it back up and placing it in a location I'd be able to find with ease during the operation.

When the crucial moment had arrived during the surgery, I had paused and pretended to look at the pack Sandra had brought out. 'Those are the wrong cc.'

She frowned. 'Really? I don't think so, I—'

'It's fine, don't worry. I'll get the right ones.' I had picked up the pack I didn't want to use, took it back and collected my pre-prepared one. I 'opened' it en route, so she was none the wiser that I'd already been in it, and pulled out the implant, making sure the 'F' was on the underside and out of sight before quickly inserting it.

'There we are! Job done.' It wasn't standard procedure, but I wasn't having Stefanie complaining afterwards that she felt asymmetrical, shape wise.

'F'. I scanned the menu again. F for flat and Fowles... Ha! And 'O' for orientation, 'W' for wall... I glanced up to see Ben returning from the loo, grumpy little sod. What was it with these boys? Sam cheeking Hamish. Ben with a face like a slapped arse. I watched my son pass through the busy, fairy-lit room, tables full of families and friends, laughter and excitement. What did he have to be petulant about? Anticipation of Christmas is the best bit – two weeks and this whole hotel would be cold and dark. Hamish's sister took the sting out of having a family run hotel that stayed open right throughout Christmas, by closing it completely for January and sodding off to Barbados – but Ben wasn't feeling the festive spirit at all. I wondered briefly if it was due to the school unpleasantness. Alex had looked upset too when we'd all parted. I wondered if Julia was even considering the chaos she'd caused? Or did she have other, more important things on her mind than ruining lives?

Ben arrived back at the table and slumped down, flopping back in his chair.

I leant over and said in a pleasant but firm voice, 'Sit up properly, please.'

He wrinkled his nose and waved his hand. 'Can you not get so close? You smell of whisky.'

'Just do as you're told and sit up.'

'I don't see why I even had to come to this.' He lurched up to a sitting position, jogging his cutlery with his elbow.

'Because it's a family thing, that's why.' I straightened his fork for him.

'Not *my* family. Or yours – no matter how hard you try.'

I glared at him – his finger pushing right into the bruise as only your children are capable of – but managed not to take the bait, contemplating instead how much simpler my life would now be if I didn't have Ben. At the very least, I'd quite like someone to take him away every now and then to give us a break from the mood swings. I might even miss him.

And just like that an idea shot into my head.

A *brilliant* idea.

*

After dinner, Hamish and I popped into the freezing hotel garden to have a cigar and a cigarette. We walked across the frosted lawn to the end of the grass and sat down on a hard bench overlooking the peaceful, moonlit bay. Puffing reflectively, we stared at the dark water stretching out beneath us, the noise of revelry drifting down from the hotel. It was so cold, it almost hurt to breathe the sharpness of the air drifting off the calm sea.

'Beautiful, isn't it?' Hamish gestured at the water.

'Very.'

'Thanks for inside – cutting Sam down.' He sucked hard on his cigar. 'He's a little sod.'

'All of them are, Ham. They don't know they're born.' I blew several smoke rings. 'It's not their fault, I suppose.'

He grunted. 'Not sure I agree with that, but anyway… as of today you're suspended?'

'Yes.'

'Anyone else know?'

I leant forward and squinted at a tiny boat, no bigger than my fingernail, quietly coming into the harbour. 'Just you at the moment.'

Hamish sighed. 'Even I didn't think Julia would go this far. She has proven – unexpected.'

I laughed. I couldn't help it. 'Yes, she has, but I've had an idea.'

'Oh?' Hamish pulled on his cigar again. 'Go on.'

I jumped up eagerly. 'When something terrible happens, what is the first thing people say? *It puts everything else into perspective.* That's what I need to do for Julia; help her understand that this filming allegation just isn't important. If her son were to go missing, she'd realise that, I think. And then, if he were to return, if *I* found him, I'd be her hero.'

Hamish scratched his head. 'You want to abduct her son?'

'No!' I held up a hand. 'I'm not going to do anything illegal. I'm going to *persuade* him to go missing. At the very least, I think my bringing him back will make her reconsider her allegations.'

'Right.' Hamish exhaled a cloud of smoke. 'When did you come up with this plan, might I ask?'

'Just now!' I said happily.

His eyebrow flickered. 'Well, while your motivation is clear enough, I'm not sure you've thought it through. If her son were to disappear, I can see someone like her would go completely over the top with panic; police, the works.' He crossed his leg thoughtfully. 'If said son turned up safe and sound again, it would certainly make her look prone to drama, exaggeration and crying wolf. It would nicely reinforce the story behind the beach picture and it would certainly make Julia vulnerable. Even better if she told the police *you* were responsible for the little bugger going missing, only for him to pop back up like a nice shiny button.' He laughed, adding with relish. 'Enough rope to hang herself with. She'd look cuckoo.' He wrapped his mouth around his cigar again. 'But just so we're clear, you're not actually going to do this? You can't – you do know that?'

I sat back down on the cold bench. 'I've got to do something. I can't just let it all happen. I'm frightened.'

'We've already got the picture of the two of you. That's all we need. You just relax.' He looked over his shoulder and lowered his voice. 'The knife I saw you drawing on Michelle…'

'Drawing on *myself*,' I corrected him quickly.

He held up a hand. 'All I wanted to ask was, you did clean it thoroughly afterwards?'

'Yes, of course.'

'Good man.' He patted my shoulder. 'Well, like I said. Don't panic and I'd sleep on everything, if I were you, but I suppose I'll stand by to hear more…'

'You do that.' I finished my fag and flicked the end over the hedge in front of us. I felt calmer already for having a plan. I made my voice quieter. 'Thanks for getting Michelle home safely last night, by the way. No dramas?'

'None,' he said. 'She was fine. Bit green round the gills today but that's all. Turns out she lives with a long-term boyfriend, so I think you're safe there. He was away last night, hence why she had her party knickers on – then off. She's not going to want to rock the boat.'

'Well, that's something, at least.'

'Any port, Nate. Put it behind you and move on.'

I nodded and glanced back to see Storm standing in the doorway of the hotel watching us. 'Time to go in.'

I started to walk up the garden, feeling suddenly more confident, hands in my jacket pockets. Storm was looking very attractive, I realised. A new dress: some russet affair, like the mass of my tenners it probably cost, clinging to her body.

'Tell me again, for the millionth time, what is the point of social smoking?' She crossed her arms as I approached. 'You're not addicted to the nicotine. You don't need to do it.'

I hesitated, before moving right up next to her, snaking an arm round her waist, pulling her tightly to me and placing the chill of my lips against the warmth of her neck. 'It makes me feel *dangerous*,' I whispered.

'Nathan!' she exclaimed, half admonishing, half laughing.

'In my head, I'm James Bond and not a sad, mediocre, middle-aged doctor with a wife far smarter and talented than I'll ever be.'

She turned her head away, but I felt her tremble as I gently kissed her throat. I reached out and took her hand, twisting her wedding ring up so I could see my initials branded on her skin.

'You do it because you know it makes you look ridiculously glamorous.'

'That too,' I admitted. 'I am – as you know – exceptionally shallow.'

'Not true. Quite often I think I don't know you at all. I've not even come close to the real you.' She wasn't smiling anymore.

I sighed and released her. As ever with Storm, all possibility and promise coming to nothing. But I didn't care. I briefly touched my fingers to my lips, blowing her the smallest of kisses before leaving her to her disappointment in me and making my way back into the room in search of Ben. I wanted to talk to him about how we might get Alex on his own.

CHAPTER THIRTY

Julia

'You don't know Dad's different this time. Anyone can make promises then break them. He only has power over me if I let him.'

I frowned. 'What? Where have you heard?—'

'I don't want to see him!' Al insisted.

'But Dad's come all this way!'

He shrugged. 'I didn't ask him to. I'm not going to come down and talk to him and you can't make me.'

*

'He's right. You can't, and I wouldn't want you to.' Dom's hands were wrapped round a mug of tea as we sat quietly at the kitchen table. All I could hear was my grandmother's cuckoo clock ticking on the wall. I'd finally got around to hanging it.

'I'm sorry,' I said. 'I'm sure it won't be like this forever.'

Dom smiled sadly. His face had lost all its puffiness and his clean-shaven skin and neatly cut hair looked better than it had in a long time. He reminded me of a baby bird, fresh out of the egg.

'It's just going to take time before Al trusts me again. I have to earn it – it's cool.' He shot me a look. 'Jules, I'm so sorry about sitting outside the house and speaking to the neighbours, and all that nasty shit I said to Ewan about you cheating on him, last time I was here.'

'Thank you. New start now.' I took a mouthful of tea.

'Sounds good to me.' He reached into his pocket and pulled out a small box. 'Will you give Al this? The iPad wasn't a hit, so I thought I'd go a bit more traditional. Have a look, tell me if you think he'll like it?'

I snapped it open to find a very beautiful, elegant man's watch – sitting on blue velvet cushion, the second-hand ticking round.

'It was Dad's; he used to wear it every day. I don't know if you remember? Anyway, he left it to me and I want Al to have it. I want him to know, all the time I've got now is his. Just like Dad did for me.'

'That's a very lovely gesture.' I thought of my former father-in-law, one of the world's last true gentlemen. 'I'll explain all of that to Alex.' I closed the box gently.

He drained his tea. 'I better go.'

'You're going to go straight back to London?'

He nodded, and I winced.

'Don't – it's not your fault, or his.' He stood up and swung on his new coat. A grown-up overcoat.

We walked down the hall in silence. He turned at the front door and briefly kissed my cheek. 'Have a lovely Christmas and here's to a happy new year for all of us. Tell Al I love him.'

Once I'd shut the front door, I leant my forehead on it, closing my eyes for a moment.

'Mum?'

I looked up to see Alex peering through the bannisters, in the hall upstairs, like a little boy again. 'Has he gone?' he asked in a small voice.

'Yes,' I held out the gift. 'He wanted you to have this. It used to be—'

'I heard.' Al came down quickly, grabbed the box and disappeared back into his room with it, closing the door behind him.

*

We spent Christmas itself travelling around: Ewan's parents for the big day and Boxing Day, then Ewan flew to Norway with Cass to Lise's family, while I went to my cousin's with Alex. I suggested meeting Sorcha and Dom in London as an alternative to Alex going to stay with them, but Alex flatly refused. We had the sum total of two evenings and a day back at home in Devon, reunited with Cass and Ewan, although the kids spent it at a friend's whose parents had been mad enough to say they could do an open house, before then driving to Wales to spend New Year with Ewan's brother, wife and children. It was fun and worth the effort, but we were all pretty tired and grumpy when we arrived home on Thursday, the third of January, immediately splintering off to do our own thing.

Ewan dropped Cass off at a friend's then went for a swim, while Alex immediately jammed on his headphones and got stuck into *Fortnite*. I attacked the unpacking and sorting out. I was *very* glad to have stipulated a full two-week break over Christmas before starting my contract. I needed a couple of catch-up days to get organised.

Friday morning saw me busily loading dirty school uniforms into the machine, when both kids appeared in the doorway, coats on. Alex had a bulging rucksack over his shoulder and Cass was carrying a bag.

'We're going to get the train into Exmouth,' Cass explained. 'I'm meeting some of the girls from school for a hot chocolate.'

'And I'm going to take some photos and do some sketching.' Alex held up the camera Ewan and I had bought him for Christmas.

'Great idea!' I said enthusiastically, straightening up. I was delighted to hear I wasn't going to face a second day of hauling

Alex off *Fortnite* and that he voluntarily wanted to leave the house. 'Are you going to travel back together too?'

'Probably not,' Cass said. 'Al might want to come back earlier than me, or the other way round, but we've got our phones so we can check?'

'Sounds sensible,' I agreed. 'Do you need some money? There are two £10 notes in my purse, so you can buy yourselves lunch. And take hats, won't you?'

'Don't worry, I've got everything,' Al said earnestly. 'I'm taking boots, waterproof trousers – just in case the weather changes. But it's meant to be fine until later this evening. I checked.'

'Well done,' I agreed. 'You've got drinks too? And your phones are charged up?'

'Yes,' Cass sighed. 'It's only Exmouth.'

'Well, have fun. What do you fancy for tea later – anything in particular?'

Alex shrugged. 'Sausages maybe? I don't know.'

'I'll see what I can do. Don't go further than Exmouth Beach, Al.' I blew them both a kiss, turned away and reached for the washing powder. I don't know if they blew me a kiss back. I wasn't looking properly, but once I'd switched the machine on, wiped my hands on my jeans and turned back again, ready to start the next job, they'd gone.

CHAPTER THIRTY-ONE

Nathan

'OK, Ben, I'm going to trim the engines up and slightly beach the bow,' I instructed. 'Get ready to help pull him on if need be.'

Ben moved obediently to the front of the boat. The sea state was calm, just as if I had ordered it: perfect conditions. I edged closer still and held it steady as Alex splashed towards us in his wellies and threw his bag into Ben's open arms. Ben stowed it in one of the crates under the seat before turning to help haul Alex on. Predictably, the poor kid was useless – grippy hands and lanky legs as Ben landed him, immediately trying to clamber to his feet and slipping all over the place, shivering like mad.

'Hello again!' I grinned. 'Welcome aboard and well done!'

Alex rolled up his sleeve and proudly looked at some old-man watch he was wearing, tapping the glass. 'Exactly the agreed time!' he said happily, still trembling – although perhaps because he was excited. 'It's all going to plan!'

'Certainly is!' I agreed. 'Now, time you two got out of sight – leave your bag there with ours, Alex.'

They did as they were told, Alex nearly banging his head on the doorway to the cockpit as he climbed in. 'Better take your glasses off,' I said. 'Don't want them getting scratched. Is the case in your bag?'

He nodded, blinking like a baby owl as he removed them.

'I'll sort it.' I held out a hand and took them from him. 'OK, chaps, we need to make a move now and it's going to get *cold*.' I put the glasses away carefully and rested his bag on the seat next to me. 'So I'm going to shut the cockpit door for a moment or two, OK?'

Once I'd closed them in and I was sure they couldn't see me, I gave it some speed and as we began to bounce over the waves, I chucked Alex's bag overboard. Glancing back, I saw it floating in the wash, but it would submerge before long. Goodbye mobile phone. Phase one complete.

The door opened again and Ben reappeared. 'He says he feels sick.'

I rolled my eyes. 'Get him a bag. Inside my rucksack.'

Ben moved over to the crate and noticed immediately that Alex's bag was missing. 'Dad, we've lost his stuff!'

'Oh no! We haven't?' I pretended to be shocked. 'How on earth did that happen?'

'I don't know because our things are still here?' Ben said slowly.

I shrugged. 'Never mind. By the way, Ben, your phone is definitely off?'

He nodded. 'But I was thinking. Won't they be able to trace us anyway?'

I shook my head. 'Nope. I've turned the AIS off. We are invisible!' I started to go faster, and Ben's eyes began to water in the wind as the coastline flew past on our left. 'Get back inside with that bag!' I shouted above the motor. 'I don't want him redecorating the cockpit.'

Ben re-emerged twenty minutes later. 'He's still feeling rough. Can we let him come out here for a moment?'

'Only if you go inside first, so in case anyone *did* somehow get an image of us, it will look like there are only the two of us on board.'

Ben disappeared, and moments later a decidedly pale and wobbly Alex emerged.

I patted the seat next to me. 'Come and have a go at the wheel!'

He managed to stay upright, and once he was alongside me, I pointed at the horizon line. 'Fix your eyes on that,' I called above the rush of wind. 'You won't be able to stay out too long though, you'll freeze without the proper gear.'

He squinted ahead – blind as a bat. No wonder the poor sod was having a rough time at school. He was just the sort of boy one could imagine having 'kick me' stuck to his back.

'Want to helm for a moment?' I offered, but he shook his head nervously.

'My tummy feels a bit squiggly. I'll just stand still if that's OK?'

His tummy was a 'bit squiggly'? I could just hear Julia using a phrase like that. She really wasn't giving him a chance.

'Ready to transform into the local hero?' I shouted, and his face broke into a nervous smile. 'People are going to think you're so brave!' I continued. 'Abducted, kept in a secret location – only to escape unscathed! Everyone is going to think you're *amazing*. People at school are going to want to be your friend for sure.'

'You'll come back to let me out tomorrow night, though?' His voice was just audible. 'And then I have to walk *some* of the way back to Exeter – so it looks like I escaped on my own? I'll be back by Sunday morning?'

'Exactly! We won't forget about you, and you'll have enough food and drink to keep you going. It'll look better if you're missing for two nights though – more realistic, and impressive. People are going to want to interview you and everything! You might even be famous by the end of it!'

He bit his lip, shy and excited. 'My mum will be so proud of me. She's always really brave; I'd like her to feel that about me too. Thank you for helping me do this!'

'Hey – I'm just a lift. It was your idea, really – you're doing all of the hard work.' I patted his back. 'You should go and swap with Ben now you've got a bit of colour in your cheeks. I don't want you getting too cold out here.'

He gave me a double thumbs up – so innocent and uncool, bless him – and once he'd disappeared, Ben came back out.

'Alex looks better, Dad?'

I nodded. 'He'll be fine.'

'But I still don't get it.' Ben came to stand alongside me. 'What's in it for him being rescued by me?'

I cleared my throat. 'He's just very easy to please. Let him do it if he wants to, because the BEST way to get Cassia's attention is to rescue her brother. She's going to love you forever!'

In spite of the chill, I saw him blush. 'We just leave him in the hotel, then I come back to get him tomorrow night?'

'Yup!'

'But how am I going to do that on my own? Will I?—'

'Don't worry about that now.' I cut him short. 'It's just logistics. I'll fill you in on that later. We've got to get him *into* the hotel first, without anyone seeing, before we worry about getting him out of it.' I looked at my watch.

Ben glanced up at the deepening sky. 'Are we going to get back into Exmouth before tea?'

'We might need to do a bit of the run in the dark, but not much.' We'd already passed clusters of holiday chalets and caravan parks, tucked-away houses with incredible views. Stretches of empty shingle beaches broken by jutting red cliffs, waves crashing at their foot, became smaller, secret inaccessible bays cast in deep shadow as we roared past.

'Just go and check on Alex again, will you? Tell him not long now. Not long at all.' I smiled.

*

Alex did well not to vomit, holding on to it the whole way and only turning properly grey when it got a bit lively as we moored up on the outside of the harbour wall.

'You're almost on dry land now,' I whispered as I helped him out of the cockpit once Ben was safely tucked out of view. I led him towards the back of the boat, and he paled slightly on spying the ladder attached to the green, slimy stonework while we bobbed up and down.

'I've got to climb that?' We both looked up it, leading to the top of the Cobb as the waves slapped against the side of the RIB.

'You'll be fine.'

He hesitated and tried to keep his balance as the boat lurched suddenly.

'Once you've got your first foot on, you'll have no problems. It's just we need to get up into town without the harbour master seeing us on the CCTV in their office, or us popping up on the webcam they've got on that pile of rocks over there.' I pointed to our right. 'That's why we've come in *behind* the harbour wall, rather than going inside it, which is why I'm afraid it also means no steps, just this ladder. When we get to the top, we're going to nip behind the buildings at the back here, then hug the wall of the Cobb – that's the one dodgy bit on view and only about fifty metres. Just keep your hood up and your face down – until we make it to the park where all the boats are stored. There are no cameras from there, so we can walk straight up the Cobb road. Any questions?'

'Yes. What's a Cobb?'

'Ah, sorry!' I grinned. 'That's just the name for the man-made wall we're going to walk along – it juts out into the sea like a sort of brick pier. It's a famous feature of the town we're in, which is called Lyme Regis.'

'Oh!' Alex said immediately. 'I've been here! I bought a fossil. Also, can I have my bag and glasses?' He smiled anxiously.

'Bit of bad news about that. We lost them at sea. But hold on to my hand if you need to.'

'Oh. OK.' Alex tried to smile again.

'You really don't need them!' I assured him. 'We've got this. Brave, remember? You're going to be a hero! Just stay there for one minute…'

I ducked into the cockpit where Ben was huddled under a blanket and wriggled out of my oilskins, grabbing my coat instead.

'Well done, pal.' I winked at him. 'Keep warm and out of sight. I'll be back within twenty minutes.'

*

I got Alex safely up the ladder, despite his welly slipping on one of the rungs, at which he let out an audible squeal. I gritted my teeth though, and soon we were behind the buildings.

'Remember, head down,' I instructed. If anyone saw us, or someone asked to look at the CCTV footage at a later date, they would see two figures – a father and son. They wouldn't be able to identify Alex without a clear look at his face.

I pulled his sleeve gently, and we disappeared through the gap in the wall into the deserted boatyard. The wind was picking up a touch and I glanced at the sky worriedly. I didn't want a choppy ride back. Some loose tarp covers on the stored boats were flapping and gusting in the wind as we ducked between them, thwacking down on the decks before lifting again, accompanied by the clanking and swaying of ropes attached to masts. Alex was a little on edge at the unfamiliar noises, but I found them comforting.

Before long we were on the pavement. Of a late afternoon in summer, this part of town would be packed with tourists licking ice creams, children riding bikes, dogs pulling on leads and seagulls ready to swoop and steal battered fish from open papers. Today, the chippy was closed, the amusements shop shut – completely devoid of its displays of buckets and spades, fishing nets, hats, and stands of cheap sunglasses. The fresh fish shack was boarded up, and the random clothes shop Storm always liked to poke around had a sign hanging in the window saying it was shut for January. The forlorn seafront was empty, apart from a few dedicated dog walkers further on. Perfect.

'Come on.' I drew Alex closer to me as I pulled my slipping bag back up onto my shoulder. 'Head down. We're going up this steep hill now.'

Alex started to puff as we climbed. We trudged past some holiday homes and the empty car park on our left, until we hit the T-junction with the back road, heading out of town towards Sidmouth. We turned right, however, and dropped down the street about a hundred yards.

'Here we are!' I said cheerfully, my heart lifting at the familiar sight of the hotel.

Alex glanced at the board. 'Fowles… It says it's closed for January.'

'That's right,' I agreed. 'There's no one here, but I've got a key to the staff entrance.' I reached into my pocket. 'Come on, round the back we go!'

I let us in through the commercial kitchen, still smelling faintly of bleach. Hamish's sister had obviously had a deep clean before packing up shop. We pushed through the swing door into the main function room in which we'd sat for our pre-Christmas dinner, when I'd first had my idea, just two weeks earlier. The lights were off, the tables and chairs all stacked at one end of the room, the trees taken down. It was also cold and Alex shivered.

'Don't worry, we're not stopping here.'

Our footsteps echoed as we walked on through to the deserted reception. I reached behind the desk and picked a bedroom key at random. 'Let's go with lucky number 7.'

Alex was looking around curiously, sticking his head into the silent and still drawing room – the blinds all pulled, fire neatly laid.

He creaked across the wooden floor of reception and peered into the bar area with its six tables, leading into the main restaurant. 'Where is everybody?'

'On holiday. The lady who owns it won't be back for two weeks. She's the sister of my friend, and he comes and checks on it for her while she's away, but he won't be visiting until Tuesday next week, so no one will disturb you.'

'I'll be here completely on my own?' His eyes widened.

'Yes, but you'll just be staying in one room because otherwise people walking past will see lights on in the hotel. It might give us away and we don't want that. To impress everyone, you've got to make it look like you've escaped, haven't you?' I looked at my watch. 'Come on. Let's get you set up. Kick your wellies off for a moment.'

He did as he was told and followed me up the main staircase, padding quietly in sensibly thick socks. The light was starting to fade and the large landing was gloomy as I quickly pushed through the door to my right, towards room 7. It became darker still as we entered the narrow corridor and I began to fumble with the key.

'So no one is in any of these rooms at all?' Alex suddenly rattled the door handle opposite.

'Don't do that!' I said sharply, and he stepped back immediately.

'I'm very sorry, Mr Sloan.'

'No, no – *I'm* sorry. I didn't mean to startle you.' I noted how obedient and pliant he was. This was a child who simply wanted to please.

I finally got the door open and we stepped in to the immaculate room with a sea view, TV, and two twin beds. Perfect.

'This is nice!' Alex looked around him. 'I just stay in here and watch TV until you come back for me, I guess? Can I go downstairs and get food as long as I keep the lights off?'

'You're not sleeping in here, Alex. We're just going to get a couple of bits. Here, you take the duvet and the pillow.' I pulled them off the nearest bed and bundled them into his arms.

We headed back downstairs with me dragging a mattress and Alex carrying the bedding. At reception, I reached behind the desk and felt for the next key I needed.

'Where *am* I going to sleep then?' Alex glanced through the window in the small office behind the desk and, paling, noticed the folly in the gardens, stood between several forlorn bare trees. 'Not in that tower?'

'No!' I scoffed. 'Of course not – you'd freeze for one.'

'Phew,' he shivered. 'It's a bit – creepy.'

'Don't worry, you'll be very cosily tucked up.' I found the key I was after and stuffed it in my pocket. 'This way. Don't forget to grab your boots again.' I nodded at them. I wasn't going to screw this up for the sake of a ten second lapse of concentration.

I pushed through a door to my left, holding it open with my foot and started to drag the mattress. Alex held it as I opened another, then finally we reached a locked third.

'Oh wow!' Alex exclaimed, having followed me through and seen the sign above the doorway. 'Hidden cinema?'

I nodded and winked at him. 'Welcome to your home for the next almost two nights! Check *this* out...'

I unlocked the door and fumbled around for a switch. It lit up the small foyer, containing a mini fridge full of ice creams, cans of drink and bottles of water. To the left of that, was a candy-striped stand stacked with tubs of old-fashioned sweets and a red popcorn machine complete with trolley, albeit switched off, empty and clean.

Alex pushed past the mattress in amazement and tapped on the fridge glass. 'Can I eat these?'

'Yes, you can... while you're watching... a movie!' I pushed open another door behind me and flicked the switches. The twenty-four-seat cinema lit up, the white spotlights in the ceiling revealing the soft leather chairs and royal blue velvet walls, carpet and pulled-back curtains either side of the blank screen. I hauled the mattress in and plopped it down in front of the seats. Alex stood in the doorway and gasped.

'I know. You're going to have the best time *ever*,' I agreed. The last time I was in here, I had a cute blonde straddling me while I sat in the back row and a not-so-family-friendly movie played. But that was then. This was now. 'There are loads of films back there.' I pointed up at the small projection room. 'And just here,' I squeezed past him back into the foyer and opened another door, 'there's a loo and sink. You've got everything you need. It's all completely soundproofed; there are no windows. No one is going to know you're here at all.'

I beamed at him and took the bag from my shoulder. It was starting to dig in. Placing it down on the ground, I pulled out a bag of foodstuffs, the tape and my knife.

'Best way to think of the next couple of days is just that you're playing a game,' I continued conversationally. 'Which I know you're really good at. That time you explained *Fortnite* to me at the rugby weekend was the first time I properly understood how it worked! You're a really good teacher and this is *such* a clever idea of yours.' I shook my head as if I couldn't articulate how impressed I was.

'You were the one that thought of coming here.'

'It was a team effort.' I smiled. 'But honestly, I had no idea you were this smart. Everyone at school is going to be *amazed* by you once you've escaped. You're going to be super popular.' I held the tape aloft cheerfully and sat down on the mattress. 'Shall I do your wrists or legs first?'

*

I hung the key to the cinema on the hook at reception and hurried back through the kitchen, mentally checking my list. I'd removed the hotel phone from the projection room. He had food, water, bedding, a loo. He'd also calmed down and stopped crying at being locked in and taped up. A child as old as thirteen will hardly be left with abandonment issues from an experience lasting just a few days. He was going to be fine. I'd been firmer than I'd thought I was going to have to be when I brought the tape out and he almost changed his mind, but I really didn't want him wandering around and fiddling with things in my absence. He would be far safer if his movement was restricted.

I marched back down the hill towards the harbour. It had rained while I was in the hotel – the ground was wet. The weather was turning slightly ahead of the forecast; we *really* needed to get going. I glanced critically at the sea. No white horses, but nonetheless, I wasn't up for a dangerous night ride back with Ben. That said, a little bit of light rain would have clouded over the CCTV trained on the Cobb wall nicely. When I'd watched a live stream of the harbour in the peace of my office, to see what I was dealing with, it had been apparent immediately that the slightest bit of rain or spray rendered the images so blurry it would be almost impossible to pick out anyone's identity with confidence. One could barely make out the fishing boats, never mind faces.

Back on the flat, I ducked through the boatyard, hugged the wall again and was climbing down the ladder onto the RIB within mere moments. I slung my bag down triumphantly. We'd done it. Glancing across to my left, I could just see the back of Fowles through the trees. Alex was in there right now. I looked away and opened the cockpit to see Ben huddled in the corner, wide-eyed with fear.

'It IS you.' He breathed out. 'I wasn't sure.'

'Of course it's me!' I reached past him for my oilskin. 'Saddle up, we're going home.'

'Alex is in the hotel then?' Ben moved forward to the edge of the cushions. 'Is he OK?'

'He's fine!' I pulled a 'why wouldn't he be?' face. 'He's excited!'

'I don't understand though, Dad, he kept saying on the way over that he was going to be a hero. How can he be if I'm rescuing him? I don't get it.'

'Forget what Alex says!' I skirted around my having played them off against each other. 'He's got himself confused – he's not the sharpest knife in the drawer, is he? All you need to worry about is Cassia thinking you're amazing when you rescue her brother.'

Ben hesitated. 'Alex *is* clever actually – he's just not practical.'

'He'll be fine.'

'But Dad, when we were at Oscar's party the other day, before you came to get me and talked to Alex, he was making some toast – which is weird anyway at someone else's house in the middle of the afternoon – and it got stuck. He set off the smoke alarm and was going to put a knife inside the toaster to get it out, only Cass stopped him.' He bit his lip worriedly.

Thank God I *had* taped him up. 'He'll be fine,' I repeated. 'All he's got to do is eat and watch movies.' I stepped back out of the cockpit. 'We, on the other hand, really will be in trouble if we don't go *now*. Get your gear on and come and push us off. It's high time we were away from here.'

'We're coming back for him tomorrow night, though?'

'Absolutely,' I said smoothly. 'Tomorrow – for sure.'

CHAPTER THIRTY-TWO

Julia

'I wasn't worried at all. He seemed his normal self when he left.' My phone lights up. 'It's Dom!' I snatch it up. 'Where have you been? I've been trying and trying to reach you!'

'I'm on my way back to Mum's.' He sounds bewildered. 'It's my aftercare day and we're not allowed mobiles. I went for a meal in Oxford with two of the other blokes when we were done. I've just switched the phone on and there are all of these messages from you and Mum saying to call? What's happened?'

'Alex is missing. He went into Exmouth this morning and he hasn't come back. You haven't heard from him? Or seen him?'

'No. I'm not in his good books, remember?'

'Can you ring me immediately if he does contact you?'

'Of course. Does he?—'

'I've got to go,' I cut across him. 'The police are here.'

'At your house?' His voice sharpens with fear. 'Hang on, so he went into Exeter this morning—'

'Exmouth,' I correct. 'I'll call you right back, OK? I need to finish talking to them first… sorry about that.'

I return to the two uniformed officers still looking around Alex's bedroom, carefully picking their way over discarded bits of Lego from his brand-new Millennium Falcon – barely started – on the carpet. 'My ex hasn't heard from Alex or seen him.' I try not to look at the empty bed. 'Sorcha was right: Dominic has been on his rehab aftercare programme in Oxford all day.'

'I'm really sorry, but I have to mention this,' Ewan says. 'Alex's father has made a few unscheduled visits to the house since we've been here. On one occasion, he bought giant stuffed toys as presents for the kids in huge, oversized black bags – big enough to fit a person in.'

I stare at my husband.

'I'm just reporting facts. You said at the beginning,' Ewan addresses the officers, 'whatever we think of, however odd it might seem, we should say it. Dominic was unhappy about us bringing Alex down here from the start.'

'That's true, but I do think his behaviour then was erratic by the nature of his addiction. Things are different now. Alex's passport is still here,' I remind them, 'and I don't believe Dominic would hurt him. Plus, he's just told me he's been hundreds of miles away all day. That's pretty conclusive.'

One of the officers opens the drawer in Alex's bedside table, and Ewan sighs tersely. 'He's hardly in there, is he?'

The policeman shuts the drawer again. 'I understand that you're worried, Mr Wilder, and want us to get out there and find him as soon as we can, but this is all part of building an overall picture. Have you got a loft space? This seems quite an old house, so does it have a cellar area too? We'll do in here first, though.'

'Are you going to want to look in my daughter's room again, or can she go to sleep now? In fact, can I leave you to it so that I can go and sit with Cass again for a bit?' Ewan looks at me.

I nod, and he disappears. 'I'm sorry about my husband,' I apologise. 'He's just very frightened, that's all.'

'Could I ask you for some recent images of Alex?' the female officer says. 'Two or three would be ideal. Ones that show him as close to how he looked this morning. I'd also like to have your permission to take his toothbrush, if that's OK?'

'For a DNA profile?' I am lightheaded with fear.

'The vast majority of items we collect in searches never see the inside of a forensics lab,' she replies gently. 'It's a precaution, that's all.'

*

Once the police have left, Ewan calls me into Cass's bedroom. She's sitting up in bed, tear-stained and pale, twisting a tissue into a spike between her fingers. She starts to cry again as I come into the room. 'I'm really sorry, Julia! You *told* me to stay away from Ben and I didn't. If I'd gone with Alex when he left the marina and not stayed behind with Ben, I would have seen where he went! This is all my fault!'

'It's not at all, Cass.'

'I did go looking for Al when Ben's dad turned up and told me you wouldn't want me on the boat with him and Ben, but I couldn't find Al anywhere by then.'

'This really isn't your fault,' I say truthfully. 'And you gave such a helpful description of what Al was wearing to the police. You've done brilliantly, don't worry.' I move to the door. 'I've got to go and phone Dominic now, but Dad will stay with you and I'll come and say goodnight in a minute.' I give her a reassuring smile and hasten off downstairs.

In the quiet kitchen, I open the back door for a moment and stare into the dark. It's raining. Just as Al predicted yesterday, the weather has turned and the temperature has dropped significantly. Shivering on the threshold, I glance at my screen – now full of messages from a vast number of people 'hoping everything is OK?' wanting to know what's happened and asking if there's anything they can do to help, in response to the Facebook status – requesting people contact me if they've seen or heard from Alex – that I posted earlier. Friends I haven't spoken to in months, school mums from this and the last school, former colleagues whom I'm pretty sure weren't speaking to me when I left, current colleagues – they are all suddenly there; pings going off in my pocket when I most want my phone clear for Alex himself. I didn't think it through; I just panicked, but no one has seen or heard from him.

I take a deep breath and phone Dom. He picks up instantly.

'The police have gone.' I don't bother with hello. 'They've said they're going to keep in touch throughout the night. Partly because he's never done anything like this before, and his age, where he was when he went missing and the weather turning, they're treating him as a high-risk case—'

Dom swears.

'…so it's search dogs, helicopters, the coastguard – everything.'

'Shit!' he says over and over again. 'Oh shit! They'll want to speak to me then. They're going to think I've got something to do with this.'

'Promise me you haven't?' I can't stop myself.

'Of *course* not! You know how much I love him? Anyway… I can prove where I was, so don't worry.' He sounds confused. 'Um – I'm sorry. That's really knocked me, you asking that.' He clears his throat. 'Can I come up? I want to be there to help. To look for him.'

'Maybe don't drive right now. You're upset – I don't want you rushing and crashing. Why don't you leave first thing tomorrow, if we still haven't heard anything?' *But that's not going to happen; Alex is going to come home. He has to.*

'Jules, I've done some stupid shit in the past, but I promise you – not this. Never *this*. Stay strong. He'll be OK. He's a tough kid.'

But he's not! He's a trusting, naïve, innocent boy, barely mentally more than ten years old, in a gangly, thirteen-year-old body, out there somewhere in the dark, frightened and needing me. 'I've got to go. I'll call you if there's news.'

I hang up and swing round as I hear a cough behind me. Ewan steps forward. 'I had to say something about Dominic. You understand that, don't you?'

'Body bags, though?' I reach for a tissue and wipe my nose. 'Really?'

'Yes. Really. I don't have the same historical bias that you have towards Dominic – through no fault of your own,' he adds quickly as my mouth falls open. 'I'll be chuffed to bits when I'm proven wrong – at which point it won't matter that I said it anyway, will it?'

I don't answer, just move to the dresser and pick my car keys off the hook. 'I'm going out to look.'

'I'll go,' he says. 'You stay here and—'

'No!' I say instantly. 'I can't bear it, Ewan. I need to do *something*.'

'But you're frightened…' Ewan moves towards me desperately. 'You'll be no use to Alex if you take risks and get hurt.'

'I just want to drive around. That's all. I'll have my phone right next to me the whole time. You won't leave the house with Cass, will you? Or go to bed and lock the door?'

'Go to bed?' he says incredulously. 'Al's missing. How could I possibly sleep?'

*

I know exactly what he means. I'm driven by a mad energy that makes me examine the streets of Exmouth with a forensic intensity that has no regard for the fact that it's nearly half past ten and I ought to be tired. It's like a ghost town for a Friday night, but it's also January. No one with any sense is out tonight.

Eventually, I return to the front, pulling up by the beach, feeling sick to see the coastguard building all lit up. The boat is out there now, cutting through the waves, searching. I open my window and a light drizzle buffets into my face. My hair whips up on the chill wind as I shiver involuntarily – the stuffy warmth I've built up inside the car bleeding away. The front is deserted and I can just make out the sound of the waves against the backdrop of a distant hum moving closer… echoing across the empty space of the sea. A helicopter… combing the open water and coastline for my son. I should feel reassured. They are looking, people are helping us, but the reality begins to hit me as the noise grows louder and louder, the vibrations moving through my body until it roars right overhead, and I scream against the volume of the blades cutting through the air, bright lights flashing, the search light beaming down onto the dark water as it blasts past. For Alex? This is for *my Alex*?

The tears are streaming down my cheeks as it heads off in the direction of Sidmouth and the sound becomes a low-level burr again. I have covered my mouth with my hand and am shaking uncontrollably when headlights pull right up behind me, illuminating my wide, terrified eyes in the rear-view mirror.

I'm aware of someone getting out of the car and walking towards me. I hear the radio crackling and voices talking, before a face appears at the open window. The police end up escorting me home, and I am furious at my own selfishness. I've pulled a car from the search when it should be out there looking for him.

*

But I'm back, alongside the sea, at 7.30 a.m. It's still dark, I haven't slept and I told Ewan I wanted some air, but we both know I'm here to start looking again. Having parked up on Marine Drive, at the furthest end of Exmouth Beach, I march up the South West costal path, hands in pockets, one wrapped tightly around my mobile phone. I start to puff as the climb becomes steeper. The track levels out on top of the cliffs and I pass Orcombe Point, the Geoneedle landmark on the most westerly part of the Jurassic Coastline, the sea majestically sweeping out in front of me. I don't care about the view or photo opportunities today. It's starting to get light, but there's a clotted dullness to the sky that suggests it could go either way. It might not bother at all.

Where are you, Alex? I scan the fields to my left desperately, while trying not to look out over the edge of the cliffs to my right.

My unbrushed hair keeps escaping out of my hood – pulled by the cold wind to swirl around my head – but remembering a hat wasn't exactly a priority. I plough on. Sandy Bay sits below me as I stride towards the Devon Cliffs caravan park, growing hotter and sweatier by the second in my puffer coat, despite the fine drizzle that's appeared in the air.

The holiday park is closed for winter, and static in every sense as I walk down into it; each lifeless little box with curtains neatly pulled. I'm reminded of the rugby weekend and swallow a lump in my throat at the memory of Alex happily walking off to the pub with Nathan and Ben, chatting away. All I can hear is the sound of the sea, gulls wailing overhead and my own breath. There must be hundreds of virtually identical units here. Is he in one of them? Can he see me now?

'Alex?' I shout desperately, turning in a semi-circle, scanning rows and rows of holiday homes, but my voice carries away on the wind and no one answers. Not a single soul appears. It's completely deserted. 'Alex!' I cry again, my hair blowing into my mouth, making my eyes smart. I turn towards the sea into the direction of the wind to clear my face.

'Julia?'

I whip round so fast at the sound of my name, I almost fall over, to see someone standing between two of the caravans where there was an empty space seconds before. I breathe in sharply. 'What are *you* doing here?'

CHAPTER THIRTY-THREE

Hamish

Julia looks like absolute shit. I recognise the waxy sheen to her face that means she's been up all night. I've seen countless parents like her over the years, waiting for their children to come out of surgery or jolting awake on that crappy fold-out hospital chair that doesn't quite make a bed, when I appear to do my morning rounds. They are all the same: exhausted to their bones, yet on anxious alert the second I pull back the curtain, hopeful that I have the answers they want to hear.

And you know what? I do have some of the answers, Julia. I don't know exactly where your boy is, but I'm ninety-nine per cent certain I know a man who does.

I shove the keys to the caravans in my pocket as Max bounds across the grass to her, wagging his tail, leaping about, putting muddy paws all over her coat and shoving his nose in her crotch, making her wobble on her feet.

'Come here!' I call sharply, but the silly sod ignores me, continuing to nudge and sniff, forcing Julia to step back.

I pull a lead from my other pocket, march over and clip it to his collar, yanking him well away from her. 'He's still struggling with doing as he's told. He'll learn.' I look her up and down. She's now plastered in mud. 'Send me the dry-cleaning bill.'

'It doesn't matter. I'd rather you didn't call me a cunt than offer to clean my coat, to be honest.'

Her tone is factual. I frown and stare out to sea. She's not trying to point score, rather in that place where nothing else matters but the emergency you are mentally trying to deal with. You'll say anything to anyone. But a measured *response* is required. One that suggests I care. One that won't raise the alarm. 'You're looking for your son.'

'Yes.'

'I was sorry to hear that he'd gone missing,' I say. 'Professionally, I know there's no love lost between us, but you must be very frightened at the moment.' I try to scoop my hair back over my head, only for it to lift almost vertically on the wind again. 'It's a line we trot out at work all of the time – but I'm sure everyone is doing all they can.'

'Thank you.'

'I'm equally sure he'll be found.' *Because I WILL make Nate appreciate the sheer lunacy of what he's done, how dangerous it is.* 'I'm due to join a bigger search party in about an hour, in fact, a bit further on from here.' I point east. 'Although I'll be taking the dog back first. I've just been checking the units I own.' I glance at them over my shoulder. 'Nothing, I'm afraid.' I hesitate, 'although you're welcome to come and look for yourself?'

She recoils, and I curse myself instantly for making a stupid, off-the-cuff invitation that could easily be repeated to the police as being weird.

'What I mean is, I know you're aware I don't like you, but I *did* look properly,' I clarify. I really did, terrified that Nate might have the kid shoved in one of them, once I heard that the last place the Blythe boy had been seen was on these very clifftops. In any case, if I wanted to hurt Julia, there would be far easier ways of doing that than luring her back to one of the caravans. I glance at the cliff edge, mere feet behind her. All of that space, stretching away. It would be so easy.

'Thank you as ever for your candour, Hamish.' She shakes her head and widens her eyes dramatically, which have started to fill up. Always bloody crying this woman.

I reach into my pocket, pull out a packet of tissues and start to stride quickly towards her, my arm straight and outstretched, but something has caught her attention and she gives a little gasp, twisting her head away from me.

I glance and see it too: movement on the beach below us, right at the far end. People, like little black ants, crawling over the rocks. Uniformed officers. I stop immediately, within touching distance of her.

She wobbles on her feet, actually staggers back at the sight of them, and my fingers spring to life, curling round the fabric of her coat, grabbing at it roughly and snatching her inland. 'For God's sake come away from the edge! You'll fall!'

'I'm sorry! I'm sorry!' she bleats. 'It's knowing they're looking for *Alex.*'

I step back, hands up and clearly in the air where they can be seen by anyone who might be looking. 'I need to go now and I can't leave you here like this, so either you come down with me, please, or you walk past the shop,' I point to a path leading further inland, 'which will take you down to the beach to join them.'

'I'll go down to them.'

I nod and wait for her to do as she's told. She puts her head down and walks off without saying goodbye. She stumbles on the path at one point, almost trips. I watch her descend. Architect of our misfortune. Will I look back on this as a missed opportunity, I wonder?

'Come on, Max.' I give his lead a tug and head back to the car, to go and meet Nate and ask him what the hell he thinks he's playing at.

CHAPTER THIRTY-FOUR

Julia

I look back over my shoulder when I reach the closed café, but Hamish has gone. At a fork in the path, one branch of which leads down onto the sand, I take a deep breath, watching the uniformed police in the tucked-in furthest eastern corner of the beach, still over by the rocks. It's impossible to get around the headland there via the beach, and on the top is an open area called Straight Point, which the marines use as a firing range. I researched the coastal hike from Exmouth to Budleigh back in October, but we didn't do it in the end, because the online reviews said it was a bit unsafe what with there not being a fence all along the edge of the cliffs in the caravan park.

Walking down the path to the beach, I lose my nerve at the bottom when I glance the other way and see a tumour of black uniforms at the furthest *west* point, where the cliffs jut out into the sea and the strip of sand is much thinner. They are clustered around something they appear to have found.

My head is suddenly full of a mixture of images so distressing – Alex stumbling out onto the firing range, disorientated for some reason and a volley of gunshots going off – or simply falling from the cliffs, arms outstretched like the Angel of the North – that I crumple to the ground. I must look like I'm sitting down to watch the search, because one of the officers spots me and starts to approach.

I want to get up, but I'm terrified of what they have discovered – I can't move. This is not how I find out, is it? Have I been drawn to this spot because I knew on some subconscious level that Alex was here? Except, if my instinct were that good, I'd have known something awful was happening to him yesterday and done something about it, rather than staying at home, completely oblivious to my child needing me.

'I'm afraid the beach is sealed off today, madam.' The policeman speaks politely even though he must think I'm some mad rubbernecker walker, out at crack of dawn and striking lucky with some drama. 'Normally, you'd be able to do the loop and walk back to Exmouth via the beach while the tide's going out like this,' he gestures to the west, 'but not today, I'm afraid. Sorry about that.'

'Have you found a body?' I breathe.

He frowns.

'Please tell me. It's my son you're looking for. Alex Blythe.'

His mouth falls open and I watch him visibly swallow. 'Can you wait here a moment, please?' He manages. 'I'll be right back.'

CHAPTER THIRTY-FIVE

Nathan

'So *that's* where we're at,' I say quietly, hanging back from the rest of the search party. I think this is the earliest most of the men around me have been up on a Saturday morning for a long time, judging by the bleary, baggy eyes on display. Good job Alex isn't actually relying on this lot. I'm not sure half of them could find their pants in a dark room, never mind a missing child along miles of coastline, but I poke at the long grass with my stick nonetheless, so as not to stand out. 'We can't go ahead with the annual meet-up tonight. You're going to have to cancel the girls, Hamish. I'm sorry because I know that's going to be a disappointment to you, but there we are.'

Hamish pauses and squints up at the thick white cloud above us. 'I've already paid half up-front.'

He's furious at missing out on a shag. This was to be expected.

'There's just too much police activity around me to risk it,' I explain. 'Ben and I have already been questioned because we went out on the boat yesterday, and Ben was one of the last people to see the Blythe boy. They don't believe we've got anything to do with him disappearing for one minute, but on the off chance they were to follow me to Lyme tonight – do you really want them discovering prostitutes at your sister's hotel? I think they'd have a few questions.'

'You misunderstand me. I'm wondering if my already having paid the girls anything at all is worry enough in itself.' He rubs the back of his neck. 'I'd have cancelled it far sooner had I realised the police proximity to you.'

'I *did* tell you not to pay them,' I remind him, 'but I don't see how you could have called it off any faster than we are? None of us knew Julia's son was going to go missing, did we?' I glance at Tan pointedly.

'OK, so how exactly am I supposed to let the Toms, Dicks and Harrys know that it's all off without arousing suspicion?' Hamish doesn't look at me, returning instead to prodding at the grass. 'Some of them will be on their way, I imagine. We're going to be very unpopular.'

I roll my eyes. 'Hamish, this isn't *CSI*. I know I said this would be the safest place to meet up and chat without needing to use phones or possibly incriminating text messages,' I glance around us at the fifty or so other locals, 'but I don't want you to worry that we're facing imminent arrest. Just phone the "Toms, Dicks and Harrys" – excellent alias use by the way – and tell them tonight is off. That's all you need to do. Calm down. You've nothing to worry about.'

Hamish straightens up, chews on his lip for a moment then squints across at the horizon. 'We're poised to entertain some very well-respected, well-known and connected men with a lot to lose, ourselves included, at *my* sister's private hotel in a matter of hours, with the police crawling all over the place, and you tell me to calm down? My God, and now there are camera crews arriving?' He nods at a small knot of people approaching along the path and wipes his brow. He's sweating profusely, despite it being bitterly cold up here on the exposed cliff top.

'Do you want this back if we're not going ahead now?' Tan pulls his Fowles key from his pocket, and Hamish nearly faints on the spot.

'Put it away!' He can barely get the words out.

'It's just a key?' Tan is confused.

'I don't want it visible on local TV, you idiot! I'll take it back another time. You keep yours hidden too.' He shoots a livid look at me and wipes spittle from the corners of his mouth.

To say I'm surprised by his reaction is an understatement. He's acting like he's got a body buried under the patio, when I'm the one with a kid taped up in a hidden cinema.

'In fact, Tan, can you walk a little bit further ahead without making it obvious that I've asked you to? Keep looking like you're searching for him. I want to talk to Nate.'

Tan sighs but does as he's told. Hamish waits a second or two before beckoning me closer to him.

'I went down to my caravans this morning, just to check that no one had thought to put a missing child in any of them.' He looks at me beadily. 'They were clear – I'm very relieved to say – but I bumped into Julia while I was there and—'

'You saw her?' I interrupt. 'How was she?'

He looks away. 'As one would imagine, in absolute pieces. Please tell me her son going missing has nothing to do with you and that this is one giant, impossible coincidence.' He swallows painfully. 'Tell me you haven't actually gone through with your insane plan?'

I hesitate.

Hamish closes his eyes briefly. 'Oh, Christ. Oh good God.'

'Well, it's not as if you didn't know about it. I told you – remember? In the garden at Fowles? You said you'd stand by to hear more. Well…' I gesture at the people around me.

Hamish stares at the ground for a moment, then puts a hand on my back, patting it, before stepping away, pulling a small bottle of water from his pocket and taking a sip. 'Let's not make it look like we're having a row, shall we? You were pissed at Fowles.'

'I was not!' I retort.

'Yes, you were. You don't even realise when you get that bad anymore. You were also angry. And I understand why! You'd just been suspended because of her – but I thought you were just shooting your mouth off. I didn't think for one minute you'd genuinely do it.'

'You agreed with me! *You* said we should use it as an opportunity to make her look mad!'

'Have *you* gone mad? If people discover you are responsible for this…' He nods at the search party. 'You're finished.'

'But I'm NOT responsible,' I argue. 'I haven't done anything illegal. Alex went of his own accord. It's going to be fine.'

'But what about the rest of us that you've now put at risk without a second thought? You must have known you were going to do this yesterday, and you *knew* what we had planned for tonight in Lyme… and now the police are everywhere!'

'But that doesn't matter because *nothing illegal has happened.*' If I keep saying it, maybe it'll finally sink in. 'The boy is playing a game. Hiding out. I just helped him get there, that's all. You heard for yourself what everyone's saying: his bag washed in this morning – a tragic accident… but he'll be back in his mother's arms before you know it. Similarly, we're cancelling tonight. You can't get in trouble for something you haven't done, so relax. And I was *not* pissed when I came up with this!'

'You're losing sight of so much, Nate.' He shakes his head. 'I'm genuinely concerned for you. What Julia has triggered in you, I…' He trails off momentarily. 'You're starting to scare me, if I'm honest.'

I roll my eyes because I can't laugh. It's not the done thing really, when you're all searching for a missing thirteen-year-old boy everyone suspects has fallen off the cliffs… but he seems serious. 'I'm scaring you? Why are you being so unusually melodramatic? This wouldn't normally faze you at all. Sure there's nothing *you* want to tell *me*?' I put a concerned hand on his shoulder, but he shakes me off.

'Don't try that. I've known you too long to fall for your… oh SHIT.' Hamish freezes, the wind still whipping around us. Tan looks up and glances over his shoulder as Hamish faces me. 'He's at Fowles, isn't he? *That's* why you don't want us there tonight!'

I shoot a quick look at Tan, but I'm pretty sure he hasn't heard. 'I have no idea what you're talking about.'

'You stupid, selfish bastard,' Hamish whispers.

My mouth falls open. He's never spoken to me like this. Ever. Even when I shagged Serena and he was technically still her boyfriend, all those years ago.

Tan arrives alongside us. 'You might want to keep your voices down.'

'That place is my sister's livelihood,' Hamish continues.

'You mean apart from the other thirty-odd properties she's got to fall back on?' I say it lightly, but he doesn't smile.

'I do not want the police *anywhere* near my family or me.' He takes a step closer and jabs a finger into my chest. 'You get him out of there tonight or I'll report you myself.'

'Hamish!' I'm astonished by his aggression. 'What have I?—' But before I can continue, the camera team, led by a local newsreader I've met at a couple of charity events in the past, start gesturing towards us. We all immediately get our heads down and start looking like we're searching for the answer to world peace in the long grass.

My face is calm and impassive, but my heart is racing. First Julia… now *Hamish* is going to 'report' me? My oldest friend… since when does his family not include me? I glance up and out to sea, at the miles of cold, silver water. Fittingly, I can see one vessel, entirely alone. Why hast thou forsaken me? I think of Alex briefly. And then I experience a memory of me as a small boy I have not had for years and years – if ever – but it is suddenly so clear and close I can smell the damp in the air, feel the tightness in my chest. I am running flat out down the long school drive, the vast building a blur behind me, green of the playing fields either side. I am no more than nine. My arms are going like pistons because as well as being able to hear my panicked breath and my school shoes pounding the tarmac, there is the distant hum of a car behind me, growing ever nearer. If I were to glance over my shoulder, the large lump of it would loom into focus. They have seen me. They are going to catch me and take me back. There is nothing I can do to stop this from happening. I am powerless. I hear the car stop, a door open – angry shouts and the sound of much quicker, adult male feet. I shriek and try to run faster, but strong arms reach around my waist and I am lifted sheer off the ground, kicking and screaming, calling for the mother so far across the ocean she either never heard me, or chose not to listen.

I blink and there is the sea again. Wavering on the spot, the sudden tears I wipe away hastily are ones of loss and fury. My heart starts to leap in my chest, my breath speeds up and I feel faint. I've waited such a long time for someone to come for me. My fingers reach into my pocket and curl around my knife. I don't want it anymore. I draw it out, focused on the sea below us, my arm slowly starting to arch back as Hamish looks up at the movement. His face blanches and he starts stumbling up towards me, struggling to get a foothold on the soft grass, before grabbing my hand and snatching the knife away, shoving it in his pocket.

'What the hell are you doing?' He is breathless with shock. 'You can't chuck knives off cliffs in front of camera crews and the police! Pull yourself together, Nathan! Other people are relying on you!'

'I don't want it!' I gasp. 'You have it! I don't want to—'

'Shut up!' he orders, pulling me down to a crouching position, masking me from the sight of everyone below with the bulk of his body. 'Just shut up! Don't say anything, get your head down and breathe. So you don't want the knife, that's fine, but you *don't* throw it in a grand showy gesture and take all of us with you!' He leans his head towards mine – close enough for us to be touching. 'I will not let you do this. Do you understand? I told you to stop scaring me!'

I nod, tears streaming down my cheeks.

'Wipe your face. Now!'

I do as I'm told and after a moment he lets me go.

'Just get the boy out of there tonight! That's all you need to do.'

'I've made a bit of a mess of this, haven't I?' I try to laugh, but it sounds more like a desperate whimper. 'I said something about Julia that I didn't mean to, I—'

'I don't want to hear it!' He puts up a hand. 'I don't want you to mention that damn woman to me ever again. This ends tonight. He's to be out of the hotel by tomorrow morning. No more excuses. No more lies.'

He walks away, leaving me crouched down in the grass, alone.

CHAPTER THIRTY-SIX

Julia

'You're certain as you can be that this is Alex's bag?' The Investigating Officer, wearing gloves, holds it up and twists it so that Ewan and I can see it from all angles.

I picture it slung over Al's shoulder as he and Cass told me their plans while I was sorting the washing. 'Yes,' I confirm as Ewan holds my hand tightly, next to me on our sofa.

'And the contents? Nothing is missing, as far as you're aware?'

I look at them, laid out in their line of individual plastic bags. His phone is there. His trainers. A virgin sketch book, the pages completely soaked and crinkled by the sea; the new camera we bought him for Christmas; a folded-up, sodden £10 note; an apple; his glasses and their case.

My son in eight objects.

'Everything is there.' I put my hands together like I'm praying and cover my nose and mouth with them, closing my eyes. 'He can't see much without his glasses.'

What on earth would he not want to see? Why would he carefully take them off and put them away? Was he meeting someone? A girl? Did she not come? Was it a hoax? Was there a group of them giggling at the thought of Alex Blythe hanging around in the cold for nothing?

'We do now know that Alex *was* on the coastal path yesterday,' the IO says gently, and I moan aloud. 'A resident of Fox Holes Hill, which is the last road of houses backing onto the path, saw him walk past at about midday, in the direction of the caravan park.'

'I told him not to go as far as that.'

'It's our last known sighting of him,' she continues. 'Records show that Alex's phone was connected to mast 9661 in Exmouth town centre, but at 12.38 it disconnected.'

I close my eyes.

'We've been through his social media and phone messages via his service provider, and there's no evidence that there was a problem of any sort; he'd not had any contact with anyone of significance. We have foot searches ongoing today, assisted by the dog unit. We'll be doing more helicopter searches, and we're still working with the coastguard and the marine dive unit to search the coastline. They can't, unfortunately, enter the water yet because the weather is really taking a turn and it's too dangerous, but as soon as they can, they will. So, given we've found his bag—'

'If someone goes over the cliffs,' I open my eyes and look directly at her, 'is it usual for belongings – like a bag – to wash up, but no body? Is that what you think is most likely to have happened?'

'It's one possibility, yes.'

'He slipped,' I say incredulously – but then my skin ices over – 'or jumped?' Blood starts to crash in my ears.

He told me he was struggling at school. I knew he was unhappy about Dom. Why didn't I do something? Too busy worrying about other people's lives yet again, not noticing my own son's, right under my nose?

The doorbell goes and Ewan jumps up. 'I'll get it.'

'Is this the way the enquiry is moving at the moment then? That he's had an accident of some sort, or hurt himself?'

Before she can answer me, Ewan reappears with Dom and Sorcha in his wake. Dom looks pale and frightened. Sorcha's warmth and familiarity as she envelops me in an embrace almost make me break down completely.

Before I have a chance to say anything, Dom spies Al's bag and the contents on the table in front of us. 'What's all this?'

'It's Al's.' I'm there first, before the police. 'It was found this morning. He was last seen walking on the cliffs. The tide brought his bag in.'

Dominic covers his mouth with his hand. 'He fell?'

I swallow. 'Or—'

'Or what?… Kids of thirteen don't *kill* themselves!'

A tear escapes down my face. 'Of *course* they do! Don't you watch the news?'

He looks at me, bewildered. 'But Al wouldn't do that. He was all right! I mean he was angry with me, but all teenagers hate their parents. Al is a softy. He's gentle and kind…' His voice starts to break and he shakes his head. 'No. This is wrong. It isn't what's happened.'

He clears his throat. 'I read online last night that when a kid goes missing and they've been abducted, it's statistically probable that it's someone he or she knows.' He sits down opposite the police. 'Just so we're all clear, I've proven I was in aftercare all day, then at a restaurant where there was CCTV, right? You've checked that, obviously? And what about you two?' He looks first at me, then Ewan. 'You were here? Well, come on! Were you?'

'Yes, we were here!' I get a flashback to Ewan and I naked in bed, gasping and giggling, taking advantage of having the house entirely to ourselves. The guilt makes me feel hot with shame.

He stares at the items on the table, putting his head in his hands. 'Now I'm freaking out that he's hurt himself though, because why did he take his glasses off? He can't see without them.' He looks up. 'People wanting to harm themselves usually happens quite quickly and by the time *you've* been told someone is missing,' he nods at the police, 'they've probably already done it, haven't they?

I read that too. Shit. Oh shit. I made him upset the last couple of times I saw him. This is my fault. This is all my fault.'

He jumps to his feet and walks over to the window. 'I want to go and look for him. Can I?' He turns back to the police. 'Is there some way I can be involved in the search?'

'A volunteer search team *has* already started up. They were out last night and this morning,' the IO says.

'Really?' I whisper in disbelief. 'We've only just moved here. That's so kind.'

'…and we do understand everyone wanting to help,' the IO says, 'particularly those closest to Alex.' She hesitates. 'Would you perhaps like to do a public appeal? We don't always suggest TV, it's not ideal to publicise a child's age, name and photo in the media, but in this case, we think the pros outweigh the cons. We don't know why Alex is missing, if it's an accident, foul play or something else, but in some cases a public plea can result in tips or information that can help find the missing person. It gets the message out to as many people as possible. It would be good to do this nice and early while events are fresh in people's minds. It tends to lead to information that's more accurate; someone who might have been going about their daily life and witnessed something at the crucial moment.'

'Of course we'll do the appeal,' I interrupt, looking to Ewan but then realising I should include Dom too.

'Can we do it together?' Dom suggests. 'Present a united front, so Al knows he's not in trouble if he sees it? Or maybe it should just be you, as I've upset him so much?'

'No, I think you're right. It should be both of us.'

'Can I be in it?' says a small voice from the doorway, and we all look up to see Cass standing there, her jumper sleeves pulled down over her hands and her pale face tear-stained. 'I want to do something to help. I want him to come home.' She wipes her eyes with her sleeves, and Ewan gets up immediately to hug her as she bursts into tears. I hope to God she didn't just hear everything Dom said.

*

'So to reiterate, while I'm not saying this applies to Alex, it can be really useful in cases where someone is being held against their will to use their name as much as possible while you speak.' The police search advisor concludes her briefing. 'It tells the abductor that you love and value Alex, forces them to see him as a person rather than a captive. It will also help humanise Alex to the public at large. We want this story to stay in the headlines. We want as much publicity as possible. So are you ready? Do you have any questions?' She looks at us.

I shake my head. We're led into a room with a white table and three chairs. On the other side are about twenty people with cameras. I'm clutching my piece of paper as we sit down, and I hear the Senior Investigating Officer accompanying us introduce me and ask me, in my own time, to begin.

I clear my throat. 'Somebody knows what has happened to Alex. Someone watching now may know something vital and not even realise it.' I can hear my own voice as I read the words on my sheet, only it feels like it's coming from someone else, not me. 'Please call the police with any information you might have – because we need Alex to come home. His sister misses him very much. She wants him to know she normally can't sleep because of all the noise Al makes, but now it's too quiet without him.' I look up briefly to clicks and flashes going off. 'Alex is really tall, so he might seem older than thirteen, but actually he's young for his age. He's kind, gentle and he's at his happiest when he's at home with all of us, just playing *Fortnite*. We *need* him to come home. He is very precious to us.'

I lift my gaze again and look right into the cameras. 'Alex, if you can hear this now, please, please get in touch, sweetheart. It doesn't have to be me… or Dad.' I motion to Dom next to me. 'Message anyone you feel you want to. Please just let me know you're safe. You're not in any trouble… but my heart is breaking not knowing where you are.' My voice is getting higher and higher. 'Just call me so that I can come and get you, please?'

I know that I'm crying, but I don't realise I've reached desperately for Dom's hand until he squeezes it back. I glance at him to see that he's crying too. 'I do also want to say thank you to everyone for their kindness,' I remember to add, looking back down at my notes. 'The police, the coastguard, the dog team, the helicopter team, the members of the public who we've been told are out looking for Alex, please don't put yourselves at risk, but thank you – everyone is offering us so much support during this impossible time. Thank you for helping us find Alex… but if you're watching and you know anything at all,' I beg suddenly, looking up again at the cameras, not wanting to stop now I have my chance, 'please help us.'

*

I'm in a closed cubicle, wiping vomit from my mouth with a tissue when I hear two women come into the ladies, chatting.

'That poor woman looked like she was in the seventh circle of hell. I don't know why they make them go through this shit.'

''Because it makes the families feel like they're doing something to help. They have to say they tried. I'd do it in their position – heaven forbid.'

'But he's so obviously drowned! Why give them that false sense of hope when the body is going to wash up in a couple of days' time? I don't get it.'

'Because you never know… until you know – I guess. Are you filming the intro to your report outside, by the way?'

'No. I'm done. I'm just putting this on because I look knackered. Too many late nights and eating Christmas crap. You go for it.'

'Thanks. He looked so cute.' She sighs. 'Such a shame he's not a girl.'

I burst out of the cubicle to catch them both redoing their make-up in the mirror. They freeze in horror at the sight of me, but I don't care about their embarrassment.

'Why do you say that? What do you mean it's a shame he's not a girl? Tell me, please!'

'Because people respond better to missing girls than boys,' the older of the two women, the one who thinks Al has drowned, says eventually. 'There's a misconception that boys were probably in some kind of trouble if they disappear, or that they can handle themselves better than girls. People basically just care more if it's a girl in jeopardy. Young, female victims always get the most media attention.'

Wow. *That's* when it pays to be female? It's one of the saddest things I've ever heard.

'You did a great job,' the younger woman says earnestly. 'I really hope they find Alex.'

'Thank you.' I bang out of the bathroom, shaking.

At least she remembers his name.

*

Once Dom and Sorcha have gone back to their hotel and the house is quiet, I am lying on my bed, staring out at the now-dark sky, when there is a creak of a floorboard and I turn my head to see Cass standing timidly in the doorway.

I hold out my arms and to my surprise she rushes into them, forcing me to sit up. She hasn't let me hold her like this since Lise died.

'I didn't look after Al.'

'It's OK.' I rock her and kiss her hair. 'Alex is not your responsibility, and I'm so sorry that there have been times in the past when I made you feel like he was.' I mentally curse every single careless drop-off at school in Surrey where I said to Cass quietly, *'keep an eye on Alex for me?'*

I let her cry some more. 'Is Ben your boyfriend now?' I stroke her hair. 'It's OK if he is.'

'No!' she says. 'That's the thing. I wanted to tell Ben that I think I do like him after all. That's why I went to meet him when he asked if I wanted to go to Exmouth. I was going to ask Ben out, but his dad turned up at the marina before I had a chance and it all got really awkward. I should have just listened to you. I'm not going to speak to Ben ever again now though, I promise. I just want Al back. I heard what Dominic said about people hurting themselves.'

'Dominic's just frightened.' I try to reassure her. 'You say things you don't mean when you're scared.'

'But Al is going to come home, isn't he?'

I can't lie to her any more than I could when Lise was ill. 'I don't know, sweetheart. I really, really hope so.'

*

She eventually falls asleep next to me, and as I allow my eyes to close for a moment, I become aware that I'm *moving*. Opening them again, I'm thrown to discover I'm actually on a trolley, being wheeled by two porters up a corridor. A woman in blue scrubs is walking alongside me, chatting away. I glance down at myself to see I'm in a hospital gown and tucked in by a blanket. I feel drowsy and confused. I've just had an operation? I lift my left hand up to try and block out the bright overhead lights and then I see it. The whole of the skin of my left hand is slipping up like an ill-fitting rubber glove, starting to float free having filled with water. It's going to completely slough away from the flesh underneath. I reach out, horrified, with my right hand and try to pull it down – keep it over the stumps of my fingers – but as I let go it simply starts to drift away from my bloodied wrist again. I'm going to lose it. 'My hand!' I try to say to the woman. 'They've forgotten to stich the skin where the edges meet!' I nod at the separated cuff. It looks like the briny edge of a boiled ham.

She laughs. 'No, they haven't! It's supposed to be like that!'

'It's not.' I try to sit up, starting to panic. 'It's going to deglove. We need to tell someone, quickly!' I start to grope about the bed with my good hand, for a buzzer to call someone, but I can't find it! Someone has to help me! Why can't she see what's happening! I need my hand! I need—

*

I sit up with a gasp in my dark bedroom. Cass stirs in her sleep next to me. The doorbell is ringing downstairs. Feeling sick and shaky, I get to my feet while trying not to wake her. Squeezing my left hand into a fist and releasing, I hasten downstairs into the hall. Ewan is already opening the front door – to reveal Dom on the step again. I have to lean on the wall to steady myself, still disorientated.

'Can I come in?' he asks. 'Mum has already gone to bed; she's exhausted. I was hoping to see if they use the appeal on the news, but I don't want to disturb her. Do you mind if I watch it with you, and then I'll go again?'

Ewan puts the TV on and the headlines begin. We learn that a twenty-four-hour tube strike has begun. A ship in the North Sea has lost 270 containers in rough conditions, and then there am I, addressing the audience directly: 'If you are watching and you know anything at all about where Alex is, please help us.'

'Parents of a vulnerable teenager in Devon appeal for more information', the news reader announces, 'after their son goes walking on the cliffs near popular local beaches and is now missing…'

CHAPTER THIRTY-SEVEN

Nathan

'I can't wrap my head around this.' Storm sits forward on the sofa and stares at Julia's face on the screen. 'It's hard enough when you see any parent going through it, but when it's someone that you know.' She shakes her head. 'He's fallen and drowned, hasn't he? Or God – thrown himself off. Nate, I just see Ben…' She reaches out and grabs my hand.

I don't want to discuss Julia with Storm. I am fixated on the image in front of me; she looks devastated, tear-stained, frightened… in need. Storm squeezes me more tightly, stricken. 'I'm so sorry! I shouldn't have just blurted it out like that, about him drowning. You know that there was nothing you could have done, don't you? It's not your fault. I expect you're thinking if you'd just got to the boat ten minutes earlier… but life doesn't work like that, my darling.'

My darling? Wow. 'You're right. I could have just driven all three of them home, then none of this would be happening…' I take my hand back. 'I'd like to go and see Julia quickly, if that's OK? Not because there's anything going on between us, but I really do feel I owe her an apology for not being there sooner, when I could have prevented all of this.' I want to see her. I need to. I hadn't planned to, but it feels right. I can build the momentum a bit; promise her I will stop at nothing until I find her son.

'It's ten o'clock at night, Nate! Wait until the morning.'

'I don't think she's going to be asleep, do you?'

Storm flushes. 'Perhaps not, but you probably shouldn't drive anyway?' She nods at my empty whisky glass on the side table under the lamp.

'I'm fine.' I wave dismissively. 'I've hardly had anything. I'm going to be twenty minutes. I simply want to say sorry and let her know if there's anything we can do to help, we will.'

I hurry out into the hall to get my coat. Ben is sitting on the stairs, picking at his nails anxiously.

'You all right?' I pull the sitting room door to. 'I thought you'd gone to bed?'

'I just heard you say to Mum you're going out?' he whispers. 'When are we leaving to get Alex?'

I put my finger to my lips. 'Later tonight. I'll come and wake you up when it's time to go, OK?'

He looks visibly relieved. 'OK. Should I sleep in my clothes to make things quicker?'

I pretend to consider that. 'No. I think we'll have time for you to get dressed. Go back up to bed now. Stand by for hero rescue.' I wink at him, and he allows himself a small smile before disappearing off upstairs. My own smile fades and I reach for my coat, pulling it on with urgency.

I could feel her pain and fragility reaching out to me through the screen. I take a deep breath. This is it; the moment where I turn everything around.

CHAPTER THIRTY-EIGHT

Julia

'This is so surreal,' Dominic whispers as the full news report begins; a still of Alex, smiling happily on Christmas Day, then shots of the cliffs and a helicopter flying over the sea, the lifeboat launching. They cut to footage of what must be this morning's search, dog teams on foot in the daylight and local people out looking, in amongst whom I clearly see Nathan, Tan – and Hamish, struggling to keep up at the rear in his flat cap and wax jacket, as they stride through fields calling, but just as he said he would be, he's there, looking for my son. I jump with shock as the front door bell chimes again. This time news, surely?

'Oh God. They've found him…' Dom takes a deep gulp of air – like he's sticking his head above water – then moans and clutches at his chest, bending forward as Ewan rushes past us to get the door.

'Dominic? Are you OK? Sit down,' I order, taking his free hand to steady him. 'Are you in pain?'

'I'm fine,' he gasps. 'It's just the shock and the fear. It's just…'

Ewan comes back in. 'It's not the police. It's Nathan Sloan for you, Julia. Says he wants a quick word.' He looks at Dom in alarm. 'What's happened?'

'He's all right, he just needs a moment to steady himself.' I move towards the door. 'Can you stay with him while I speak to Nathan?'

'I'd rather come with you,' Ewan says. 'Can you hang on and wait for me?'

'I'll be OK, just keep an eye on him.' I motion at Dominic, lying on the sofa.

Nathan is huddled on the doorstep in the rain, hands in his overcoat pockets, collar up. 'Come in,' I offer automatically, and he accepts, shivering as he steps into the hall.

'Thank you. That's kind. How are you bearing up?'

'So, so, thanks.' I can't bring myself to say more than that. 'But on the subject of being kind, I just saw you on the news with Tan and Hamish, searching for Alex. Given the circumstances, that's decent of you and I'm very grateful.'

'It was the least I could do.' He scans my face, concerned. 'You're going through hell. I'm so sorry. I just wanted to say, any help we can offer you – have Cass over or something like that – just let us know.' He reaches out and briefly squeezes my arm. His touch returns me to standing outside the school on the last day of term when he wouldn't let go of me and our children were watching… I don't want to have to think about that now. I have no room in my head for anything that isn't Alex.

'You know what, Nathan, I would ask you to come in properly, but we're all a bit…' I move instinctively to the door and open it again. 'Thank you for coming and it's appreciated but… I'm sorry, I hope you understand.'

'Oh!' He looks taken aback. 'Of course. I just felt I should apologise too. If only I'd arrived at my boat a bit earlier when Alex was still there. I could have brought them all back with me. I'm so sorry that I didn't.'

Does he think it helps to hear how close I came to keeping hold of my son? 'You couldn't have known.' I open the door wider. *Please just go now.* 'But thank you.'

'If only I could wave a magic wand and make this all OK again in a heartbeat…'

Enough! 'Yes, wouldn't that be good,' I manage. 'Thank you, but—'

'No, don't dismiss me,' he says sharply. 'You don't understand. I'm here to tell you I can help. I'm going to give Alex back to you.'

The hallway seems to expand around me, or I shrink down. Everything becomes misshapen. '"Give Alex back" to me?' I repeat. 'What do you mean?'

'Get,' he says quickly. 'I said get.'

'No, you didn't.' I step forward. 'You said give! Do you know where he is?'

'Of course I don't!' He draws away from me, but I see real fear in his eyes. 'I shouldn't have come here. I've upset you.' He turns to go, but I fly round him and block his exit, spreading my hands over the door frame.

'You know where he is! I can see you do!'

He tries to push past me, so I grab at him instead. 'Where is he?'

'I came to tell you I wanted to help, that's all!'

'No, you're lying. Tell me! Where is Alex?'

CHAPTER THIRTY-NINE

Nathan

This was a huge mistake. It was crazy. My mind is scrambling for an explanation of my catastrophic slip of the tongue, but she's holding my arm and I am distracted by her touch. Turns out Hamish was right, just being a hero isn't enough for her. I try to remember what he said I *should* do, in the garden at Fowles. Fowles... the ornate letters of the menu swim uselessly in my mind. **F**ront. **O**rientation – think, Nate, think! You're hitting a **W**all...

'Tell me where he is! *Why* have you taken him? Oh my God!' She covers her mouth with her hands. 'Is this because I reported you?'

'No! I love you!' I exclaim. This is all going badly, badly wrong... Fowles. He's in FOWLES. He's...

'You love me?' she repeats. 'I don't care! I want my son. Wait—' she gives a sharp inhalation of shock. 'You think "giving" Alex back to me is going to make me *love you?*'

I go very still – **s**een. **E**xposed. **F**uck. **F**uck, **F**uck.

'I am *never* going to love you!'

I can feel the hurt... the pain rising in me, and I have to close my eyes.

'I am *never* going to be yours.' She's almost choking as she spits the words out.

I swallow and everything settles within me; a terrible, cold levelling of my blood.

'Nothing you can do will *ever* change that. Give him back to me!'

I open my eyes and look right at her. 'I've hidden him. It's part of a plan. I've written six letters on the back of six breast implants in surgical pen – all of which are now inside the last six women I operated on. Collectively, they tell you where Alex is. So go to these women. Ask them if they'll let you unpick their stitches and slice open their scars. I think you'll find they say no because *they* like the way *I* have made them look.'

She recoils from me. She can't believe what she just heard. 'What did you say?'

The second the words are out of my mouth, I'm horrified too. I am not that man anymore! What part of me, what deep, awful part of me do these lies come from? I am not normal to have something like that on the tip of my tongue. What did my mouth just say to the person I love most?

'You've put clues to Alex's whereabouts *inside* six of your living patients?' She repeats and it sounds… mad. She sounds mad. I can see Hamish puffing on his cigar approvingly; *it's your only way out now, old chap…*

'I'm sorry?' I let my mouth fall open, pretending to look confused. 'I didn't say anything about patients or clues?'

The panic rips from her in a shriek. '*Ewan!*'

He appears in the doorway at the far end of the hall, Dominic behind him. Ewan rushes towards me as she falls back. He grabs at the front of my coat, pushing me up against the door. 'What have you done to her?'

'He says he's got Alex!' She babbles, incoherent with fear. I feel dirty and sordid as I watch her start to wind the rope I've handed her around her own neck. 'He's hidden clues inside his living patients! Letters – a code! Call the police! Quick, one of you!'

Ewan's grip lessens, just a touch, as he turns to look at her. 'What?'

'WHAT?' I shout, in unison, pulling myself free. I make a show of putting my hands on my head in amazement. 'Why would you even say something like that?' I look directly at her. 'OK, I *won't* tell him!' I move my hands into a surrender position. 'You win, Julia! But you can't make up shit like that! That's evil! Of course I don't know where Alex is! And putting clues in patients? What the hell? I won't tell him, OK? I swear!'

Ewan reaches out and grabs me again. 'You won't tell me what?' He almost lifts me off the floor, despite my being as tall as him. 'Tell me what?'

Everything I've gleaned about you, Ewan, everything I know you're terrified of hearing.

'Please don't hit me!' I plead, genuinely hoping he won't because he is really bloody strong. 'Julia and I are involved! I'm so sorry. I had to come and see her tonight. I couldn't let her go through Alex being missing without me. She needs my support!'

He shakes his head. 'You're lying.'

'I'm not!' I scrabble in my pocket for my phone. 'See?' I find the picture and hold it up for him. He has his back to Julia, but *I* witness the pain explode across his face. He drops me and I cut deeper.

'We need to tell the truth here, Julia,' I say. 'It's too important!'

'No,' Julia whispers, moving backwards down the hall away from us, in Dominic's direction. I wish with all my heart that I wasn't having to do this, and I want to shout to her that I'm so sorry. If only I could explain that I don't have a choice.

'It's not true, Ewan. I told you about this photograph, remember? He's set it all up,' she says very carefully, before turning to me. 'Nathan, are you on any medication at the moment?'

'*Me?*' I laugh. I have to hand it to her, she's more than up to the challenge. We are meant to be together. 'I tell you I love you and you try to destroy me, making up allegations about me *filming patients* and now putting *clues* inside them?'

'You have been filming your patients. That's a fact. We are not in a relationship and I'm deeply concerned that you seem to believe we are.'

'You can't pretend this didn't happen, to protect him,' I hold the phone aloft. 'It's not your fault Lise did this to Ewan too!'

Ewan shouts with rage, his hand flies back and I brace, but Dom suddenly rushes forward and shoves him so hard Ewan loses his footing and smashes into the sideboard before falling to the ground.

I manage to stay on my feet, staggering backwards, shoving my mobile back in my pocket. 'Thanks, mate.' I nod gratefully at Dominic. Best hundred quid I ever spent.

'You're welcome,' Dom replies. 'Hang on.' He turns and hastens off to the kitchen as Ewan manages to get to his knees, pushing Julia away as she tries to help him.

Dom returns with a glass of whisky, which he holds out to me. 'It takes guts to walk into another man's house and admit you're seeing his wife. Your nerves must be all over the place. She did the same thing to me, with him.' He nods at Ewan.

'What?' Julia gasps, staring at her ex-husband as if she's living in a parallel universe, or having one of those nightmares that are so vivid they feel real. I want to wrap my arms around her. I shouldn't have come. I have messed all of this up because of my *ego*.

'Dominic, what are you talking about?' she whispers. 'You *know* that's not true!'

'Here.' Dom offers the glass to me again. I hesitate but reach out and take it. I could do with calming down.

'Thank you.'

'No problem,' Dom slaps my shoulder, 'but then maybe you should go, yeah?'

I nod. He's right. I need to get the hell away from here. I knock it back and hand him the glass.

'No! Stop!' Julia steps forward. 'We need to call the police! He's just told me he's abducted Alex!'

'I'm going now as well.' Dom ignores her. 'You two,' he motions between them, 'need some time alone to talk things out, by the sound of it.' He pulls his keys from his pocket, stepping to the front door to throw it open. 'I'll let you go first, Nathan. You're blocking me in.' He nods at my Porsche in the opening to the drive and steps out into the night, walking round to a small, red car.

'Dominic, stop!' Julia calls after him. 'You have to believe what he's just told me!'

He climbs into his car and starts the engine, waiting for me to do the same. I turn to Ewan, now sitting on the hall floor, with one hand clutched around his middle. 'If you start coughing up blood or have shortness of breath that gets worse, go to A&E,' I tell him. 'It might mean a broken rib is doing more damage to you.'

'Don't you *dare* do the caring doctor bit!' Julia's voice is shaking, but a tiny movement at the top of the stairs catches my eye and I look up. Cassia is watching us silently through the bannisters, crouched down in her nightie, terrified. 'Ewan, I think your daughter needs you.' I nod up at her. 'I'm very sorry that she saw all of that. It wasn't my intention.'

Ewan drags himself to his feet, gasping as he clutches his ribs and starts to climb the stairs.

Julia turns to me. 'What have you done?'

'I didn't do or say anything. I told you I wanted to get Alex back for you. That's all. You're under immense strain at the moment. Of course you are. You've barely slept. I didn't say anything about knowing where Alex is, or "clues" in patients. I just love you. That's all.' I look at her face searchingly. She is so beautiful.

'No.' She shakes her head. 'I will not be manipulated by you. I know *exactly* what you said.'

Chastened, I turn and leave. Starting the car up, I begin to pull away slowly. I was a fool to have come here. One slip of the tongue and– *shit!* I lurch forward violently in my seat and have to slam on my brakes. It takes me a second or two to process that Dominic has just driven his car right into the back of me.

CHAPTER FORTY

Julia

Dom throws his door open – his mobile aloft – and starts taking pictures of Nathan climbing out of his Porsche.

'What the hell?' Nathan exclaims at the sight of the mangled metal that moments ago was his pristine back bumper. 'What are you doing? You just rear-ended me!'

'No *mate*, you're mistaken. You slammed your car right back into mine! You been drinking or something?' Dom has already started dialling. 'Police, please! Someone's just reversed into my vehicle.'

'No, I didn't!' Nathan starts to raise his voice. 'What are you talking about?'

'Yeah, that's him shouting now. Can you blue-light it, please? He's drunk, aggressive and at the home of my ex-wife. We're the parents of the missing boy, Alex Blythe. This man has just turned up and said he's abducted our son. His name is Nathan Sloan. Quick as you can, please. I don't want to get done for having to defend myself against him.'

Dom slips his phone into his back pocket, walks straight up to Nathan and punches him hard in the stomach. Just as Ewan did, seconds earlier, Nathan doubles over with surprised pain and drops to his knees – a genuine reaction this time.

Dom bends down and gets right up in Nathan's face. 'Who you trying to be, hey boy?' He speaks softly. 'I've known Julia the best part of my life. For a long time she *was* the best part of my life. You couldn't even begin to understand what's made her who she is, so you shut your mouth with your dirty lies about her cheating, you hear?'

He gets closer still, grabbing Nathan round the back of the neck and pushes his forehead so hard into his cheek that Nathan exclaims aloud. 'You can never be the richest, most powerful person in the room, but you can be the kindest, and she's it. She's a *good* person and you want to hear the truth?' He straightens up, staring down at Nathan. 'She wouldn't look twice at someone like you because, these days, she can spot a fuck-up at five paces. And you, my friend, are one of those, all right. *Now* I know what the cash was about.'

Dom turns to me. 'That afternoon when I was wrecked outside the school, Mr Sloan here paid me a hundred quid to go home. I should have told you before but I wasn't exactly proud of it, you know what I mean?'

'You paid Dom a hundred quid?' I'm completely bewildered. 'But I'd only just met you? Why would you do that?'

Nathan says nothing, just rolls onto his side, lying on the ground, clutching his stomach, gasping.

'Oh, behave yourself!' Dom says. 'It doesn't hurt that much. When the police get here, I'm going to show them my pictures of you behind the wheel, and you'll have to do a breath test. You're going to be *that* man, because you're pissed, I can tell… Where's my son?'

Nathan continues to lie there and closes his eyes.

'You're going to hear them coming soon,' Dom says. 'You're running out of time. You think you can do this – I can see you do – but trust me, you can't. You're going to fuck *everything* up. You've got kids yourself. Don't do this to them. Just tell me and Jules where Alex is, we'll go and get him, nice and quietly. We won't tell anyone you told us. We'll say he ran away and came home on his own. We'll say it was me that drove into the back of you. All of this can go away.'

I hear the distant wail of sirens.

Dom stiffens. 'Here we go… that's for *you*. Next thing, it's blue lights up in your face. They'll be here and it's going to get real quickly. Just tell us. This is the moment you're going to look back on, where you wish you took the lifeline I'm offering you now. Don't be a dick. Come on – this is your chance…'

The sirens are getting closer.

'Come on, COME ON!' Dom urges him. 'Just tell us! Do the right thing!'

But now they *are* here, and Dominic exclaims in disgust at Nathan's continued silence, leaning forward and whispering: 'if you've hurt my son, there won't be a surgeon in the world able to put the bits of you back together.'

*

After Nathan is arrested for angrily refusing to perform a breath test, and taken off in one of the two squad cars, the other attending officers move his Porsche to the opposite side of the road. Ewan is then able to take Dom back into town, so that he doesn't have to drive Sorcha's battered car and leave it unattended in the hotel car park. Once they've left, I go to check on Cass. She's still awake, eyes wide open in the dark.

'You all right, sweetheart?' I sit down on the carpet beside her.

'I didn't like seeing Dad and Ben's dad fighting.'

'Of course you didn't. It's horrible seeing adults behave like that.'

'Dad was protecting you.'

'Yes, he was.' I try to smile.

'He loves you.' A small hand reaches out from under the duvet. 'We both do.'

I catch my breath. She has been holding my heart in that hand of hers for such a long time now. I reach out tentatively. 'I love you too, Cass.' I stroke her gently. 'You, Alex and Dad mean everything to me.'

'I want Al to come back.'

'Me too.' There is nothing more I can say, so instead I start to sing her the songs I have sung Alex since he was a baby and then to both of them when she and Ewan first came to live with us. She doesn't tell me it's OK, I can stop. She listens quietly to rhymes of silver nutmegs and golden pears, boats laden with treasure, lavender blue and green, twinkling stars… and her eyes begin to close. I wait until her body relaxes and I'm sure she's asleep.

Slipping away from Cass into Al's empty room across the hall, I close the door gently behind me. His stuff: school books; the twist of his unplugged phone charger; dirty clothes; *Fortnite* magazine; scattered Nerf gun bullets; Lego constructions everywhere; the bag containing the Hollister top I bought him for Christmas that needs to go back because it's too small. I pick my way over to his bed and lie down, closing my eyes and concentrating on what it feels like to hug and hold him: the uncontrollable limbs; bashing cheekbones; floppy hair and slipping glasses. There is no protesting, busy, wriggly boy small enough to scoop onto my lap anymore. The warm baby sleeping on my chest – his downy hair covering the delicate, pulsing crown of his head that I would softly whisper-kiss – has gone too. But I am in no doubt that Nathan knows where Alex is. I saw it in his eyes. My son is out there and he needs me. There are letters within patients that will tell us where to find him and I am a surgeon. There must be something *I* can do.

*

'Happy?' I ask the anaesthetist and she nods. 'All OK to begin.'

'Right. Here we go.' I raise my voice to address the audience behind me. 'I chose my incision site earlier, as denoted by these marks on the skin under the crease of each breast, so it won't leave a visible scar. I'm now going to carefully make the three-centimetre incision using a scalpel.' I lean over and begin. 'I'm slicing through the skin surface in one clean line, and as it parts, returning with smaller strokes to divide the tissue beneath. We'll briefly swab at this point, and you can see I'm being assisted while I use this thing like a pencil with a wire attached to it' – I hold it aloft briefly in my right hand – 'which is a cautery device to control the bleeding, but that can also cut the tissue.'

The students behind me crane in their seats to see.

'Luckily, this patient has a thin pocket of scar tissue so we don't need to remove it,' I continue. 'I've cut through the pocket now, we've put a retractor in and I'm going to remove the implant itself by grabbing the corner of it with what look like these long, blunted blade scissors, and simply pulling it away cleanly through the incision.'

I reach in, but I can't find the edge of the implant. There's nothing there. I fish around in empty space with the blades until I finally feel something. I clasp it and draw whatever it is towards me, and as it emerges through the incision, I realise to my horror it's a tiny finger, on a baby's hand… a small arm follows, flopping wetly through the cut only to lie limp on the table, the fingers slowly spreading open, looking for something to clasp… oh my God…

The students are on their feet, talking, whispering, pointing. Someone cries out.

'Get me a paediatric team!' I shout, panicking. Now a shoulder is relentlessly emerging, in slow motion. I don't know what to do. No one told me she was *pregnant*. I try to push it gently back, but how is this happening? How is?…

I wake with a gasp, to find Ewan holding my arm, his hand on my shoulder, whispering my name. I am still in Al's single bed: another horrible, horrible dream, or hallucination.

'What's happened? Is there news?' I sit up immediately, dazed but already alert.

'No, I just thought you'd be more comfortable in our bed. You were thrashing around. Come on, let's take you through.'

He helps me to my feet and leads me into our room. 'Why don't you get properly changed and under the covers?' He watches me as I sit on the edge of the bed. 'I can stay up by the phones. I'll do tonight and we'll swap first thing tomorrow morning. Come on, at least lie down.'

'Ewan, everything that Nathan said to you about me and him—'

'I know it wasn't true. It was just the shock of seeing the picture for myself, that's all. Get some rest now, please?'

I do as I'm told, but when he leaves the room I stare up at the ceiling, unable to get that tiny, reaching hand out of my mind.

CHAPTER FORTY-ONE

Nathan

'I have to let my wife know what's happened. For one, I need her to go and collect my car. Could someone call her for me? Is *that* allowed?'

The police officer looks at me impassively, and I do my best to try and remove the acid from my voice, but this is ridiculous. I'm sober! I *must* go and get Alex!

'Look, I'm sorry,' I try. 'I don't mean to be getting frustrated, but this is just a misunderstanding. I couldn't explain why I didn't want to give a breath test in front of my colleague outside her house – why the result would be inaccurately spiked – but now that she's not here, I'm comfortable to disclose that I'm on antidepressants at the moment. I've not had a drink with them before now, but I can confirm I had ONE unit earlier on. It's Christmas, after all, but yes, it was unwise. This particular type of medication does skew blood alcohol readings and would have given a false positive roadside result. I'm sorry that I wasn't willing to explain that then and there, but there's unfortunately still a huge stigma around doctors needing to take medication for mental illness, and it's just not something I want this particular colleague knowing. Sadly, she wouldn't hesitate to use that knowledge to professionally damage me. We were involved personally and it ended badly. Anyway, I just wanted to explain, ahead of Paul Gainsford, my solicitor, arriving. Unless you can just let me go now I've told you that, of course?'

Disappointingly, there's no reaction to my mentioning Paul's name, despite him being a local bigwig and no comment on my being released either.

'I'm really not trying to be difficult, and I completely understand why you had to arrest me and bring me in.' I look around the small interview room I'm stuck in – damn Dominic! 'But as I say, there really was a good reason for my needing to refuse the breath test. I'm not likely to be here very much longer once Mr Gainsford has arrived though, am I?' I smile ingratiatingly.

'We do have a few questions for you, Mr Sloan,' the officer replies, 'but we'll do our best to conclude everything as quickly as we can. Obviously, you'll be aware that things take a little longer at this time of night. We thank you for your patience.'

My smile fades. A few questions? So she's told them what I said about the letters and now they have to investigate it. Why, WHY did my mouth say that? It was a total spur of the moment overreaction on my part. This is what happens when you lose focus. I *have* to get to Fowles tonight! Alex must be walking in through the door tomorrow morning. That HAS to happen, or I really am in serious trouble. If I don't turn up tonight, he's almost certainly going to panic – I would, if I were him – and then what? Plus, Ben is going to start asking questions. There are too many loose threads now. They all need to be tied off. I really could kill Dominic for winding me up in here, the crapped-out waste of a man!

'Can I contact my family so they don't worry about me?' I continue to smile.

'If you give me your wife's name and contact details, we'll let her know that you're here.'

I think I might detect a slight thawing, which is a start. Frustratingly however, I realise I don't actually know Storm's number off by heart, which doesn't look great.

'Actually, can you call Hamish Wilson?' I'm forced to request. 'He's a friend of mine and he'll be able to reach my wife for me.' This is not good either. Hamish is going to go *nuts* given his warning while we were at the search earlier. This is about as far from keeping the police away from him and his family as it's possible to get. Although… couldn't HE go to Lyme for me? My heart thumps with excitement. He already knows exactly where Alex is!

The officer sighs. 'I'll allow you to contact this friend of yours if you're sure you know *his* details?'

'I do, I promise!' I'm a little too eager in my response, but they let me go ahead anyway. For a terrible moment I don't think Hamish is going to pick up, but just as I'm expecting his voicemail to kick in, he's there with a terse but resigned 'Hamish Wilson'. It must be the No Caller ID – he thinks it's the hospital calling.

'Ham! It's me! Listen, I'm really sorry to disturb you with this, but I've been arrested and I'm just down at the station now.'

There is a sharp intake of breath, and before he can say anything incriminating, I add quickly, 'it's all a misunderstanding over a breath test, but could I possibly ask you to call Storm for me and explain what's happened? She'll be worried because I popped out to do something important and never even made it there!' I pray that he understands what I'm actually saying to him. 'I'm so sorry to have to ask *you* to clean up my mess for me, but will you step in and sort it all out instead? Ham? Did you hear me?'

'I heard you – but no way. I'm not doing that.'

'I understand it's annoying, but I really do need your help.'

He simply hangs up without another word. I smile at the officer. 'There! That's all done. Thank you very much.'

Ham is angry, but when push comes to shove, twenty-five years of friendship will out. He's more than family to me. He's the only person I have ever been able to truly rely on. He won't let me down.

CHAPTER FORTY-TWO

Hamish

'You *bastard*!' I yell in the darkness of my car, having been *dispatched* to Lyme in the middle of a freezing January night, the rain lashing so heavily at the window the wipers are barely achieving anything. I'm having to concentrate furiously just to stay on the damn road.

I've come the back way, to avoid traffic cameras, cursing Nathan repeatedly as I swerve to avoid a small, fallen branch lying in the middle of the twisting and weaving Ware Lane, leading down into to Lyme. I didn't have to come, of course, but I can hardly have a special kid like the Blythe boy crashing around Fowles, unaccompanied, doing God knows what, panicking and trying to break out when no one arrives to rescue him. He could burn the bloody place down, with him in it! A murder enquiry with a charred child's body in situ. Wonderful, Nathan, you absolute *cunt*.

Not only is Nathan not robust enough at the moment to withstand intensive police questioning – he'd probably tell them he discussed the abduction with me in the garden – *everything* else would come out the second the police start their interviews. I shift in my seat as I think about Michelle. It wasn't even worth it, a moment of lapsed judgement, but more importantly, with Nathan's newly evangelical quest for the truth, I can't rely on him to back me up and say that he was in the bedroom at the house before Christmas with us at all times and didn't see me do anything. Michelle has said nothing so far, and obviously at this stage, there will be no forensic evidence to back up any allegations she might make. I'm not stupid: I removed her underwear, dress and tights after taking her back to her house and putting her to bed – disposing of them thoroughly once the taxi dropped me off at home – but there's still too much risk of the floodgates opening should the police decide to question Michelle about Alex's mother, Nathan or me – and I can't have that.

Why must it always fall to me to find solutions? Nathan never *thinks*! He's made a catastrophic balls-up of all of this – losing his head completely over Julia bloody Blythe and leaving me no choice now but to clear up after him and attend to the boy.

I glance at the passenger seat to make sure the Domosedan gel and oral plunger I swiped from the stables before I left is still there. I'm not scrabbling around in the pissing rain and wind, moving seats back trying to find them in the footwell when I get to Fowles.

Glowering out of the windscreen, I try and formulate my thoughts. I'm going to need to just get on and *do* this once I'm there – not hang around making decisions on the spot. Shit – I did turn off my mobile and the car GPS, didn't I? My heart seizes, but I know I did. *Calm down, Hamish, calm down.* So, it's twenty to forty micrograms per kilogram of body weight to sedate a horse; it's going to be next to nothing for a skinny thirteen-year-old kid. I just want him initially compliant enough not to mind getting in the boot of my car.

From what else I gleaned when I hurriedly logged on to Cecily's laptop – it takes about ten to fifteen minutes once the sedative has gone under the tongue of the horse to take effect. I should probably allow for that with him. The only bit I really don't like about all of this is not knowing the half-life of detomidine. I could only find one study online, relating to the accidental poisoning of a farmer attempting to inject a bull with detomidine before paring its hooves. In that case, he barely got any of it in his system by mistake but was significantly drowsy. Much more and it could well have stopped his heart. It's potent stuff. Would a toxicology report pick the gel up if they tested Julia's son? But in reality, would they even order one? Full forensic post-mortems are horrendously expensive – it would be a huge chunk of someone's budget, especially when I'm going to give them exactly what they are all expecting to find: a drowned boy with no tell-tale signs on his body.

Of course, I've still got to get him out of the hotel, into the boot, drive him back past Beer and Branscombe and down to Westmare caravan park without anyone seeing me. At least by then he should be out cold. But am I really going to be able to carry his heavily sedated body down a pebbled beach and walk him into the sea? I mentally compare him to the build of my stepson Sam; try to imagine myself hoiking that ungrateful lug down a beach, although – I grit my teeth – I think I'd find a way. Sam is also built like the proverbial shithouse, whereas the Blythe boy is a lanky runt of a thing. He barely managed to run the length of the pitch on his Bambi legs at the rugby weekend. Mummy's boys, the lot of them.

Well, I've no choice anyway. I can hardly collect him and simply drop him at home in Exeter, or even at some point en route. Julia's son knows who I am. He'd identify me. If I turn up in a balaclava, he'll freak and try to leg it – every avenue leads to police questioning. I need to shut this whole thing down, for good; although it's also worrying me that a corpse that's been in the water for two nights will present differently to one that's been in the water for one night… but again, that's supposing the body washes up at all. Plenty don't. I sat in on an inquest years ago – a former patient who had chucked herself into the sea in Cornwall – and only one limb was recovered. She was identified by a very helpful tattoo on her wrist. The coroner told me afterwards, it's unfortunately all too common that only body parts are found.

The conditions are also perfect tonight. The tides and winds will almost certainly carry the Blythe boy out to sea rather than take him east or west along the shore.

Lyme itself is deserted as I drop noiselessly down the hill – sending an almost completely silent prayer of thanks to Cecily for insisting we get an electric car. Pulling into Fowles' empty car park, I drive around the back to the goods entrance, before killing my lights. Reaching into my coat pocket, I slip on my gloves, check for my torch, then collect the gel and plunger. We are all systems go.

Letting myself in via the kitchens, I reach for the lights instinctively as I shake the rain from my jacket, before catching myself just in time, feeling for the torch in my pocket instead. Closing the door quietly behind me, I shine the beam on the lock as I twist the key and try the handle to make sure it's secure, just in case he appears and makes a sudden run for it. There's no alarm to deal with after the last one went off so randomly and often the residents started complaining. Lyme is hardly a hotbed of crime, in any case. Not usually anyway.

Turning round, I lift the beam and scan the shapes of the kitchen: hanging pots and pans; closed cupboards; large ovens. It's spotless and silent. Now, where would I hide a thirteen-year-old boy? I push through the swing door into the main function room.

'Alex?' I call softly, the strike of my heels echoing as I walk slowly across the wooden floor, pointing the beam into the shadows cast by stacks of chairs and tables, before emerging into the dark reception area.

'Hello? Master Blythe? Are you there?' I gently push into the drawing room and jump as I see my own reflection in the mantelpiece mirror. Idiot. I shine the light across the rest of the room in a sweep, catching the gleam of the ship in its bottle, neatly stacked wood for the swept and laid fire. Side tables with fans of magazines, numerous fat sofas and chairs all plumped, ready to be sat on. He is not here.

I draw back out and wander into the cold restaurant. The rain has started up again and is thwacking relentlessly against the conservatory windows. I think savagely of Nathan, back in Exeter, as I walk through to the bar area. I shine my torch over the rows of gleaming optics, tempted for a second to draw myself a measure of something, but lip marks on a glass? No.

He must be upstairs, but in which room? I return to reception and move behind the desk, the metal hooks and keys glinting as the torchlight catches them. Every single one is hanging where it should be. I groan aloud. Christ, am I going to have to try all of them individually? I don't have time for this! What if by hideous bad luck something has come into work, and because I'm on call the trauma team is contacting me *right now*? Didn't think of that, did you, Nathan, you selfish prick. Suddenly furious again, I grab the first twelve keys and hurry off to rooms 1 to 12, the beam bouncing as I puff up the shallow stairs. Turning right at random and pushing through the door into the first long, dark corridor, I have to balance the torch on a small table to illuminate my hands as I feed through the keys looking for number 6. I'm itching to put the light on but I daren't. It's too risky. I drop the key on the carpet as I'm fumbling to get it in the lock and curse my sister for being too tight to invest in card systems like any other normal hotelier. The dark is creeping in around me. I don't think many teenagers could spend a whole night and day here on their own. He must be *really* special.

I finally get it open and burst in. Just the virgin gleam of a pristine expanse of white duvet as the moon shines in through the window on to the professionally made bed. No boy. I swear silently and lock it up again before moving on to number 7.

This room tells a *very* different story. A mattress is missing from one of the single beds, the valance all rucked up as if it's been dragged off. The duvet is gone and one pillow is on the floor. I shine my light on the en-suite bathroom door. Has he locked himself in there?

'Alex?' I call softly.

No response. I cross the room swiftly to double-check, but it's open and so small you couldn't possibly get a mattress down anyway. He's got to be somewhere where there's a bigger floor space. I glance out of the window and the dark spire of the folly catches my eye. Nathan wouldn't have put him in there, surely? It'd be bloody arctic for one and there's not even a TV; he'd have nothing to do except wander around, and the whole thing is wall-to-wall windows. He'd be seen in a heartbeat. So bigger floor space and yet shut away from nosy neighbours. I close my eyes and run through the hotel floor plan in my mind – my face breaking into a wide smile as it dawns on me where Alex is. The secret cinema. Soundproofed, no windows, endless movies on tap. Of course.

I rush back to reception and grab the keys, practically bursting into the mini foyer once I've unlocked the door – Nathan locked him in? – then into the screen room itself. Sure enough, there is the mattress on the floor, the duvet scrumpled up and empty bottles and chocolate wrappers littered around. The whole thing could be in the Tate Modern.

'Alex?' I raise my voice, peering among the seats as I click off my torch, struggling to see properly in the subdued lighting. 'Don't be frightened. Nathan sent me.' I put my hand in my pocket and my fingers curl around the plunger. 'Come out and I'll take you back to Exeter.'

Nothing. I frown and walk up to the mattress, bending over and placing the back of my hand on it. Very faintly warm. He's been lying on this recently. He's here.

'Alex?' I try again. 'I'm not going to hurt you. Please come out, wherever you are.' I look around me and my gaze alights on the door leading into the small loo. It's closed but there is a much brighter light shining out from around the edges. I smile, walk across to it and knock on the door. 'Alex? You can come out now. I'm here to rescue you.'

CHAPTER FORTY-THREE

Julia

'I've been thinking a lot during the night and there are some important points I wanted to raise.' I sit opposite the Investigating Officer in a small room at the police station, squinting as the sharp winter sunlight shines directly in my eyes.

'Did you *run* here Julia?' the IO asks, looking at my trainers and gym gear. 'It's really cold this morning?'

'No. I went to the gym earlier, but I drove straight over after that because something occurred to me.'

'Earlier?' She looks at her watch. 'It's not quite nine a.m., on a Sunday. Have you slept at all?'

'Yes.' I try to keep the irritation from my voice. 'I'm fine. So these letters – or clues – that Nathan Sloan has written on the back of the breast implants and put inside some of his patients… Since joining Nathan Sloan's team, I've personally dealt with two cases of encapsulation – that's where the body forms a pocket of scar tissue round an implant that becomes too tight and painful – which affected both patients within six months of their original surgery. That's unusual. Both women had their operations performed by Nathan Sloan. Encapsulation can be caused by infection. Now, Mr Sloan must have handled the implants of the six women in order to write on them unnecessarily – so there's an increased chance he's now exposed *them* to infection. That gives you a medical reason for needing to contact these women, which gets round any issue of patient confidentiality, assuming there was one.'

The IO stares at me. Is she just going to sit there? 'Do you need to note that down?' I suggest. 'Or should I keep going – and then we can recap?'

She blinks. 'It's fine, you tell me the rest.'

'OK.' I shift on my chair uncomfortably, my leg muscles starting to cramp where I didn't stretch earlier, just jumped straight in the car. 'I formally reported Nathan Sloan to the Medical Director of the private hospital he's affiliated to, for filming his female patients without their consent, on Thursday, the twentieth of December, in the afternoon. I saw him in person back at the EM, immediately afterwards, because he was going out with Hamish and Tan – two of our other colleagues. So, he *wasn't* operating that afternoon. I know he was suspended from surgery literally as he was finishing up his fourth procedure on Friday, the twenty-first, because he told me so himself. Therefore, it must be the women on his Thursday list, and the first four women from his Friday schedule who have the letters within them, because I first confronted him on the evening of *Wednesday* the nineteenth.' I stop and take a breath. 'You're still with me, right?'

The IO nods. 'Yes. Yes I am.'

'But the really important point is, I *know* one of the women he operated on that Friday!' I lean forward eagerly. 'I realised when I was trying to piece it all together last night! I bumped into her in person on the Wednesday when I went to confront Mr Sloan at his office. Her name is Stefanie. I've met her socially, and she told me herself she was having a breast augmentation on Friday, the twenty-first of December. She's a really nice woman and I'm sure she'd be very willing to help you.' I take a gulp of my water from the cup the IO gave me when I arrived. 'Now.' I place it back down. 'If she *were* to agree to have further immediate surgery, to identify the letter Mr Sloan has on her implant or implants, I would happily confirm that I think there are medical grounds for it to go ahead, given the increased infection risk I've already outlined to you. Obviously, it would be inappropriate for me to perform the surgery myself, but I'm sure this is something I can talk to the department at the EM about, although I confess I've no experience of needing to 'fast-track' surgery like this when it's not a life-threatening scenario… for Stefanie at least. But it's a starting point, isn't it? One of the colleagues I already mentioned, Tan Husain, is an excellent, very kind surgeon. I'm sure he'd be happy to perform the surgery. Stefanie would be in very safe hands.' I stop and draw breath – waiting for the IO to start running herself with everything I've just given her.

She hesitates and scratches her head. 'OK. Julia, this is all very helpful, thank you. I'll pass it on to the DI and one of the team may well want to talk to you further about what you've said once I've—'

'Hang on.' I put a hand out. 'You're going to talk to Stefanie today, right? Because I'll need to start contacting people at work. Operations don't just "happen".'

'No, I appreciate that. Let's hold back on you doing that for the moment though.' She smiles. 'At least until I've spoken with my Senior Investigating Officer.'

I stare at her and scratch my arm suddenly. 'I'm sorry, but I feel like you don't seem to think what I've just told you is important? Alex has been missing for two nights now. While it's obviously a huge relief that he *hasn't* had some sort of accident, my son is still being held against his will, possibly without enough food or water and, as you pointed out moments ago, the temperature has significantly dropped. So for me to just give you the information that will enable you to find the letters Nathan Sloan has—'

'Julia, I can see you're frustrated and frightened right now, and I totally understand why, but—'

'No, you don't,' I interrupt. 'I'm sorry, but you really *don't* understand what this feels like.'

'What I meant to say was I appreciate why you are frustrated, but we're not able to discuss all of the ongoing developments in this case with you at the moment.'

'So there have been some?' I seize on that.

'As soon as we can, we will,' she says firmly, 'and please be assured that we are working tirelessly to find Alex. What I *can* tell you is that Nathan Sloan is here at the moment as a voluntary attender – this is a phrase that isn't used all over the UK, so you may not find it if you google it – but it means that he's here with a solicitor and is being interviewed under caution, not arrest, at the moment. You can trust us to do this, I promise.' She looks at me sympathetically.

I shift in my chair again. 'It's got nothing to do with trust. Why wouldn't I trust you? After all, you're not sitting there thinking I sound mad, are you? You're thinking this very sensible, rational woman is telling me something so unusual and awful I have to investigate it, because why would she lie about it? You trust *me*, right?' I sound too aggressive. I see my mistake the second I've finished speaking.

She raises her eyebrows. 'I hear you and I promise that we're helping you, Julia. We are doing everything we can.' She stands up.

'Look, it's not that I'm saying you're all doing a bad job.' She's pissed off with me now, I can tell. 'I'm not trying to be rude to you. Yes, I'm used to being the person in control. No, I don't like not being able to do anything – but none of this is about that. I'm very uneasy that what Nathan Sloan told me last night will be dismissed – because he'll now be denying he said it – but as we've already discussed, *why* would I make up something as bizarre as that? Here, I'm going to give you Stefanie's details, so you can speak to her as soon as possible.' I reach into my hoodie pocket for my mobile. I find the number and hold out the screen to the IO, forcing her to note the number down.

'I'm sure we'll have updates we can share with you soon.' She gestures to the door the second she's done it. I've been dismissed.

I'm left with no choice but to get to my feet too and let her lead me back to reception… only as we're walking down the corridors, I glance through an open door to see Ben Sloan and Storm sitting on one side of a table, accompanied by some man in a suit. A solicitor perhaps? I can't help myself; I double back and stare right at them. Ben looks up with red eyes – he's obviously been crying and the second Storm clocks me, she looks astonished.

'Julia? What are you doing here? Are you?—'

But before she can continue, I hear someone else start speaking, the door closes and the IO hurriedly leads me away.

'Why is Ben here?' I ask immediately. 'What's he got to do with any of this? Is he under arrest?'

'When we can discuss developments with you, we will.'

*

Back in the car, I sit in the driver's seat, staring out of the windscreen in frustration. I've done this all wrong. I should have gone to see Stefanie first and explained everything to her; that way, she could have come down to the station *with* me, which would have forced the police to act then and there. But I've already passed the information on. I'm going to have to leave it to them. I can't go and see her now… can I?

I hesitate and start up the car. I could go and see Tan though. I can at least ask him if he'd be prepared to help in the event of the police needing someone to operate at short notice… but it's Trishna who answers the door when I knock.

'Julia!' She's understandably shocked to see me. 'Oh my goodness!'

'Hello.' I try to smile. 'How are you? I'm sorry to be turning up out of the blue like this, but I wondered if I could speak to Tan?'

'He's at the hospital, I'm afraid. There was a mix-up at work; he had to go in and cover an on-call for Hamish. Shall I get him to call you when he gets back?'

'No, it's OK. Don't worry. I might pop down to the hospital and see if I can catch him there. Thank you, though.'

'Julia?' I turn back and she's holding the door wide open, beckoning me in, her kind face etched with concern. 'Would you have a cup of tea with me? We saw the appeal on television last night. I can't imagine what you are going through right now. I think you are so brave. Do you have time to stop for a moment?'

That draws me up short. I don't know. I don't want Alex to have to be without me for a moment longer. I want everything, *everyone* to be urgently searching everywhere. I want the police to be on their way to talk to Stefanie now and yet, perversely, I have too much time because, ultimately, this search is beyond my control and I can't bear it. The seconds and minutes and hours are ticking over and over and over and still he's not here.

'Thank you.' I force myself to smile again. 'I probably won't come in, though.' I gesture down at myself. 'I ought to get home and sorted out. I'm a bit of a state!'

'No, you're not. Whenever you are ready. We are here for you,' she says simply, and I have to turn and practically run back to the car before I break down at her kindness.

Once I'm sitting behind the wheel, I suddenly change my mind. I *am* going to see Stefanie. She will come with me to the station right now, I'm sure of it. She was so kind to me about Alex, too. She will understand.

I drive too fast to where I think I remember she lives, but have to crawl around the leafy streets, looking at the identical white Georgian house fronts because I can't remember exactly which one is hers. I double back a couple of times uncertainly, before trusting my judgement that I've got the right place.

'Julia!' She throws the heavy door open before I've finished knocking. She's immaculately made up and dressed in a soft, tight cashmere jumper tucked into black jeans to emphasise her new shape: big breasts, tiny waist and lean legs… even her hair is hairdresser bouncy, she looks almost computer generated. 'I was upstairs when I saw you driving past, then back again. I was going to lean out of the window but… anyway, come in.'

I step into the hallway, and as she closes the door I get a waft of fresh coffee and toast. My stomach rumbles involuntarily, and she raises a stern eyebrow.

'You need something to eat. You should be keeping your strength *up* at a time like this. Come on.' She turns and I kick off my trainers before following her. She's already pouring me a coffee in the huge, chilly kitchen and pushing a small jug of milk across an island when I walk in, but I hesitate, worried suddenly that I'm making a mistake, that I should leave this alone and not interfere. I don't know how to begin.

She sits down on a high stool and waits for me to join her. 'You must be exhausted. This is all too ghastly for words. I saw the appeal last night. How horrendous for you.' She's one of those people who doesn't shy away but becomes brisk and practical in a crisis. 'Has it yielded anything yet?'

'Yes,' I say uncertainly, and she sits up straighter. 'Oh?'

I join her at the island. 'Nathan Sloan came to see me at home last night. He told me something that I'm afraid involves you.'

She doesn't move for a moment, then puts her hands in her lap. 'Me? I can't imagine how?'

I clear my throat, unsure if I should continue… but I've started now and if the police are taking me seriously, why have I beaten them to this? Why aren't *they* here, telling Stefanie what I'm about to? 'Nathan confessed he's hidden Alex from me.'

Stefanie almost drops her coffee. As it slips in her grasp, she spills some of it down the front of her caramel jumper. 'Damn!' She jumps up, still holding it and more liquid lurches from the cup onto the white marble worktop. She slams it down and rushes to get a cloth, scrubbing furiously at the stain before throwing it back in the sink and turning to look at me again with an odd, bright smile. 'I'm so sorry. You're saying Nathan has *abducted* Alex?'

'Yes. When Nathan did your operation just before Christmas,' I plough on quickly, 'he wrote a letter, using a surgical pen, on one of the implants he put inside you… and he did the same thing to five other women he operated on. These six letters together reveal where Alex is. Nathan has deliberately and callously stitched them inside your bodies. This was utterly premeditated and a deeply shocking thing for him to have done. I told the police this morning that I know you are one of his patients, so they'll be contacting you – to ask if you would consider having some additional emergency surgery to recover the letter and help us find Alex.'

She stares at me for a moment. 'You want me to have another general anaesthetic so you can cut me open again, when I've only just started properly healing, to see if there is a *letter* in me?'

'There definitely is. He's already told me.'

'Would you do it?' she asks suddenly. 'If you were sat where I am now?'

I hesitate. 'If it meant finding a missing child, yes, I would.'

'Don't be ridiculous! No, you wouldn't! Of course I'm not willing to have another major operation on the basis of what you've just said! Are you totally mad?' She gets to her feet.

I hold up a hand. She's freaking out, and I get that. Who wouldn't? 'I appreciate it's very hard to hear that you're one of his victims, but—'

'Victim? Goodness, that's a strong word.' She folds her arms. 'These implants all carry serial numbers on them now, I believe, so they can be registered on a national database as a safety measure?'

'Yes, that's correct.'

'So even if he did write on them, how is that any different to the serial number? Nathan didn't write *on me*. That doesn't make me feel like a victim.'

'It's completely different! Nathan would have removed the implants from sterile conditions, handled them unnecessarily when he tampered with them and placed them back in boxes before your surgery. That places you at a significantly increased infection risk, something Nathan would be very aware of. He also did it with the single purpose of you needing to be opened up again to remove it. He's treated you like a human storage facility.'

She doesn't take her eyes from me. 'Have *you* ever written on the back of an implant you've used on a patient?'

'It's not common practice. I've marked the skin of patients with surgical pen, yes, but with their permission and not in the way Nathan—'

'Just yes is fine.' She cuts me off. 'Sorry. Once a barrister… I'm just really struggling here.' She picks up her coffee, walks to the sink and chucks it away. 'If someone was presenting this to me to see if I'd represent it, I'd be saying a firm no… He's marked something that's been placed within my body, that already carries markings in the form of a serial number. Do you see? So all you're left with is asking me to undergo emergency surgery on the basis that YOU say this letter, that he may or may not have written, may or may not carry some sort of significance.' She gives me a bland smile. 'So as I've already said, it's a no from me. What do the other women say? Has *anyone* else said yes to your request?'

'You're the first victim I've asked.'

'There with the "victim" again!' She winces. 'I'm really not sure you can get away with that. I'd be careful if I were you. Did you choose me first because you know me socially and I'm also a mother? You thought you'd exploit that?'

My mouth falls open. I appreciate she's shocked, but that's downright hostile. 'I understand that asking you to have more surgery under these circumstances *is* very extreme, but—'

'You know, when Caroline asked me to have you to dinner, I was only too happy to help out,' she interrupts, her tone conversational. 'A mutual friend in need and all that. She explained that you'd had a rough time of it before moving here, all of the press intrusion with your court case, and I won't lie, I googled you. I read some of the things you alleged about your former colleagues, dead rats and the like, and I thought that *poor* woman. How horrendous. Who would treat a colleague so badly?' She picks a piece of lint from the front of her jumper and flicks it away delicately with her fingers. 'But now here you are, sitting in my kitchen, telling me that a very good friend of my husband – and mine – who I trust enough to perform surgery on me, has abducted your son and put clues to his whereabouts inside people. Now, I don't deny that you must be under enormous strain and I can see it's had a material effect on you. You look exhausted: you plainly haven't slept or washed.' She glances at my gym gear. 'But Nathan would *never* do something like that to me – to anyone,' she adds quickly.

'He's also been filming all of his consultations in his office; women undressing, himself intimately examining them. Women in a state of vulnerability, who trusted him. Did you give him *your* consent? Surely, as a barrister, *that* concerns you?'

The expression falls away from her face. 'How do you know that?' Her voice is little more than a whisper.

'I saw the cameras for myself and consequently reported him. He's already been suspended by the private hospital that his practice is affiliated to.'

'Is this common knowledge yet?'

'I don't think so, no.'

She exhales shakily. 'Well, I'm sure there is a reasonable explanation for that too. I wouldn't want to comment without having spoken to Nathan himself first.'

A reasonable explanation? I try again. 'He's played God with your bodies, and I am truly sorry that his feelings for me have been expressed in such a twisted way, but—'

'His feelings for you? Are you in a relationship with Nathan?'

'God no!' I draw back. 'I'm married for one, and for two I respect myself too much to let him anywhere near me. I'm well aware of his reputation, that he'll take any opportunity with any woman who stands still long enough.'

'My, my. We do have a high opinion of ourselves, don't we?' She is starting to breathe a little faster. 'You say you've already reported him for filming his patients? So this will all be made public soon?' She is starting to look flushed. 'You really are a nasty little stirrer after all, aren't you? I'm afraid I'm going to have to ask you to leave.' She's actually shaking. I didn't expect her reaction to be anywhere close to this extreme. 'I am at a loss to know why you would be making up such extraordinary and insane allegations about a trusted friend of ours. I do hope they find your son soon, of course. Perhaps then you can all go back to where you came from?'

*

My eyes are still red when I pull up outside the hospital. Stefanie might have said no, but if the police identify the other five women, there is still a chance one of them will say yes. I should have let them handle it. I am a fool. Stefanie is a barrister. She would have responded so much better to the police than me. It would have made it less personal, less of a tug of loyalties given her husband and Nathan are friends. I didn't think it through. In a way she's right: I did think I knew better than everyone else.

I walk up to the office, but Tan isn't there. I must have missed him. I try the other plastics office instead, and as I stick my head round the door, one of the nicest of their team looks up – his face registering surprise to see me.

'Julia! Hello! We weren't expecting to see you back here for a little while. Er, how are things? Any, any…' he struggles for the right words, 'update yet?'

'Not yet, no. But thank you for asking. Jim, I was wondering if you'd seen Tan?' I move us both on quickly. 'He was in here covering Hamish's on-call last night. I thought perhaps he might still be around if it was something big.'

Jim frowns. 'Nothing big came in last night that was mentioned when I did the handover a couple of hours ago? And Tan wasn't covering for Hamish. Hamish was in earlier. He's gone now, but you could catch him on his mobile?'

'Thanks, but it was Tan I specifically wanted.' I pause. 'I must have got my wires crossed. I'm pretty tired to be fair.'

'Of course you are,' he says sympathetically.

'OK, well thanks anyway.' I give him a redundant wave. 'See you soon.'

'I really hope you get some positive news before too much longer. We're all thinking of Alex.'

'Thank you.' I envy him simply going back to his paperwork and the rest of his day, with a longing so overwhelming it makes my head swim.

*

I try Tan's mobile but there's no answer. There's nothing for it but to go back to the house. Nathan is telling me the truth, I've no doubt about that, so what if the other five women refuse to help me? What if they react like Stefanie did? What will Nathan do then?

As I reach the village, it starts to rain: a fine drizzle misting up the window. I told Cass I would be back by the time Ewan woke up, having done the night shift of staying awake while I tried to rest, so I can't be late. I don't want him, or her, to worry. Dom and

Sorcha are arriving in half an hour. I need to get showered and changed. Ewan also wants to go to the shops with Cass to pick up some food, but no one likes to leave the house empty, just in case.

I pull up on the drive and open the front door, calling instantly, 'it's just me, that's all.'

'I'm getting dressed,' Ewan calls down. 'Had a quick shower after I woke up. Cass said you came back and got the car to go into town?' He appears at the top of the stairs in just his trousers, rough-drying his hair and pausing to look at me worriedly. 'Where did you go?'

'The police station. I had a few thoughts.' I can't bring myself to tell him about Stefanie yet, how badly I handled it. 'I saw Ben Sloan and Storm being interviewed. The IO said she'll be in touch again soon as they can tell us what's going on. I don't know what that means, if anything.'

Cass appears from the sitting room. 'The police were interviewing Ben?' She looks frightened. 'Why? What's he done?'

'I don't know, sweetheart,' I say truthfully, walking off down the hall as she follows me. 'Perhaps they had some more questions to ask about—'

But I don't finish my sentence as I round the corner into the kitchen, because there, in the back doorway, kicking off his wellies like some exhausted, beautiful, damp angel, is Alex.

Cass and I both scream in unison; I don't know how we cross the room so quickly, but somehow my son is immediately in my arms. I am *holding him again*, stroking his hair and weeping. I can hear Ewan shouting upstairs in alarm, and Cass shrieking 'he's here, Daddy! Alex is here!' and I can't stop kissing him, laughing, crying and gasping, 'Oh thank God!' over and over again. Cass rushes and throws herself at us too, sobbing, and I look up over my children to see my husband leaning weakly on the door frame, his hand over his mouth as tears of relief course down his face. I have never experienced such instant release from pain in my whole life. The *love*… heaven appearing in the corner of an ordinary, messy kitchen, on a rainy Sunday morning in January.

A moment I will never, ever forget.

CHAPTER FORTY-FOUR

Nathan

Emerging into bright sunlight, jacked up on coffee, uncomfy in the clothes I've been in for more than twenty-four hours and jittery from anxiety and no sleep, I am on hyperalert… If I closed my eyes, I could be a junior coming off nights all over again. I wish I was: perhaps I'd make a better stab of this second bit of my life if I had my time over. Instead, I cross the police car park towards a Range Rover containing my wife and son, which is going to be like climbing into a giant inflatable bubble full of shit that I will then attempt to walk uphill.

On the plus side, the police have released me. There were 'voluntary' questions about Julia's allegations, which sounded even more bizarre when recounted aloud to me. Wearily – that wasn't a stretch – I denied them all. I admitted it had been unwise to go to her house in the first place, but the truth of the matter was Julia Blythe and I – until recently – had been involved in a relationship.

'I very foolishly went to her house again last night after I saw the TV appeal because I was worried about her. We're not together now, for various reasons, but you don't just stop loving people overnight. I wanted to make sure she was OK, but things got out of hand. I ended up telling her husband we'd had an affair… and

Julia just panicked. She went into full-on defence mode, via attack. She started just spouting these lies that I'd abducted Alex.' I had put my head in my hands. 'She's under immense strain, our relationship didn't end well and she's very angry with me. She's making all sorts of allegations that simply aren't true.'

I'm pretty sure they bought it – but I have plenty more problems to solve. My mobile is completely dead. When they returned my belongings, it wasn't switching on or off. 'We wouldn't have touched it,' the plod handling my discharge had said firmly. 'If your battery was low it would have just run down organically.'

Organic my arse. They left it on deliberately to see if anything interesting came in, message-wise. I'm not that stupid. I have everything set to private. No partial message displays at all. But it does mean I don't know if Hamish got to Fowles last night and let Alex go, and I am *shitting* myself about that. If he hasn't, I don't know what I'm going to do. Alex will have panicked. I keep thinking about what Ben said about Alex sticking a fork in a toaster at the party. He's really not the full ticket. If he's done something *really* stupid, my fingerprints are going to be literally all over him and the tape around his wrists and ankles. Ben is also sitting in that car I'm about to climb into, wondering why I didn't wake him up, as promised. Storm is going to want an explanation of what exactly would land me in the nick all night. If I'm to stand a chance of getting out of this in one piece, I need to stay sharp on my feet and remember exactly who knows what.

I take a deep breath and open the door to the car.

'Hi gang!' I smile. 'Thanks for coming to get me! Did you ring to see what time they were letting me go?'

'We were already here,' Storm replies flatly as I climb in.

Alarm bells begin to ring. 'Oh right?' I say casually. 'Why's—'

'Dad!' Ben bursts, pushing his phone through the gap between us, unable to contain himself a second longer. 'Alex is back! Cassia messaged me! He's at his house, Dad!'

I haven't had a rush like this in a *very* long time. The relief and euphoria flow through me like psychedelic rainbows. He did it! Oh Hamish, you beautiful, beautiful man! Thank. Fucking. God.

'That's brilliant news!' I exclaim, twisting to look at Ben as Storm starts the car and pulls away. He looks back at me, completely confused, and I widen my eyes silently, pleading with him to get the message.

'Sit back and put your seat belt on, love.' Storm glances at our son in the rear-view mirror.

I watch his expression change in front of me like clouds scooting across the sun; urgency is turning into frustration, which quickly becomes disappointment and finally, powerless resignation. He flops back into his seat and deliberately turns his head away from me. But he is at least quiet.

I twist to face the front again. I can rescue this when we get home; it's nothing that fifty quid won't solve. He'll get over it. The main thing is Alex is back. Hamish stood by me. I lean my head on the rest and close my eyes for a moment. Everything else can be dealt with. It can all—

'So who did you make your one phone call to, out of interest?' Storm's terse tone cuts through my thoughts.

'I couldn't remember your number. I asked Hamish to contact you.' I frown and look at her. 'You're saying he didn't?'

She nods slowly. 'That is correct. The police came to the house for an informal chat this morning with Ben. You were nowhere to be seen. I assumed on a run or something. I called your phone and got your voicemail. So then I called Paul Gainsford straight away because I didn't want to let Ben speak to anyone without checking the legalities first. Paul told me the best thing to do was to ask for any discussion to take place at the police station because he was already there – with you.'

'OK,' I say slowly. I twist to look at Ben again. 'You all right, champ? The police were nice to you?'

He stares out of the window. 'Yeah. They wanted to know if we'd seen Alex when we went sailing on Friday.' He turns and looks right at me. 'I told them we hadn't.'

I give him a quick wink. He looks away.

Why didn't Hamish ring Storm? I don't get it. I need to speak to him ASAP. I turn back and look at my dead phone in my hands. 'So you won't have picked the car up yet?'

'Excuse me?' Storm shoots an incredulous look at me. 'From outside Julia's, you mean? No, Nathan. We have not picked your car up yet.'

'OK, well let's swing by and get it now.' I've got a charger in the car, and I can call Ham in privacy on my way back. As long as I'm careful and don't say anything incriminating, I think that would be OK? Almost more suspicious if I *didn't* call, in fact?

'You're serious?' Storm says. 'That's what you want to do first of all. Get your car.'

'Yes,' I say patiently. 'Then I'll come home and we'll sort everything out. OK?'

She doesn't say anything to that. When we finally pull up at the top of Julia's road, I simply open the door. I don't attempt to kiss her because she's making it very clear which way she intends to play this.

As she roars off, I reach into my back pocket and blip the Porsche, which was moved onto the other side of the road by the police last night and is now opposite Julia's house. I walk round to the driver's side and look across at her parked-up Mini. The Christmas wreath is still on the door and the real tree up in the front window, lit and twinkling. It all looks very pretty and inviting. The house of a happy family. I glance again at the tree. That needs to come down today though. It's Twelfth Night. Bad luck otherwise. I scan the windows searchingly. No sign of movement. A police car turns into the top of the road, so I quickly get my head down, climb in, start the car and pull away as they approach.

I don't stop until I'm back in St Leonards, where I pull over at the end of my own street to plug my phone in and call Hamish. The second it switches on, it updates with new voicemail. That has to be him… but when I dial in, it's Storm wondering where I am and then a calm, measured message from Stefanie, asking me to call her back as she's had a visit at home from Julia, who has made all sorts of outlandish allegations about me and her missing son that I really ought to be aware of. But there is nothing at all from Hamish.

I call him. It rings… and rings and rings. He is not picking up. I leave him a voicemail, asking him to call me, then once I hang up, I ring again. It goes straight to answerphone. He's listening to the message. I sit there confidently waiting for him to ring back once he's done, but more than enough time passes and he… doesn't. So I ring again.

He picks up.

'Hey, it's me!' I begin, but there's a silence. I can only hear him breathing. 'Hamish? Are you there?'

'I'm here and I want you to listen to me very carefully. Our association is over.'

'Our association?' I laugh. 'What are you talking about?'

'From here on in, we are colleagues for the time being and that's it. You don't contact me informally again.'

'But this is crazy! I—'

'No, Nathan. This weekend has pushed me beyond my limits. I don't want you in my life anymore. It's as simple as that. You're selfish, you're a liability and you're on your own now. Do not bring anything else to my table, you understand me? Not a single bloody thing.'

He hangs up. I put the phone down in shock, only to see Storm walking slowly towards the car, watching me. She opens the passenger door and climbs in.

'I've dropped Ben with one of the school mums for an hour. We need to talk. No more lies now. Can you do that for me, please? Why were you arrested last night?' She doesn't look at me.

'For refusing to give a breath test.'

'I've been told by an old friend at the EM that there are rumours of you having kissed a work colleague—'

I hesitate. This could be that someone saw me with Michelle at the club, or it could be the photo of Julia...

'Have you been having an affair?'

Ah – back on safer ground; Stefanie. 'Yes, I have.'

She closes her eyes and a slow breath of pain escapes from her lips. 'Is that who you were just speaking to?' she whispers.

'No. That was Hamish.'

'Who is she?'

'It doesn't matter.'

She winces silently in the way that the braver patients cope when you do something to them that *really* hurts, and wraps an arm round her stomach, clutching it tightly. 'It matters to me.'

'It shouldn't. It's over.'

'Do you love her?'

'No. I don't.' I cannot believe what Hamish has just said. Alex is back! It can be like the weekend never happened! I didn't come out of it Julia's hero, and it was never my intention to discredit, anger or hurt her, but things could have been a lot worse. Although there is also no way she will drop it about the filming now, and I'm going to have to deal with the allegations alone. I can't!

I feel like I'm sat on a board, paddling out to sea... I can see it all inevitably coming towards me; a bloody great wave that's going to pull me under until I don't know which way is up.

'I want us to leave,' Storm says suddenly. 'I will stay with you – for Ben's sake. I'll try again, but I'm not doing it here. It would be too humiliating. I want us to go to America.'

'*America?*' I turn to her. I did not see that coming.

'I'm not staying here to worry that it's started up again and you're seeing her again behind my back. I want to get as far away as possible. You could easily get work there. I want to go this week. The girls can come and visit as much as they like… your daughters,' she clarifies. I must have looked momentarily lost but really, I'm thinking, it's not the worst idea. Would they bother to try and haul me back from the States to face charges over the filming when I'm an American citizen? Don't they have to apply for extradition or something to do that?

'The girls are almost sixteen,' I say slowly. 'By the time I was their age, I'd lived without any of my family for nine years. We'd probably see *more* of them. America versus Devon. Not much contest.'

We sit there in silence for a moment longer, both wondering if it could work, staring ahead. We must look insane to anyone watching. Motionless in a stationary car, outside our own house. This is a total, heartbreaking mess. I put my hand on the door. I'm getting cold. 'Let's go in and we'll talk about it some more.'

'Nathan?'

I stop and turn back.

'I need you to tell me it meant nothing to you.' She is hugging herself tightly. 'I need to know it didn't happen like it did with us.' She turns and looks at me desperately. 'That you weren't fascinated with her like you were me. Not having me drove you mad, remember? Do you remember how often you used to call me?' She tries to smile.

'Yes, I do.' I *was* infatuated with her for a time, it's true. Storm was the hospital beauty from the second she arrived. I had to have her, but it was nothing like what I feel for Julia.

'Do you love me, Nathan?'

Luckily, before I have to answer there is a tap at the window and one of our neighbours walks past, waving and clutching a paper.

We both force bright smiles and wave back. 'We need to go in.' I open the door, climbing out. 'I have to call Hamish back.'

We walk up to the house, and I wait patiently alongside her on the doorstep while she feels around for her keys in her pockets. She struggles to get it to turn in the lock once she *has* found it, and starts tugging the door towards her to force it to give.

'Here. Let me.' I place my hand over hers to help, and at my touch, she turns and collapses into tears on my chest. I put my arms round her automatically and kiss her black hair as she sobs. 'Hey! Hush!' I say quietly. 'You're OK. Let's go inside.'

'Promise me that we will try our hardest to make this work in America, that all we need is each other and Ben?'

Bleakly, I think of Julia and being on the other side of the world to her. I spy another neighbour across the way coming out of her front door, ready to go for a run, looking curiously in our direction as she pauses on her doorstep to stretch her quads. 'Let's go inside now. I don't want to give anyone anything else to talk about.'

CHAPTER FORTY-FIVE

Julia

'I am really sorry. It was just a game.' Alex looks at the officer sitting opposite us on the sofa with wide, frightened eyes as I hold his hand. 'I didn't think it would be this big, that Mum would be on TV and everything.'

'We're not angry.' The DC gives him a kind smile. 'We just want to make sure we understand what happened, that's all. You don't have to answer me if you don't want to. This is just a chat now you've come home, so we can update our records. What was the game about?'

Alex pulls his hand back and starts picking his nails nervously. 'I wanted people to miss me. I wanted them to notice I'd gone and be pleased when I came back. I wanted them to think I was brave and that I'd escaped. People at school mostly.'

'Escaped from what?'

Alex looks anxious again. 'I was going to say someone kidnapped me.'

The DC nods thoughtfully. 'And did they?'

I hold my breath.

Alex shakes his head. 'No. It was all made up. I'm sorry!' His eyes fill with tears. 'It was really, really stupid of me.'

'So what did you do after you left Cass and Ben on the boat?' The DC leans back on the sofa, casual, relaxed.

'I went into town, up on the coast path. I lost my bag but then I hid.'

'You lost it?'

'Yeah, I don't know exactly what happened.' He scratches his head. 'I think it fell off the...' He stops himself quickly, flushes and adds, 'cliff.'

'Where did you hide?'

Alex pushes his spare glasses back on his nose. 'You said I don't have to answer? I don't really want to say, if that's OK?'

'In case you want to hide there again?'

He looks alarmed. 'No! I'm *never* going to do this again.'

'OK, well that's good to hear. But it was somewhere that had food? You were warm? You had somewhere safe to sleep?'

'Yeah.'

'How did you know how long to stay there though, because you lost your things?' He leans forward, sounding interested, as if Alex has been really clever. 'You didn't have a phone, so how did you know what time it was?'

Alex lifts up his arm and proudly shows him Dom's father's watch. 'I had this. It helped *a lot*.'

'Ah. I see! That explains it.' The DC hesitates. 'Alex, nobody has hurt you or made you afraid to tell us the truth about what really happened, have they?'

'No. No one hurt me. I just wanted people at school to like me for being brave.'

I put my arm round his thin shoulders. Hearing that is almost more than I can bear.

'I understand. We're all just really glad you came home. So how did you get back today?' The DC starts looking around him, patting his pockets as if he's preparing to go and these aren't really even questions anymore, just the end of a friendly exchange.

'I walked along the coast road, then back on the estuary path, where all the people cycle?' He looks the DC right in the eye. 'It was just a game. Please don't be angry.'

*

Once Cass and Alex have disappeared into the kitchen to find something to eat, and Ewan has taken his place on the sofa, I turn back to the DC. 'So what happens now?'

'We'll update his records in case he does this again and—'

'You believe everything he said to you?' I interrupt. 'You think this was "just a game" too?'

The DC pauses. I can see he's picking his words carefully. 'When a misper comes back, we always continue investigations to either prove or disprove an offence, if there is one. Just because a juvenile says "no one hurt me" doesn't mean we automatically take their word for it, but there isn't anyone else in this case saying "yes someone DID hurt him". We don't have any evidence that Alex isn't telling the truth.'

'Except for what Nathan Sloan told *me*,' I say quietly.

'Your statement said Nathan told you this was part of a plan. Let's say for sake of argument that's what happened – it's still not an offence if Alex went along with it willingly. It's very misguided, but not illegal. And of course, when we questioned Mr Sloan, and his son, both of them insisted they were sailing together all afternoon around the time Alex went missing and didn't see him at all. Mr Sloan denies saying anything to you about any plan or clues hidden within his patients' bodies. He cited a personal relationship between the two of you that ended acrimoniously.'

'That's not true,' Ewan says. 'I expect he probably showed you a picture of my wife apparently kissing him? It wasn't how it appeared.'

The DC looks politely at the floor for a moment before lifting his gaze again. He's feeling sorry for Ewan, thinks he's deluded – I can tell. 'The trouble is, there's no evidence of foul play here,' he reminds us. 'Alex insists that it was a game and he was hiding. Mr Sloan and his son insist they were sailing together all afternoon on the Friday that Alex went missing. There's nothing to say they weren't all doing what they said they were – except your allegation.'

'What about forensics?' I say desperately. 'If you tested the inside of Nathan Sloan's boat, rib, whatever it's called – I'm sure you'd find evidence that Alex had been in there, while he took him to wherever he hid him?'

The DC nods. 'I'm sure you're right, but then there would be evidence of Alex having been on the boat anyway, because he joined Cassia and Ben there before going off on his own, didn't he?'

I open my mouth to protest again but give up. This is pointless. They don't believe Nathan has done anything wrong. He's going to get away with what he's done to Alex.

Men like him always do.

*

'Dad and Granny will be here in a minute, so let's find you a clean top to wear.' I open Al's drawers as he stands shivering in his jeans, hair damp from the shower and arms folded self-consciously across his bare chest. I find a T-shirt and hand it over. 'I'm so sorry that I didn't see how unhappy you were, Alex.' I glance out of window and realise Nathan's car has gone. I shiver. When did he come to get that?

He frowns. 'It wasn't *you* I wanted to notice me. It was people at school. I'm not – popular. Can we just not talk about it anymore? I just want to get dressed.' He pulls the top over his head and moves away. 'I didn't mean everyone to get angry.'

'Al, I'm not cross.' I reach out to catch his wrist as he passes. I'm about to tell him we need to talk about what really happened, but his skin is all sticky.

'What's on your arm?' I frown as he snatches back away from me. 'Nothing!'

But it's too late, I'm already inspecting his other wrist too. That's tacky as well. I look more closely and can see tiny lumps of what looks like glue. It's not unusual for Al to not wash properly, but… 'Your hands have been taped!' I look up at him in horror.

'No, they haven't!' He pulls them back again and puts them behind his back.

My heart thumps. 'Al, enough now. Forget what you've said to everyone else, this is me. I'm your mum and I KNOW this was a plan – or game – between you and Nathan, Ben's dad. I know this because Nathan told me himself.'

Alex stares furiously down at the floor, refusing to meet my eye.

'Please tell me what happened? Or even just where he hid you? *He* taped your wrists up, didn't he?'

He laughs suddenly. 'I don't think he told you anything! You're just trying to trick me!'

Oh Jesus – he doesn't get this at all.

'OK, you got me!' I nudge him, trying to change tack with a grin. 'Tell me who "rescued" you instead then? I know *that* wasn't Nate, but you couldn't have got free on your own! Come on! Who else was there? How did you do it? It's driving me crazy!'

'No. Not telling.' But he grins.

Oh, he is so bloody naïve. Do I say I know it couldn't have been Nathan who freed him because he was in prison last night?

'I won't tell anyone else, I promise!' I cross my heart.

His smile fades. 'But you *always* tell on people!'

'Oh Alex, come on!' Frustrated, I change again. 'Cass thought you weren't ever coming back! She was devastated. The police thought you'd fallen off the cliffs – especially when your bag washed up with your glasses in it.'

He blushes bright red. 'My glasses were getting scratched, so I put them away then my bag fell off the boat.'

'Whose boat? Nathan's?' I pounce on that quickly, but he's already shaking his head.

'Please Mum, *don't ask me*. He made me promise not to tell. He said he'd get into really bad trouble.'

'Who did? Nathan?'

'No. The man last night.' He holds up his arms. 'But you can't tell I even said that! Not to Ewan or anyone. Promise me! It's really important!'

'I promise. Do I know this man? Was he at the rugby weekend?'

'Yes! But I'm not saying *anything* else.'

Hamish. 'Is he the man who?—' but before I can push any further the door opens gently and to my enormous frustration Dom appears in the gap.

'Ewan said it was all right to come up, but…' His face softens at the sight of Alex. 'Oh! It's so good to see you!'

'It's good to see you too.' Alex looks embarrassed. 'I'm sorry that I—'

'Hey!' Dom comes right into the room. '*I* say sorry here, not you.' His eyes well up and he wipes them quickly. Alex looks horrified and flings himself at Dom, almost knocking him off his feet.

'Please don't cry, Dad! I'm sorry! I didn't mean to frighten you.'

I watch Dom fold his arms around Al then twist to kiss his hair. 'It's OK. You're home, that's all that matters. I love you so much!'

Al rests his head on his father's shoulder and smiles blissfully. I can't help but think he's starting to believe this has all turned out pretty well really.

I've missed my moment. He's not going to tell me anything now.

*

In desperation, I try Cass later, to see if Al has confided in her, but apparently not. 'He just said it was a game,' she shrugs as I scream inwardly.

'How long does it take to be a doctor?' she asks suddenly.

'Five years to be a doctor, ten years minimum to get to where I am. A bit more sometimes if you want to stop and have children or do a PhD. Do both, like me, and takes forever.'

'*Ten years?*' she repeats in disbelief. 'That's a really long time to do the same thing.'

'It's not *all* the same. Why do you want to know, anyway?'

She shrugs. 'No reason. Alex didn't say anything about where he was. Can I speak to Ben now, please?' She holds up her phone.

'Of course.' I can't stop her. It wouldn't be fair. 'It's fine for you to talk to him again.'

'Yeah, I know *that*,' she says. 'I mean, can you leave my room, please?'

*

When everyone has finally gone home, the phones and doorbell have all stopped ringing, and Alex and Cass are both in bed – right where they are supposed to be – I sit at the kitchen table with Ewan. We simply look at each other in exhausted, stunned silence.

'That was quite the day,' Ewan says eventually. 'I think we—'

There's a noise in the doorway and we both look round to see Cass, shivering in her pjs, eyes red from crying.

'What's the matter?' I hold out my arms as her face crumples and she rushes across the room to me, in tears. 'Ben's moving!' she weeps. 'He's just messaged me. They're going to go and live in America!' I stroke her hair while her heart breaks and look at Ewan, over the top of her head.

He's running away.

Tell me that's not the action of a guilty man with something to hide.

*

I march across the work car park the following morning full of righteous anger. I have my arguments prepared and I want answers.

While it's clear Nathan's going to face no further action over what he did to Alex, the small issue of the filming is a different matter. Nothing has changed *there*, so how is he being allowed to disappear? He's already been suspended from private practice. Everyone should know about it by now. He cannot be allowed to slink off so that they avoid a scandal. It isn't fair, it isn't right and I won't let it happen. I'll literally yell about it if I have to.

Several people accost me on my way in, to let me know they are so pleased that Alex 'decided' to come home, like it was all no more than some hormonal teenage flip-out. I bite my tongue so hard I'm almost in tears when I run into Jim, who is sweetly delighted that Alex is safe.

'My sister's son ran away for a bit too,' he confides as we cross on the stairs. 'I didn't like to say when I saw you yesterday morning because I didn't want to draw comparisons that might not have been helpful while he was still missing. We don't always know what goes on with our kids behind closed doors, do we? Especially with social media the way it is. It's so hard to police what they're up to.' He smiles at me kindly. 'I'm not surprised you still feel shaken up.'

'It was Nathan,' I blurt. 'He took Alex and helped him hide somewhere. I don't know where. Then he came to my house and told me if I wanted Al back, I'd have to recover six letters he'd written on the breast implants of six of his living patients. Then he told my husband we've been having an affair. We haven't, whatever he might be saying otherwise.'

Jim stares at me, speechless.

'I know.' I shrug miserably. 'The trouble is, I don't have any proof of what he said and Alex is back now anyway, so… it's been horrendous, frankly.'

Jim struggles with what to say. 'Have you told anyone this? Here, I mean?'

'The police know.'

'I think you should tell the Clinical Service Lead too,' he says seriously. 'Proof or not, you want that on record. *Please* get that on record, won't you?'

'You believe me?' It's my turn to be stunned.

'I trained with Storm, Nathan's wife – before she left. We were good friends, nothing like that, well not on her part anyway.' He smiles sadly. 'Just mates. Do I believe you? Yes. I believe Nathan will say whatever it takes to get his own way… and you should tell someone.' He looks over his shoulder to make sure we're still alone. 'He's the worst kind of man.'

*

I positively slam into the office, making Michelle jump as the door bangs off the wall. She quickly shoves her phone away. 'Hi Julia! Happy New Year! I saw your son is safe? That's great! Congratulations!'

'Thank you.' I sit down, my mind reeling at what Jim has just told me.

'I saw you on the TV appeal too. I thought you were so brave.' She jumps up. 'Let me make you a cup of tea or coffee! What would you like?'

'I'm fine,' I begin but she looks crestfallen. 'Oh please!' she begs. 'I really, really want to! Go on, tea or coffee?'

I'm slightly thrown by her enthusiasm… 'OK. Tea. Thank you.'

She rushes off to the kettle and moments later returns, proudly carrying a very full mug, which she places down on the desk next to my keyboard. 'I saw this and thought of you,' she says shyly, pushing it towards me, slopping some of the tea on the desk in the process. 'It's a thank you for when you stood up for me just before Christmas.'

'That's very kind.' I grab a tissue and glance at the shiny new mug while I'm mopping up. It reads:

Heroes.

Friends.
Mothers.
Daughters.
Visionaries.
Queens.
WOMEN.

I sit back, genuinely touched by the sentiment.

'I really did think you were so brave on the TV.'

I stand up and spontaneously hug her. 'I love it, thank you.'

'Christ, what's the matter with you two?' Hamish sweeps in, holding his ringing mobile phone and glares at us, shoving his bag down on his desk furiously. He's had the most extraordinary haircut over the Christmas break, like someone used dirty bacon scissors, causing his pale straw hair to stick out in slightly greasy, blunt-edged clumps at random angles.

'And what in God's name is that?' He squints bad-temperedly at my new mug on my desk. '"Visionaries, queens, women",' he reads aloud in disgust before flinging his phone, unanswered, into his bag. 'Jesus wept.'

I had been going to thank him for his presence at the search for Alex, but the words die on my lips. We seem to be back to 'normal' again. 'Perhaps if you haven't got anything nice to say, Hamish, don't—'

'Just shut up, Julia.' He speaks over me, doesn't even look up. 'Know when not to push your luck.' He yanks a laptop from his bag, peers at it, mutters and shoves it back in the bag before pulling another out instead. 'Stay away from me today, all right? Or I'm going to end up doing or saying something I'll regret.'

Before I can respond, Michelle suddenly grabs my mug of tea and with a gasp of rage, flings the hot contents all over Hamish. Thankfully, he steps back, but it still hits his chest. Howling, he lurches instinctively towards Michelle. I reach out and pull her towards me.

'Don't you *dare* touch her!' My eyes are wide with fear.

'I had no *intention* of touching her!' he exclaims. 'I'm the one who has just had scalding liquid thrown in my face! Learn to bloody well control yourselves!'

'It went nowhere near your face.'

'I'm covered in it.' He pulls the front of his shirt away from his skin as Michelle stares at the large tea stain, horrified. He makes a show of needing to pull the shirt tails from his trousers, briefly revealing a wobble of white, blond-haired stomach – like a side of raw pork. Michelle visibly retches, covers her mouth with her hand and turns away from him.

He glares at her again. 'That was a mistake. A *huge* mistake.'

She looks back at him, visibly shaking. 'What are you going to do to me that you haven't already?'

I come to my senses and step forward. 'Michelle. Let's leave the room now.' I gently take the mug from her fingers and put it down, before starting to lead her away. 'People will hear what you have to say, but let's not do it this way.'

'Oh really?' Hamish starts to raise his voice. 'People will hear! Because it's Julia doing the shouting and everyone must listen?'

I ignore him and lead her out. She's trembling violently. 'It's OK, take a deep breath.' I stand opposite her, my hands on her forearms as she clings on to me for support. 'That's it. Well done. And another… I look up to see *Nathan* rounding the corner in his overcoat and striding towards us, holding his mobile.

'Is Hamish in there?' he pants, pointing at the office. 'Yes or no! I really need to speak to him!' He glances at Michelle, noticing her tears. 'Why are you crying?'

She looks at the ceiling and gives a half laugh. 'You mean he hasn't told you? I thought you two share everything.'

Nathan looks confused as Hamish appears in the doorway, wiping his front with a tea towel.

'Don't say anything you might regret.' He points at Michelle. 'And you, just get in here, now.' He nods at Nathan, who pushes past him and the door closes in our faces.

Michelle starts to shudder again. She seems to have gone into shock. 'I think I'm going to be sick.' She *has* turned completely white; her skin is clammy. I look around for a bin, anything, as Tan arrives too, bike helmet swinging on his arm, backpack on his back. 'Tan!' I call. 'Go and grab my rubbish bin! Quick as you—' Before I can continue, the sound of muffled shouting from behind the closed office door reaches the three of us. I look at Tan worriedly and he frowns.

'Who's in there?'

'Nathan and Hamish.'

Tan draws back.

'Ohhh!' wails Michelle, looking at the ceiling. 'I'm going to be...' She gags and covers her mouth as we turn our attention back to her, Tan shoving his bike helmet under her mouth, while I hold her hair back. We are distracted from the noise on the other side of the door.

CHAPTER FORTY-SIX

Nathan

'I don't want to talk to you! I've told you that repeatedly! I have nothing to say to you. We are DONE, Nathan!'

'You don't just end a twenty-five-year friendship overnight, Ham. I know you're pissed off with me, but—'

'Pissed off?' he repeats. 'You simply don't get it, do you? *I've had enough.* We are no longer friends.'

'Oh come on!' I retort. 'That's ridiculous. We're not kids. You can't just "stop" being my friend.'

'I can and I have.'

'No, you're stuck with me!' I joke, feeling panic rising in my chest. I'm about to tell him that I'm going to need his support as I face these allegations. I also want to ask his opinion of my moving to America, maybe for six months or so until this all calms down. 'I'm not going to let you!'

'You don't have a choice!' He rounds on me furiously. 'You stay away from me or I will show them all of my files. You're in pretty much every single one. Looking at the camera and laughing in some of them.' He points at his laptop.

It's like someone yanking a dressing from skin it's become stuck to. I gasp as I feel the scabs give way, exposing raw flesh beneath. 'You kept the files? I thought you'd deleted them!'

He shakes his head. 'Don't push me, Nathan. I mean what I say.'

'Why are you being like this?' I stare at him, trying to make sense of what he's saying. 'What's happened? You're not yourself. You're threatening people left, right and centre. Michelle just now, for example.' I jerk a thumb at the closed door. 'What was she talking about, we "share everything"?'

Hamish flushes bright red. He's sweating profusely. 'I'm not discussing that girl with you or anyone!'

I hesitate, recalling him lurking in shadows of the bedroom, watching me with Michelle, staying there when I left her on the bed. 'You didn't...' The penny drops and I'm horrified. 'Shit, Hamish! Was it because everything else was stopping? You thought you'd go out with a bang? *That's* why you haven't wanted the police anywhere near you!'

'Shut up!' he hisses, glancing over his shoulder in panic at the door. 'Someone will hear you! I swear to God, if you breathe a word to anyone... You were the one who cut her leg, remember?' He reaches into his pocket and pulls out my knife. A trapdoor springs under me. I feel my legs going.

'You said you'd take care of that!' I whisper.

'I have. Very good care. If you say a single thing about what happened after the club back at the house, I will put you right there with me, injuries to her inner thigh and all.'

'Hamish, this is *me* you're talking to!' My voice cracks. 'We're family! I love you, pal!'

'No, you don't!' He exclaims. 'You only ever think about yourself. You hid a child in my sister's hotel. You rang me in the middle of the night from the police station, when I *told* you to sort it out yourself!'

I hold up my hands. The laptop is just sitting there on the table. I can see it out of the corner of my eye. 'I'm truly sorry about that, but I didn't know I was going to get arrested, did I? And it all worked out fine. You let him go.'

He looks at me like I'm cracked. 'What are you talking about? I drove all the way there, on my on-call night – just stop and think what would have happened if an emergency had come in at work – and he wasn't there! Just a mattress in the cinema and loads of shitty chocolate wrappers everywhere that I had to tidy up! I checked every room, marched up every corridor before having to turn around and drive home again.' He steps closer to me, scarlet in the face, his eyes bulging with rage. 'I was going to put him in the sea, let his body wash up. That's what *I* was going to do because of *you*!'

'Calm down,' I instruct him. 'You're just ranting now. You look like you're going to have a heart attack or something.'

'You don't think, do you?' His hand is gripping the closed knife. 'Someone else always cleans up for you and you act like it's no big deal. *A kid hidden in the hotel that police forces up and down the country are looking for.* Your recklessness beggars belief. You're nothing but a child yourself!'

'I didn't understand why you were so afraid of the police getting close to you. If I'd realised that—'

'No, Nathan. I don't trust you anymore. We're done. I know where your loyalty lies now and it isn't with me.'

He turns away, but I'm too quick for him. I dart over to grab the laptop, but he blocks my path. Stumbling slightly, we bash into the edge of the desk and he drops the knife, snatching up the laptop and wrapping his fat arms around it like a vice while I try to yank it from his grip. He's surprisingly strong and shoves me back, but I manage to pull it clear. He gasps as I triumphantly step away with it, then grabs at his right arm, his face screwed up in pain.

'Come off it. I didn't touch you.' I roll my eyes.

He bends forward suddenly, taking a few staggering steps like he's in an imaginary ruck – minus the rest of the pack – pausing before stepping back, straightening up and looking at me, his eyes wide with fright. Fuck, is he actually having a heart attack?

'Hamish? Are you all right?' Worried, I lower the laptop and step towards him, at which point he lunges for me. I twist away and elbow him, shoving him hard, but he loses his footing and stumbles sideways, crashing into one of the desks and hitting the side of his head on the corner, before falling to the floor, eyes closed.

'Nice try.' I scrabble for the knife and shove it in my pocket. I have everything now, thank God. Panting, I watch him for a moment… but he doesn't move. 'Hamish? Stop messing about!'

No response.

I put the laptop down and am next to him in seconds. 'Hamish! Can you hear me? Hamish?'

CHAPTER FORTY-SEVEN

Julia

'What was that noise?' I frown at Tan, who moves quickly to open the office door. Hamish is unconscious, with Nate kneeling over him calling his name. 'Hamish? Hamish, can you hear me?' He looks up panicked. 'Call 2222! He hit the side of his head hard and he's out cold.'

I dart to the nearest phone. 'We've got an unconscious adult. We need the cardiac arrest team.' I give my location, name and extension number and, hanging up, I move over to Nathan, who is loosening Hamish's collar and checking his breathing, muttering 'don't do this, pal! Can you hear me?'

Michelle is in the doorway, hand covering her mouth, and more staff appear alongside her.

'Don't just stand there! Has it been more than two minutes, people?' Nathan shouts. 'Repeat the 2222, Julia! Tell them I said to get a fucking move on!'

I move to the phone again, but the crash team are already arriving, spilling in through the door, asking what's happened, getting a trolley, ringing Resus to say Hamish is on his way.

*

In theatre, they open his skull, go in through the dura mater and remove a massive clot with suction… but there are complications.

Acute subdural hematomas have one of the highest mortality rates of all head injuries, and Hamish is not one of the lucky ones. He dies mid-afternoon with his family and Nathan by his side.

*

Later in the day, as it's starting to get dark, I'm sitting outside on a low brick wall with Tan at the back of the car park by the entrance to A&E. We are holding lukewarm tea in takeout cups that neither of us is drinking. It's cold and I'm trying not to shiver, but I'm not going to say anything because Tan is in tears and I just want to sit with him. It's hard though, to comfort someone without touching them, or speaking. Eventually I crack.

'I'm so sorry for your loss. It's really shocking when someone you are close to dies in a location that you're used to seeing through professional eyes.' I wonder whether to tell him that Lise died in the hospital that I was working in at the time, and how difficult I found that to deal with for years afterwards, how complicated my grief became in my mind as a result, but like Jim earlier this morning, I'm wary of sharing – because I don't want him to think I'm making this about me.

He doesn't reply, just looks at the network of industrial pipes snaking up the outside of the building, pumping fat clouds of steam into the grey sky. I can see him trying to find the sense in what has happened.

I don't know I'm going to say it. I've no idea if it's *my* shock at witnessing a colleague dying in front of all of us only hours earlier – yet again seeing how quickly we can lose the opportunity to say important things to people on the twist of a sixpence – but I blurt: 'thank you for joining the search for Alex on Saturday morning. I saw you on TV with Nate and Hamish. And thank you for rescuing him on Saturday night, because I think it was you.'

The words are out of my mouth before I remember what I *promised* Alex. He said I always tell… and he was right. Horrified,

I glance at Tan, who is now biting his lip, hard, and staring at the ground.

'I should say Alex didn't name you,' I add immediately. 'And I haven't discussed what he said with anyone at all. He only told me that someone from the rugby weekend helped him. It was all my assumption after that.' I am making this worse. 'The thing is, Nathan spent Saturday night at Heavitree police station, so that ruled him out. I went to see you at home on Sunday morning, and Trish said you'd been called in to cover Hamish's on-call. Only at the hospital they said you *hadn't* been there?' I shoot another tentative look at him. 'And as Hamish *was* on call, it was unlikely to be him who went to rescue Alex, and he wasn't exactly my number one fan in any case. Although – if it *was* Hamish, you're going to be sitting there wondering what the HELL I'm talking about!' I give a wobbly laugh and put my cup down on the floor so I can reach into my bag for a tissue.

'Alex was hidden in the secret cinema at Fowles, the boutique hotel in Lyme Regis that belongs to Hamish's sister,' Tan says suddenly. 'I found your son on a mattress, in the dark, on the floor in front of the screen, taped up and locked in.'

I straighten back up very slowly and turn to face him. He doesn't look at me. His eyes are closed, his cheeks wet. He's put his drink on the floor. His hands are now pushing down onto the wall either side of him, as if he's braced for impact of some sort. 'There were no windows, no phone – just a loo off the main room. It was a good hiding place. Alex had some water bottles, a duvet, but he didn't have any more food that I could see.'

'How did you know he was there?'

'Every year, the first weekend in January, Nate and Hamish quietly hold an "event" at the hotel for some selected male "friends". We all have our own keys.' Tan glances at me quickly. 'Paid women, yeah?'

I nod to show I understand, but I'm completely shocked. Tan?

'I don't participate; I want to make that very clear. I'm simply expected to attend, in case they need someone sober; a driver, a doctor – you get the picture. Nate cancelled it because he felt there was too much police activity. It was going to be a very,' he pauses, 'significant gathering this year. Hamish was agitated. I heard them talking – Hamish told Nate to sort something out by Sunday. I wondered, and I was right. When you saw us on television looking for Alex, we were actually discussing cancelling it all then. Nate felt the search was a good opportunity for us to talk in person without having to do it over the phone or via messages, in case anyone was monitoring our activity.'

I gasp.

'I know, it's deplorable. That picture Nate has of you kissing him at the beach, the one Hamish took?'

'*Hamish?*

Tan nods miserably. 'They have a picture of me like that too, but more graphic. The first year I joined the department, Nate and Hamish asked me to come to their "select gathering" in the hotel. I was flattered to be asked. We had just moved to a new area. I wanted to ingratiate myself and make some friends. I imagined men playing cards, cigars, whisky – no wives. Too much testosterone and not really my thing, but I wanted to make an effort.' He shrugs. 'And at first it was like that. I got drunk. I'm not a drinking man. Then suddenly there were women arriving. I was *very* drunk… more than that; I was not really able to move. I was on a hotel bed, very confused.' His eyes close again. 'I remember hearing laughing and cheering. The next morning, Hamish shows me a picture of what appears to be me penetrating a naked woman straddling me. I don't believe I possibly could have been doing anything, but that's not what it looks like, what it would look like to Trish, to my family. I have never, ever committed adultery. I love my wife.' His voice starts to shake. 'I love my children.

'Nate and Hamish *would* have destroyed everything for me. They bought my silence and I am ashamed. I am bitterly, bitterly ashamed. And I am so sorry I brought you and Alex into this.' He seems unable to stop his confession now that he's started it. 'I really did want you to come here because I thought that perhaps *you* would stop them. You wouldn't be weak like me. You had taken on a whole hospital before coming here. You wouldn't turn a blind eye to the way these men operate… but I truly did not realise there was *nothing* they would not do. After you reported Nathan and Alex disappeared… I couldn't stand by. He's a child! I found him, I drove him to Budleigh and I told him to walk back along the coast road as if he had reappeared.' He turns to me urgently. 'But you understand why I couldn't say anything, right? They still have that picture of me – they would use it if they knew what I'd done. They are monstrous men… but now to see Hamish dying like that in front of me and feel nothing but relief?' He places his hand on his heart. 'I am a *doctor*.' He starts to weep again. 'I am supposed to preserve life and all I could think was, please die!'

'That doesn't make you a bad person, Tan. It makes you human.'

'They are both in this together – you understand?' He barely seems to have heard me. 'Nate lets Hamish receive the films. It's not just examinations: Nate has relations with women there and Hamish watches. He calls himself Fat Uncle Ham. He knows these are not women he would attract himself. It is disgusting. They have been doing all of this for a long time. There are things that…' he pauses suddenly, seems to change his mind about what he was going to say. 'You heard that arguing upstairs?' He looks at me and I nod. 'Nathan's going to America; you know that too, yeah? But you watch… now that Hamish has died? Nathan will say it was Hamish doing the filming, not him.'

'I know that's not true. He knew the cameras were there. He told me it was to protect himself legally.'

'That won't matter! He'll deny it. He *will* say it was Hamish, I guarantee you. There is no loyalty in death.' He stands up suddenly. 'And that's another thing – so Hamish just dies like that? I mean, OK, he is not healthy, but he collapses where nobody else but Nathan sees? You'll think I'm crazy, but I'm not. I swear to you!'

He looks around us urgently and bends down to whisper to me. 'Nathan is a very dangerous man. He is unhinged. He doesn't have boundaries. He is used to doing what he likes, he doesn't know where to stop. He took your son to a hotel. He bound his legs and arms! That's a man you'll wake to find standing by your bed in the middle of the night, watching you. He terrifies me. Say nothing to anyone. Let him run away to America. This is so much bigger than you realise, Julia. Let him go because you do not want him looking at you anymore. For my part, I am so sorry for the pain I have caused you, and I hope you won't tell anyone else now, because I don't want him looking at me and my family either. The shame I live with every day is my punishment. I just want to protect my loved ones. Thank you for listening to me.'

He walks back towards the hospital, head down. I watch as he approaches an anxious elderly woman paused outside the double doors, leaning heavily on a frame, while she works out how to navigate stepping off the kerb. He notices her, stops and helps guide the frame down carefully, taking her body weight as she leans on him too, until she finds solid ground. She gratefully says something and he stops to listen, nodding politely and making time for her, like he isn't falling apart inside. Eventually he goes back in through the doors. She continues on her way, but she now is smiling, relieved – grateful for the kindness.

I understand what Eleni meant perfectly now.

He is a good man.

*

And a wise one.

When the news breaks first in the local, then national press, Tan's prediction comes to pass:

Local plastic surgeon Hamish Wilson died from a subdural hematoma yesterday at the EM hospital, Exeter following a confrontation with a colleague over the alleged sexual assault of a staff member. Allegations have also emerged that Mr Wilson had secretly been filming patient examinations, conducted at private plastic surgery premises owned by the Wilson family. Images were discovered on Mr Wilson's laptop by the executor of his will, Mr Nathan Sloan, who referred his findings to the General Medical Council. A spokesperson for the GMC has confirmed an investigation is underway into Mr Wilson's 'potential professional misconduct that may have compromised patient privacy, resulting from the collection and storage of images without patient consent'. Police have also confirmed that they are investigating an alleged breach of the Human Tissue Act after a collection of human bone fragments was discovered at the property Mr Wilson shared with his wife and stepson.

Michelle is not named, but it quickly becomes common knowledge that she's the 'staff member' in question. I'm devastated for her, and as for the *human bone fragments*? Rumours begin to circulate that Hamish liked to keep private mementos of some of his patients, which confirms – if it were needed – that he was very much, in his own right, a narcissistic psychopath.

But what can we now do about Nathan? Tan was aware that the filming happened, but he was not directly involved. He has no evidence or proof that Nathan was responsible for the installation and use of the cameras. And he is very frightened.

'What if Nathan uses the image of me? I would be risking everything when I'm not sure it would achieve anything. That's bad enough, but,' he looks at me, terrified, 'Hamish is *dead*. They won't have spent money on an expensive Home Office post-mortem when it looks obvious what happened. They'll have just done the standard hospital one, and any subtle bruising on his chest from being pushed, or marks on his wrist from being pulled down so that his head hit the desk will have been missed; but this was not an accident, whatever Nathan says. And even *if* an examination was conducted to the "highest" standard, I wouldn't trust the conclusion. The truth would be covered up. Hamish had *human bones* at his house. You are talking about dangerous men, Julia. I just want Nathan to go away, as far away, as soon as possible. I want him away from my children and my wife!'

I won't argue with that. It wouldn't change Tan's mind if I did, and I'm starting to worry about his mental health in all of this. Tan is worth a million Nathan Sloans… but it doesn't mean watching Nathan get away scot-free doesn't cause me considerable distress: it does; the only positive outcome is at least we never have to see him again.

Until he denies us that too.

Cass comes rushing into the kitchen after school on Friday, to tell me that Ben has messaged her. After a week's absence he will be back in school on Monday after all! No America! No broken heart! She is ecstatic. Ewan and I are horrified.

He waits until she's disappeared back up to her bedroom then turns to me. 'You don't believe for a second that this was all Hamish and not Nathan, do you?'

I shake my head. 'Nathan told Joan, the clinical nurse specialist at work, that he didn't know the cameras were in the office until *I* spotted them. He's somehow managed to make it look like I *helped* him, rather than whistle-blew on him. The way he manipulates everything and everyone is astounding. We're going to have to leave though, if he's now staying. You know that, right?' I take my husband's hand. 'I can't work alongside him like nothing has happened, watching him treat patients who have no idea what he's like – and that's before I even think about what he persuaded Alex to do. Tan's terrified of him. He thinks—'

I stop talking as Alex walks in, happily clutching the new phone that Dom bought him. 'Mum, Ewan – is it all right for a couple of friends to come over tomorrow afternoon? We're going to do a survival assault course in the garden!' He grins, looking delighted when I nod. 'We are all systems go!' He holds the phone to his ear. 'If you've got a camo net too, I think that would work.' He legs it and we hear him thundering upstairs to his room, still chattering away.

Ewan sighs heavily.

'I know. Don't,' I whisper. 'I don't want to have to do it to them. Of course I don't. They're never going to forgive me, but we don't have any choice.'

*

I leave them all sleeping in the morning and slip out as soon as it's light enough, for a quick 5k along the estuary path. I know my knees will complain, but I want the mental space. It's not what I'd hoped for – a damp rather than crisp, chilly winter morning. The tide is in, and I'm running under the cover of a cold mist that feels oppressive. I don't mind that all I can hear is the thud of my feet on the track at the water's edge and the sound of my own breath. I'm not bothered by the rustling in the reeds to my right and the ripples that spread across the surface of the otherwise flat water as a result of some animal or bird moving about nearby, but I *am* unnerved by the sudden appearance of another runner heading in my direction out of the gloom – an unmistakably male shape. I glance behind me. We are alone. There is no one else to hear or see us. It's a split-second thing, but I suddenly turn on the spot without even knowing that my feet are going to do it, and start racing away from the stranger, picking up my pace, pushing my body into a sprint until my muscles are screaming and I've no choice but to stop completely, unable to take enough oxygen on board. I glance back over my shoulder into the fog, gasping, he must now be some distance away – and as soon as I can, I resume a gentle jog over the bridge, towards the level crossing.

I am safe but now I feel foolish… and suddenly very angry… What the hell was that about? Now I just abandon everything on a whim, just because some random man is there? I need to calm down. I need to not see threat *everywhere*. I head back to the house, but at the last moment I change my mind and turn onto the main road instead, running into town.

I keep my head down as I pass the new-build housing sites. I pound past the crematorium, the golf and country club, where men of a certain age are already arriving in their large gleaming Jags, clubs carefully packed in the boot for an early morning round. I head over the roundabout, past the barracks and swing right, as if I am making my way up towards the hospital, only instead I turn left at the crossroads and into St Leonards, arriving at what estate agents might breathily refer to as one of Exeter's most desirable addresses: the home of Mr Nathan Sloan.

I hesitate in the driveway, hands on my hips, chest rising and falling as I try to get my breath back – but my rage is already getting the better of me. I crunch over the gravel, past both cars and ring the bell. It is not right that he faces no consequences. *It's not right!*

The door opens and it's him. I haven't actually seen him since Monday, when he was standing over Hamish, looking down at his friend's body in disbelief. In place of his usual shirt and chinos he's wearing a faded, misshapen sweatshirt over baggy jogging pants. The casual look doesn't suit him, neither does it appear age-appropriate. Fittingly – he looks like he's trying to be something he's not.

'Julia!' He seems genuinely astonished to see me. I appreciate I must look slightly manic… but I don't care.

'You said before Christmas that someone like me could save you, so that's why I'm here,' I announce, my voice shaking. 'I've come to respectfully ask you to leave after all.'

'Leave?' He looks astonished. 'You haven't come to apologise to me then? For incorrectly reporting me filming my patients when, in fact, it was Hamish?'

'Apologise? *Me?*' It's all I need him to say for my fury to bubble over completely. 'YOU have lied about everything, to everyone. *I* know it, *you* know it. I sat there in your office and you told me that you'd installed those cameras to "protect yourself". You knew they were there. Just like you told me to my face that you'd put six letters in six of your living patients. We both know that happened too!'

'Oh no, no.' He holds up his hands. How is he so calm? 'I lied about *that*. There were never any "clues". I said some things in the heat of the moment that I shouldn't have. I'm very sorry, Julia.'

'I don't believe you.'

'It's true! I'm trying to be honest with you!'

I laugh incredulously. 'You don't know the meaning of the word! I know who rescued Alex. I know that my son was taped up and locked in a cinema. You are a dangerous, compulsive liar, Nathan. You have fooled everyone – even yourself – and congratulations, because somehow you've managed to get away with it all. You've kept your reputation intact. You can still practise medicine, which is horrendous – both for you and your future patients – because you are incapable of seeing women as anything but sexual objects. You will say and do *anything* to have your own way.' I take a breath and wipe the sweat from my eyes. 'In an ideal world, I'd like to see you admit your crimes and take responsibility for all of the—'

'Crimes?' He interrupts.

'Yes! Watching female patients for your own sexual gratification, without their consent, is a *crime*. It doesn't go away just because you pushed the blame onto Hamish. You *need* to stop! You can't work in an environment where you're in control and women have to trust you, because you abuse that. God – you can't even see it, can you?' I watch him lean on the door frame as if he's intrigued but confused by what I've just said. 'Walk away from surgery! Don't practise anymore. Just STOP.' I exhale and try to calm my breathing. His deliberately relaxed stance is both insulting and utterly enraging.

'Please consider it,' I try again. 'At least then you would have learnt something from the damage you have caused so many people.'

'People meaning you?'

'I'm one of them, yes. Alex is another. I don't want any of us around you – not knowing everything that you've done, what you're capable of and the company you were keeping,' I think of Michelle, the bone fragments at Hamish's farm and shudder. 'Leave and go somewhere else, because if you don't, *I'll* have to and I want to stay – despite everything, Alex and Cass are settled here now. It's the least you owe Alex.'

'Alex is happy now!' He straightens up and takes a tiny step towards me. 'He's *popular* because of what happened.'

'He only survived because someone saved him! He—'

'Oh come on! No one "saved" him; he was never in any real danger!' He is becoming exasperated. 'Ben's told me Alex has come out of this a rock star! And what *about* Ben? Doesn't he matter as much as Alex and Cass? He doesn't want to leave Cass any more than I want to leave you. He loves her – like I love you. No, don't look like that, I mean it! I love you with all my heart.'

'You're not capable of love!' I say it without hesitation.

'That's a dreadful thing to say!' He looks devastated. 'Of course I am. I haven't always been the man I should be, you're right, but I want to clean my soul, so help me do it!' He inches forward again, closer still. 'I'll leave if you come with me. Please.'

'Clean your soul?' I repeat in disbelief. 'Nathan, that son you just mentioned and your *wife* love you. You start again with *them*!'

'Storm and I are done. We've been done for a long time. There's nothing there anymore, it's all imported Italian baths – you've seen it for yourself. She knows it too – in her heart of hearts.'

Exhausted, I close my eyes briefly. He is going to keep on and on…

'It's you I want! It's you I *need*!'

'No, Nathan.' I open my eyes and immediately notice Storm, standing at the back of the large, dark hallway behind Nathan. She very slowly lifts her finger to her lips, urging me to keep her presence secret.

'You're the love of my life,' he insists, oblivious to his listening wife.

Storm turns and silently vanishes back into the house.

'I shouldn't have come here,' I say eventually. 'I'm sorry, but please think about what I've said. Stop practising medicine. Leave. Go as far from all of us as you possibly can. And don't come back.'

I turn and walk away. He has learnt nothing. I, on the other hand, feel something close to despair as it dawns on me that I am saying this to him twenty years too late. That is the real problem here. It is *too late* to re-educate men of his age. They cannot change; it's just lip service on their part. I am shouting into the wind. He can't see it but watching him break Storm like that – so casually dismissing his own son and wife, squashing their needs down to meet his own – is almost more than I can bear.

CHAPTER FORTY-EIGHT

Nathan

Having completed my Sunday morning worship at the temple of pain otherwise known as the seven a.m. HIIT class, I'm putting my sweaty gym gear straight into the washing machine, in the chill of Storm's impossibly neat and gleaming utility room, when the grief is there again. It's been following after me like an old dog. I turn around in the middle of something ordinary, like making a cup of tea, to find it's suddenly off its bed and wanting a walk after all. In these moments, it seems extraordinary that Hamish is no longer here and I will never see him again. I keep hearing him laughing in my head – which is just like him, the irritating arse.

When Storm – years ago now – suggested I have counselling for my parents' death, I patiently pointed out they were both very much alive, so it seemed a little premature.

'I just worry about what's going to happen to you when one of them eventually does go.' She'd stroked my hand. 'The loss of the possibility of the relationships you've never had is going to hit you hard, I think – far more powerful than losing the person themselves. If you're determined not to contact them again, and I understand you don't want to keep being rejected and pushed away, I think it would be sensible to take some preventative measures to protect yourself. There are only so many compartments that one person has to shut things in.'

So I've been encouraged to discover that my response to losing Hamish has been very normal. I've felt profoundly sad and empty at times, but I suspect this is because I don't really have anyone to talk to about him, and also because I haven't been working. When I return tomorrow and get back into the routine – giving me physically less time to think – I know I will find things easier, although it will be very, very odd to be at the EM without him. In truth, I'm a little frightened of it. I miss him very much. I take a deep breath and start opening all of the head-height cupboard doors, looking for the washing powder.

I wonder what Hamish is making of my having turned the spotlight from my own face to shine it directly onto his cold and immobile features. Zip up the body bag because the case is closed; he was a fucking idiot not to get rid of his collection, I did tell him, but it's also helped me out no end. Add that to sexually assaulting a colleague… and now secretly filming my patients. I know it's morally dubious of me to bolt it all together, but does it make me a bad person to take this second chance? Hamish's genuine assault of Michelle would not be made any the less without the other charge. It was an unfathomable thing for him to have done to her. Deeply, deeply shocking. He crossed a completely unacceptable line. *I* truthfully never touched any of my patients inappropriately, or without consent; not once did I engineer intimate examinations of them. I only looked again at what *I had already been voluntarily shown*. I accept that the context of the subsequent viewings is not irrelevant, but a huge part of me just wants *all* of it to die with Hamish. His death has freed me. I can be the person Julia says I ought to be, now. Surely it's better that something good comes out of this? I see Hamish taking the blame for the filming as the last, posthumous gesture of our friendship. I've cleaned everything up.

I scoop up a large cup full of powder and frown at the front of the machine: do I put it in the drum? Or is there a little drawer it goes in?

I very much regret that we had hostile words and Ham was so distressed just before he died, of course I do. Had he told me how frightened he was about Michelle, I would have tried to help him. I understand now why he was panicked – all of that nonsense about going to the hotel and pretending he couldn't find Alex, just to make it seem as if it had been even more of an ordeal for him. He didn't need to do that. Knowing what I know now, I get why it was such a big ask. It was brave and kind of him to go at all.

Which is also why I don't believe he really would have betrayed me with the files and the knife. He was just very badly shaken indeed by the police proximity to him, maybe even having some sort of breakdown, but for God's sake, if he hadn't gone for me like that, I wouldn't have pushed him! He wouldn't have fallen. He would still be here!

My hand jerks involuntarily, scattering some washing powder over my feet like snow. I have to place the cup on the shelf and lean both hands either side of the utility room sink, taking a few deep breaths as I stare at the plug. I miss him. I feel very alone.

At least Julia herself has emerged unscathed by all of this. Whatever whispers there might still be about her incredible 'letters in patients' theory will fade away with time, before becoming nothing of consequence – everyone is too busy talking about Hamish to remember what accusations a desperate mother cried in the middle of the night. Her reputation won't suffer. Alex is fine, too. I wish to God I could convince Julia that he was never in any danger… but she doesn't believe me. I understand why she wants me gone, but it's important that I'm *here* to help support Hamish's family through this difficult time. I can't move to America and leave them now. I can't just run away. It wouldn't be right.

I bend to look at the bewildering array of buttons. Twenty-minute wash? That'll do, but as I straighten up, cramp kicks into my left calf. I went too hard at the gym, agitated after Julia's left-field visit yesterday morning, pushing myself until I nearly dropped.

I can't possibly give up my career either, however much Julia wants me to. It's a ludicrous suggestion. Financially I'm in very good shape, but I'm only fifty-one! Surgery is all I know how to do; it's who I am. It's enough that the slate has been wiped clean, surely? I really think that I can make a proper go of things professionally this time; do some good.

I wander back through to the warmth of the kitchen to make some coffee. Storm is sat at the kitchen table drinking a cup of tea. Not reading or on her phone, just sipping, and waiting… which knowing her as I do, makes me instantly wary.

'You all right?' I ask. 'Where's Ben?'

'He's upstairs.'

I look around and see an absence of evidence of Sunday lunch. 'Want me to make a start on peeling some potatoes?' I offer, hungry and determined to make an effort.

'Can you just sit down for a moment, please?'

I knew it. Something's afoot. I do as I'm asked. Has she been crying? I think she might have been.

'Since your recent arrest things have been… challenging.' She holds onto her mug with both hands. 'I discover you've been having an affair; we decide to make a fresh start in the States. Then Hamish dies and suddenly you can't go and leave the Wilsons and the department in the lurch after all. You want to stay. It's all been very confusing and unsettling for me, and Ben, but then I heard what you said to Julia on the doorstep yesterday, about you and I being done. How we are nothing but imported Italian baths, and your motivation for a lot of things became crystal clear for me pretty quickly… I was standing right behind you. You didn't see me.' She takes a mouthful of tea.

The bath thing is too specific a reference to be anything but the truth. I don't react, however. I just wait to see which way she is going to play this.

'You told her she's the love of your life. I told *you* very recently that love was my red line. While you were at the gym,' she continues, her tone flat, 'I told Ben you're not going to be living with us anymore, and he started crying. He wanted to know if it was because of what he saw on your computer a little while ago when he came back early after swimming was cancelled; a film of you having sex with someone in your office at work and I quote: "laughing over his shoulder at me and winking". Ben told me it was Stefanie. He saw other images of women too. It made him feel confused, and angry. We discussed how it's really hard to talk to your parent about something like that, and you sometimes end up trying to forget about it instead.'

An unpleasant cold shiver ripples through me. 'I'll speak to him…' I begin and she laughs.

'Like you did when you told him you knew something that would cheer him up? He would be the "hero" when you went back to get Alex from Fowles?'

Shit. He told her about that too? I shift in my seat, starting to feel a little agitated.

'He didn't know what to think when he woke up and you weren't here because you'd been arrested.' She looks at me steadily. 'He still lied to the police for you, though – only now he thinks he's going to go to prison for that and you are too.'

'OK, let's cut to the chase.' I return her gaze. 'What do you want from me, Storm?'

'Go to America, but without us.'

'No.' I shake my head. 'I can't do that. I'm sorry. You want to leave me, *you* go.'

'I had a feeling you might respond this way.' She sips her tea again. 'Ben took a screenshot of you and Stefanie in action. He gave it to me, and unless you're gone by tonight, I'm going to give it to Julia Blythe. I imagine she'll give it to the police.'

I look at her, astonished. The knife has gone in but I can't feel the pain yet. I have not cleaned everything up as well as I thought. 'Can I see it, please?'

She raises her eyebrows. 'You're calling your son a liar? That's a bit rich, isn't it? You might have a job convincing people you really knew nothing about the filming, given you're winking at the camera over your shoulder – you disgusting, arrogant bastard.' She speaks calmly but her hands tighten around the mug.

I breathe out deeply. 'Please don't show it to her. That's not who I am now. I don't want her to see me being that person.'

Storm closes her eyes briefly. 'Then go. Or I will ruin you.' She stands up. 'I'm going to take Ben out. I think it would be better if you're gone when we get back. My solicitors will be in touch.'

She turns and starts to walk out of the kitchen. I watch her retreating back and am momentarily furious.

'I've never loved you,' I find myself calling after her, 'to tell the truth.'

CHAPTER FORTY-NINE

Julia

Looking through NHS jobs with a cup of tea, rather than the papers, is not an especially relaxing way to spend a Sunday morning, but needs must. Cass is laughing at something on her phone, and Al wanders into the kitchen in his pjs, with Dom on FaceTime, to ask if it's OK for the two of them to do a Dartmoor walk the following Saturday. 'Dad is going to book a hotel but wants to know if that's OK with you first. We haven't got plans already?'

'That's fine. Thanks for checking though, Dom.' I wave briefly and return to my laptop. One 'Locum Consultant Plastic Surgeon' position in central London with a specialist interest in 'Breast Reconstruction and Microsurgery'. Something similar but permanent in Newcastle: 'a team of fifteen consultants, on-call commitment...' but Newcastle. Miles away. Two posts in Birmingham: 'a twenty-six strong team; special interests Orthoplastic Trauma'. At the other end of the scale, there's a small team in north Tyneside. I'd be expected to be predominantly involved in the skin cancer and microvascular breast reconstruction services, plus assisting in the general plastic surgery emergency and trauma service.

Could I maybe commute to Birmingham from here? But that wouldn't solve the kids seeing Nathan at school. And I don't want to be away from them during the week. They need me. I need them. Wearily, I rub my temples with my fingers. I don't want any of these jobs. None of them excite me at all… and yet I cannot work with him. I just can't.

'How about I book us lunch out somewhere?'

I glance up to see Ewan looking at me worriedly. I try to smile. 'That sounds nice.'

'And a quick walk on the beach afterwards before a movie back here?' He is already picking up his phone.

'Lovely.' And it *is*. I don't want us to leave.

The doorbell rings. Ewan briefly covers the phone's mouthpiece. 'That's probably my Amazon delivery. Would you mind getting it… Oh hi. Yes, I wonder if you've got a table for Sunday lunch?'

I get up automatically and head down the passage, still deep in thought. I fling it open expecting only to have to sign for something, to discover Storm and Ben standing on the doorstep. They have very obviously both been crying.

*

'Thanks for this.' Storm shivers as she holds the cup of tea and looks around the room, her eyes alighting on the piano. 'Do you play?'

'I used to.'

'Is there anything you can't do?'

I'm not sure what to say to that, so I just look down at the floor.

'Sorry,' she says. 'That was unnecessary. It's a nice space.'

'Thank you. I haven't got around to sorting it properly yet.'

'You need an interior designer,' she remarks drily. 'Listen,' she continues before I have to answer that, 'can I talk to you?' She looks at the door. 'In confidence?'

'Yes, of course. They can't hear us when they're in the sitting room,' I assure her. 'The walls are too thick.'

She takes a deep breath, sets her tea down carefully and clears her throat. 'After I heard what Nate said to you yesterday, I had a think. I slept on it – I didn't say anything to Nathan himself, just waited. Once he'd gone to the gym first thing this morning, I told Ben that very sadly, Daddy wasn't going to live with us anymore.' She begins to absently twist her wedding and engagement rings. 'Ben started to cry and asked me if it was because of the film of his father having sex with Stefanie in his office at work – you'll remember her from that charming dinner we all shared – on Nathan's computer? He went into Nate's study at home to borrow his laptop charger and told me, "Dad was on the screen, looking right into the camera and smiling".'

'Shit!' I swear aloud before I can stop myself. No wonder Stefanie was so hostile to me! She must have been terrified when I told her about Nathan filming his patients… although she was sleeping with him and he operated on her? Urgh!

'I know. It wasn't Hamish doing the filming – at least, certainly not alone. My husband is not a very nice man.' Storm picks up her tea again. 'I've changed since I married him too.' She takes a tiny sip, as if it's too hot. 'The first time a nurse friend told me about the rumours he was having an affair with one of his patients, I thought it was because she was jealous that *Nathan Sloan* fancied me. I'd started seeing him on the quiet by then and only she knew. When I got pregnant, she said he'd end it, but Nate left his wife. *That's how much he loves me…* I can actually remember thinking that. I can also remember listening to Nate on the phone to his daughters when we were newly living together, telling them he hadn't made a *promise* he was going to see them that weekend, it was only ever a maybe, and I didn't think anything of it. I should have run as fast as I could, but I loved him. That's *my* mistake. It's not Ben's. He doesn't deserve any of what has happened.' Her eyes shine fiercely and she puts her mug down on the table. 'I've told Nathan he's to go to America without us. The further away the better. Anyway there's a reason you need to know this.'

'Storm, whatever Nathan says he feels for me is not—' I begin, but she holds up a hand.

'I told Nathan that Ben took a screenshot of him having sex with Stefanie and looking at the camera, and that I have that picture now. If he isn't gone by tonight, I'm going to give it to you. He's desperate for you not to see the image…' She exhales deeply.

'It's the police that you should give it to, not me!'

'I would if I had it, but I don't. Nathan just thinks I do.'

My eyes widen. 'Oh, Storm!'

'I know!' she says, raking her fingers back through her hair, resting her elbows on her knees. 'That's why I was wondering… if he calls my bluff – would you maybe be prepared to lie and tell him you've seen it?'

'Except the trouble is he knows I would take that to the police. I can't do that if it doesn't exist. He'd realise very quickly that you'd lied to him. Your best shot is threatening to show it to me, but I wouldn't say I've already seen it. I'm sorry.'

She bites her lip and gets to her feet. 'No, you're right. I didn't think of that.' She points at the window. 'A heavy velvet would be nice. Nothing ever did happen between the two of you, did it?' She turns to face me again.

I look her in the eye. 'No. It didn't. He tried to kiss me on the beach at that rugby weekend. Someone took a photo of us.' I wait to see if she's going to admit it was her, but she turns away.

'Wow. So I'm the only woman in my husband's life he *didn't* want on film.' Her voice is light with the sharpness of pain.

Instinctively, I reach out and put my hand on her arm. 'Why don't you leave Ben here with us? Come back for him later?'

She clears her throat. 'It might be better if he doesn't have to see Nathan angry. If you're sure?'

I take my hand back. 'Of course, but are you OK going back there on your own? You don't want Ewan to come with you, just in case?'

'Thank you, but I'll be fine.' She wipes her eyes and gives me a grim smile. 'That said, if I don't turn up later, you know who to suspect.'

*

She's joking – at least I think she is – but all through lunch, as the three children happily chatter away and mess around on their phones, I'm quiet, remembering how it felt to watch Dom leave, knowing there was no going back... being sure it was the right thing, but feeling like I'd failed Alex very badly. Storm is angry and hurt enough at the moment for that to carry her through this first bit, but what about Nathan? He will be feeling cornered by Storm right now. And what will happen then? Tan's voice urging me not to challenge Nathan myself echoes in my head.

By the time we get home, I'm starting to panic that I let her go back there on her own. Nathan's behaviour has been indulged for such a long time and been allowed to become so extreme, I don't think he even knows how to stop anymore. Sitting at the kitchen table, I try to concentrate on reading the more detailed job spec for the London post, but all I can think about is: what if Nathan turns up at our house and says *he's* come to collect Ben. Do I let him go? Do I call the police? When the doorbell goes, my chair scrapes the floor I get up so fast.

I actually laugh with relief when it's Storm I find standing on the step. Alive. Safe. I lean on the door frame, weakly.

'I did message Ben,' she looks at me warily, 'but he didn't reply? Sorry – have I interrupted something?'

'No, not at all. They're all upstairs. Do you want to come in?'

She shakes her head. 'I won't, thank you. We probably should get back. It's done. He's gone. He flies to America tomorrow. I've no idea where he'll be tonight, but...' Her eyes fill with tears and she wipes them away quickly. 'Sorry! He kept asking to see the picture and I kept refusing. In the end he just – accepted it. He said he hoped one day I'd forgive him, and he didn't blame me for what I was doing, I was right to protect Ben. That was one of the reasons he married me, apparently, because I'm so strong and determined.'

I can hear the sadness in her voice and *that's* the power of someone like Nathan: gently stroking the side of your face with one hand while slicing the scalpel with the other.

*

Joan is in our office in tears the following morning. 'It's so sad!' She sniffs into a tissue. 'He's such a beautiful man! He called me himself last night to explain because he knew I'd be worried about him when I heard the news that he'd resigned. Isn't that kind? Thinking of others even at a time like this! He just can't be in the hospital anymore. It's too painful for him to think about working here without Hamish, and I can see that. They were like brothers, they really were. So they're letting him go on gardening leave, and he's going to work in America now. I said to him not to make any rash decisions and that grief is a funny thing, but he said it's made him reconsider a lot and you only get one life – which is true enough, I suppose.'

Tan listens without a word, arms crossed, then walks over to the kettle and puts it on. 'Well, good luck to him,' he says shortly. 'Can I make you a tea, Joan? It's obviously been a shock for you.'

'No, thank you, my love!' Joan lifts her glasses to dab under her eyes. 'I need to go and tell the other team now; they won't have heard yet, I shouldn't think.'

'That's him now!' Michelle says suddenly, looking out of the window, and we all get up to look. Sure enough, I catch my breath. There's Nathan walking across the car park in bright sunshine, against a brilliant, blue sky. He has his back to us, but that relaxed, confident swagger could only belong to him.

'Oh my word! He must have come in to dot the i's and cross the t's before he leaves!' Joan clutches her chest. 'The little lamb!'

'He didn't *have* to do it in person,' Tan points out. 'I know they like to see you, but he could have got away with an email.'

Joan frowns. 'You have to have closure, Tan! It's healthy.'

No. Tan's right. He has to have the last word. That's what this is. He's learnt nothing.

It's as if he hears what I've just thought. Nathan suddenly stops, turns and looks up directly at the office, smiles... and blows a kiss.

'Oh bless him, blowing *me* kisses!' Joan says firmly – before blowing him one back. 'You take care, my sweetheart!'

I open my mouth to point out that he can't see in through the glass. The lights aren't on. He has no clue if she's here or not, but that would be unkind.

Michelle drops back quietly as Tan pointedly walks away too. Joan looks over her shoulder then whispers to me, 'I destroyed the photo. Nathan asked me to. We'll say no more about it, all right? I didn't tell a soul, just so you know. To have loved and lost, Julia. To have loved and lost...' She squeezes my hand, spins on her heels and leaves.

What on earth did he?... I twist back. He's still there, staring right up at me, but no longer smiling.

He can't see me! I turn my back on him, furiously. I've got work to do.

CHAPTER FIFTY

Nathan

I wait until I've driven several streets away from the hospital before I pull over, gasping, and cover my mouth with my hand. What if that *really* is it? What if I never go back there again? I close my eyes and see Julia stood in the office doorway, handing over the coffee she bought me. Smiling gently.

I am at sea. I don't know how to be this person... all of my mooring ropes have been cut overnight. Surgeon, best friend, father, husband... this time tomorrow I won't even be in this country. I'll be climbing the three steps to my parent's picture-perfect Queen Anne shingle home. Crossing the porch to knock on the door; a moment I used to fantasise about all the time.

My phone rings and I glance down at it. Stefanie. I decline her call and instead open my photos. I find the one that Hamish took at the beach. I've permanently cropped it so that Julia pushing me away is not visible. Now we are simply kissing. Tears flood my eyes and I have to blink them away so I can see the picture properly.

I've not even left yet and all I want to do is come home.

NINE MONTHS LATER

SEPTEMBER 2018

CHAPTER FIFTY-ONE

Julia

'Excuse me… Julia?' One of the sparkier female students who has hung back at the end of the tutorial approaches me. I can see that using my first name is a bit uncomfortable for her, but debunking the hierarchy and pseudo-importance of 'Mr' and 'Dr' as early as possible in an educational setting is so important. 'I just wanted to say that was really interesting, thank you. Can I ask, though – don't you miss clinical practise?'

I smile. 'Thank you, and no – I don't. The change has been good for me – plus, this way I get to shape and define the programme you're studying!'

She wrinkles her nose and I laugh. She reminds me of Cass: incapable of hiding her feelings.

'But my real driver is to change outcomes for *all* patients by doing my research here,' I continue. 'I've got some exciting stuff coming up. I'll tell all of you about it next week.' I hold the door open for her. 'Have a good weekend.'

She grins and bounces out, like Tigger, calling cheerfully over her shoulder. 'You too!'

I'd like some of her energy for the drive home. I am tired. Turning to my desk to pack up my things, I glance out over the faculty lawns, where plenty of the students are relaxing in the late afternoon sunshine, enjoying the Indian summer and planning their Friday night. I should get going or the M5 is going to be a killer – but as I'm shutting down my laptop, my phone buzzes with a message from Tan. The inquest into Hamish's death has just concluded. Thankfully, we were allowed to supply statements to the coroner rather than attend in person to hear her rule that Hamish's death was a result of unavoidable complications from a subdural hematoma. He tripped and hit his head on the side of the desk. No one was to blame. Just one of those freak occurrences.

A tragic accident...

Unlike most texts when it's hard to gauge a sense of tone, Tan's implication is clear. I send him a 'X' to acknowledge his message. I'll call him over the weekend. I hope he's OK. I'm just glad he wasn't forced into a face to face with Nathan, who we were both shocked to discover yesterday, is now permanently back in the UK and working for one of the London Trusts. Broaching this news with Storm – I have no idea if she knows – is also on my to-do list this weekend.

It's mercifully a clear run home. Before long, green fields start to flash past me; the early evening sun is high and bright enough to need sunglasses, but even with them on, I'm still frowning, trying to focus my mind on something other than Hamish. The air is warm and I'll be home in time to help Ewan fix tea. We can eat outside in the garden. I flip around the radio stations in search of songs I can turn up loud, which will drum the thought of Nathan being back in this country and seeing patients – asking them politely to slip off their things, placing his hands on them – out of my head. I do not want to think about him.

It's a choice of Friday night request shows: callers ringing up to talk about their weekend plans for birthdays and barbeques. I force myself to sing along to a couple of classic songs, windows wound down. I fancy heading to the beach tomorrow with Ewan, as it's just the two of us. Al will be with Dom at the flat and Cass is at Ben's for his birthday… but try as I might, I keep coming back to the Exeter Memorial Hospital; Hamish shouting at me and Michelle…

I will message her too later, to let her know I'm thinking of her. I think of her often. Her mug has pride of place on my desk, and lots of my students remark on it. Sometimes it sparks some interesting discussions. On my first day at the university, when I was hiding in my office ahead of giving my first lecture, terrified and wondering how on earth I ever thought I could upstream into academia, Michelle messaged me to wish me 'happy joint-first-new-job day!', adding she knew I was going to be brilliant, she wished she'd had teachers like me.

I got my act together after reading that and did the lecture. I have no doubt now that I made the right decision to stop practising medicine to research and teach it instead.

I pull up outside the house and let myself in. 'Hi gang! I'm home!' I try to sound cheery, slinging my bag down, and wander into the kitchen, to find Holly sitting at the table with Ewan, still in her scrubs.

'Hello!' I'm surprised and pleased to see her, although my next thought is that I must have forgotten some plans we made, but then Ewan pulls out a chair for me and places a glass of wine on the table in readiness.

'What's wrong?' I walk over slowly and sit down. Ewan leaves the room, closing the door gently behind him, and my friend reaches out to take my hand in hers.

'This afternoon I removed a woman's encapsulated breast implants.' She holds my worried gaze steadily. 'She came in as an emergency: sepsis symptoms. I went down to see her after she'd consented but before the op, because she was in a right old state – more than just feeling like complete shit – there was obviously something else. So I asked her if there was anything she wanted to discuss with me, as she seemed really distressed. I got the husband out of the room, in case there was something going on there, and the second he was gone, she made me promise to tell her afterwards if there was anything unusual about the implants. She said she was "very detail orientated" because she's a barrister.'

I gasp.

'YES!' Holly exclaims, 'Stefanie!'

I cover my mouth with my hands.

'I know! So now I'm looking at her and thinking about the horrendous story my new friend told me when I first arrived at the hospital, about the *insane* male surgeon she used to work alongside, who told my friend he'd written clues on the breast implants of living patients – one of whom was a local barrister he was shagging on the side. Anyway, we got her into theatre. Julia...' Holly leans forward and squeezes my hand more tightly. 'The left implant has a bloody great letter F on it. He did it – the bastard absolutely did it.'

I think of Alex lying on a mattress in a small dark cinema, under a blank screen, taped up, trusting Nathan to return... the skin of my back tightens, sending a rush of sensation up my spine that reaches over my shoulders and around my neck, before I briefly taste vomit I manage to swallow down. Nathan meant every word that he said to me.

'I bet there are five other women out there somewhere with letters written inside them too. I took a photo of the implant. Look!' She passes me the phone, and there it is. A clear 'F' – for Fowles.

'Oh, love!' She gets up and puts her arm round my shoulders. 'Cry because of what you know he was fully intending to do, but then we get strong, OK? We're going to hold him accountable, even if he is in America!'

I stare at Nathan's handwriting on the bloodied, misshapen implant. He did this to a woman he was sleeping with; sliced into her and hid a clue in her body. He took my child and hid him. He filmed female patients undressed. He is at his most dangerous when someone is in an acutely vulnerable state – anesthetised, naked, alone – around him. It's as if he has a compulsion to abuse their trust. 'He's back working in London. I found out yesterday.'

Holly is astonished. 'What? Wow – that says it all, doesn't it? You'd think he had the sense to slink off quietly, thank his lucky stars and stripes and stay put. The arrogance of the man!'

I shake my head. 'We should probably be more surprised that he stayed there as long as he did. It's not in his nature to be told what to do – especially by women.'

'Well, bad luck him, because times are changing.' She squeezes my hand again. 'Times are changing.'

CHAPTER FIFTY-TWO

The Independent, 25 September 2019

A plastic surgeon who recklessly and excessively handled the breast implants of two patients, was today found guilty of Actual Bodily Harm at Plymouth Crown Court and sentenced to an eighteen-month suspended sentence. The court heard how Nathan Sloan, 51, removed the implants from sterile conditions in December 2017, marked them with surgical pen and, in one instance, returned them to containers open to bacterial contamination. The hazardous implants were then inserted into the bodies of two anaesthetised patients during private surgery. Sloan's actions came to light when the first of the implants was removed in September 2018, by an NHS surgeon, after one of the women required emergency surgery. The surgeon dealing with the follow-up procedure noticed the unusual pen mark. Prosecutors argued that there was no clinical reason for Sloan to deface the implants, and in doing so he had knowingly and recklessly caused the two women harm by exposing them to serious infection risk.

Mr Sloan tendered his resignation from the Exeter Memorial Hospital in January 2018 before moving temporarily to Boston in the USA, returning to work for the NHS in London in August 2018. There is no suggestion any improper conduct occurred at any NHS hospital.

Carolyn Merrit QC, prosecuting, said the two surgeon's victims felt 'violated' and one of them, referred to in court as

Patient A, having already had breast cancer, was left suffering from psychological harm. The court heard a nurse from Sloan's private practice witnessed Sloan mark three implants with surgical pen during surgery on Thursday, 20 December and Friday, 21 December 2017. She questioned the markings – a letter O, W and F. Sloan told her the letter 'O' was to assist him in 'orientating' the implant, and during the second procedure told her he 'didn't trust' the efficacy of the national database and was considering creating an informal record of 'my girls' so that he could 'identify them and look after them if anything went wrong at a later date'. She assisted Mr Sloan again on the morning of Patient B's surgery on Friday, 21 December 2017 and did not see him mark any implants, concluding that Sloan 'must have done it before the surgery started, put them back in their boxes and put them in the patients so that I couldn't see the letter on them'.

Mr Sloan denied that he had, over his twenty-five-year career, potentially marked hundreds of women, creating what Ms Merrit referred to as 'an astonishing "club" that not one woman had given her consent or any indication of her wish to join'. He also denied that he had on any occasion intended the markings to create any form of 'possession, message, clue, mission state-ment, manifesto or plan', describing the assignation of any letters as 'a completely arbitrary index' as denoted by the letter marked on the implant of Patient A being a random 'F' and the letter marked on Patient B a random 'O'.

The Judge, Nicolas Fremantle QC, told Sloan: 'You have been unable to provide any satisfactory evidence of the indexing system you say was your explanation for marking Patients A and B, and that this action took place at a private hospital rather than an NHS one, where it would have been almost impossible for you to remove the implants from sterile conditions without raising the alarm, as a serious deviation from normal procedure, is noted.

'The court has heard evidence of your sexual relationships with both former patients and female staff at the hospitals you worked at, in a position of power. These relationships, while consensual were certainly inappropriate. That it may have been your intention to construct some sort of code hidden within one of these women – as was alleged to the General Surgery Clinical Lead at the EM Hospital, Exeter and the police in January 2018 – as part of a dubiously motivated "plan" to withhold information relating to the whereabouts of a colleague's missing child, for your own personal and possibly sexual gratification – is deeply disturbing. You insist no such plan ever really existed, but you are a man who likes to tell stories. It is my belief you have told yourself a story in this instance which belies your actions as an accomplished liar and manipulator.

'You are also a man who likes to demonstrate ownership, Mr Sloan – from your wife's tattoo of your initials on her wedding finger, to the "smiley faces" you draw on patients' skin, to the letters on implants.

'I am satisfied, therefore, that your actions were reckless but premeditated, and not without risk of which – the court has also heard – you were fully aware, having discussed your typical approach to the insertion of implants on a separate occasion as "I did what I always did; out of sterile conditions, straight into her. No messing". These women were not "your girls", Mr Sloan. They do not belong to you despite your actions demonstrating you believed they did. You abused their trust in one of the most important relationships in society, that of patient and doctor.'

In a private hearing, the Medical Practitioners Tribunal Service found that Sloan had 'failed to demonstrate any insight into the damage caused to both his victims and the reputation of the health service as a whole'. The disgraced surgeon was removed from the medical register with immediate effect.

The Goldtree Hospital said Sloan had not worked for it since it changed ownership in March 2018.

CHAPTER FIFTY-THREE

Nathan

I was, of course, the only person in the courtroom capable of appreciating the irony that I had been found guilty of something I *hadn't* done, but it's frankly outrageous that the case made it to trial in the first place. I was told by at least one barrister he couldn't even see what crime I had committed. The marks I made on the implants were to ensure the women's safety! The world really has gone mad. We now prosecute innocent medical staff for showing the diligence patients are entitled and deserve to expect when placing themselves in our professional hands. I have been found guilty of *taking too much care*. I was genuinely incredulous when I was stopped – mid-surgery – and the allegations dear Stefanie had made were put to me, kicking off the second suspension of my career.

I actually thought, when they walked into theatre, that Storm must have found out I'd pulled in a few favours and come back. I reasoned that I must have misjudged how angry she could still be with me after eight months, before concluding that she'd shown my new Medical Director the screen grab after all and I was toast... but then they started blathering on about letters. I kept expecting them to produce the screen grab as time went on, but they didn't... and finally the penny dropped that there was no screen grab. I admit I was pretty furious about that.

But the bit that hurt the most? Watching Julia stand there in court and under oath, tell everyone about my 'plan' to mark women with clues inside their bodies.

Who the hell would do a thing like that in real life? It was an *absurd* story, something I said in the heat of the moment; too far-fetched to be true even in the most idiotic of minds. Julia cannot have believed I meant it. Not really. She knows me better than that and yet she painted me as a monster. Her performance in the witness box was every bit as accomplished as I imagine she was during *her* trial. She certainly didn't come across as a serial destroyer of male colleagues' careers, maliciously whistleblowing for a second time. Hamish was right about that, in the end.

All three women worked together against me. It was a witch hunt. I could see it of Storm and Stefanie – but Julia? Her betrayal was devastating. I had hoped once I'd put in some credible time in the London Trust – and she'd seen that I could do it – perhaps we might have… talked. I looked right at her when my sentence was passed. We both knew that my being struck off was now inevitable. She had got what she wanted; I would no longer be able to practise.

She couldn't even look me in the eye.

I regret that I called her name as they led me away. I would have liked to talk to her afterwards, but one of the conditions of my sentence prevents me from having any contact with her, as if I'm some sort of criminal low-life. I find that very frustrating. It's made me angry that *everyone* has simply walked away as if I no longer exist, as if I don't matter.

I glance down at the empty aspirin blister packs on the side of the filled bath, then up at the condensation gathering on the obscured glass of the large window. If I *could* see out of it, it would reveal a glorious sea view – the USP of this single-storey holiday cottage, right on the beach. Although, of course, it is now dark. I duck back and have a last quick check around the bedroom –

scattered clothes everywhere, TV on, mobile on the side, keys, letter for Julia – although she will almost certainly decline to read it – ditto Ben, the girls, Storm and Serena. There is also cash to cover the damage done to the front door should the police gain access by breaking it in. It will also pay for professionally cleaning the bathroom because – I return to the bathroom and glance at the scarlet water – that's a lot of blood. Final flush of the loo.

I pick up the penknife and make the last cut, letting it fall to the floor, the rubies catching in the light before it lands on the tiles with a clatter. I drip a bit over the sill as I push the large window open and drop my rucksack through. I don't want to go through the front door and leave it unlocked. I intend to buy myself as much time as possible before the alarm is raised.

I can hear the sound of the waves crashing onto the beach. Hamish's idea of a body claimed by the sea was a good one.

They'll get what they all want. I shall disappear.

CHAPTER FIFTY-FOUR

Julia

It was just the most enormous sense of guilt and confusion when I heard the news. I've known medics who have taken their own lives, but Nathan? I just couldn't see it of him. It's true that the aftermath of a trial is difficult to navigate. You feel exhausted and weirdly lost without the routines of court, plus being struck off was always going to hit him hard and Christmas/New Year is a difficult time for a lot of people under normal circumstances... but for the Nathan *I* thought I knew to do that made no sense to me. Although perhaps that's entirely the point of something so desperately sad – it can never make sense. I am so very, very sorry for what his death has cost his three children and the people who loved him. Watching Ben these last few weeks learning to navigate the loss of his father – being comforted by Cass having lost her own mother, has been heartbreaking. I don't know how you ever come to terms with your father booking into a holiday cottage a handful of miles away from you, bleeding into a bath, then walking out into the sea. Those poor children didn't even have a body to put to rest and say goodbye to.

So I've also felt very angry with Nathan. I refused to read the letter he left addressed to me. I wouldn't let anyone else open it either. Ewan said outright he had no idea how I could simply pretend it didn't exist. Wasn't I curious? Didn't I have to know what Nathan wanted to say? A confession? An apology? I pointed out it could just as easily have been something designed to do even more damage. He shouldn't have been writing to me at all.

Whatever it said, I wasn't prepared to let Nathan have the final word. I threw it away, and now, he isn't able to hurt anyone, anymore.

FEBRUARY 2020

MEXICO

EPILOGUE

The hot new guy is very good. Small stitches – she'll have a neat scar. I glance up at the clock – and he's fast. We're going to be done much earlier than I thought. He steps back, rolls his shoulders. I reach out to remove the tray, but he says 'OK – now the other side!'

Huh? I thought this was a single not a double mastectomy? I open my mouth, but he's already started the incision… OK. I give a tiny shrug. He is the surgeon, not me. I glance down at the inert body in front of us. To be truthful, this woman is lucky to be having her cancer removed at all. She will probably be among the last for a while. Everyone says there is a storm coming. The hospital is buzzing with it.

'You OK, Isabella?'

'Yes! Sorry!' I focus back on the job in hand. He's frowning down at the breast tissue he's cutting away, but he doesn't seem annoyed with me. More like he was actually asking how I feel. That makes a change here. I hesitate, 'I was just thinking how people are saying life is going to be different for a bit.'

'It is,' he agrees. 'Very. We should all have fun while we can. Life is too short.'

I stare at him for a moment. 'What do you like to do then… for fun?' The second the words are out of my mouth I blush behind my mask and my heart thumps – but with excitement. I know I sound suggestive, but perhaps he's right. Better to burn fast and bright…

He carries on cutting, calmly. 'I like the usual things.'

The flame fizzles out. In another lifetime he asks me out to dinner. We talk all night and fall in love, but… I scowl down at my scrubs. It is impossible dressed like this! Another moment or two of silence passes. Just me, him… and the unconscious woman with her chest open, between us. I sigh inwardly and stare at the clock, willing the hands to move faster.

'I could pick you up at eight tonight?'

I turn back, surprised. He is still frowning down, busily working. Did I imagine him saying that?

'Would you like to come out with me?' He drops a piece of bloodied flesh in the tray, but because I see that sort of thing all the time, I am not distracted.

I bite my lip, suddenly shy. 'OK.'

Finally he looks up. His mask might be covering his mouth, but I can tell from the way his eyes are crinkling at the edges that he is smiling. And damn – those eyes! One light, one dark. Heaven and hell at the same time.

'We'll do dinner. Drinks,' he says. 'Maybe a film. We'll see…'

A LETTER FROM LUCY

I wrote *The Secret Within* way before Covid-19, but I had just enough time to tweak the ending to reflect the arrival of real-life events we're all now living through. During these unprecedented times, my fascination and admiration for all things medical is now off the scale and I hope you've enjoyed my fictional tale of the bad apple in the barrel.

I would be very grateful, if you had a spare five minutes, to write a review of *The Secret Within*. Feedback allows me to see what does and doesn't work in books and also makes a huge difference in helping new readers discover one of my books for the first time.

If you'd like to contact me personally, you can reach me via my Website, Facebook, Twitter and Instagram. I love hearing from readers, and always reply. If you'd like to keep up-to-date with all of my latest releases, you can sign up at the following link. Your email address will never be shared and you can unsubscribe at any time.

www.bookouture.com/lucy-dawson

Thank you very much for deciding to spend some of your time reading *The Secret Within*. I look forward to sharing my next book with you very soon, when, let's hope, life will be more 'normal' again.

With all best wishes,
Lucy x

lucydawsonbooks

@lucydawsonbooks

www.lucydawsonbooks.com

@lucydawsonbooks

Printed in Great Britain
by Amazon

61468459R00226